SAFE AND SOUND

Every con in the Max had his own handcuff key. There was a guy who made them for dust, a pro who ran a metal lathe and could turn out a tiny key that would pop a Teflon Smith & Wesson set quick as you could say "it."

Bunkowski had one made out of hard plastic, which he carried in his stash: an often-moist, stinking, secret skinfold crease that hid under the huge, ugly truck tire that overhung his groin. He carried all kinds of goodies in there: money, a postage stamp in plastic, a combat bandage, some monofilament line, a plastic mini-grapple, and his handcuff key. Nothing would set off a metal detector, and although they loved peering around in his mouth, his nostrils, and his ears, nobody ever thought to pull up that hard hunk of rubbery fat and check out his safety-deposit drawer. . . .

D1570645

PRAISE FOR REX MILLER'S
CHAINGANG

"An unflinching, ground zero look at how child abuse builds monsters the way no recombination of DNA ever could. . . . All the more terrifying for its core of truth."
—Andrew Vachss

"Rex Miller's potential, there to be seen from the start by anyone who had the stomach for it, is fulfilled in chilling, chance-taking *Chaingang*. . . . Rex's characters *all* come to life on his pages—at least, for as long as it takes Bunkowski to annihilate them! . . . Miller's *Chaingang* knows everybody is complicated as hell—and in *this* world, the shadows are gigantic, and come out *after* you!"
—J. N. Williamson, author of *Monastery* and *Spree*

"*Chaingang* is outstanding! In the character of Chaingang Bunkowski, Miller has created the quintessential killer. Chaingang makes Hannibal Lecter look like Mr. Rogers."
—R. Patrick Gates, author of *Tunnelvision*

Books by Rex Miller

Butcher*
Savant*
Chaingang*
Iceman
Stone Shadow
Slice
Profane Men: A Novel of Vietnam
Frenzy
Slob

*Published by POCKET BOOKS

BUTCHER

REX MILLER

POCKET BOOKS
New York   London   Toronto   Sydney   Tokyo   Singapore

An *Original* Publication of POCKET BOOKS

POCKET BOOKS, a division of Simon & Schuster Inc.
1230 Avenue of the Americas, New York, NY 10020

ISBN: 0-671-86882-9

First Pocket Books printing December 1994

10 9 8 7 6 5 4 3 2 1

Cover art by Steven Stroud

Printed in the U.S.A.

"What I fear is being in the presence of evil and doing nothing. I fear that more than death."
—Otilia de Koster

BUTCHER

1

Kansas City—1959

The Snake Man was drunk and slobbering mean, and the child feared what might be next, as the man who was his foster mother's current live-in companion hammered out the breathing slits in the Punishment Box. It was a metal trunk, just large enough to hold the eight-year-old child. The shirtless drunk, whose hairy upper torso and arms were writhing nests of serpentine tattoos, cursed and hammered. He'd made crude slits with a small cold chisel, and was in the process of pounding the razor-sharp steel edges of the openings more or less flat.

"I'll teach you to talk back to me," the man ranted. The boy, cowering with his mongrel pup on the urine-soaked floor of the locked closet, tried to swallow back his abject terror. The sound of the metal trunk slamming shut was followed by heavy footsteps. The door opened. Blinding sunlight. A rough hand squeezed his arm, jerking him painfully forward as the little dog whined in fear. The Snake Man, which was how the child thought of the monster with his blue skin-map of jailhouse serpents, held the boy in steely claws.

"Danny gets scared in the dark," the man mocked him in a harsh voice. "Little Danny cries for his mommy." He shoved the frightened boy into the metal box. "Let's see how he likes this. A nice hot, dark Punishment Box." The words made the child's skin crawl, as the lid slammed down on him. There was no air. He would die in the suffocatingly hot box. The metal seared his skin where it touched him.

The bright sunlight illuminated a crudely-made open-

1

ing, and he put his face as close as he could to the lid of the box without actually touching it, supporting his little body so that he could breathe the foul air in and out, and he fought with what was left of his sanity to survive.

He had learned about the thing he had, which one day he would know was termed claustrophobia, while he'd been kept for hours in the pitch-black closet. To keep himself alive he had first learned to communicate with the little dog, whom the man also hated, and it was but one of many mental gymnastics Daniel would ultimately master.

For the sake of his survival, he'd learned about the secret room inside his head: how to enter it at will, where the trap door was, how he could mentally key it and walk down the long flight of black stairs that led into the core of the imagination, where his teachers lived. Crosshairs, the Buzzsaw, Big Sister, the Doctor, they were all there to hold his mind, to give solace and strength, to stanch the flow of tears, to teach him the ways of the dark places.

They'd taught him that claustrophobia, which he'd felt acutely that first day in the stinking closet, was at the front and back of the mind. In the center, one could escape it. Was there enough air in the closet to breathe? Yes. Was there not a crack under the door? Yes. Breathe the air slowly, the doctor told him, and as you take each breath into your lungs freeze the front and back of your thoughts.

He tried it, and it worked. He learned to slow . . . still . . . slow his vital signs, to freeze the panic, to control his thoughts, and he tried to teach Gem, but the dog never quite got the hang of it. He learned to comfort the animal with soothing, slow strokes, and whispered gentlings, which he communicated inside his head. His ability to speak to the dog, to make it understand, using only his brain, was quite real. Deep in the center of encroaching madness, he found his neural key, and unlocked secrets of the mind few would ever know.

Buzzsaw, the fearless one, the killer, taught him, as the child reached out for his comic-book friend in the screaming fear of the stifling metal box, what payback was. He would survive the Punishment Box, he would be strong, and then Buzzsaw would help him do what had to be done.

"The Snake Man will kill you if you do not do what I say," Buzzsaw snarled at the child.

"I'm so afraid," the boy said, crying inside the hot, airless trunk.

"Fear *nothing*," the killer said, and he showed Daniel how fear existed only as thought; it was not real. Heat was real, yes. Air was real. But the heat would not destroy him if he remained calm. The man would take him out of the box soon, if only to use him again. There was air.

"What can I do? He is strong, and I'm small."

"All is known to you, Daniel, all of the things that are. All secrets are in plain sight, you must look for them with your mind. You must remember. Where is there a weapon?"

"In the basement . . . downstairs?" Daniel remembered a room of mysteries in the cellar of the old tenement building.

"Yes."

"A hammer."

"No."

"The smoky bottles?"

"Yes," Buzzsaw said, helping the boy visualize the small pharmaceutical bottles with skull-and-crossbones warning labels. "Acid," he snarled.

Not long after that, Daniel Edward Flowers Bunkowski, age eight, was sent to a Kansas correctional institution for children for blinding his stepfather. The boy was said to be incorrigible.

Then

Daniel Bunkowski
and Raymond Meara

The hunter-killer unit of Operation Green River hid in deep woods roughly ten klicks north of LZ Mary, a forward base for clandestine ops on the Ca Mau. The official parent of record, Alpha Company, carried three platoons on its books. Each of these subdivided into three squads, a squad being, theoretically, three four-man fire teams and a squad leader. That was on paper.

In reality, one of the forty-three-man platoons, Alpha's recon outfit, was a cover for a two-squad insertion probe being run by the mysterious USMACVSAUCOG, a group mandated in the secret pages of a National Security Council directive to the Joint Chiefs of Staff, or a "non-skid jacks" in the spook parlance. Sensitive wet work was their specialty of the house: over-the-fence deals and "special" actions such as Operation Green River, which were meant to stay off the books.

The hunter-killer unit, a fire team in itself, was unique. It consisted of only one man: a sociopathic, heart-eating behemoth named Daniel Edward Flowers Bunkowski, a serial killer and mass murderer who'd been turned and set free in the field to take care of Uncle's dirty laundry. He was happy in his work.

The "unit" was approximately the size of a large freezer stood on end and rounded off, six feet nine inches tall, four hundred sixty-odd pounds of unrelenting ha-tred, an abused and tortured child who'd grown up with a talent for destruction, and owned a well-earned reputa-tion for having taken a human life for every pound of his weight.

Chaingang Bunkowski, whose jailhouse nickname had derived from his killing tool of choice, a three-foot, tractor-strength chain wrapped in friction tape, did not care who died just so long as someone did. He was an equal opportunity destroyer, and he would waste a human without regard to race, color, or national origin. At the moment, hiding in the deep woods near an intersection of map grids designated Snake Eyes, he was enjoying a scene of bloody carnage. Two dozen of SAUCOG's finest were getting their asses lit up, and he was enjoying it fully. He hated his own men as much as he did the little people. They were all human—his natural enemy as he saw it. It pleased him to watch them die.

This was Charlie's AO, a dangerous place of twelve-foot tides and stinking mangrove swamps, and the night had come full of spooky moonlight, fog, mad moths, and kamikaze mosquitoes the size of tarantulas. The previous day, a hellish time of fear and ceaseless bug swarm, Mr. Charlie had stalked the insertion team and suckered them into an ambush, and Operation Green River was now merely one more fucked-up Vietnam disaster.

Inside the strange mind of the beast, Snake Eyes stared out of his memory. The grids were so named because, on a military map, the intersecting features, a river and canal, vaguely resembled blue eyes on either side of a long nose of rice paddies. The mission had brought men in on foot because the passage of watercraft was made impossible at each low tide.

Chaingang was slightly to the southwest, in woods that bordered a ridge bank and slough parallel to the nearest canal, which was where the two squads had been ambushed. Only their tail man, who lagged behind the column and moved at his own snail's pace, and one other hardy camper survived the ensuing firefight, such as it was.

As a secret spectator, Bunkowski's only interest in the swift and unilateral contact was, first, in surviving, and then perhaps in assessing the degree of vulnerability to whatever easy targets might present themselves.

The other Caucasian to live through the ambush was a grunt named Meara. He was alive, but badly injured. Terminal screaming pain, the kind of eschatological stuff that surrounds and hurts without mercy, had him in its lock. Deceptive, coming first as smoke, wispy and bearable pain snaked out at him like the tendrils from a flame. Then it became dangerous and oily and it frightened him with its unforgiving nature. Billowing, dense, impenetrable clouds of pain choked him; suffocating end-of-the-world pain blanketed Raymond Meara, half-assed mercenary.

He felt it next as fire. It lingered in his throat and lungs, a double-barreled burn that one bit into like a chili pepper, a thing so hot that a single seed tasted like sucking on the end of a flame thrower. He felt it deep in his military fillings; tasted the scorching pain on his tongue. It enveloped him with the intensity of turbs, after-burners, blast furnaces, refinery flame-off, back-blast, this oilfield-Armageddon-hot pain.

He began to lose it with the heat mirage shimmer of agony. Ray Baby Meara, cut off from his fellow ground-pounders, who were lost somewhere back behind him, swallowed by the earth, was befuddled by the pain that burnt him as it screamed in his ear.

"Callsign to handle, you copy? Over." It shrieked at him over the radio.

"Bounty Hunter, Pallbearer Six Actual," crackled through the fierce heat.

"Most frigging affirm, Pallbearer Six." The Command Post. Six Actual, the Man his own self: *Dai Uy* (Viet for captain) McClanahan, who lived in a trailer called Der Bunker. Twelve feet below ground level, within B-40 range of Monster Mountain, Dai Uy held Meara's life in his hand. Dai Uy would work the magic for Raymond Meara and save him.

3

The beast sensed something, another presence, a thing that went unidentified, but these were the important nudges that he always listened to with the greatest care. The thing that had saved his life innumerable times poked him again, and told his life support systems to saddle up and hustle.

He moved, an apparition in the darkness of the woods, a freezer-big thing in a cammoed tarp the size of a small vehicle, loaded with a ruck most men would not be able to lift. In one enormous gloved hand he carried a belted M60, the other held his master blasters and det gear. His huge, meaty chest was covered with grenades, many of which were short-fused and meticulously taped to him. A massive fighting Bowie hung upside down from his Alice unit, and everywhere you looked there were claymores strapped to him. One custom-made 15EEEEE bata boot sprouted its own "hush puppy"—a silenced .22 sentry-duster, and across the back of his humongous duffel a sawed-off twelve gauge topped off the ensemble. Unlike the usual combat loads, Chaingang's twelve was filled with a curious mix of sabot-sleeve and fleshette loads. The first shell was a power-load behind a hardened lead slug in polyethylene—it would penetrate an engine block at close range—and the next capped a hot load behind twenty needle-nosed nails. They fanned out at three thousand f.p.s. Tree-cutters.

Bunkowski was literally armed to the teeth: Part of his arsenal was a martial technique he'd perfected during long, hard time in the slams, a vile thing called the

Breath of Death. There was no more deadly hunter-killer team than this lone assassin.

Stocked with enough freeze-dried long rats, the so-called LURP rations that were a specialty of the house with recon patrols out in the superbad bush, Chaingang could go for weeks without resupply, living off the fat of the land, so to speak, taking a bit of protein here and there . . . roving and killing.

The big death dealer silently blended into the blackest pocket of shadows and was gone.

Time shifted. Tenses commingled and became confused. Then was now. Past was future. Raymond imagined that he keyed his radio and whispered for blessed relief from those nagging aches and pains.

Bounty Humper One, he thought, calling in air support, we got mystery aggressors. Phrases wobbled and curved grotesquely in the heat, and Meara's imagination distorted them like the visions in a funhouse mirror.

They're on the way, Bounty Mountie One. Gut up and hang tough! The phantoms were coming. Phantoms streaking out of Udorn; fast movers that would come and get some. Light up slopes. Kick dink butt. Take serious names and dig big gook graves. It was blazing noon inside Meara's head.

He fought to get his bearings. He knew that he must prepare precise coordinates. He tried to think. He thought he was roughly northwest of the VNSF compound, home of the dreaded Look Deep Duck Back. To the south was the buried trailer of Dai Uy McClanahan.

No, that wasn't right. Southeast? He and these other fools, they were proudly lost. Pathfinders, Rangers, Airborne, headhunters, and assorted scouts, all wearing the double-bad bloody skull patch of Deathsquad Recon, lost to the mothering world.

A quartet of specks materialized in the sky of Raymond Meara's imagination, shattering his fantasy with pain as noise, the noise of a hundred earthquakes and a thousand sonic booms. They brought pain as smoke, heat, discord, and, the worst of all, pain as napalm. Hell-hot, death-black, stinking petrozap of oxygen-sucking napalm exploded Raymond's world. It killed Look Deep Duck Back, Pathfinders, Rangers, Airborne, headhunters, scouts, brave soldiers, cowardly lions, and buried the Dai Uy dead in his air-conditioned double-wide beneath twelve feet of concrete, steel, sandbagged berm, rubble, and Monster Mountain real estate.

Pallbearer Six Actual? Anybody? Only pain remained to answer him in the stinking petrochemical afterbirth. Snake Eyes.

He shivered, captured by the misery of icy, intimidating silence. Pain so terrible and cold that it made him forget the hottest flames, isolated him, shocked his brain into numbness, and paralyzed its victim for the slow kill.

Imprisoned, gripped in the chilling claws of death, caught inside the heart of agony as formidable and unassailable as a sheer ice cliff, frozen immobile like some fossilized, prehistoric biped, Meara's fantasy of pain allowed him to whisper but not to breathe, and he knew it would make him die slowly, as it tortured him inside the freezing mass of glacier-like hurting.

Help me, he begged, into the darkness of his imagination. But no one responded. The phantoms were gone. The captain was gone. All his good buddies were gone. From whence would cometh the magic? He had never felt so alone, trapped and terror stricken inside the ice-cold walls of silent, crushing pain.

"God Six Actual, this is Bounty Hunter One," he whispered in desperation. "Do you have a copy on me,

God?" Heavenly Father, who gave your only begotten son, Jesus, please forgive me for my sins.

Staunchly devout agnostic Raymond Meara prayed that God would make the magic happen, that He would forgive him and save him.

He wanted to hear the thunder crack, see the clouds speared by shafts of gold, hear God's majestic voice shatter the block of pain.

"Ray!" he wanted God to say "I didn't recognize you."

Meara tried to attach some thread of reason to this newfound ability of his to suddenly suspend all disbelief. For the first time he was quite prepared to believe in the power of prayer, and that one might obtain a miracle. What about the weeping religious icons? Those magical pictures that teared up and cried on cue? Weren't these miracles? He thought about the power of secret incantations. The shroud. The ark. The mystery of the robe. The laying on of hands. The dark virgin of the basilica of Guadalupe, whose fabled tears had been witnessed, impossibly, in the cornea of the Virgin Mary's weeping eye. Surely not all of these inexplicable miracles were ecumenical hoaxes.

A man doesn't think about getting shot. Sure, he thinks about it, but he never believes a projectile will really hit him. Maybe that other dude, that guy over there, maybe he'll catch a bullet. But nobody thinks it will actually happen to them. Certainly not to that closet Christian, Raymond Meara. Fight it, ace, he thought. Don't slip away yet.

The monsoons had cut through the woods like a giant backhoe and there was a good-size slough, there at the edge of what would have been called a deep ditch bank back in the little Missouri country town he was from.

They'd been moving parallel to it when Charlie hit them from the woods, coming through the other side soundlessly, underlining the oxymoronic nature of the phrase military intelligence once again. First and second squads. Recon—what was left of it—totally lit up.

Meara had been running toward the nearest trees when

he'd been back-shot. It was liked being smashed in the kidney by a wrecking ball. You're history. Never any doubt how bad it was. Every breath made him want to scream.

The moon that had been far away, hanging out there in the black velvet so pale, back when they were moving along the ravine's lip, now seemed to shine like a searchlight pointed at him. He kept listening for his bros, listening for returning fire in the mad minute of noise.

I know why you weep, dark virgin. I, too, cry from a weeping eye. Hail, Mary. Full of grace. The Lord is with thee. Mary, Mary, quite contrary. A steel door slammed on the irreverent doggerel before it could utter a sacrilege. Reverent Ray.

An inane loose thought.

It snakes across his brain.

From out of left field.

A thought-burst from a girl whose name he's forgotten.

Mary, Mary . . .

"It's almost Christmas," she's telling him. It was December back in the world. "Wal-Mart's is like a battlefield," she tells him.

Wound-trauma trivia. What was it like there on the battlefield, Ray? Oh, it was sort of like Wal-Mart's. Nobody would get it. Pain knifed through him before he could finish the joke and he cried out, unable to catch it in time.

Still noisy. That's good. But all the same kind of fire, and that's not so good. He could only hear the Soviet-made AK-47s cracking away nearby. He tried to force himself to think about something other than the pain and his mounting fear.

AK, he thought to himself. Spell it out. He tried to see a piece of paper and write the letters AK with his mind, but he couldn't spell Avtomat Kalashnikov and midway through the exercise the fear broke through and took over again.

He knew he was shot bad. It never dawned on him that

he'd been hit twice. All he could concentrate on was the one he'd taken in his lower back. He knew what he had to do. Get a battle dressing out. Get the wound covered. Lie chilly.

His brain told him to move and he started to and his body told his brain, I'm going to take a short nap. *Don't do that,* he said to his body. *Fight it.* He thought about the assault rifles. Caliber. Operation mode. Type of fire. Cyclic rate. Muzzle velocity. Components. Reliability. "The AK-47 utilizes a curving, staggered-row, thirty-round box magazine."

He would survive. Go into publishing. Become a competitor of *Playboy.* His publication would be called *Box Magazine.*

Sporadic shots. A sustained burst. You never had to doubt what kind of weapon was firing, the AKs had their own distinctive crack. Box magazine is loaded by hand. Cartridges depressed the spring. Make sure the forward end is pointing first, then insert into the feed port on the bottom of the receiv—Jesus! The pain was bad. Charlie had sure snookered them good.

How easy it would be to go to sleep. The pain jolts were coming closer together, but that was a good sign, no? He wondered how much blood he was losing. He knew he should fight the dizzy feeling.

Another snaky image—he felt his heart pumping, and for an instant his heart was his enemy—as he visualized his blood squirting out into the night.

Move the operating handle to the rear. He was seeing the words *recoil spring guide* in a weapons manual just as he heard the footsteps. They were coming through the woods. No sixteens. No forty-sevens. Just feet.

Move, his brain told him. *Can't,* his body replied. *Do it or die,* it told him, and he started moving, inching forward.

The lightning bolt of pain shot through the layer of gathering cobwebs and he was wide awake and alert for the next few seconds. He was hurt bad. He was going to die. He made himself grit his teeth and keep moving down under the awful thing that he was touching there in the shadows. Moving down under the wetness.

He passed out but came to almost instantly, or so he believed, and saw figures in the deep shadows cast by the huge trees, under the seemingly bright Asian moon. He knew Charlie was right behind him looking at him. With a weapon. He hoped they'd shoot him well. Give him a clean head shot.

He tried not to think about getting a blade in the back, but all he could focus on was an AK-47 with a bayonet on the end. He wondered if it would be quick. A bayonet shouldn't hurt too much. Nice sharp thrust. In and out. Maybe they wouldn't hit anything. You could survive a gook bayonet. Stab wounds weren't any big deal.

Raymond Meara had no last rush of insight. Nor did he see his life flash before his eyes. His last thoughts were of the smell of blood and stink of the body that he'd pulled himself under, and Charlie's fish smell. He willed himself to freeze, willing his breath not to come in loud, ragged gasps, willing his heart not to beat.

And it was then that a huge, soft, swift-moving black thing came fluttering over him, enveloping him like some immense black Manta Ray swimming over a tiny fish, and he went under completely.

5

The beast was inert, vital signs locked down, frozen motionless . . . waiting. The gigantic clown warrior had nearly waddled out of the deep shadows but something touched him, signaled his mental computer, and he stopped in his tracks.

A big, bright Kate Smith moon shone down on the Southeast Asian jungle that butted up against the woods. Blue feature to one side, jungle in front, open rice fields to the other side. He continued to wait, unhurried and untroubled, ignoring the swarming things that fed off him, impervious to assaults of such insignificance.

They appeared, sure enough, in a patch of saffron moonlight, perhaps a thousand meters in the distance. His weird mindscreen absorbed it in through the sensors, tasting the information and finding it palatable, chewing over the data, swallowing and ingesting the relevant aspects, then, when the cud was assimilated, expectorating it into the maw of his hungry computer. A meter was 39.37 inches, more than a yard. Ten football fields? A thousand meters. He was terrain-aware, shadow-cognizant, environmentally alert to woods, moon, jungle, darkness, rhythms of movement, textures and permutations of sight, smell, sound. He silently acknowledged their noise discipline. More than a squad. The remains of a broken platoon, perhaps, caught in the dangerous moonbeams.

He gathered in and collated more raw information, but the mindscreen functioned on its own, computing and assessing even as new data were factored: one klick was a kilometer, sixty-two hundredths of a mile. One metric yard was . . .

Their version of force recon? The ambush team? Of no consequence to the massive figure, who, unfortunately, was not currently predisposed to engage these little people. He would have enjoyed taking the last one down, squeezing off a big nasty wet one and putting the tail man to sleep. They would flatten, chitter, jitter-jive like monkeys as they hit the jungle floor. He had genuine affection for the little people, as he always thought of them. He really liked them. He really liked to kill them.

The images of the distant shadow men danced like faraway campfire silhouettes. His mental computer continued to take in and process the snap of each twig, the crackle of the leaves around him, the pop of tree limbs, the bug buzz, monitoring his own safety as he watched the passing parade, his thoughts a warm fuzziness of command-detonated claymores.

It was such a shame not to do them. The imagined taste of a salty warrior heart made him salivate. Pleasant fantasies to make the moments pass.

They melted away into the night and yet he remained completely inert. The sensors still glowed red inside his mind and he ignored them at his own peril. The life-support and maintenance system that had evolved in closets, trunks, interrogation "interview" rooms, and solitary-confinement cells breathed deeply of the ambient darkness, absorbing and analyzing everything from the possible existence of toxic thiophosphates, to *nuoc mam,* to Agent Orange. Satisfied, data collated, the beast took his first normal breath in several minutes, and resumed his route of exfiltration.

It was still morning by the time he reached the edge of the sprawling U.S. fire base that provided support and resupply for such surrounding elements as LZ Mary, but the sun was already high in the sky and the pierced-steel planking reflected retained heat like a griddle. He'd breached the childish perimeter security without breaking a sweat.

A sergeant stood shielding his face with a manifest clipboard as a combat attack chopper lifted from the baking military surface. At that moment Chaingang Bunkowski began to make his move, and the man didn't hear him. When the wind-whipped debris had abated, the supply sergeant returned to itemizing goods for an immense C-130 cargo monster that waited not far away.

Another immense monster materialized from the shadows around a nearby Quonset hut, startling the man at his work.

"This is off limits, troop," he growled, warning the huge apparition.

"Sergeant, I'm supposed to rance a trason over here, do you know whether they crayled or not?" Words, accompanied by contortions of a rubbery face, the face of a born actor, timed to simulate genuine concern; non-words that sounded like words spoken fast, slurred, said with a beamy, radiant Pillsbury doughboy smile. A verbal onslaught rumbled from the depths of a basso profundo gutbox, by something so large and immediately menacing it discombobulated as well as frightened.

"Tracers? Say what?"

"They said over at the connus I was supposed to race a trishon or—" the metal links snaked out of the big, reinforced canvas pocket like an uncoiling steel rattler, each link wrapped in black tape, propelled by a killing arm the size of a foot-wide sewer pipe, putting an end to one Sergeant Fellows, who had always watched his weight, played the game, kissed officer heinie, got his malaria, typhus, and hepatitis shots, and done his damndest to stay a safe REMF till he could DEROS. But this was one Rear Echelon Melon Farmer whose Date of Estimated Return suddenly got reupped to the Twelfth of Never.

Fingers like gigantic cigars had the sarge in a death grip, and even as his lights were going out, the monster was pulling him back into the shadows to feed.

_____ **6**

The room was in soft focus, diffused, pleasantly warm.
He remembered being in triage and hearing the corps-
man say something and another guy looking at his face
and going "Holy shit."

Raymond Meara had wanted to make a joke about the
guy's bedside manner needing some work, but he
couldn't move his mouth, and they were hooking up a
glass thing and he caught his image in a random reflec-
tion, a bloody mess of meat that was no face at all and
as he passed out he thought, *Yeah, well, more great
news. I was hit in the face, too . . . but the important
thing is . . .*

He'd blacked out before he could remember his other
wounds.

"That red-haired little whitey never done nothing but
brag on hisself and talk about buyin' a new 'vette when
he got back and we—"

"—twenty-second and he comes back with this short-
timer stick and they tried to get him to go down to
battalion—"

//////////////////////////

"—met her in the geisha house. She's buying this good
Thai stuff and we're goin' over to get—"

"—listening to the ball game and I hear somebody yell
incoming!"

"—says thirty and a wake-up and you boys can wave
goodbye. He says, my man, I'm a double-deuce goose,
and I—" ///////////////////////////////////

20

"—got a sump in there. Check that drain every—"

"—IVs, and we've got the dextrose and the blood—"

//////////////////////////

"—with the Fifth Special Forces Group. So these Airborne dudes come in and—"

He hears their harsh phrases in a blurring cacophony of snatches. Snatches of dialogue. Snatches of conversation. Dark and hairy and mysterious snatches. Strange *///////////////////*'s of blunted pain, swimming in the finest dope.

"You alive or what?"

"Huh?"

"Say, Monk, you coming to the party, man?"

"Say what?"

"Are you alive, my man?"

The face is foreign, distorted. The voice is slope.

"Are you VC?"

"Are you kidding me or what? If I was VC you think I'd be layin' in this bed next to you, Monk, my man? VC! Shee-it!" Laughter. Two faceless forms seen through blurry fog.

"How come you call me a monkey?" he asked, but his voice, which seemed to resound out of a deep cistern, came out distorted, like *hah nah nu naw ne ungy?*

"I didn't say you was funny, bro." He tried to make himself understood and felt the surge of something coursing through his veins, heady and powerful like smack or morphine.

"We been callin' you Monk, cause your head is shaved, dig? One of them little round places like a monk but over on the side." They'd shaved a kind of tonsure on him to operate, a bald spot like a monk's shaven patch. Patch . . . snatch . . . words sat still and the room revolved slowly around them.

"I tell you about them monkeys?" The two men nearby resumed their conversation.

"I dunno, man, what monkeys is that?"

"North of Dau Tieng." He saw Iron Triangle on a field map. But the combination of words was meaningless. Just more useless information. Dau Tieng. Iron Triangle. Parrot's Beak. Plain of Jars. Death Valley. Just words to sit in the midst of a dark, revolving room.

"—jungle and there was so much noise. All of a sudden man, it's going *RRRRRRRROOOOOOOOOOO-OOWWWWWWWWWW* and we figured Charlie. Big assault force. We was overrun and this was their psy-ops, dig? You ain't never heard such a racket, and you know what it was? It was *monkeys.*"

Another word. A word like bananas. Rubber Trees. The Monkees. Another useless piece of information to spin the room around.

"No lie, blood. Howler monkeys dukin' it out. Scared me half to death, bro."

Then the voice came in so clearly, and he was totally coherent. Meara in harmony again with meaning—for only this moment. He sensed a logical consistency fastened to a congruous unity of thought as the words fused, adhered, penetrated:

"That's where we found the big piece of cement up in the tree. They had about a four-hundred-pound chunk blasted off a pagoda or whatever. Big steel rods in that mother and, you know, way, way up there, man. Trigger was a tree bent over and tripwire running to it. And this white boy we call Red, he goes—"

But then the glue came loose and the meaning began to disintegrate on him again, the room finally slowing to a tippy stop. He felt himself sinking down through the incredible softness of the bed, submerging right into the mattress, unable to hear the voices, so he never did learn what the white boy called Red had to say there in the jungle of the mad howler monkeys.

In the cargo hold of the C-130 it was suffocatingly close, but if you are the sort of cargo that thrives on blast-furnace heat, the kind of human mutant that evolved from a child kept for the first eight years of its life in such places as a urine-stinking darkened closet, what the hell is one more suffocatingly claustrophobic box?

It had been many years since he'd needed Big Sis to hold him in her strong, imaginary arms, or Buzzsaw to help him key the secret inner room of his mind. He could now simply concentrate with the full brunt of his powers, and he was gone within himself, respiratory rate and heartbeat slowed . . . stilled . . . slowed to a crawl.

This particular box was headed for JUSMACTHAI, and then on to Hawaii—the big island. JUSMACTHAI was the Joint U.S. Military Assistance Command Thailand, and the shipper was one USMACVSAUCOG, something else again.

The military stencils looked very proper, right down to the painted legend Perishable Solids across the front of the container. Four hundred and sixty-some pounds of perishable solids would soon be off the in-country books and carried as requisitioned training ammo by ICS, the armed services' infamous Inventory Control System. The full system designation for the container of perishable solids was:

23

APC612901–500–C1873   39192–2
LMG 30 R1892–200–71U   710–34
HMG M2 01A198–YAD   852420–47

The number of the beast, in this case.
Daniel Edward Flowers Bunkowski. Coming home.

Now

Bayou Ridge, Missouri

Meara came home to nothing. He'd become invisible both to the residents of the rural Missouri town where his folks farmed and to those who lived their sanitized lives "back in the world."

There were vague months in California, then a return east, a mission overseas with some other vets, and various and sundry warm bodies who'd hired on as mercs. It proved to be an abortion.

He kicked around for a few years until, in 1981, he was notified that his folks were now dead and what remained of the family farm was his. That was the first time he learned his dad had been dead for over two years. The three hundred acres were now a hundred and sixty, the best hundred and forty having been liquidated to pay bills. The rich bottom ground was gone.

The choice was simple enough: either sell off what little was left and blow the money, or try to eke out a living with the ground. And this was how Raymond Meara had become a farmer.

He'd been working on the fence that ran through the woods bifurcating his primary soybean ground and J.J. Devenny's farm. J.J. had a couple of horses and it seemed as if there was usually fence down someplace in the woods. If you farmed, there was always something to do, and in your free time you could try and keep your fences up. There was an old axiom—good fences make good neighbors.

The winter sun felt good. He laid the heavy spool of

wire down and walked over to the door of the pickup, pulling out his battered billfold and counting money and checks onto the front seat. His badly worn wallet was stuffed thick with unpaid bills, important papers, receipts, even a check or two. His file box.

One hundred and forty-two dollars in cash. Doug Seifer's check for two hundred he'd been holding for a couple of weeks. He squinted at the post-dated numbers. He'd deposit it today when he went in to get the fan belt. The old John Deere was still running, that was something. He'd have to put some money on the seed bill. Hell, he thought, why not go ahead and pay it? Have to sooner or later.

Meara reached over with a grunt of effort and dug a stump of pencil out of the glove compartment, adding up numbers silently for a minute or so. Then he wrote down what he had left of the money from the gin, less what he'd been docked.

He crammed all the bills and paper back into the beat-up leather and shoved it back in his hip pocket. He might make it through the year without borrowing. If he hadn't added wrong. If he didn't eat anything. If his tractor didn't break down again. If the weather didn't conspire to screw him. If he got his wheat out and put in early beans behind it and if he could manage to keep the Johnson grass out and if his preemerge worked and if his poor ground'd hold still for yet another crop and if the gin didn't dock him too bad for moisture and if he could get this combined and that levelled and if . . .

The big if was the one on the letterhead of the Committee on Public Waterways in the U.S. House of Representatives. He snatched the pile of crumpled papers out again, spread them in front of him, and read that the chief of engineers, in the interest of "flood control, commercial navigation, and related purposes," had been requested to undertake the Clearwater Trench Reconnaissance Study. It was an undertaking long since completed. Meara had heard their choppers over the farm a dozen times. His crumpled pile of papers included their assessment, and he looked at the line map that accompanied it.

The drawing was roughly in the configuration of a pistol with a misshapen trigger guard, the barrel of the gun beginning at the inflow point in Illinois, north of Cairo. The blue feature was the Mississippi River, as it traveled down past Columbus to the curving trigger guard, Bayou City. The sides of the pistol were a pair of levees: the set-back main line levee on the west, the front line levee to the east. The blue line divided Missouri from Kentucky as it headed south. Raymond's ground was pinched between the two levees, a small dot approximately where a screw would go on the grip of the pistol. Screw, to be sure, was the appropriate nomenclature.

The study's conclusions were that it was indeed feasible to divert floodwater from the mighty Miss by cutting, by means of high explosives, the front line levee and so allowing excess waters to bleed off into the relatively unpopulated lands north of the pistol's butt, Clearwater Trench. This act, however, would place Raymond Meara's bean and wheat fields at the bottom of the Mississippi.

He put the papers back where they belonged, thinking things couldn't get a whole lot worse, so they'd have to get better. But, once again, he was dead wrong.

9

New Madrid Levee, Missouri

The number of the beast is twelve, but he cannot fathom why. There were twelve letters in Udanax Xanadu.

His mind is stranger than a glass hammer. It does, or tries to do, many things simultaneously: receive and transmit impulses, assess and collate, identify, compute, extrapolate, measure, recall, plan, direct, monitor, safeguard, but the infinitesimal data stream has been dammed to a trickle.

One piece of information computes: his mouth is dry. Two: he is hurt. How badly? This fails to compute.

There was an op in the mangrove swamps of the Rung Sat, where even angels feared to tread. UC123Bs defoliating the trails with Agent Orange, poisoning all who traversed them, an equal opportunity toxic agent, entering the bloodstreams of the Ranchhands and Charlie alike. His mind fed him the fringes of a '60s arc light strike, when he'd been concussed in the blast pattern of the B52 Superforts.

For no reason his wobbly mind locks onto a line of errant poetry. Something he'd read in a stolen library book, something that caused him to smile his fierce parody of a human grin, tear the page from the book and eat it, which he sometimes did to things that pleased him.

Udanax. A pharmaceutical trade name. He knew that it was Xanadu reversed, and his shaky brain reached out for the poem:

> *In San Antone did Keebler's can,*
> *A tasty weatherdrome puree,*
> *Where Alice Sager's reefer band,*
> *Played taverns' pleasureless Duran,*
> *Into a funhouse free.*

He tried to shake it off and saw the word cauterization imprinted, like a sign, above his thoughts. Twelve letters . . . no, thirteen in cauterization: to make insensible, dead; to sear, burn, or destroy tissue. Had he undergone cauterization? The number of the beast was thirteen.

Bunkowski tried to focus, searching for memory of cauterizations past, as a caustic envelope of sunrays, reflected or refracted by the curved surface of his broken computer screen, catoptrically mirrored the reflected light.

BUTCHER

A catalyzed cataplexy had left him catabolized, catastrophically catatonic on the catafalque of his categorically catadioptric catechism.

What this cat wouldn't give for a mouse!

~ **10**

Bayou Ridge

She is beautifully slender. Her skin is perfect. Flawless. Only under magnification will one see the microscopic imperfections. A tiny curlicue against the skin, a single wispy tendril. She is so lovely. Run your hand down her length and feel the pleasure of her shape. Smooth, sleek, and shapely. She is a work of art. He labors over her, moving back and forth, grunting with effort, and a drop of his sweat falls onto her skin.

Her skin glows with a thin sheen of oil. She is his . . . and soon he will take her and hold her as he screws her, and she will hardly make a sound.

The tiny silver curlicue is gone now as he removes her from the metal lathe. She is delicate and he caresses her silvery skin, removing invisible metallic hairs. He will look at her again now, closely, in the strongest light, searching for anything that might interfere with her perfection.

Her insides are already mounted on the receiver of the piece in one of his heavy-duty workbench vises, turned carefully, meticulously, her inner core true to the thousandth of an inch, and soon her strange innards will be covered by this beautifully shiny tube of skin.

She is baffled, double-walled, packed, stacked, mounted, milled, fastidiously turned, scrupulously calibrated, and now it is his pleasure to slide her outer body over this intimacy of washers, one-eighth-inch space expanders, and coiled steel wool.

Slowly he eases her skin into place and screws her tight. She is a perfect fit with her insides. Both of her parts have been cut from the same block of aluminum. Her metal curls litter the floor like the shorn hair of a silver-tressed woman, and at last she is in place. Silver and slick and streamlined—a perfect creation that looks like a glistening extension of the barrel. Her tiny, dangerous mouth is open and ready. The exquisitely shaped lips form a hard permanent O.

His income tax returns do not read "Raymond Meara, gunsmith." Meara is a farmer by occupation. But there are four perfectly turned suppressors to belie this, and under his hand-hewn cedar barn, packed in their original Cosmoline sheaths, wrapped and sealed in four-mil plastic, then sealed again in a watertight, airtight coffin, are ten assault rifles.

Tonight he will sell some of these pieces—these collector's items. It is not something Meara looks forward to with any degree of pleasure. The man who buys is extremely dangerous, and of a disposition that at best might be called tricky. Meara has promised to deliver a half dozen of these illegal weapons, for which he will receive nine thousand dollars in cash. Raymond Meara is what the jargon terms a runner. He runs guns.

He has paid seven thousand dollars for the ten pieces. Why, you might well ask, would he put himself at risk for two thousand dollars? There are two reasons, three really. He needs money. The farm from which he derives his main livelihood is located in a floodway that may some day be dynamited. Meara owes money, and must have more money still to operate.

But he does not make this move for the two-thousand-dollar immediate profit, but for the four pieces he will keep. For these four pieces, with their custom-made sound suppressors, he will net another eight to ten thousand dollars. He will probably move three. Take a quick six thousand dollars. Keep one for hard times.

In theory the math supports Raymond Meara's venture. The problem, the unknown element, is always the point of exchange. Meara gambles.

Raymond has some degree of trust for the man *he* buys from. But for his supplier perhaps he is a potentially dangerous, necessary risk the seller must take. Similarly, the man tonight is a calculated risk.

Meara will concentrate on the eight-thousand-plus that will be his profit on an investment of seven thousand dollars and a bit of his time, skill, and expertise.

He will concentrate on wiping out his debts with this money that he has not yet earned. This is what Raymond Meara, farmer, will think about until it is time to exchange the iron for the butter.

He will not think about the possibilities of being ripped off or arrested and jailed or hurt or killed, and certainly he will not think about Jesus SanDiego.

Meara will save all of this for tonight, when he will think of nothing else beyond staying alive.

For now he turns off all the equipment and the lights, and returns to the house. He picks up the paper to kill some time and there is his horoscope, the first thing he reads. It says: "scorpio (Oct. 24–Nov. 22) If you deal with the wrong kinds of people you are going to be left at a disadvantage."

11

Night came with a buzzing presence. Meara waited, as instructed, at the top of the steep ravine leading down into Blue Hole. The air was alive with biting flies, mosquitoes, and vicious, microscopic sub-gnat annoyances that kept a man wiping, slapping, and fanning at his face. They went for the mouth and eyes and ears and nostrils, and they thought mosquito repellent tasted like Coors.

He'd dug worms up here at the top of the barrow pit at sundown on a bad bug night and gone home a solid, red mass of angry welts; a festering, itching nightmare.

It reminded him of a time back in-country, when he and another dude walked into some picturesque bug-tussle that instantly covered them in everything from leeches to unknown entomological mutants. They hit like iron filings clinging to a bar magnet. Stuck to skin the way ice cubes stick to a wet sponge. Meshed to flesh the way maggots are drawn to freshly-spilled intestine. It had been a bloodsucker of a nightime ambush and now this word ripped out at him—Ambush!

He fanned micrognats as he moved toward the stand of willows, automatically thinking in terms of broken silhouettes and target opportunities. Moving into the terrain, thinking about possibilities.

He had a chance to save this big boy nine thousand bucks. All he had to do right now was get real stupid. Or be careless.

A man could put a sniper down in these woods a ways.

A patient man who could wait under netting and camouflage until the boss wipes his forehead or adjusts his package just so and the shooter takes his first clean head shot.

Somebody very good. Put them up on that knoll over there, or deep in the darkening woods. Give 'em a thou. You could still save eight.

The imagination was a terrible thing.

Jesus "Sandy" SanDiego was a very bad boy and he played on a tough court. But Meara discounted half of the stories. Sandy had an extremely unfortunate reputation. They said he liked to hurt people. He had been in Farmington once, and they let him out and not long afterward he was dealing in various things. There was talk of a dope burn that had gone sour. A torture death. A pair of corpses left incinerated down by the junction of two old county roads was said to have been Sandy's work.

But would he take a man off for guns he hadn't seen? Raymond slapped at a mosquito, mashing it against his neck and flicking off dead insect and blood. Damn. Another hungry devil bored into his scalp and he scratched at his head.

That night of the bad ambush the leeches had been the worst he'd ever known all the time he'd been overseas. Aggressive and as lethal as you can imagine.

Wisdom: the ultimate catheter nightmare is a hungry, hemophilic worm threading the eye of the penis, or a leech penetrating the puckered anal rosebud.

He felt his neck crawl and his hand was moving when a voice behind him said, "Yo," and he almost let a burst of pee loose in his britches.

"Damn!"

"S'matter?" SanDiego, moving quietly out of the woods, something in his hand, coming from the direction of the river. Meara a perfect silhouette against the top of the pit.

"Damn, Sandy. I didn't hear you comin'."

"You ain't slowin' down on me, are ya, chief?" The hand moved out of the shadows into Meara's face. It was a can of Bud Light. "Better have one of these."

"No thanks," Meara said.

"Okay," SanDiego said, shrugging. "Let's do the thing."

"Yeah." Ray moved to the pickup and popped the tailgate latch. He reached in and slid the crate onto the gate. Even on the old piece of slick rug-runner it was all he could do to move it. "There you go." The huge man tossed the can away from him absent-mindedly.

SanDiego looked around a little. Glanced down into the pit. Back towards the highway. Meara heard the one in the woods before he saw him and eased on around behind the truck, standing at the right side of the vehicle, the pickup between him and the willow trees, as Sandy examined the pieces.

The skinhead came out of the trees with a goofy look on his face, as if he'd just seen something he shouldn't, and kept moving toward the truck.

Meara tucked his hands under his arms and leaned forward against the truck bed, saying softly. "This boy with you?"

"Huh?" SanDiego looked up and then back to the goods. "Um."

"'Spose to be just you 'n' me, Sandy. That was what I understood."

"It is. You don't want you 'n' me to have to carry these clean across the bar pit, do ya, Ray?"

"No."

"Well, there you are."

"Where you parked, Sandy?"

"I'm over yonder." He nodded in the direction of the farmland to the south of them.

"Oh." That was another thing about him. He ran with some of these skinhead weirdos. This one was up beside the truck. Saying nothing. Just staring at the guns.

"Nine large," the big man said, staring down into the unwrapped assault rifles.

"Right."

"Take a check?" The skinhead kid laughed, a braying mule noise. Meara smiled.

"Maybe another time."

SanDiego laughed mirthlessly and slowly slid his right hand into his hip pocket. Meara was conscious of the stillness. Even the gnats seemed to be holding their breath. He still had his hands tucked under his arms, but he wasn't leaning forward.

"Nine large," he said, laying the envelope on the tailgate and looking at Meara. Raymond moved over and took the packet with his left hand, steadying it on the side of the truck and fanning it quickly. Ninety hundreds had a nice, thick heft to them.

"Count it, man."

"With you, Sandy? No need. I'll have some more stuff in a couple of weeks."

"Yeah?"

"Including a couple more of these babies with suppressors." Ever the salesman.

Jesus SanDiego took hold of the crate and slid it to him as if it were a bushel of apples.

"Grab holt," he said, and the skinhead took the other handle, the pair of them swinging the heavy crate off the truck and moving toward the river. Meara didn't even shut the tailgate, just came around and opened the door, got in, started the motor, and backed down in the direction from which he'd come, his envelope on the seat beside him.

A hard mothering deuce, he thought, wiping his hand on his Levis. He roared out onto the blacktop and cranked every window open, flailing at the swarm of bugs that had joined him in the cab of the pickup. He took a deep breath of the hot night air. Now he could think about the rest of that easy-spending money he hadn't made yet.

12

New Madrid Levee

Daniel had experienced it all during his hellish life, always on either the giving or taking side of pain. He'd been beaten, burnt, taunted, tortured, squashed, stomped, struck, steamrollered, jumped, jacklit, spat on, suffocated, sledgehammered, and damn near snuffed, but this was something else.

The enormous beast had come to believe that yes, though he could be hurt, he would always bounce back. Not so this time. The human battle cruiser had sunk.

The aftermath of something all-powerful, like an exostosis of impacted bone spur working its way out of the root of a rotten tooth, broken during amateur extraction, tried to make it to the surface of his battered awareness. No dice. He'd been freight-trained, he knew that now. His brain had quit on him.

It had to be the beating. It was the only thing in his experience that approached the level of his present condition, as best as he could assess it. It had convinced him that when it comes to mortality, one could forget size, heft, strength, muscle, resolve, grit, race, religion, or sex. When it came down to it everybody bled. Everybody cried.

The remembered pain of the beating warmed him with encouragement, as it was the first thing that came back with any degree of detail. He'd brought it on himself, coming back from the doctor's office, or on his way, fully jacketed, shackled, restrained, black boxed, cuffed, and locked to steel bars. He could vividly picture the guard.

"Lookee here," Spanish had whispered near the biter,

*which was a kind of helmet and fencing-mask–type
contraction, "the Goodyear blimp's back on its tether. You
gonna get a taste now, you ugly mountain of shit." He
struck at the sore ankle but Chaingang managed to move
just enough to deflect the worst of it. He said something
and the guard froze. It had all been calculated, right down
to the hour and minute, everything but the suffering.*

*"What the fuck did you say?" he said, lips curled into a
drooling snarl. Chaingang whispered something again
and the man flew into the predicted rage, whipping the
baton across the head of the bound man again and again,
trying his best to kill him.*

Blackness again.

13

Bayou Ridge

Raymond Meara came back from the woods with maybe
a half a rack of chainsawed oak, and broke his second
sweat of the day unloading it, throwing the ash and gum
off to one side. It was cold and the perspiration hurt the
bad side of his face a little, so he turned and worked with
his back more to the wind.

He split it all down into quarters, using a plain wedge
and sledge, and then he took a maul and did the smaller
pieces. He took a very sharp double-bitted axe out of the
pickup and made a stack of kindling, and carried an
armload into the house, hearing the phone make a ping
as it quit ringing. It rang a second time while he was
finishing up stoking the wood stove and he picked it up
on the fourth ring.

"Yeah."

"Ray?"

"Hello." It was Rosemary.

"I called a couple times before but I guess you was out."

"Yeah. I just came in."

"We gonna do somethin' tonight?" she asked.

"I gotta go to the spillway meeting. You wanna go with me?"

"Sure. I reckon so."

"Then we'll come on out here when they finish," he told her, unnecessarily. It was all they ever did beside go out to eat once in a while.

"All right. You gonna pick me up?"

"I'll be by about seven-thirty."

"What should I wear?"

"Clothes," he said, hanging up. Rosemary was pretty. Divorced, with three small children, bleached blond hair, and a tight little shape lots of guys around Bayou City liked the looks of. Meara promised her nothing, and she didn't ask for much more. As long as they kept it that way he figured he'd enjoy her company. He picked her up in the driveway of the ramshackle trailer court where she had a mobile home.

"Hi," she said excitedly, sliding in beside him. She seemed small and proud under her beauty-parlor hair.

"This'll bore the pants off ya," he told her.

"Promises, promises." Her mouth had a lot of mileage on it but she gave a smile easily. It was just that her eyes stayed in neutral.

"Atta way," he said, reaching over and patting her leg. He felt pretty good. His back and face were acting up some but that wasn't anything. It smelled good in the pickup with the heat on, a mixture of soap scents, Rosemary's perfume, and truck smells. He didn't feel like getting out when they pulled up to the meeting hall.

By the time the meeting was over, Raymond wished he'd stayed in the truck. Some of the troubleshooters for the Clearwater Trench project tried to defuse and/or deflect every question with big, long-winded spiels about "hypothetical flooding scenario number thirteen," and a lot of technical stuff about "reservoir gauging" and "overflow dispersement." Nobody knew what the hell they were talking about. Finally he'd had enough and he stood up and they recognized him.

"My name's Meara. I got a farm right there in the spillway. You blow that levee, I'm wiped out. So are a bunch of other farmers in there. But look here: Clearwater Trench is dead bang over the New Madrid fault line. You're gonna' set off a massive explosion right on top of the fault? How do you know you're not gonna' trigger one of the worst earthquakes in history?"

"Come on," the man chuckled patronizingly, "it's not like we were dropping a hydrogen bomb on it. We're just talking about cutting the levee."

"By cutting you mean blowing, and I know something about demolition. You people wanna' pop the caps on three hundred tons of DBA-105P, some of the most powerful slurry-type explosive made. The truth is you really don't know what the reaction's going to be when you explode that much right on top of the fault line.

"What about scour? What about blue holes? Have you thought about that? What if the Mississippi diverts right through the hole you blow and here comes all that water, is the set-back levee gonna' hold the entire force of the river? You have plans to evacuate all of Bayou City? You got that many helicopters and pontoon craft standing by? Any idea how fast that water's gonna' come slammin' in on top of these folks? Ever been in a real bad flash flood? That's nothing to what it'll be like. You got a lousy deal here." Meara sat back down, red faced, his scar aglow like a white brand.

"I understand your concerns. And, no offense, you aren't exactly without a vested interest, considering the location of your farmland. However, all of these factors you mention are being looked at. We are going to study on all of this. Next?"

Ray felt helpless and trapped in the flow of something as certain and unavoidable as the tide.

"Rosemary James," a man's voice said as they walked

outside after the meeting. "I do declare, child. You're getting so pretty I can hardly stand it, you know that?" It was Milas Kehoe, a wealthy rancher and landowner. Meara's companion smiled and kept moving toward the truck, but Kehoe stepped in front of Meara and said softly, "Ray?"

"Yeah."

"What do you think?"

"I can't really say, man."

"Kinda' makes that offer of mine look a little on the high side, now, don't it?" He doubled over and started roaring with laughter as if he'd told the funniest joke of all time. Meara just walked around him and went over to the pickup and climbed in beside Rosemary.

"What was all that about?" she asked.

He repeated the one-liner.

"Kehoe tried to buy the farm a couple of times. I guess that's his idea of humor, rubbing it in that the ground isn't worth as much now that it might get flooded."

"That's terrible."

"Oh, well," he ground the ignition, "it was getting flooded with backwater every couple of years anyway. I guess that's why it's called the spillway, eh?"

Some dark, troubling thing was dogging his trail. He felt it close at hand, ominous and unswerving. Something bad was coming. It grated like a loud, unanswered phone, and Meara put the truck in gear and floored the accelerator, driving straight into its teeth.

Then and Now

Dr. Emil Shtolz and
Anna Kaplan

STEN MELLER

~~ 14

München—1944

The kindly looking physician in the white smock bids the two armed Waffen-SS guards to leave the room. They are the ones the patients whisper about, the ones they call Ignorant and Knowing behind their backs—*Schoppen* and *Wissende*. He nods in the direction of the operating bay and the nurse takes one end of the table and the two of them push the wheeled work surface, rather like a gurney, next to some lab equipment. He begins reading as she plugs tubes into vials and retorts, attaches electrodes. There is little sense of what is about to come.

He is glancing at a translation of a paper on gerontomorphises. His interests are wide and he studies the words with interest, feeling a light touch as a power cord brushes against his smock, hearing an almost inaudible "Excuse me, Herr Doktor." He steps back a bit and looks up from his reading material. The patient's eyes are riveted on him. He smiles into the man's gaze.

"You're being a fine, cooperative patient." Through the door he can hear Ignorant and Knowing laughing together out in the hallway, their voices loud and grating.

The man on the wheeled table, small, with salt-and-pepper hair visible where the head has not been shaved, makes a movement with his mouth like a grimace and the physician smiles again.

"Nothing to worry about," the doctor begins to say, soothingly, as he feels something strike him. He looks down at the spit, gets a tissue, and wipes it from his white coat.

"Nazi *pig,*" the patient says, and curses him, telling

him to lie in the ground and burn. The physician looks at the man sadly. "You treat us like animals because you have power now, but you will not live forever. I will go to my spiritual reward, but *you,* you will—"

The nurse places an object over the man's mouth and his words are muffled as he says, "rot in Hades. God will not forgive your crimes!"

The man in the white coat leans near and says in soft, gentle tones, "It will not help you to struggle," as he observes the patient straining at the leather straps. "Listen to me a moment. It is only natural that you are afraid, that you feel hatred and fear. But please do not be afraid. This process will be virtually painless, I assure you." The man's eyes look daggers at him. "You have no way of knowing how important you are. You're part of a scientific breakthrough that will someday benefit all mankind."

"You're wasting your breath, I'm afraid," another man says, coming out of the operating bay and hearing his colleague. "I've tried to do the same thing with these people and they seem incapable of understanding."

"If they could only know. We're all making history together here."

"That's right. And of course no one wants to undergo surgery, however painless or scientifically valuable their contribution might be." The younger physician moves into the bright light that floods the doorway. "But better here than in the Auschwitz Special Treatment Units, eh?"

The older physician nods and raises his bushy eyebrows in agreement. The young one turns, and the man on the table sees the sign of the devil on his face and his heart almost stops with fear. The younger one with the reddish-purple mark on his face, what the patients call the Tear of Satan, is the one they call the Boy Butcher.

"Just think," he says to the wide-eyed patient, nodding to the anesthesiologist, "our contribution to medical science could be the one that leads to a new dawn for the race of man. Perhaps your name will live on for eternity. Bring the baby in," he tells the nurse.

The three persons begin attaching more apparatus to the man who is strapped to the wheeled table. The younger physician begins to make marks on the patient's freshly shaved skull. In a very soft voice he tells the man what to expect, telling him in that manner he has that is at once solicitous and threatening.

"You will lose your sensitivity but you will not lose consciousness at first," he says, almost in a lover's whisper. The bright light glints on bone saws and drills. "So don't be surprised at some slight discomfort as we begin the discorporation process." The man on the table faints as the Boy Butcher whispers gentle words of unspeakable promise.

This is Riestermann's play-pretty, the younger physician thinks. Doomed to instant failure, of course. Uncle Hans, which is how he thinks of his avuncular mentor and benefactor, is caught up in a series of tests involving the discorporation of human infant brains, in which attempts are being made to keep fresh brain transplants living in a host. Literally countless animals and now babies have been unsuccessfully discorporated. The series clearly cannot succeed, yet Uncle Hans perseveres. This dead Jew will be nothing more than numbers in a ledger, lines on a graph. Number cipher cipher, of Adult Non-Aryan Male Host Subjects/Infant Brain cipher cipher. Empty, dead numbers.

Next week looks much more promising, he thinks. They will turn out a lot of skullcaps next week. That is their little joke between them. They make real skullcaps for the Jews here.

He does not see himself as a monster, this Boy Butcher. In Emil Shtolz's twisted mind he is the perfect Renaissance man, German by birth, Italian by spirit. A genius, they say, a young star of the Reich. Learned. Suave. An elitist who already is master of the operating room, the drawing room, or the bedroom. Especially the latter, where he can give free reign to the other Emil, the one to whom a tortured scream is music. In his mind he knows he is far above the laws that constrain lesser mortals, and even beyond the laws of God. Men like Emil are a law unto themselves.

When the operation is finished, he discards his cap, mask, gloves, and bloodied gown, and leaves the surgical bay, passing the lab annex and his office, and turning to walk quickly down the hallway. It has excited him, all the blood, the feeling of power when he exposes the brains, knowing that he and Uncle Hans are free to have their fun, all in the name of the program. He is very excited by the time he pulls his heavy ring of keys out, fumbling with the locked door of room number three.

"Hello, my darling," he says, and the little girl runs to him, her arms outstretched.

15

The first premonition of what he would remember only as the bad times came a couple of weeks later, unexpectedly. He was in his office, reading, when the older doctor's voice caused the younger man to look up from his papers. He heard a nurse saying something to Herr Doktor, and Riestermann saying "Danke," as he came around the corner and into view.

"Busy?" asked Riestermann.

"Just reading."

"Who have you scheduled for tomorrow, the host subject?"

"Um, I have Number Twelve."

"No. I don't want Twelve yet. Get that little one you

like. What's her name?" Shtolz looked at the physician who'd become a mentor to him. "The little fair-skinned Jewess you're so partial to? Let's use her."

"We've discussed this," Shtolz said, swallowing. "Don't you remember? Twelve is all prepared."

"Emil," the old physician said softly, "I don't mind your little games. But you're growing attached to Number Three." He stepped all the way into the small room and pulled the door shut behind him. "Pleasures of the flesh can become self-destructive when a person isn't careful. It's all right to indulge but the key is moderation," he was almost whispering. Shtolz could feel himself reddening.

"I don't know what you mean." The words caught in his throat.

"Let's not embarrass one another, Emil. I wouldn't say anything to you but," he gestured toward the wall, "you know how things are around here. I'm just watching out for your welfare." He smiled paternally. "Agree? Good." He winked his Uncle Hans wink, opening the door and moving out into the hall.

Shtolz had the oddest sensation that he'd dreamed the moment between them. It was the closest the two had come to anything resembling an argument since Emil was brought into the program.

In spite of the degree of closeness imposed by the work they did, the empathic bond that two evil kindred spirits might establish, Riestermann was someone Shtolz was sure he'd never get to know. Nonetheless, the older man normally treated him as an equal, a respected partner. He didn't give a damn which subject they hooked up to the brain tomorrow. Shtolz was sure he knew what this was about. It had come from those black-shirted dumbheads in the front office.

There was one officious swine in particular, a suspicious and excessively observant clerk type from, according to the grapevine, the complex on Prinz Albrechtstrasse in Berlin. Eyes and ears for Internal Security, or the Staatspolizei, or even Himmler himself.

Emil understood the need, obviously, for the program not to be compromised. But this thing he felt for the little girl whom Hans Riestermann referred to coldly as Number Three, defied logic or regulations. She was something he had grown attached to.

He loved it when she would kiss his face, arching up on little tiptoes to "taste his strawberry," touching her warm, moist lips to his birthmark. The way she was so quick to forgive his excesses when the heat of his perversions caused him to inflict pain.

He wanted to take his girlchild and escape from a world that he sensed was beginning to collapse. Politics had no meaning to Emil Shtolz. Science was everything. He would envy the progress of the program, so long as it lasted, as it transcended any lowly morality, but there were practical matters of survival to deal with, both his and the object of his passion's.

The Waffen-SS clinic was within a quick hop to the border and he was not one to be without ways and means. It would be easy, he thought, getting up decisively and leaving his office, turning down the hallway outside the laboratory annex. They'd expect him to head for Switzerland, which was enticingly close, but Poland was only the narrow width of Czechoslovakia from there. He could melt into the crowds with his beautiful love toy and soon the Tear of Satan would be forever obliterated.

He stopped before her room and removed his keys, unlocking the heavy security door. The hallway smelled of equal parts of fear, formaldehyde, and insanity, as he closed and locked the door behind him.

"Hello, my darling girl," he said, waiting for the child to run to him with outstretched arms as he had taught her.

"Hello, Papa," she said. They kissed. There was only a bed, toilet, and a ceiling light fixture shrouded in steel mesh. The shelf of the old-fashioned water closet was several feet off the ground, nearly as high as he could reach. He gripped her tiny waist and with considerable effort sat her up on the shelf.

"Stand up on that, darling," he told her.

She shook her head no, the long, beautiful hair gently falling against the smoothness of her perfect, blemishless, oval-shaped face. Not defying him, but afraid.

"Do what I say," he coaxed her, gently, smiling with pleasure. He had learned she had a great fear of heights. *"Do it!"* he barked, putting some authority in his tone. "It's only a few feet off the floor. Just stand up."

He loved her pained expression as she forced herself to stand on the small ledge. Her hands were outstretched at either side, pressed against the wall.

"Please, Papa, let me come down now."

"I will, darling. That's what I want you to do. Come down," he almost laughed with glee. "Put your hands out like this," he said, showing her what he wanted. She complied instantly, but looked as if she were about to cry. "Jump into Papa's arms. Papa will catch you, you know that." The girlchild trusted him. She stepped off like someone stepping into a shallow swimming pool.

"No, no," he corrected, catching her thin body and sitting her back on the shelf in one motion, not even noticing the effort. "That's not it at all. I want you to dive into my arms, like a little bird." The child, whose name was Marta, simply sat on the shelf, shaking in terror and confusion.

"Please," she began, tears trickling down her face, making him even more resolved.

"Get up there, you vixen. Stand up! That's it. Put the arms again like so. . . . Now, *dive* into the air like a bird." She was frozen to the spot. "Do it, you bitch, flap those wings and fly to Papa. Come on!"

The girl, her thin arms held to her sides, flung herself into space, and of course he caught her and sat her back on the shelf.

"Do it again and fly this time," he said, his voice thick.

"Please, Papa, please let me come down," she begged, sobbing.

"Come down then, darling, flap those arms and fly

down here to Papa." She dove off but this time he waited an extra quarter beat, keeping his hands down long enough to cause her heart to come up in her throat, snatching her just as she nearly smashed into the concrete floor, and the scream that his next kiss trapped inside her was what he'd been waiting for. For the Boy Butcher, this was his foreplay to lovemaking.

~~ 16

The morning's events had been a slow montage of daydreaming. Riestermann had called off the scheduled experiments because of some minor technical problems, and Shtolz had spent the day idly, his thoughts often returning to the object of his lust. He was almost ready to make the break. Their escape route was mapped out, and it had become a matter of biding his time until the vagaries of fate favored the logistics.

He'd been concentrating on the young sex slave he'd constructed inside the dark hollows of his imagination. Marta as she would look in three years, and Marta as she might appear in womanhood. He visualized the beginning roundness of her breasts as they might look when they began to blossom. He thought about the nipples, as yet undeveloped buds, how they might take on shape. The way in which they might change texturally in his devoted hands, under his particular tutelary influence.

The fantasy simmered as he went about routine chores. Clean-up work around the office and in the lab annex. He thought about ways he might discipline the girl. He hardened at the thought of how certain implements of the surgical trade might be employed. The word forceps came and perched on the tongue of his imagination, tasting of salty blood and hot jism. He tasted the edges of his thoughts, biting into another twisted daydream.

As he did so, Dr. Emil Shtolz chanced upon a stack of three fresh cadavers. The fruits of Uncle Hans's morning? He wondered if his mentor had worked in the O.R. after all. Oh, well. He would clean up after his colleague. Wouldn't be the first time. He would roll each corpse onto . . .

He recognized the body subconsciously at first, the look of the bony, mutilated cadaver in the lab morgue tagged "Human remains: Host Subject No. 3," bearing Riestermann's loopy, hand-scrawled addendum.

The horror of it smashed him like a wall, burying him in the dirty rubble of shock. It was a pounding, merciless wave of hard data that his mind tried first to reject. He wanted to cry but only a lewd, inarticulate, choked thoracic gargle left his lips. Shtolz tried next to yell but the wall of undigested raw input stifled his rage.

And the God in whom Emil had not the slightest shred of belief, this God who suddenly chose to intervene and assert himself, declaring as he did so that he chose not to be a merciful God, took the black core of Emil Shtolz deeply into madness.

Bayou Ferry—1949

The man and the woman had their four youngest children, three boys and a girl, all packed into the wagon. The man had fashioned a crude seating arrangement on the front so that he could use the wagon for a family buckboard of sorts.

Two red-brown-colored mules were hitched to the doubletree, and the man took up a bit of slack in the reins and leaned to the side.

Both the man and woman in front had faces like earth, tanned so deeply they were almost a solid, dark brown. The woman, in a sunbonnet and a garment like a duster; the man bareheaded, in a faded blue work shirt buttoned to the throat and overalls that had seen a lot of hard wear. Both adults wore work shoes. The children riding in back were all dressed alike, the little girl tomboyish in T-shirt and frayed jeans, all four of the children shoeless.

The man and his wife had been quarreling. She had complained to him about the way he treated the cows. She could not stand to hear him beating them. He was a hard man, who had led a hard, rough life, and he had no patience with recalcitrant animals. Then the accident the day before. So often the fates conspired against him. The muscles in the side of his face twitched as he thought about his problems, wondering how he would make this small bit of ground he owned grow sufficient crops to feed the seven hungry bellies that were his responsibility.

They were heading up a rutted country road, little more than a worn path. He thought if the mules failed him now he would take the axe handle from the back of the wagon and kill them both dead in their traces, beat them both to death on the spot. They obligingly pulled the wagon up the slight incline, as if they could read his fierce thoughts, bouncing the occupants of the wooden wagon each time the wide, iron-rimmed wheels slipped off a hard mud rut.

"Pa, there's the cabin up yonder," one of his boys said. The father made no response.

The one they were coming to see lived in what was left of the log cabin old man Thurmond had built before it burnt down. The Royal feller had built him a sort of lean-to up against what was left of the logs, mainly one wall and a great fireplace of river stones.

The man spoke for the first time, a single, deeply uttered syllable that sounded like "haw," but it was enough to stop the mules. They recognized the tone. These were the same mules that had been foolish enough to balk as they pulled a breaking plow through black gumbo, and they weren't likely to ignore their master's voice. Years of failure, frustration, abject poverty, and bitter hopelessness were distilled into the monosyllabic command. He might control little else but by God he would control his mules.

He dropped to the ground and slid the heavy crate out of the wagon, moving in the direction of the cabin, but stopping as the woman said, "Earl!" in her barking, harsh tone. He turned, irritated, and saw he'd forgotten something. He went back and let her drop the huge onions into the crate. He was approaching the dwelling when the man inside pushed the crudely curtained doorway open and stepped from his makeshift cabin into warm sunlight.

"Howdy," he said, his voice loud in his own ears. The man coming toward him nodded slightly, but neither he nor the brood of kids spoke. A woman sat in the wagon looking straight ahead. He did not recognize any of them.

"You Royal?" the man asked him.

"Yes."

"Wanted to thank you for what you done yesterday."

The one called Royal stared without comprehension, shaking his head slightly.

"What's that now?"

"That was one of my boys you saved yesterday." A kid had tried to dive off a railway trestle into deep water. He had broken a shoulder, collar bone, and several ribs. He'd been lucky he hadn't broken his neck.

"Glad I was nearby. You must be the Ledbetters?" The man nodded. The word "was" came out "vuss."

"Cain't pay ya for the doctorin'," Earl Ledbetter said, bluntly, voice raspy like a file on metal. Without further ceremony he set the crate down, turned, and began walking back to the wagon.

The crate contained fresh garden tomatoes, some of the biggest he'd ever seen. Squash. Two enormous onions. Potatoes.

"Thank you," he said. The "thank" sounded as if it were spelled with an *s*. He had learned to speak their language beautifully. His idiomatic English was nearly flawless, and he'd already lost a lot of his accent.

He had heard about the man. Heard some men joking about Earl Bedwetter, making fun of the man's name. A man who apparently had a reputation for not paying his bills. He didn't care a damn about that. He had only one interest, in creating an impenetrable legend of disguise.

"If you ever need medical attention, just come see me. I won't charge you anything," he added, hastily, knowing "any-sink" was one of his bad ones. The *th* sound was so awkward for him. He thought the man might have nodded before he picked up the reins and started back home with his family.

Solomon Royal had only one thought. He wanted to wash his old identity away. He'd been working downriver and had seen a tattered scrap of newspaper, an advertisement for a tiny rural community that was without health care. It was a chance to start over. To build a new reality.

Hard eyes narrowed as he watched the wagon from behind the rag of a curtain that hung over the doorway of his rough-hewn cabin.

"Auf Wiedersehen, Herr Bedvetter," he said quietly, scarcely moving his small, red lips. "See you," he added, for practice. The girl in the wagon would fuel the heat of his imagined fantasy that night.

~~~ 18

New Madrid County, Missouri

More than forty years ago, when he'd first come to this soil, a man in hiding, he'd selected his safe haven with the greatest care. There were, in the final analysis, only half a dozen geographical areas that beckoned. The big, teeming industrial hubs of the American Northeast, mass melting pots where accents blurred and went unnoticed; the booming Midwestern blue-collar cities like Detroit, with their ghettos and ethnic communities, and the impoverished agri-villages of the heartland and the Bible Belt South. He'd gravitated to the latter, and worked his way up the Mississippi River to a rural area in dire need of a medical clinic.

Shtolz's goal was to create an identity that could be sculpted into something invulnerable. Oddly, the cosmetic surgery he'd undergone in South America had not been a total success. The birthmark and the reshaped cheeks should have been augmented further. The eyes and mouth and ears needed to be changed, but by then time had become a pressing factor. He was one of the most hunted men living, wanted not only by the fanatical Jews but by his own people, and he'd made his way to North America without a moment to spare.

The young Boy Butcher considered many things, but while it would have been the prudent course to forsake any further work in medicine or the sciences, he'd been somewhat reassured by the lack of curiosity in him by the locals. The state of Missouri was as war ravaged and poverty stricken as parts of Europe. The small agricultural communities were in great need of farm labor and skilled artisans of any kind. Emil Shtolz could do many things well. After a short stint as a manual laborer, working every waking hour to absorb the peculiarities of idiomatic American slang, he decided on his plan of action.

It was common at the time for illegal aliens to obtain "tombstone I.D.s," which were easily and inexpensively created. Shtolz found a number of deceased residents resting in obscure county graveyards who'd been born around the time he had. Setting up a "genealogical research firm" involved nothing more sophisticated then renting a mail box number out of the busy Memphis postal zone, and within a few weeks he'd come up with a handful of candidates. Individuals who had vanished more or less without a trace, persons without living relatives or obtainable histories. One of them particularly appealed to him because of the name.

Solomon Royal pleased him greatly because of the play on the first name. The Seal of Solomon. The Magen David. King Solomon was, indeed, a Solomon Royal. So within a few days an application was filed for a replacement birth certificate, and Emil Shtolz no longer existed.

The next step was to obtain documentation. Like the officials of his mother country, Germany, the petty bureaucrats in the U.S.A. respected paper. Using a variety of techniques ranging from mail-drop correspondence schools who sold diplomas to forged documentation, Solomon Royal became the learned and lettered Dr. Solomon Royal, complete with a fabricated past that implied he might be of Jewish descent. The truest thing in his story was the fact that he'd "escaped from the Nazis." But Solomon Royal escaped them as they were on the brink of war, in the late 1930s.

A natural manipulator, Royal used media to build a legend to reinforce his web of lies with checkable pictorial proof. Before long there were pictures of him "taken in World War II" as he worked with American servicemen, photos captioned with dates that could then be reproduced in other stories that repeated the same mythology and cushioned and insulated the lies with another generation of journalism. As the years passed, those who knew Royal, or who had been treated by him, repeated the legend until it became part of the community folklore. Dr. Emil Shtolz, product of his own brilliant imagination, had successfully reinvented himself.

At the moment, the legend was driving slowly into a chat-covered driveway some fourteen miles from his clinic and turning off the ignition of his humble used car.

"It's Doc Royal," the woman inside the farmhouse said in that pleased tone people reserve for the individuals for whom their affection is greatest. She turned from the window to the elderly man seated at the kitchen table. "I tell you that man has been so good to us. We could never have kept Buck home without Dr. Royal helping the way he has. He's wonderful!"

"I know he's a real blessing to this community," the man said in a surprisingly deep, resonant voice. It was a voice used to commanding the attention of a congregation from the pulpit, and the years had not dulled its powerful thunder, but it was too loud in the small kitchen and he noticed it. "I've heard some wonderful things about him, Mrs. Jenks, I truly have."

She was pushing back the folding doors that separated the front room from the kitchen. A chrome hospital bed was the only object of furniture in the small front room and a white-haired man occupied it, staring unblinking at the ceiling.

"It's Doc Royal, honey," she told the man in the bed. Even though they said the signals didn't get through she thought maybe sometimes he might be able to understand, so she still spoke to him as if he could comprehend.

"I thank you for the coffee and I'll just go on directly," the man said, pushing away from the table and standing with considerable effort, old, brittle bones popping loudly. "I've got to drive to Caruthersville."

"You're welcome to stay now," she said.

"No, no. I'll go on."

"I do appreciate you coming out like this, Brother Peterson," she said, and they chatted amiably until the footsteps and the knocking punctuated their conversation.

"It's open. Come in," she called, moving in the direction of the back door as it swung open.

"Hello," the Jenks's family doctor said, coming in to the familiar kitchen. "Hello," he said again, nodding to the man with her.

"Doc, this is Brother Peterson from Canalou," she said, smiling at their old friend.

"Oh, we see each other around."

"We sure do, we sure do," the older man shook hands with Dr. Royal. "I'll go on, Mrs. Jenks," he said.

"Don't let me run you off," Royal said.

"I've got to be going," he responded, moving with octogenarian singleness of purpose. The woman walked to the door with him and when she got back Dr. Royal was already standing in the front room looking down at the man in bed.

"Buck asked for Budrell Peterson to preach the—" she started to say funeral but the word stuck and she said "—the service for him when it's time."

"Oh? Well, that's nice."

"Brother Peterson's Pentacostal," she said.

"He'll give you a dandy. I heard one he preached not long ago and it was quite eloquent. Hello, Buck," he said, putting his hand on the bare arm of the man in the bed. Fiery blue eyes blazed from a gaunt, haunted stare.

"Look who's here. I wish you'd get me out of this gol' dang thing."

"What gol' dang thing is that?"

"This heliocopter," the bedfast man said, a bandaged hand weakly simulating the pattern of a spinning blade.

"They land this dang thing in the field where the wolves are and stir them all up."

"You're not in a heliocopter," the woman said sharply, "Buck, you're at home."

"That's a hydraulic lift," Dr. Royal said, pointing to the large device that stood beside the hospital bed. "That's how Naomi gets you up to change you. You're at home, Buck."

"How many wolves you kill today?"

"Would you please fix me up with a pan of warm water?" he said to the woman.

"Sure," she said. "He heard some coyotes by the house the other night. That's what set him off." She went back in the kitchen.

"Them wolves hurt me," the man said.

"We'll fix that," Dr. Royal said. Naomi Jenks was running water. He had a syringe out and put it on the bed where the man's emaciated legs were carefully bound with soft cloth. He pushed at the man's gaunt flank very gently.

"How many wolves did you kill today?" the man repeated. Royal swiftly injected the contents of the hypo into the man's exposed anus.

He felt a surge of power akin to a sexual thrill as he returned the syringe to its case. He wished he could be present when the solution worked its way through the man. He loved working with the elderly, animals, and the very young—anything that was helpless. Nursing homes and hospices were particular favorites for his games, which for many years had acted as the surrogate for his perverted drives.

The woman came back in the room with a pan of warm, soapy water. "There you go," she said, smiling.

He took some paper towels, tenderly cleaning the man where he'd soiled himself. The bowel movement was like an infant's, Royal was pleased to note, and he cleaned the fragile, parchment-like skin with the greatest tenderness.

19

Bayou Ridge

Solomon Royal parked at the bottom of the steep incline and began his slow ascent. He was just past seventy and still in good health, physically, but it was a cold day, it was a pretty fair climb, and he took his time. The Aters house—if you could call it a house—was an old share-cropper's shack on the edge of a small farm owned by a lady who lived in Florida. Locally it was called the Lawlesses place, though Ferg Lawlesses was long deceased.

The new owner never got around to tearing the shack down. The Diamond Ranch outfit farmed the ground for its absentee owner, and their foreman had let old Mr. Aters and his family move in.

Aters was gone most of the time, a drinking man he was, and his wife, a woman in her fifties, their six children, and assorted livestock somehow survived on this piece of barren ridge. No electricity. A hand pump. Dr. Royal knew they lived rough.

He was breathing hard, blowing pretty good, by the time he reached the top. Tar paper on boards, just this side of a shanty. Coal oil smell . . . kerosene. He recalled what it was like to live like this.

A girl of about ten with a dirty face opened the door for him. She had old eyes already. He entered without asking and spoke to the room, "Where is he?"

"Over here," Mrs. Aters said. She was stout and had a doughy face with the same wary gaze as her child's. She pushed a filthy cloth back and he saw the little boy. He moved over toward him, still with his coat on, and set his bag down beside the bed.

"I need the lamp," he said, and they moved the strong light beside him. Huge shadows shot through the room and the pungent smell took him back to another time, as he prepared to ply his trade.

"Appreciate you comin' all the way out here. You bein' sort of retired and all," the woman spoke from the shadows.

"Um hm." He bent to the task at hand. He glanced back and saw the little girl watching him. "How old are you, my dear?" She stared at him, transfixed, too shy to speak. "Hm?"

"Tell him," the woman commanded, adding, "she's nine."

"Nine! Well, that's nice. What's your name, my sweet?" The child mumbled something. He worked with the boy. Finished. "He'll be all right." Royal gathered up his things and as he walked by the dirty-faced girl he cupped the back of her head in his hand, looking at the stout woman and smiling.

"I think I should give all these kids of yours a good, thorough, routine checkup. Tell you what. Call the office and we'll set up a schedule for you to bring them in."

"Can't afford to," she said simply. About the ten thousandth time he'd heard that one.

"I'm not going to charge you anything for the visits. We'll start with the little girl here. My, you are dirty. May I have a washcloth?" he asked. The woman turned, got a filthy rag from the sink, and walked heavily across the room and handed it to him.

He took it and rubbed at the dirty cheek, then permitted himself to roughly rub it across her full, pouty lips.

"That's much better. Next week I'll give you a complete examination . . . no charge," he repeated to the Aters sow, on his way out the door.

20

Bayou City

The man still walked with a sprightly step considering his age. Observing him from a distance one would find it impossible to determine either his age or occupation by watching his back as he walked. He had the gait of a person twenty years his junior, and from the shiny, black, poor-boy suit, one might have pegged him as a preacher from an impoverished congregation, a third-world missionary, or somebody down on their luck. Nobody would have surmised, from watching the back of Dr. Solomon Royal, that they were looking at one of the most successful physicians in southeast Missouri.

The man in the wrinkled and worn black suit walked briskly through the doors of Van Estes's Funeral Home.

"Howdy, Doc," the greeter, who doubled as chief medical examiner/embalmer for Bayou City, Eddie Roddenberg, said in his professional whisper of respect.

"Howdy, Eddie." The men smiled and the doctor went to the left, a pathway he'd traveled many scores of times. Between the two of them they'd seen more death and pain than any fifty men would normally encounter in a lifetime. Both were older men, reasonably at home with the social graces, but perhaps each sensed the aura of darkness around the other and they tended to communicate as little as possible.

"Emily," Dr. Royal said to the first woman he saw in the room where his former patient was being viewed, "my condolences to your family." He hugged her and she responded with the same feeling of tenderness and warmth she felt toward her own kinfolk.

He shook a few hands and walked over to the open coffin and looked at what was displayed between the two large groupings of floral arrangements. He bowed his head.

Across the room two women of the town watched him.

"What a fine man. I just love Dr. Royal. I don't know what Bayou City will ever do without him."

"He delivered me, did you know that?"

"Did he really?" The woman had to bite her tongue to keep from adding, "I didn't know he was that old."

"He's like my own family."

No he's not, he's not an alcoholic, she thought, smiling a wicked little smile. She said, however, "Same here. The man's such a saint. I hope he never quits. You know, I hear he still goes in every day, rain or shine. You almost have to force money on him. Such a dear, sweet man."

"A real saint. I agree." The two women who secretly hated one another stood watching the kindly physician across the room from them.

What Royal was thinking, as he looked down at the cadaver in the expensive box, was Brother Roddenberg got a bit rushed there with the jawline. Barbaric custom. Open casket rituals were nonsense to begin with, but this cancer-ravaged corpse would be displayed only briefly prior to cremation: what was known in the spade trade as a "shake and bake."

"He looks so good, doesn't he?" a man said, patting Royal on the back.

"He does. How are you, Bob?" *You idiot.*

"Fine doc. You doing okay?"

"I'm good."

"I'm sure gonna miss him."

So shall I. Royal thought it had been rather enjoyable taking him through the final weeks of structured agony, ringing the changes on him with a carefully orchestrated regimen of injections calculated to send him screaming to the utmost wilderness of his pain threshhold, bring him back, send him out a little further, bring him back, send him out again. "I miss him already," he said.

"You know what, Doc, you'uns brought him some relief there at the last, and that was a real blessing," the smiling man patted Royal again, as if he were a dog.

Take your wretched hand off me, you drooling imbecile. Or would you prefer I amputate it at the wrist?

"I did what I could," he said, softly.

21

Tel Aviv—1960

The prosecutor emanated righteousness and ratiocination; the truth and nothing but, so help you God. His posture and kinetics were those of an avenging angel of the court.

Witness number 113 for the State in the special investigation of Nazi war crimes before the War Crimes Tribunal of the State of Israel, was a woman of indeterminate age, a witness for the prosecution against one Emil Shtolz, being tried in absentia.

"Anna Kaplan is your name?" She was his witness.

"Yes."

"You also go by the name Anna Purdy, do you not?" he asked, carelessly.

"Alma Purdy, yes."

"Alma Purdy," he corrected himself. "And would you tell us why you go by this name?"

"So that I keep my identity to myself."

"Yes. I understand. But you don't you want your identity known?"

"I don't like people to know my business. I keep to myself, that's all."

"Isn't it true that you don't use the name Anna Kaplan

because it sounds Jewish, and you think the name Alma Purdy sounds less Jewish?"

"Yes."

"Are you an American citizen, Miss Kaplan?"

"Yes."

"By birth or naturalization?"

"I have naturalization papers."

"And what country were you born in?"

"Germany."

"Where were you in 1944?"

"I was in Germany."

"Where specifically in Germany?"

"München."

"And what were you doing there in 1944?"

"I was a patient at the Clinic for the Fatherland."

"What was this clinic?"

"A medical clinic for the care of women and infants."

"Did this clinic provide room and board for pregnant women?"

"Yes. I believe so. Yes."

"And did it provide room and board and medical care for other women who were not pregnant?"

"Yes. In some cases it did."

"Isn't it true that the Clinic for the Fatherland provided free medical care, room and board, and other accommodations for you, Miss Kaplan, when you entered the program?"

"Yes."

"And what service did you perform to obtain this free care the clinic provided for you?"

The witness mumbled an inaudible answer.

"Please speak louder. The question was, what service did you perform to obtain this free care the clinic provided for you?"

"I became pregnant and had a baby."

"Was the father of the child your husband?"

"No."

"Who was the father of your child?"

"I was not told his identity."

"You were required, were you not, to have intercourse with a man you did not know?"

"I . . . uh . . . was told he was an officer and that he'd met all the requirements set by the clinic."

"What organization maintained and operated this clinic?"

"The SS."

"So in 1944, you became pregnant with the child of a German officer in the Waffen-SS, or so you were led to believe. And then you had a baby?"

"Yes."

"Was this baby healthy and normal?"

"Yes, he—" Suddenly she broke down and began crying. The avenging angel of the court had seen this phenomenon many times and he said nothing. The tribunal and the prosecution waited. After a few moments her tears subsided.

"When your baby was delivered, tell us what happened next."

"They brought my baby son to me and I was allowed to keep him with me for a short while. I kept him with me for four—almost four weeks."

"And after your baby son was four weeks old, approximately, what happened?"

"They took him from me."

"For what purpose, do you know?"

"I don't know." She blew her nose. "They said I was unfit." She looked down for a beat, and the prosecutor thought she was going to lose it again, but she straightened and continued. "They said they'd discovered discrepancies in my medical history, and that I was no longer considered a fit mother for participation in the childbirth program."

"Isn't it true that you were forced to enroll in the program, that you'd had no choice in the first place?"

"Yes. They came to me and said it was required."

"Required by law?"

"Required by the SS."

"The SS needed women to be mothers?"

"Yes. They said they needed healthy German women with untainted bloodlines."

"Were you going under the name Anna Kaplan at that time?"

"No."

"What name were you using when you were recruited by the SS?"

"Anna Schumann."

"And you were using this name so that you could pose as an Aryan-born German?"

"Yes. They were rounding up Jews."

"Whose idea was it for you to use the identity of Anna Schumann?"

"It was my parents' idea. They made me leave home and take the new identity."

"What happened to your parents?"

"The SS took them. After the war I found out they were taken to Treblinka. They both died in the camp."

"And so when the clinic said you were unfit and took your baby, did they elaborate about why you were no longer a fit mother?"

"No."

"Did they tell you they had found out you were Jewish?"

"No. They just said there were discrepancies in my records."

"Were you then released from the clinic?"

"No. They took me to this other house where they said I had to stay."

"And what happened to you while you were at this other house?"

"There was a doctor who had been at the clinic and he came to the house. I was forced to do things with him."

"He had sexual relations with you?"

"Yes."

"Do you know the name of this doctor?"

"Yes. Dr. Shtolz."

"Is this the individual whose photograph I now show

you, which is prosecution exhibit 294-L? Let the record show this is a photograph of Emil Shtolz, taken in 1943, and documented by the Ludwigsburg Center for the Investigation of Nazi War Crimes. Is this the Dr. Shtolz you knew?"

"Yes."

"Dr. Emil Shtolz had a nickname while he was assistant director for the Clinic for the Fatherland. Do you know what the nickname was?"

"Butcher. The Boy Butcher."

"Do you know why he was called the Boy Butcher?"

"He cut people apart. He was a monster. Because he was very young they called him Boy Butcher."

"And you were forced to do things with this young doctor?"

"Yes."

"What were you forced to do?"

"To have sex."

"Normal sexual relations?"

"No."

"Please explain what you were forced to do."

"Depraved sex acts. Awful things."

"And isn't it true that you were told that if you did not perform these awful sex acts that Dr. Shtolz would hurt your baby?"

"Yes. He said he would kill my baby if I didn't do what he wanted."

"And you believed him?"

"Yes."

Anna Kaplan, witness number 113 for the State in the special investigation of Nazi war crimes before the War Crimes Tribunal of the State of Israel, felt as if she'd been questioned for a week, but she'd been giving testimony for less than an hour.

The prosecution was very experienced, and read exhaustion in her eyes, as well as melancholy, hatred, shame, and pain. He decided to spare her specific enumeration. "How long did Emil Shtolz continue to force you to perform these depraved sexual activities?"

"A few weeks. I . . ." She shook her head slowly, eyes downcast, as she reached back for the hideous memories, ". . . have no way of knowing. A month, perhaps."

"And then what happened?"

"When he grew tired of me he took me back to the clinic. I begged him to show me my baby, to let me hold him before they killed me. I was bound and taken into the room where they performed the experiments and he showed me what had been my baby boy." The woman started to break down again, her shoulders moving up and down as if she were having trouble breathing. She was able to stop herself somehow and managed to continue.

"He was in a case among some of the others. Some of the other babies. I wouldn't have recognized him but there was a tag on him. The babies had been operated on . . . the skulls, you know—their little heads were open."

"Miss Kaplan, you were able to escape from this clinic. How did you manage it?"

"I cut my hand very badly. I tried to break the glass case with my hand and lost a lot of blood. There was a moment while they were sewing me up that nobody was watching and I jumped through the window on the second floor of the clinic. I ran. . . ." She shrugged. "I was found by good people who helped me to hide."

"Are you absolutely certain the photograph you have identified for this tribunal is that of Dr. Emil Shtolz, whom you allege to be responsible for the atrocities you've just described?"

"Yes. That's him."

22

Bayou City

Perhaps a quarter of a century back in time, the woman called Alma—Anna Kaplan—had shut down. To lose a child in such an unspeakable manner, to endure inconceivable depravities, to survive the nightmare of evil that was the Holocaust, what were these experiences but stepping stones to a kind of quiet madness?

Her way of coping, of surviving, was to close her doors to the world, both literally and metaphorically. Part of her that shut down was the part that once felt love for children. It was a mild enough lunacy, given the circumstances of her youth. This woman, chronologically in her sixties, but mentally and emotionally ancient, lived a barren life long since reduced to the bare essentials of existence.

Once a week she would trudge the three and a half short blocks to Bob's Discount Store, a weekly stop in her agenda that included City Grocery, Bayou City Bank and Trust, and, occasionally, the post office.

At Bob's Discount, however, there was an added hazard: children. When they were out of school, or if she timed her visit wrong and arrived during the noon hour or in late afternoon, she was face to face with noisy children. Only Bob's low-priced merchandise, such as bargain-basement toilet paper, gave her the courage to brave the perils of the store each week.

There were no kids in the store when she entered, and that was a relief. She cringed at the abrasiveness of their loud, piercing voices, the blundering oafishness of their actions. They seemed to know she felt great distaste for them and it made them hate her, she suspected.

Summer vacation, teacher's meeting days, Thanksgiving, Christmas, and of course dreaded Halloween, as they called it here, these were the times she feared and loathed the most. Noisy, awful children would be running through the streets, and if you ventured out of doors they would come very close to you, threatening to touch you, sometimes shouting things. She favored inclement weather for the reason it kept most of them out of sight and out of mind, even if it pained her old and crippled bones.

Halloween, the night of October 31, was the most feared of her personal abominations. All Hallows' Eve was a time of devil worship, when the cruel calendar would conspire to pull the children forth in unsupervised clots, the spirit of the darkness encouraging their more sadistic impulses.

Alma Purdy would spend these nights quietly in the living room of her small frame house, all the lights off, the curtains and blinds pulled tightly shut, an ancient but trusty revolver loaded and clutched in her lap. She would sit this way for hours, fearing to make a sound, praying to her harsh gods they would not come to her door again—the loud banshee children, cloaked in their disguises—mean snickers stabbing through her as they threatened "trick or treat."

So when she found no noisy kids clamoring in the aisles of Bob's Discount, her first sight of the man brought only gratitude. She went on about her business, an old cripple homing in on the cheap toilet tissue.

He had a purchase in his hands and was on his way toward the cash register to pay when they met, almost colliding, two ships in the same lane, between School Notebooks! Special! and Big Chief Tablets—Save!

There was a second or two of recognition, shock to her nervous system, a startled shudder through his, no doubt or question in either of their minds. She'd seen the Boy

Butcher. He had been recognized. He knew it. She knew it. He was smoother, and managed a flicker of a smile. She could feel her body jerk in frightened reaction as she forced herself to keep going.

He waited until the old woman had paid and left the store, as he fought to get himself back under control. Adrenals in overdrive, heart thumping like a long-distance runner's, he stood in back of the far aisle, his back to the round security mirror. All he could see was that shocked flash of recognition in the woman's eyes. He forced himself to calm down and put a smile on his face, moving up to the counter to pay.

"That be all today, Doc?"

"Mmhm," he said, paying. "How's the missus doing?" The man at the register began yammering about his hypochondriac wife, and Royal nodded as if he were interested in her welfare.

"Say, that older lady who just left . . . was that Helene Caulfield?" He used the name of a former patient now living over sixty miles away.

"You mean Mizz Purdy? That's old Alma Purdy. She's the one shot at them trick-or-treaters that time. Everybody knows her. She's got about half her oars in the water," he said with a wicked chuckle, pointing at his skull for emphasis. Solomon Royal anticipated the five-minute dialogue of moronic banter that would follow any anecdote about her activities.

"Oh, goodness, that reminds me," he said quickly, pointing a preemptive finger in the clerk's direction, "I need to get Miss Caulfield on the phone." Royal mumbled something about tests as he paid and made his way out the door. His face felt red in the air.

There was a Bayou City directory, an absurdly small booklet, chained to a pay telephone outside the store. Purdy, Alma, was listed on page twenty-four, complete with address. Three or four blocks away!

He caught himself hyperventilating and willed deep breaths. He started his car and pulled out into Main

Street. The crippled woman was hobbling along less than half a block away. Plenty of time.

Royal turned at the end of the block, found the street she lived on, turned again, counting house numbers. It was a small frame dwelling on a postage-stamp lot, the house badly in need of paint. The small town street appeared empty of people, only one truck coming from the opposite direction. He saw no one in his rearview. He backed into the nearby alley, parked, killed the engine.

His heart was hammering. Too late to worry about that now, he thought, getting out of the car. No traffic, no watchers. Dr. Royal opened the trunk and looked in a small canvas carrier in the corner of the neat storage space. Removed a few items: surgical gloves, a long screwdriver, the thing he always carried for emergencies, and a small black syringe case.

He estimated about a minute to a minute and a half and old Alma Purdy—who shot at Halloween pranksters —crippled, half-demented Alma, would come dragging around the corner, see him, and scream.

But Dr. Solomon Royal would be nowhere in evidence. He was already on the way to the back of her house, moving between the Purdy house and another dingy frame dwelling. Both structures shut up tight as drums. If neighbors peered through dusty curtains they did so surreptitiously.

Doctor Royal walked up to the back door of the little house and turned the knob as if he lived there, knocking very gently as he did so. His heart still pounded in his chest and he would later recall that at that moment his hearing seemed unusually acute. He could hear several different faraway vehicle sounds, machinery noise from a small business a block away, a distant car horn, bird noises, a kind of whir not unlike a furnace noise, the sound of a small dog barking across the street, his breathing, the noise of the screwdriver in the cheap lock, the crack of the door.

Inside, he moved silently and quickly out of sight,

through the back porch and kitchenette, into the hallway, past the phone, living room, back through the bedroom, squeaking loudly across her bare wooden floor. Each room was alive with the strange pervasive odors of age, of garbage, of the woman herself, all offensive in his nose. She was not fastidious but, as best as he could tell in this cursory pass through, she apparently lived alone. Not even a parakeet chirped in the house.

He assumed she'd come in the front door. But what if she entered through the rear door, found the puny lock compromised, and began screaming for the police? His mind ran many steps ahead of her, planning his exit routes, cobbling together some plausible construct of lies should the unthinkable happen. He sensed his own panic, controlled it. He moved one of her kitchen chairs away from the window, where he could wait unobserved, and sat down.

Out of view from either door he prepared his syringe, which he carefully placed on the kitchen countertop, and arranged the other items he would need. With the weapon in his right hand he practiced standing a time or two, but he could neither stand nor move across the kitchen floor silently. He decided to remove his shoes and did so, standing again. He moved a couple of steps. Better. Pleased with the results, he sat down again, working to calm himself in the remaining seconds or minutes before she showed herself.

A younger woman, a woman with a more normal background, a less totally frightened woman, a woman whose emotional gyro had not been impaired by the horrors to which Anna Kaplan had been subjected, a woman with a keener olfactory sense might have detected some vibrations, sensed something out of place, felt another's presence, intuitively realized she was not alone, smelled the cologne of a stranger.

But it was all she could do to get her key to work in the lock and move directly toward the telephone in the hallway.

To the man who waited for her in the shadows of her

small kitchen the key in the door had sounded like a gunshot, and it was as if her screeching voice began its high wail the moment she burst through the front door.

She'd flung the door open and lunged at the phone, dialing almost as she opened the phone book to the first page where the police numbers were printed. That page was all she'd focused on since she started the long, frightening walk home, how she would open the Bayou City book and see that number listed on the Fire-Police-Ambulance page. It never dawned on her that there were two small books issued to residences, one for the immediate city limits, one for the surrounding communities, and she'd grabbed the book with the county sheriff. Sheriff, police, they were all the same.

As the words tumbled out of her mouth and she heard the laughter in the man's voice she knew it would be useless. Even before he'd finished questioning her she knew what she must do.

The thing that prolonged Alma Purdy's life was not saying goodbye. When the call to the authorities had come to an end, and the man taking her call had said they'd look into it, she simply said, "Yes," a monosyllabic grunt in the same dead, emotionless tone she'd used all the way through the conversation. As she set the phone down on the slim directory and began rummaging around in her desk drawer for a newspaper account she'd saved, the man listening patiently in the next room had no way of realizing the line had been disconnected.

There were the few seconds it took for the woman to dial when he heard the unmistakable sounds of another call being made, but he decided against a quick move, assessing it as excessively risky. There was always the chance he'd be implicated in the moments it would take him to spring from the kitchen and strike her down.

"Mrs. Talianoff?" Her screech broke the silence of the house. "It's Alma Purdy. You know the package I gave you for safekeeping? . . . That's right. Please go ahead and send it. Yes. That's right. Just tell him to mail it now. Okay. Thank you." She broke the connection and he was out of the chair, moving on his stocking feet, but she'd just dialed the 0 this time, and her high whine was already speaking again as he reached the doorway. "Operator?" He froze.

"I want to call a man in Kansas City," she demanded. The woman's voice then dropped back to the dead monotone she'd used during the rambling call to the local authorities. "No. Please get the number for me. I don't have the number." He heard more conversation about how it was an emergency.

He'd put himself in incredible jeopardy with the inane business of waiting for the woman in her filthy home. What an idiot he'd been to react in such an illogical manner. A hundred times he'd curse the fates, and himself, for not having simply run the bitch down in the street. It would have been so simple. A traffic mishap.

"A mentally defective elderly cripple lurched out in front of his car," he imagined one of his defenders would say. No one would have suspected him for a second. He goaded himself with wish-fulfillment scenes as he listened to the crone's lies, heard himself described, stood in this simpleton's kitchen fighting for composure, when he could have painlessly deducted one more bitch from the female Jew population with his front bumper.

"Is this Mr. Kamen?" he heard her ask. "Are you the one who looks for Nazis from the war?" Regrets mounted. How many mistakes had he made in the last ten minutes? He felt perspiration in his right palm, the hand gripping the weapon. He never perspired. The situation would have been ludicrous had it not been threatening. He must kill her and leave the "elderly cardiac arrest victim" to rot. "I'm calling because I know where there's a Nazi."

He heard her say his name and realized he now would not even be able to wash his hands of her simply. Now he must also make the meddlesome old bitch vanish. That meant coming back after dark, taking more chances, somehow moving the dead weight to his car. Nothing insurmountable, but each element compounded his risk factor.

By the time she finally replaced the phone and walked into her kitchen his pent-up fury lashed out at her and she died without knowing that Emil Shtolz had smashed her to death like the wrath of the devil itself.

Ignoring her frail, fallen body, he checked the directories and then tried local directory assistance for new listings. The hurried search failed to yield a Talianoff, Taliakoff, or anything close. Emil Shtolz moved on to other more pressing matters, and never found Lenore Talianoff, Bayou City's only other old Jew, and the closest thing Alma Purdy had for a confidante.

Mrs. Talianoff lived with her son and his family, the son having taken his stepfather's name, and it was to the son she spoke.

"Are you going to the post office today?"

"Not today, Mother. Whatcha' need?"

"I'm keeping a package for a woman. She called me and asked me to mail it for her, so I'm mailing it already."

"I'll get it after a while. I'm calling in a UPS pickup. Will that be all right, if it goes out tomorrow?"

"That's fine, honey. So, are you coming home for lunch?"

The package, about the size of a small book, was rectangular and wrapped in thick paper obtained by cutting apart a grocery sack. The label, printed in a somewhat shaky hand, bore the address of a man in Kansas City, Missouri. The UPS center in Earth City would, in fact, misdirect it, but so far as Lenore Talianoff was concerned the matter was ended and she'd discharged her responsibilities in full.

Now

~~~ **23**

New Madrid Levee

He sees the white line through fever, aching jaw, tooth, squinting and hurtling through the night in purloined iron. The broken white line, the yellow line, something about the car. Probably its figurative heat. It was on a hot sheet, maybe that was it.

It held the day's heat like a kiln, and he breathes in stuffiness, keeping his conscious mind on track with whatever hard grit is left to him.

He does not remember wandering away from the car, nor the protective vibes that pushed him to seek cover. He will not recall camouflaging the ride or the force of concentration it took to persevere.

A huge, injured monster lies in thick woods, his superhuman life-support system working overtime to save him.

Illinois seems galaxies away. He is a dying man, drowning in deep, black water. The whirlpool pulls him back under before he can sort his situation out.

Just as Dr. Emil Shtolz was a monster, he is a monster. Daniel Bunkowski had killed, some said, more than any other living human, but some said that about the good doctor. Each had taken hundreds of lives. Shtolz might have won had the body count included animals.

Neither man had a normal conscience. Each considered himself to be far above rules or laws. Each had only disdain for mankind. Each man was, in his own way, of superior and, in fact, unmeasurably high intellect. Each had enormous talents. Each found pleasure in the act of mutilation. Each had murdered in terrible ways and performed the vilest acts imaginable.

The psychiatric bibles, the continually revised diagnostic statistical manuals, found ways to describe such men. They were "sick." Such descriptions reflected society's lack of willingness to define, quantify, or even recognize, the existence of clinical evil. It underscored a massive oddity: many of the same human beings who believe in God refuse categorically to believe in the devil.

But perhaps there are good monsters as well as bad.

A clear image drifts past the battered memory banks: *seven paramedics, cops, monkey men and women, straining to roll his dead weight onto a gurney. The barking noise that is somewhere on the audio scale between a loud lawnmower and a powerful outboard motor starting—the closest sound he makes to a human laugh—escapes his throat. Two of them drop their handholds in fear and this convulses him further, even though the result sends his immense bulk to the hard surface.*

Black clouds of pain relent, he hears a siren wail, sees an unfamiliar vehicle roof. He is crammed into an ambulance. The authorities have found him—had he not escaped? It must have been after the beating—his head roared and one eye was firmly shut. The muddled chronology is all too confusing. His monitors sign off.

The darkness puddles into dappled green and gold fuzztone. The wounded bear is curiously mortal feeling, trembling, but from neither fear nor trauma. Cold? Surely not. Time nudges a sticky inner clock and one hand ticks through coagulated fogsleep, moves the inert gigantus forward one square, back two.

"Are we awake?" A nurse, black as his mood, and wide as a living-room sofa, white teeth smiling. "You gots to eat. Keep up your strength, big boy!" This convulses the room and he hears several persons laughing. He studies a blur in front of him. "Eat, now," she says, trying to poke something in his maw. He is ravenous and inhales the puny portion and part of her meaty hand and arm. He would like to barbecue her and pork out. Chaingang

Bunkowski, gravitationally challenged by a quarter ton of baby fat, is not what one might term a picky eater. Even he will not swallow this trash and he spits it in the fat chocolate face. She growls at him, which he ignores, focusing in on a plate of overcooked liver, something that might have been Jell-O, a tapioca-like puke. He hurls the plate in the direction of humanity.

"Food!" he demands, in a Hammond organ bass. He wants a couple of dozen pizza supremes, a few hundred blueberry pancakes swimming in hot butter and sweet syrup, a couple of sides of ribs, nurse-kabob, a hundred of those little White Castle bellybombers. He could eat wood.

He careens to his feet and against some hospital crap, bounces heavily off a wall, people are shouting, pawing at him, one massive arm knocks fools this way and that as he stumbles out into the hall. A woman recovering from cataract surgery peers out into the hall through her good eye. He sees her with his good eye. Turns, bends over. The hospital gown that barely covered his balls, much less his behemoth flanks, is wide open. The hairiest back and nastiest nether regions she has ever seen on anything, man or animal, shoots her the grossest moon in Christendom, as he shakily waddles through the screaming hospital personnel, pushing his tonnage full steam ahead, moving in the direction of vulnerability.

He grabs a small doctor, his ticket out, and together they find the biggest XXXL white coat in the building. With that halfway covering his butt, and the gown halfway covering his nuts, he and the frightened man negotiate the steps to the parking lot.

A parked vehicle feels right. The driver gives off the proper victim scent; the beast reacts, acts, locks onto the heartbeat, strikes, and drives.

Daniel dreams all of this—in deep limbo.

Aaron Kamen and Sharon Kamen

24

Kansas City

It had been a weekend of killer headaches, the worst he could recall, and he could remember some dillies. Aaron Kamen arched his neck up, then stood and stretched, putting his hands on his hips and swiveling from side to side. Saturday morning services, he'd been saying Kaddish, the prayer for the dead, when a Godzilla-like migraine had enveloped him. It had stayed with him for two days, one of those things that neither medication nor sleep seems to shake. He had to wear them off. This one started somewhere down in the shoulders and worked its way up the spine, across the top of his head, and settled above the eyes. Maybe that was it, he thought, taking off his glasses and rubbing his aching eyes. He cleaned his glasses with a tissue and put them back on. His head was throbbing. Maybe it wasn't a migraine, maybe he needed to get his prescription lenses adjusted. He glanced at the time. The two extra-strength Tylenol hadn't had time to kick in. He'd busy himself.

The tape box read Microcassette—Contains 10 Pieces, and he shook it gently, absent-mindedly, as he thought what to do about the woman. He would call. That was it. He couldn't wait any longer, it wouldn't stop nudging.

The tapes were neatly labeled in his firm printing, each title in block-lettered caps. SHTOLZ/PURDY, A. He finally got it out of the case, the small box difficult to handle in his big, thick-fingered hands. They were the hands of a man who'd labored hard all his life; beat-up, broken, rough-hewn hands with a workingman's calluses, even though he now did only paper work. Only paper work, he smiled. Nobody would believe how much work paper work could be.

Aaron Kamen felt the toll of his age, as he inserted the tape into the recording device plugged into his telephone.

"Hello," he heard himself say from the miniature speaker.

"Is this Mr. Kamen?" He pressed stop when he heard her voice again and went to find a pen. Some notebook paper. He'd already forgotten the killer headache. His tunnel vision was locked back in on the woman, on finding her and making sure she was all right. The sense of something gone amiss was very strong. He wanted to hear the tape one more time before he began with the authorities. He'd make sure he took notes this time.

"This is he," he answered. A small silver thing, a sleek machine with little holes and controls, a miracle that could record voices over a phone.

"Are you the one who tries to find Nazis from the war?" She spoke with a heavy accent.

"I try to do that," he said simply, "yes."

"I'm calling because I know where there is a Nazi. I read about you two years ago when they had a story in the paper about you finding that guard from the camp. Then I called the operator and got your number from the Kansas City phone directory, that's how I found you."

"Yes." He'd let the caller go on at her own pace.

"I was taken by them when I was a young girl in Germany. They didn't know I was Jewish at first and when they found out they . . . did things to me. They killed my son, my baby. They were going to kill me, too. It was a doctor for the SS. *Shtolz!* I saw this man again. All these years. Twice I saw him. The first time I wasn't sure, but now I've seen him again. He's the one murdered my baby." Her voice was full of pain.

"Emil Shtolz you saw?" He tried to keep his voice calm and measured, but every fiber in him was alert.

"Yes. You heard of him?"

"He had a nickname, did he not?" Kamen spoke to her softly in the German tongue she knew best. "The Butcher of Lebensborn?"

"Yes," she hissed in a razor-edged voice. "The Boy Butcher."

"You're certain it's Shtolz you saw?"

"I wouldn't forget his smiling devil's mask."

"Where is he?"

"He's *here* in Missouri." Aaron Kamen underlined her words as he printed them and chided himself for not being more thorough. He should have pulled it out of her then, but it had seemed so unlikely. "I'm in the southeast part of Missouri. A little country town called Bayou City, do you know it?"

"No. Where is it located?"

"Between St. Louis, Missouri, and Memphis, Tennessee. I don't know exactly how far but—"

"That's all right. I have maps. Listen, your name is—what?"

"Alma Purdy. I didn't know who to call so I called the police. I could tell they didn't believe me."

"You phoned the police in Bayou City?"

"They weren't going to do anything. I decided to call you," she said, exhaling deeply into the mouthpiece of the phone.

Everything about the call seemed genuine but one had to be on guard. Crackpots occasionally called and some could be quite cunning. One in particular, a man from a morning radio program in California, had pretended to have found a Nazi in hiding and had made a fool of Kamen, playing a recording of their conversation on the air as a prank. A less serious man would have found it actionable, but Aaron had done nothing.

He felt sure this was a legitimate call. Next was the question of its authenticity with respect to the sighting. Survivors of the camps saw their share of ghosts, so to speak. The voice on the other end of the line sounded

91

like a woman in control of her faculties, but . . . who knew?

"Precisely what did you say to the police?"

"This man named Pritchett took all the information, who I was, where I lived. He wanted to know about me, as if I might have done something, but he asked *nothing* about Shtolz. I knew he would not act, so I found the clipping, the one with the story about a Nazi hunter, and I called."

"You must be *very, very sure* this is the same man. The people who investigate such things are extremely busy and overworked and unless you're positive, please do not pursue it until you are one hundred percent sure."

"I'm sure. *This man killed my baby. He sawed the top of my child's . . .*" It was as if the connection had been broken. Nothing. Then there was a racking noise like a cough and her voice returned to its former monotone. "Do you think I would not know the Boy Butcher to see him in front of me?"

"Yes. All right. Please, take it easy now. I will help you and we shall proceed. I'm going to give you the number of an organization that deals with these matters. I will phone them first, myself, and have them contact you. Do nothing further until you've been called. Understand?"

"It is his turn to squirm now."

"Did you understand what I said? You must not make any further contacts as it could jeopardize the situation, perhaps even put yourself in danger or allow the man you've sighted to be warned."

"I understand. I will do nothing more." There was another line but it was garbled, and he stopped the tape, rewound it for a second, and played it back. It sounded as if she'd said, "I'm sending you something—" but he couldn't make the words out. He heard himself testing her.

"I have a small photo of Shtolz from the war years. There is something that makes his appearance unique. Do you recall what it is?"

"If you mean the Tear of Satan, which is what we called it, the ugly, red mark on his face? No. I didn't notice it. He looks different. Much older of course, but the eyes in that face are the same. I don't remember the birthmark. Maybe it faded. Or—he's a doctor—he might have had it changed."

"Yes."

"But I swear it's Shtolz. The eyes. That mouth like a curveh." A whore's mouth.

He rewound the tape again to the place he'd warned her to do nothing further, listening with the volume up as high as it would go.

"I understand. I will do nothing more," the voice said. "I'm sending you something."

What? What could she be sending, this woman who recognized old Nazis, how could she send him anything? She'd neglected to ask his mailing address, and he hadn't thought to provide it.

25

I-70, east of Columbia

The drive was longer than Aaron Kamen had anticipated. How could two hundred fifty-some miles on an interstate be such a drive? It felt as if he'd done four hundred fifty miles on a back road. His eyes ached from the glare. The excursion had left him physically tired. *Like an old man already,* he thought, giving himself a smile.

It was bright, and the Missouri sky was a hard, perfect blue. The sun was so painful he pulled a visor down and thought how quickly it all went by with the passing years.

A week now was like a heartbeat. He tried to think how long it had been since the Purdy woman had broken contact with him. He'd become very concerned.

A forty-five minute construction jam helped him decide he'd had enough and he decided to stop at the first motel he saw and spend the night on the outskirts of St. Louis, then drive on to Bayou City in the morning.

Ice was still in the fields, oddly, giving the bright, flat landscape the look of an endless skating rink broken only by occasional tree lines. The countryside and measured pace gave off a sense of reassurance, triggering old childhood recollections that came back to him as he drove.

Heading south in search of Alma Purdy—and one of the rats, one of the big boys, still living free down in the Missouri Bootheel.

~~~ **26**

Bayou City

The small-town cop genially escorted him from the building, shaking his head. "We've got a bunch of Pritchetts around town. I never thought about her calling the *sheriff*. Come on, might as well ride with me, Mr. Kamen," he said, as they stopped beside the first police car.

"Okay." Aaron Kamen got in the front seat. The car was like the building inside, spotlessly clean and shiny. Kamen was tuned to the man's vibes and the aura was professional and smart. The cop spoke good ol' boy dialect, which is to say he talked with a Missouri twang, but Jimmie Randall was no backwoods cracker. Kamen sensed intelligence and competency, and that acted to reassure him. Without needing to ask he knew this small-town police chief had checked him out thoroughly; it was unspoken in the way he was being treated. There was no hint of condescension in tone or language.

The chief had said Alma Purdy was probably off visiting kinfolk, but there'd been a file folder in a basket on his desk and Kamen had noticed he'd picked it up and brought it with him. It lay on the seat between them and he knew police never gave a civilian everything they knew, regardless of his or her credentials.

"Do you think it's possible Mrs. Purdy might have told the sheriff about the individual she thought she'd seen?"

"The Nazi from the war, you mean?"

"Right." So there'd at least been some investigation of the matter.

"We'll sure regard it as a possibility. Let's check the residence and see what we can shake loose there first, and then maybe we'll go talk to the sheriff. You know these older folks." He shook his head. "You have to see what kinda' mood a person might have been in the last time somebody saw them. You get to be that age and you also have to take into consideration senility. Alzheimer's." The words came easily to him.

"What's the normal procedure for how long a person is missing before you suspect something?"

"It varies with circumstances. Like I say, determining the mood and whatnot. Was Mrs. Purdy mad at somebody? Does she have a friend she might be staying with? Medication? Somebody that age is probably under a doctor's care, and they might be on strong medication. Was she on any kind of mind-altering substance? We can check to see who her doctor is, what the pharmacy might have sold her recently, who she might have confided in, such as a friend or neighbor.

"Had one old fellow got lost. Found him in a hotel in Memphis. You never know. She might have distant kin who came in, found her all agitated, and decided to slap her in one of the area nursing homes and just didn't tell anybody. That's happened, too."

They arrived at the Purdy house. The chief gained entry and the two men looked around. Kamen could imagine trying to go with the cops under similar circumstances with an urban force such as the KCPD. They found clothes in the closets, food in the refrigerator, stale air.

"Something must have happened to her," Kamen said.

Jimmie Randall replied, "See if there's any correspondence around. She might have had a letter from somebody or . . ." He trailed off and shuffled through a few papers. "Let's go see the sheriff."

They closed up the house, which Randall locked with a key from a ring of what looked like a hundred or more keys.

The two men chatted amiably about the weather most of the way to Charleston, driving with the windshield wipers on full. It had begun to rain, a hard blowing rain that was coming down with sudden fury. Aaron Kamen was beginning to feel the depression that comes with rainy days.

He was surprised the local cops had not asked him more about his own investigative background, and he listened for hidden nuances in the policeman's conversation but found none. They pulled up next to the county jailhouse, hurried inside, and the two local law-enforcement heads greeted one another like old pals.

"We've got this lady, Alma Purdy," Randall said, "been missing for a couple weeks."

"I spoke with her about three weeks back. I took a report on it. That was the War Crimes deal, right? She'd sighted a guy from the old concentration camp, something like that?"

"Yep."

"Um." The sheriff's face didn't change.

"Mr. Kamen here is concerned something may have happened."

Kamen spoke up quickly. "I think we have to assume that possibility—that strong possibility exists, sheriff. She thought she might have seen a former Nazi doctor who committed a lot of atrocities and . . . suddenly she goes up in smoke." Even as he spoke he wondered if the sheriff realized the singular inappropriateness of that phrase. "Chief Randall said she might be under medication or under a doctor's care, and it dawned on me, I wonder if this man Emil Shtolz might still be working as a doctor?"

"First, Mrs. Purdy didn't strike me as particularly coherent, but let's say she was. Let's give her the benefit of the doubt and assume she saw this old guy. Aren't all these Nazis elderly men themselves now?" the sheriff asked.

"He was a young man at the end of World War II," Kamen said. "He might be seventy now, but he might not appear that age. He could easily have had a face lift, and from what Alma Purdy told me it sounded as if he might have had some cosmetic surgery, assuming, as you say, assuming she did see Shtolz."

The two lawmen discussed who'd file the preliminary missing persons report with the state police in something called Bluff, which Aaron Kamen learned was Poplar Bluff, Missouri. But he knew he was hearing two conversations: one was shorthand cop talk, the other appeared to be for his benefit. It sunk in while he and Randall were heading back to the Bayou City police headquarters in the rain. He listened to their questions about the Purdy report, in tandem with a bantering about computers, how the sheriff was sick about the 2000 getting "shit-canned," which he knew referred to an NCIC computer program. "I knew it'd be a hump," Randall had said.

"I'll call Cape and let Immigration in St. Louis know." More shorthand about the FBI and other authorities whom the sheriff would bring up to speed. It had been rather smoothly executed, Aaron thought, all in the cop-shop sidebar talk, punctuated with occasional questions to him about the contact with Purdy. He realized they'd known every speck of this all along, right down to the trip to the missing woman's home. This had been something Sheriff Pritchett and Chief Randall had set up to take *his* measure. He was being investigated, and not for the first time.

"Did I pass?" he asked suddenly, turning in the seat and smiling to show he recognized professionalism and approved of it.

"Excuse me?" The chief raised his eyebrows. Aaron was not offended. The fact they'd handled him rather adroitly, that they'd obviously been on top of the case for some time, was hardly discouraging. So far, at least, nobody was laughing at the serious situation.

So he saw it as good news and bad news. The good news was a circle of light was moving in the direction of the darkness. The bad news was that a woman named Alma Purdy, who'd apparently already been through hell once, had vanished.

Aaron left Randall's office after a few conversational loose ends were tied, among them being a mutual promise of cooperation. Meanwhile, where would Mr. Kamen be staying? He gave his room number at the little ma 'n' pa motel on the highway. How long was he planning to stay in town? Not long, he said. He assured the cop that he knew his place as a civilian, that he'd notify Randall and Pritchett if he learned of Mrs. Purdy's whereabouts, all the expected stuff. The chief would circulate the two blow-ups of Emil Shtolz that Kamen had extracted from his files, one a passport photo that showed the Boy Butcher without his infamous facial birthmark. Yes, he realized it might be impossible to I.D. a person from a forty-plus-year-old passport picture. And so on.

Instead of returning to the motel, Kamen went to a pay phone and dialed Raymond Meara's number for the second time. Kamen routinely attended gun shows, firearms club rallies, and the like, with a special eye for the lunatic fringe gun collectors, from whose ranks Neo-Nazis sometimes emerged. Aaron and Raymond Meara had met at a gun club rally the preceding year. They'd exchanged opinions on gun laws, the plight of the small businessman and small farmer, and found some areas of agreement. Kamen, being a people collector, retained the man's name in his files. When Alma Purdy had said Bayou City, he had recalled having a contact there.

"Mr. Meara," he said, when a gruff voice answered after a dozen or so rings, "it's Aaron Kamen calling again. I'm the one called yesterday about Mrs. Purdy?"

"Yeah."

"I'd like to talk with you, as I said. I just finished speaking with the police and the sheriff and apparently the woman is in fact missing."

"Um. Well, like I said, I don't know zip about her. She's like a hermit, or whatever you call them, a recluse, you know?" Kamen moved under the protective over-hang of the building as he was pelted by hard, cold raindrops.

"I understand, Mr. Meara, but if I could, I'd still like to come out and talk with you. I'm trying to find another individual. It's a bit lengthy to go into on the phone. Also, I want to show a couple of photographs to you and see if you might be able to help me."

"That's okay. Pretty good drive out here from town but you're welcome to come out." It sounded as if Aaron Kamen were anything but welcome.

"If I'd be catching you at a bad time we could make it another day."

"Nah. I'm just waddlin' around out here. Come on if you want to."

Kamen extracted directions, and in spite of the off-putting and complex-sounding series of twists, turns, and otherwise convoluted instructions, he had no trouble finding the Meara farm.

Within twenty-five minutes he was pulling up in the muddy yard of a near stranger, and he saw the scarred countenance of Raymond Meara.

"You bring this down from K.C., didja?" drawled Meara.

"No, sir. It was cold up home but at least it was dry."

"Come on in," Meara said, and Aaron Kamen followed him into the farmhouse, and out of the pelting rain.

~~ **27**

The rain had become an ever-present factor in Kamen's daily plans. It slowed his driving even more, and he'd been no speed demon to begin with. But he did not enjoy driving in the rain. His unfamiliar surroundings presented yet another worry. Working his way outward from the hub of Bayou City, he'd tried for an operational plan that was geographically logical, but the locations of some of the suspects on his primary search list were deceptively placed. Seeing something on a map and finding it in rainy, unfamiliar territory, weren't the same.

Three of the closest communities had been approached alphabetically: Anniston, Bertrand, and one of the list's more promising names, a Dr. Mishna Vyodnek, working at Consolidated Labs some twenty minutes from Bayou City, had not panned out. He found himself sitting in the front seat of the car, water puddling from his raincoat, trying to make heads or tails out of his map.

There were at least two other nearby leads, a veterinarian of Shtolz's approximate age, and a surgeon with the name Raoul Babajarh. He decided to check those two out next and, if time permitted, look up a party in a community called Kewanee. That would bring him into line with New Madrid, and from there he could swing back through Bayou City. If none of his semi-leads checked out, he'd call it a day and tackle the rest to-morrow. Then he saw another stop he reckoned would be on his way and inserted it into his itinerary. With that he pulled back into a stream of trucks and headed for the vet's.

Three hours later Aaron Kamen was winding up a conversation with a retired general practitioner in New Madrid, and for the first time he found someone opening up to him a bit.

"If you don't mind my asking, is this fellow you're looking for in some kind of trouble?" Kamen's day had convinced him that physicians were even more clubby and protective of their own brethren than lawyers or cops. His methodology had been to do a quick thumbnail profile of the type of man he was looking for, one who might have background or expertise in the medical or experimental disciplines, at least fifty years old—he ruled nothing out—and he might have a slight European accent, "a little like mine, perhaps."

None of the persons he'd personally contacted could have been Shtolz, but Nate Fletcher, retired from a lifetime of private practice, was physically excluded by his size. He was all of five feet tall. Many things about a person can be altered or faked, but among the most difficult is the simulation of diminutive stature. Spinal compression notwithstanding, a man who stood nearly six feet tall in 1944 could not have shrunk a foot in fifty years. When he asked if the man in question had been in trouble, it was not in the usual AMA tone.

"The man I'm looking for was a Nazi doctor. He was tried as a war criminal for the torture and murder of many, many persons. He was in his early twenties then, and we know he made his way to North America." He told the man, Dr. Fletcher, about Alma Purdy.

"You need to go to the po-leece," the man squeaked at him in a high-pitched voice. "That's the first thing." Kamen assured him he had and showed him his list of doctors over fifty within fifty miles of Bayou City, his arbitrary parameters.

"I can name about a half dozen doctors over fifty you don't have on that list. And there'd be another two dozen between here and Cape if you'd include Dexter, 'n' places like Scott City. You want to make some notes?" He paused to give the youngster time to get his pen out and keep up with him.

"How'd he get his Missouri license? What's this fella got for a diploma to hang on his wall, one of them fakes? Here's what the real thing looks like." He gestured behind him at a wall full of framed, gilt-edged certification. "Have you thought about sales? Fella like that would do right well in sales. Probably like it, too," he snorted. "Check out your oddball ministers, too. Be a natural for him." It was clear that Nate Fletcher was not overly fond of salesmen or men of the cloth. "Fella come through here once claimed to be a Baptist minister, turned out he was nothing but a—what do you call the perverts who molest little boys? Check out your priests and ministers. Bunch of *charlatans.*"

"Well, I sure appreciate your taking—"

"And another thing, I'd run up to Farmington. They've got some older people in there. And I'd—"

"Sure do thank you, Dr. Fletcher." He was gathering up his materials. Leaving the blow-ups of the old passport and driver's license photos. "If you think of anything else—"

"Talk to some of the old-timers around Bayou City. They can give you lots of names of people emigrated over back in the olden days."

"That's a good idea," Kamen said, smiling, pulling his raincoat back on.

"I reckon you already talked to Doc Royal."

"Who's that?"

"Be sure to go see Dr. Royal. He's still up there in Bayou City. Been there all his life. He'd know all the old-timers."

"I don't think he's on my list," Aaron Kamen said, not being totally successful at swallowing a yawn as he made his way to the door.

"He's the first one I'd talk to. Been here since God was a pup. Somebody told me he still works a couple days a week. He's probably like me, a good bit past retirement age. Got the clinic there."

"What clinic is that?"

"The Royal Clinic they used to call it." He made a face. "But I don't rightly know what the name is now. Some younger fellas got 'em a practice there in town, too, so I don't really know if Doc Royal's still open but go talk to him."

"I will," he said, thanking the old gentleman and opening the door. As he headed down the sidewalk toward his car, the high screech of Nate Fletcher called out behind him.

"Don't forget some of the old *preachers!*" Kamen assured him he wouldn't and waved farewell.

The rain had slackened off somewhat, tapering to a fine mist that was just enough to keep the windshield wipers hypnotically sweeping back and forth across his field of vision. He was getting an eyestrain headache again, and felt unusually tired for no reason.

After fifteen minutes of driving along a slick levee road it occurred to him the terrain looked vaguely familiar, and it dawned on him he'd driven past these landmarks before, only from the opposite direction, when he'd visited Raymond Meara.

A pickup truck shot around him, the men in the front seat looking at him quizzically as they went around the irritatingly slow-moving car. Aaron rubbed his eyes under his glasses and turned the car radio on.

"—rain belt. Widespread heavy rain is flooding the lower Ohio River Valley and the thirty-day forecast indicates greater-than-average precipitation and warm temps for the next thirty days.

"Southeastern Missouri has been drenched with rain

for the last five days, and the Mississippi is swollen by more than ten feet, threatening to flood its banks in many places." Interference crackled. "—expected to reach the flood stage tomorrow. Flood stage there is forty feet. The Missouri Highway Patrol reports—" He switched to music and that irritated him even more, so he shut the radio off.

As he looked to his left he wondered if he'd have to drive through any water on the way back. He'd lost his directional bearings. If Aaron Kamen had glanced to his right instead of his left, far along the horizon he'd have seen a silver band glistening like a knife edge in a break between the distant tree lines. The slim, bright sliver was the edge of the mighty Miss pushing inland. He had sensed danger, true enough, but he'd looked in the wrong direction.

28

Kansas City

It was an ominous-looking day. Sharon Kamen picked up the phone in her apartment and dialed the weather number. A male announcer's voice told her in computerized neospeak that she should "ask Kansas City Federal Savings about a money-saving IRA account. Time . . . seven nineteen. The forecast is . . . cloudy with thundershowers likely. Turning colder tonight." She hung up and put the small, collapsible umbrella in her briefcase.

An invisible photographer, snapping a shot of Sharon as she walked across the room with her cute little foot-long maroon-and-silver umbrella in hand, could have captured one of those fantasy poses one used to see on the calendars in gas stations. A beautiful, near-nude woman with long, lovely legs and a traffic-stopping pair of high, firm breasts saluting, tiny parasol covering the essentials, a cutesy caption beneath the artwork.

Or catch her with the phone in her hand and wrap the cord around that showgirl body and call it Telephone Trouble. No man could walk past such a pose without doing another take. The ideal female sex symbol, posing coquettishly from all the Vargas, Petty, and Moran paintings; forty years of centerfolds, going back to the era of Mutoscope arcade cards. The eternal cheesecake shot.

Post-feminist-era Sharon stood with bumbershoot, pantyhose, black high heels, and a whole lot of Sharon, surveying the choices in her closet. She began to dress, stepping into her underpants and pulling a bra over the chest that made otherwise mature men turn goofy.

But gorgeously coiffed, marvelously stacked, model-lovely Sharon was many people, as real people are, and none of them was the big-boobed bimbo on the calendars. What you saw, with Sharon Kamen, was most assuredly not what you got.

At that moment her mind was as far from her own sexuality as it could take her, dressing for her job at the Kansas City Emergency Shelter, and thinking about the night before at her father's apartment. Missing her mother, taken by cancer, missing their cozy rural home outside Kansas City, which her dad now professed to loathe.

To others, her dad was inevitably the Nazi hunter, but to her he was the wise, good, and fearless man who represented so many positive things in her life. Others compared him to a Midwest version of Simon Wiesenthal or Elie Wiesel, because their names were known, but he was nowhere near the level of the top luminaries in the field. Aaron Kamen had achieved a degree of notoriety in the heartland by helping to find two low-level war criminals who'd been at the death camps half a century ago. People could not see beyond his notoriety so they often couldn't see the real man, just as they couldn't see the real Sharon for her physical package.

Her dad had enriched her life, to be sure, with his shared philosophy of serving others, with his caring, his genuine belief in man's goodness, and with his deep, challenging desire to help others, which he and her mother had instilled in her. Not only did she love him as a daughter loves her father, she revered him. The latter emotion was not without emotional baggage. It carried a funny ambivalence that swung back and forth between awe and irritation.

There were times she'd give anything to disassociate herself from the overpowering Judaism and Zionist zeal that had shaped such a great part of her life. On the threshold of turning thirty, still unmarried but desired by men since her adolescence, she was torn and confused inside.

This woman, who was so flattered by eye, camera, and mirror, was smart enough to know that mirrors showed nothing. The skin and teeth and hair were wrapping paper. Inside, Sharon was a woman at war with herself.

She worshipped her father but was viscerally antagonized by his unrelenting Jewishness. She knew she believed in God but sometimes she'd watch her father lighting candles and saying the Kaddish, and question why she didn't feel what he obviously felt. Sometimes he behaved as if he personally carried the weight of millions of souls. What gave him the right to impose the dictates of his moral compass or his conscience on her? Also, she found his blind orthodoxy numbing, intolerant, illogical, and judgmental. Temple, she felt, was a guilty irrelevance, and she ignored it. "Israel's rightness," and the basic implicit wrongness of the Palestinians, was one more piece of dogma that stuck in her craw.

Inside her secret heart this caring, complex, enigmatic woman was troubled by a dark, persistent fear: the daughter of one of America's most prominent Holocaust survivors was afraid she'd become a closet anti-Semite, a self-hating Jew.

Her father had called her at work and asked her to pick up something of hers he'd found in a storage box. His own belongings had remained unpacked when he'd moved following her mother's death. He'd taken the first apartment he'd looked at, and thrown some clothing in the closet and a few utensils and bare necessities into drawers and cabinets, but the rest of the household goods still sat in unopened moving company cartons.

The exception had been his files, which were meticulously arranged and cross-indexed and kept in steel drawers. When she'd dropped by his place after work he'd said he was on the track of "another one," gesturing at the files and documents that filled the apartment. He was quite animated and in one of his most Jewish moods.

"Hypothesis," he'd said loftily, sitting her down in the only available chair. "A space vessel lands and aliens disembark. Sentient beings who profess to be extraterrestrial evangelists from a planet beyond our solar system.

"They prove to the satisfaction of the scientific community that theirs is a civilization technologically superior to any dreamed of before." Her dad's accent became thicker as his excitement grew. "They espouse a religion parallel to Judaism that completely negates the precepts of all other religious beliefs. Christianity, Islam, Buddhism, they all go out the window, you see? Their version of the Talmud proves that there is but one religion, let's hypothesize. The question is this: precisely what does that discovery do to the nature of man's faith?"

"I don't know," she said, shaking her pretty head and shrugging.

"It does . . . absolutely . . . nothing!" He lit up as if he'd just won the lottery.

"I don't get it."

"Of course you don't. But it wouldn't hurt you to think about it some, eh?" They talked some more and she left him in the opening stages of his latest rat hunt. He'd given her a box of her old 45-rpm records. For this she'd driven across town.

As she dressed for work she thought about the seventies oldies that had now migrated from his closet to hers. Billy Paul's "Me and Mrs. Jones," which she'd played until the grooves had worn flat. Joni Mitchell. Steely Dan. For some reason the records depressed her even more than her father had.

Her dad's elevator stunk of urine and he didn't even have the sense to move a sofa from the house. Why couldn't he simply retire like everybody else's father? Why did he have to be the big Nazi hunter?

Then she pictured him taking her to shul and her heart was instantly so full of love for him she almost wept. Sharon realized once again that among the conflicting emotions she felt for her very special father was a core-deep, abiding, undiminished pride. So the calendar girl finished dressing, repaired her makeup, and went to work, the lyrics of old tunes in her head—"A Free Man In Paris."

29

Kansas City Emergency Shelter

"You know, I didn't do anything to provoke him. I would never flirt like that in front of him. Honest." It hurt Sharon to look at the girl. "But he got so worked up. When we left the party he called me names and stuff all the way home, telling me I was a whore and that I made a fool out of him in front of his friends. And Duane was calling me all these names and I guess I talked back to him so he hit me. You know, like in the stomach.

"I fell down and I knew I was hurt real bad. I tried to

get him to take me to the hospital and he wouldn't do it. He said the cops would investigate and because of his record he'd be thrown in jail. He said I wasn't hurt that bad, but I was bleeding and everything. I tried to call a cab and he knocked the phone out of my hand and started hitting me in the face." Stacey Linley. A twenty-two-year-old womanchild.

"Did Duane know he'd caused you to miscarry, Stacey?"

"Yes, Miss Kamen, I told him. I'd passed tissue in the commode. He joked about it. Said it was a Kansas abortion. He thought it was real funny to call it that."

"You know you're lucky, Stacey. I don't suppose I have to tell you."

"I know." Her face was a mottled collection of dark purple-blue and black bruises, but it was nowhere nearly as swollen as it had been in the police photos taken at the hospital.

"Okay, hon, first things first," Sharon said gently. "We want to get you safely relocated." The young woman was clearly frightened. "Just as we talked about on the phone, first we have to go to the Circuit Clerk's office and file the papers, right?"

Stacey Linley looked down at the floor. Sharon could see a tear in the corner of one of her blackened eyes. The bruises went down under the clothing. She'd been very lucky indeed.

"We can't put it off, Stacey," Sharon said, a bit more firmly.

"I don't want to."

"You don't?"

"I don't have to, do I, Miss Kamen?" She'd asked in the softest possible voice.

"I told you what you have to do, honey. I'll be right there with you."

"I just want to get away from Duane." The tear trickled down her cheek.

"That's what I want for you, too. We want all the law we can get on our side. We want you protected, right?"

The Linley girl only shrugged.

"Stacey, Duane is very dangerous. Look at what he did to you. You have to deal with that." It was unusually still in the office. Sharon was aware of the thrum of the outside traffic, her clock, a door closing loudly in the foyer, a phone ringing, the small refrigerator in their makeshift lounge.

"Can't you make them put him in jail and keep him there until I can get away safely?" She sniffed back the tears.

"You don't have any money, Stacey. Nowhere to run to. No resources. Nothing. How can you get away?"

"Like I said on the phone, I have a girlfriend. She'd loan me a few dollars. I could take a bus somewhere. Anywhere. How could he find me?"

"Look," Sharon said, "you're twenty-two. You don't have any money. I spoke with your friend and she said she could loan you about twenty dollars. You can't travel far enough to hide if this guy decides he isn't ready to call it quits and makes up his mind to find you. Not looking like this."

"I could wear lots of makeup and dark glasses. Just get on a bus . . ." Her TV fantasy.

"I've been through this a hundred times, hon. These guys can get very persistent about tracking people down. Duane's obviously violent. His record of prior arrests has to be considered. You need to go over with me to the Circuit Clerk. We'll file an ex parte. He won't be able to touch you, come near you, go anywhere near the apartment—"

"You don't know him," Stacey Linley whined. "He's not gonna care about a piece of paper. It'll just make him mad." Even through the discolored meat of her face, Sharon could see she was attractive. So many who came into the Kansas City Emergency Shelter were good-looking, bright, decent women. But they'd been called whores, ugly sluts, tramps, worthless, stupid bitches, and no-good mothers so many times they'd begun to believe it themselves. It was what her father termed the concentration-camp mentality, the breaking down of one's esteem, the first step on the road to domination.

Sharon Kamen was a caring and loving woman. She'd been part of the shelter since it originated. She was twenty-nine, and it was really the only job she'd ever held. She loved it and, at times, hated it for the frustrations. The Linley woman had been a referral from the Missouri Coalition's crisis team. They'd recommended Sharon immediately house this outpatient in the domestic violence ward they maintained for the extreme abuse cases.

"Thing is, we hit him with that ex parte and if he so much as looks like he's going to cross the line the police will drop him like a rock for us. We'll have all the law working in our favor. Right now this bozo is out and, for all we know, stalking you. I'll go there with you when we file. We'll come right back here so you'll be safe tonight. They're empowered to serve him as soon as we go over there."

"Serve him? What do you mean?"

"I tell the judge, they drop the ex parte on him, somebody from KCPD or County serves him with it. That's his formal notice. One violation and they'll have to lock him up and throw the key away."

The younger woman didn't bother to conceal what she felt.

"But why don't they . . . why didn't they keep him in jail? They had him locked up."

"He posted," Sharon said. "But he won't be running to the bail bondsman next time to post some nickle-dime bond. It won't go that way. I'll see to it." She could hear a commotion in the hall.

"I'll go with you, but can't I stay here for a few weeks until he gets tired waiting?"

"You can spend the night tonight but, no, Stacey, I have a full house. We have battered wives with children. Child abuse cases. But don't worry, I'll try Safe Haven for you, and we have some private homes, too. This happens to be our busy time," she smiled.

"Your busy time?" Stacey Linley at the moment looked all of fourteen.

"Believe it or not, battering seems to be seasonal. Stress and whatnot, I suppose. Partying, things like that."

"Merry Christmas," she muttered.

"Knock, knock," a large, powerful man said. He had a lopsided grin on his unshaven face.

"You'll have to leave." Georgia, the shelter's secretary-receptionist, was trying to hold his left sleeve, hoping to restrain him. He jerked his arm away from her grasp.

"Telling more lies about me, Stacey?"

"No, baby." The young woman began whimpering, begging him, "I wanted to—please, baby—" The hard fist failed to catch her fully but it smacked the side of her head, knocking her from the chair. He shoved the receptionist backward and as Sharon tried to grab the telephone to dial 911 he reached over and tore it from its connection, throwing it across the room, where it came apart in a crash of glass, wood, and broken plastic, the phone and a picture frame exploding like a gunshot.

"Georgia, call the police—" she tried to say, springing up to try to protect Stacey Linley, but he was strong and fast. He backhanded her and she fell across the desk.

"You're coming home where you belong," Duane told the sobbing, bruised woman on the floor.

Sharon pushed herself up, her head abuzz, vision cloudy, fists balled to fight. "Don't you touch her again. *Georgia!*"

"*Shut your loud mouth,*" the man shouted, threateningly. "Come on, baby," he reached for Stacey, "this bullshit's over. Let's go."

"No, Duane. Don't—"

"*Shut up.* Move it!" He yanked Stacey up by her hair, pulling her toward the door, shouting for Sharon and Georgia to stay back. Stacey was screaming. Georgia was screaming. He was screaming.

"Stop! Let her—" Sharon never saw the fist.

Once, when she was nine, the boy down the road had thrown a chunk of wood and it had hit Sharon in the forehead. It had stung badly and frightened her, the sudden pain, the stars from the blow, the momentary absence of vision and equilibrium. But with that exception the worst pain she'd ever known had been a terrible sunburn one year, or a toothache. Childhood accidents. The thrown piece of wood. Never in her wildest dreams would she have been able to imagine what it felt like to be struck in the face.

Sharon could not see. She had started crying before she could stop herself, bawling like a kid struck on the nose in a schoolyard fight, tears streaming down her face, fighting to see. Trying to get her eyes to focus. It had been like being struck with a hammer. The pain was almost overwhelming. The only advantageous aspect was that, after the first couple of seconds of numbness, the terrible pain of the fist to the face cleared her vision, which was still cloudy from when he'd slapped her.

She broke a long nail fumbling the desk drawer open, taking the gun out, the revolver her dad, the famous Nazi hunter and firearms buff, had given her years ago over her protestations.

It was heavy and unfamiliar. She knew what kind it was but had long forgotten. He'd taken her to the river and made her fire two loads, ten or twelve shots. She'd hated the noise and her wrist had ached from the kick of the recoil.

Now it weighed a ton in her hand as she staggered out into the hallway, tasting blood in her mouth.

"Let her go," she said, very afraid, as she pointed the barrel at him, head pounding, the screaming voices and the fear and the horror of the moment all one terrorizing tactile overload.

She was as afraid of the thing in her hand as she was of the man dragging Stacey by her hair, shouting his violent curses into the cyclone of the women's fearful screams. She hated guns and everything they represented, but in that first fleeting reaction, her eyes desperately searching for a blunt office object to stop him with, a cane, a paperweight, whatever, her fear for Stacey's life overcame her revulsion for the instrument of destruction she now clenched in a death grip.

From the moment Duane had barged into her office, to the backhanded slap, to the hard fist, everything had led to her reaching into the desk drawer for the iron executioner, and these events climaxed as her finger squeezed the trigger beyond the point of no return. Sharon Kamen's penultimate act of violence.

30

Months later Sharon was still haunted by the shooting. Innumerable times, in sweaty dreams, she'd prayed for the moment back, rewriting the scene each time. Once or twice, to punish herself more, in the recreation of the event she'd let the man take Stacey. There were other haunting moments.

Sometimes, especially in the shelter, shadows would loom in an ominous form, and the absence of real security would do nothing to alleviate her anxiety. They'd installed an alarm, but the one-way-view access entry, with locked door and video monitors, had gone the way of other good intentions, victims of the usual budget crunch. She felt vulnerable, both for herself and for ones like Vonetta Jackson, a black version of the Linley woman, who sat across from her recounting a tale of woes sadly familiar to Sharon.

"I'm sorry if I'm trouble," the woman said. Vonetta, unemployed and unemployable, very pregnant, had twice been the target of ghetto bangers looking to steal, or when there was nothing left to take, to rape and brutalize.

"You're no trouble," Sharon smiled. "Soon as we get you fed we'll find you a place to sleep tonight, okay?"

"I can go back to the project tonight."

"You don't want to do that." She felt herself getting angry, not with Vonetta so much as with the shadow of a man filling the open doorway inside her imagination. She was suddenly reliving the damned thing again. Seeing every indelible detail, even the trivia, like the plastic name tag of a kind young cop as he leaned over to reassure her.

"—all I got to do is fix the door—"

He had leaned over and whispered to her.

"—and I be fine." Poor Vonetta.

"Sure," Sharon said, "you'll be fine."

"You'll be fine," he'd said it just that way as the police were finishing with her. "Don't change the way you tell it. Remember what he said: 'I'll kill all you bitches dead!' Just stick to that." Chill bumps covered her arms.

"But that is what he said," she'd whispered back, very scared again, but frightened for herself this time.

"Yeah, I know," he said, in what she thought was a slightly matter-of-fact tone. "I'm saying don't change your story around."

Why would she change her story around? She snapped out of it as the phone on her desk buzzed. She picked it up and learned she had a call. Her father was on the line.

"Vonetta, hang on a second will you please? I've got to take this quick call." The girl sat patiently. "Hello." Sharon spoke into the phone.

"It's me." Her father was calling from southeast Missouri. "Could I ask a favor?"

"Sure."

"Would you go over and get my mail, please?"

"Glad to," she said.

"Wait a day. Go over day after tomorrow and see what all I have. Put it in a bag and mail it to me here at the motel, you mind?"

"No problem, Dad."

He told her he was trying to find someone who'd called him and then apparently vanished. Sharon had his extra keys.

"You looking for anything particular?" she asked.

"No. Just get it for me one time. Leave everything after that because I'll be back after next weekend, one way or the other."

"Oh, good." She brightened.

"Monday at the latest. I'm going back to St. Louis and take care of business and I'll be back home no later than Wednesday week."

"How's Bayou City?"

"Wet. Is it raining?"

"Um, it wasn't," she said, turning to glance out a window. "It's kinda grungy looking, like it could mist or something. I think they're predicting rain tonight, though." She turned back and noticed Vonetta was gone. Her sigh of exasperation was audible on the other end.

"You sound tired," he said.

"Not really," she said, not wishing to explain. She knew how concerned he was about her since the shooting incident.

"What's the matter?" he asked.

"Nothing. Really. Just the blahs."

"Well, perk up and get peppy."

"Okay."

"I'll talk to you later. Thanks for the mail and be a good girl, all right?"

"Hug and kiss."

"Hug and kiss." The line went dead. Your little girl loves you too, Daddy.

What's the matter? Oh, Vonetta Jackson is pregnant again and she has the mind of a houseplant. I'm almost thirty, unmarried, and every guy I've ever dated probably thinks of me as a ball breaker. I have a police record. My father is a professional Jew who hunts Nazis as a *hobby*. I'm depressed, foolish, ungrateful, and have a problem interfacing with my software. It's going to rain. Other than that . . .

On the other hand, as Mom used to say, she thought, look at the bright side. In most places it is legal to make a right turn on red.

31

Bayou City

Aaron Kamen was rather tired, somewhat confused, and acutely headachey. His face felt pouchy and swollen as if he were coming down with something. Ordinarily he'd never have stopped. But fate chose the moment to intervene.

He wanted to take something, perhaps find a nice glass of orange juice and ingest some vitamin C, but his immediate concern was street signs. He was looking at streets with the names of trees, looking for the road the nursing home was on, and the street a Dr. Troutt lived on as well. Was it a tree or a flower? He'd forgotten the address.

Carefully pulling over onto a side street he looked for the list, which he'd temporarily misplaced, cursing himself for possibly leaving it in the voluble Dr. Fletcher's office in New Madrid.

Rubbing his eyes, yawning, and stretching, he flipped through the Bayou City phone directory that he'd brought with him from the motel. It was a massive thing of some thirty or forty pages, and he flipped through it looking for a street map, such as directories often include in the front or back sections. He learned that when it was ten degrees Celsius it was a warm winter day, that you should hang up if you get an obscene phone call, and that B.C. Auto Is Your Collision Doctor. No map. He found the Troutt address on Cypress, looked up at a street sign, marked West Vine, and put his foot back on the gas pedal, eyes in the rearview mirror.

Cypress was the name he was looking for, he repeated to himself, as he drove by a building with a large sign out front that said Royal Clinic, and instinctively he wheeled into the parking lot, pulling behind the building. Might as well go in and talk to them as long as he was here.

Kamen put the loose papers and phone book in his briefcase, glanced back in the back seat to make sure his umbrella handle was where he could reach it, pulled his raincoat collar up and forced himself out of the vehicle and into action.

The rain was really coming down again and it felt cold. He hurried in under the protective archway and was glad for the warmth of the anteroom, even if it wasn't all that cool outside.

He felt chilled to the bone suddenly, and he realized he was on the verge of succumbing to a flu bug or some other dastardly virus.

The waiting area was full of people waiting to see the doctors. He went over to a window where a busy woman finally was able to ask him what he wanted.

"I would like to see Dr. Royal if I may."

"And your name?"

"Aaron Kamen from Kansas City."

"Okay. One moment please." She took another phone call and then began looking through an appointment book.

"How would nine-thirty be?"

"You mean in the morning?"

"Mm hm." She nodded expectantly.

"I'm not a patient. I just need to see him for a second."

"May I ask what it's in regard to?" He didn't look like a drug salesman but you could never tell anymore.

"It's a personal matter." He leaned forward, suddenly conscious that the people there in the waiting room were listening with all ears. "I'm looking for an individual and was told he might be able to give me some information."

"Let me see if he's in, sir," the busy nurse told Aaron Kamen, touching a control on the call director and speaking to someone. He heard her say, "A gentleman is here to see him," and, "No, he doesn't." She turned to face him across the counter that separated the lobby from the rest of the clinic's interior. "Who did you say you were with?"

He told her again who he was and, satisfied that he was neither a prospective patient nor a drug salesman, she told him to take a seat and Dr. Royal would be with him in a moment. The moment was about twelve minutes. A nurse came and told him to follow her please, and escorted him through the length of the building to a corner office, depositing him in the presence of his quarry.

"Mr. Kamen, how can we help you?" He was not the man Kamen had expected to find. It's conceivably a fallacy that we wear the face we've earned, the face we've come to deserve in our years of living. This was the face of a benevolent, kindly man. More Jean Hersholt than Erich Von Stroheim, to be sure. Yet without a hint of any sinister elements, without the infamous Tear-of-Satan birthmark, still Kamen chilled with the sure knowledge of the evil confronting him. Maybe it was in the eyes. He'd have been unable to articulate how he knew, but this was his quarry.

It was Dr. Solomon Royal, to be sure. Not Shtolz of the forties' passport or fifties' driver's license photographs, but on a visceral, intuitive wavelength Kamen knew the kindly, questioning face studying him through bifocals was the elderly Butcher of Lebensborn a lifetime later. Unexpectedly, though his feelings were a puzzle, he knew he'd found Emil Shtolz.

He made up his mind instantly not to play games. "I'm here about Alma Purdy," he said, putting all his contempt into the words, letting this human monster know that his freedom had finally run its course.

"Pardon?" A saintly smile. Inside the genius mind of Dr. Royal a shadow moved from under a corner of the brain and the other one who lived inside slithered out of the darkness.

"You know her, *Alma Purdy*. I fear for her safety. She did a foolishly brave thing." He watched the man pretending innocence, playacting, raising white eyebrows in feigned ignorance. Smooth, this one was. "Don't pretend you don't know what this is about, *Herr Doktor Shtolz!*" He spat the words out with the authority of a death camp survivor.

The man was very good, he'd give the devil his due. Not a flicker of recognition found its way into the sympathetic face. One shoulder went up slightly. The aging, handsome head shook again, but the eyes remained flat and unchanged. "I'm sorry, but I just don't . . . Oh! Yes!" He reacted convincingly, smiling. "The woman with the prosthesis. I'm sorry. It just didn't register for a moment. I couldn't place who you meant." Kamen listened for Munich in the consonants. Just a touch of something, a guttural quality. His own accent was thicker than this man's.

"Shtolz, what have you done with Mrs. Purdy?" In his right pocket he felt the weight of the hammerless revolver that he carried as a precaution. He was strong. More powerful than this old Nazi. He would fear nothing. Nonetheless, he wished he hadn't stopped. Wished the local law-enforcement people had found him. He wished Randall or Pritchett were here now. "The police know about you, by the way; they're on the way here." He sensed his tactical mistake as the words came out.

Shtolz turned and reached for the telephone, his face hardening into a question mark. This was what Kamen expected. He'd call a lawyer, or perhaps the cops. Try to have Kamen thrown out of his clinic. But instead, the doctor surprised him.

"Would you pull a file for me, please? I need the file on Alma Purdy. P-U-R-D-Y. She was a referral from Dr.

Levin. The lady with the prosthetic hand, remember? ... Okay." He hung up. "She'll have it in a moment."

A few seconds passed. "What did you do with her?" Aaron Kamen's voice was loud in the room. "Answer me, you smiling Nazi bastard!"

"I didn't do a thing," he said, smiling, but with that look people get when they're trying to humor an unruly person. "Mrs. Purdy came to see us for the first time a few weeks back. She was referred to the clinic because of some complications she'd been having. May I ask what your relationship is to Mrs. Purdy?" He was infuriatingly unruffled.

"I'm her friend. And I want to know where she is."

"That part isn't any big mystery. Unless she's been released she is a patient at Barnes Hospital in St. Louis."

"You mean I can pick up the phone and speak to her in St. Louis right now?" Kamen's tone was razor edged.

"I don't see why not." The eyebrows shot up again. "She has no—" A nurse came in with a folder. "Oh, good. Thanks." He got up, taking the folder, opening it up right there in front of Kamen.

"See, she has acute rheumatoid arthritis in the arm and the prosthesis was causing a great deal of pain." Kamen was beginning to wonder if perhaps this was all paranoia. What if he called the hospital and Mrs. Purdy was all right after all? He'd feel like a total imbecile. Hospitalization would explain why she hadn't called back. He'd just called the man a Nazi bastard.

"This is as I thought," Royal continued. "She was admitted to Barnes about three weeks ago. Here's the report based on our X rays. There's the note about our admission and, you see, there's her present room number.

The Nazi hunter was an experienced, tough, resolute fighter, and he was not a stupid man. In theory, he could never be so easily deceived. But theory and real life are often far different birds, and who better to convince and lull and mislead and persuade than the ultimate method

121

actor, the man or woman with more than one personality? Shtolz, long subjugated and submerged, was a genius as well as a murderer, and Aaron Kamen alone was no match for him. Shtolz, the real inner being, came snaking out of Solomon Royal's twisted mind and killed the man in a few heartbeats.

There were calming, reassuring words. Cleverly manufactured facts detailing the seriousness of the absent Mrs. Purdy's arthritic pain, a smokescreen of doctors and nurses and medical initialspeak, a convenience of contrived history swirled in front of Kamen's tired eyes. It might be argued that had he felt better he would have proved to be a more worthy adversary. But Emil Shtolz, brilliant butcher of the secret Himmler breeding farms, was fighting for his life.

He kept the thing under his desk in the office. There was one in his car, one in the bedroom, another here. Over the years he'd become proficient with them. He thought of them as his brass knuckles, but they were far more than that. Protrusions came between the fingers, a heavy tube was clenched in the palm, and the hard, sharpened striking surfaces protruded from top and bottom. Shtolz no longer remembered the name of the weapons, which he also used as grip strengtheners.

It was the simplest move to slide his right hand into the one beneath the desk, pulling the file off with two hands as he stood, speaking as he moved, the right thumb visible on the file folder, the left hand with the papers now crossing over the right as he handed the folder to Kamen, right hand curling around the powerful knuckles, focusing on a spot a foot in space beyond the man's head—hands moving, right hand at the left shoulder, weight into the blow, expert knowledge of anatomy targeting the hard striking surface as the extended fist smashed into Kamen's temple.

Even a person in his sixties, without great strength, striking a lightning-fast blow with such an instrument, can traumatize the brain with four thousand to forty-five hundred foot-pounds of pressure per square inch. It is a devastating blow to the head.

Shtolz had emerged to direct the movements of Solomon Royal the moment he sensed danger. The evil genius soaked the situation in through his pores, every movement geared to that moment when he could lash out at this intruder.

From the second he thought he'd been spotted by the old woman and he first realized that she recognized him, the long-dormant survival instincts had been reawakened. Since then, he'd been constantly prepared for and attuned to the other hunters that he knew would be coming.

He'd known when his girl had closed the door he would be safe. He kept up his soft-shoe routine, speaking to the man even as he moved, talking about the woman's prosthesis as he took the syringe out, deftly seeking and finding a vein and plunging the hypodermic needle in, filling the unconscious Jew's veins with enough morphine to kill three men.

Now the adrenals were activated and he felt the erotic charge surge through his own system, as if he'd shot the dope into his own veins, and the apprehension, excitement, and pleasure of supremacy gave him the power he needed to work the heavy body into his private closet.

He opened the office side door that faced a corner of the rainy parking lot, then, leaving it ajar, quickly opened the door of his office, and, seeing the hallway empty, he faced the parking lot and said in a loud voice, "No problem. I think she'll be fine. Give me a call if she needs anything." A pause and a glance back at the open office door. "Okay. So long." He slammed the private door much louder than necessary, immediately going back down the hallway for his next patient, thinking a dozen thoughts as he quickly sorted and compartmentalized his options.

His main regret was not that someone had come for him but that he had felt unwilling to gamble. He regretted that he could not afford the risk of keeping this solitary hunter alive for interrogation later. Aside from the pleasures of the inquiry and what would follow, it would almost have been worth the gamble to know for certain who else knew about his existence.

There would be a vehicle in the parking lot to contend with. Keys in the man's pocket would doubtless fit the ignition. He silently examined these dangerous intrusions and inconveniences, as he assessed the risks of his plan.

In the slimy darkness of his mind he felt the blood and tissue fleck his face as it flew from the bone saw, savoring the climax of the evening ahead.

When he'd spent a few minutes with a woman whose kidney infection could be treated with a simple urine analysis, routine diet, and prescribed antibiotics, he returned to his office and considered the problems at hand.

There was his fictitious Purdy folder there in the clinic files, now conveniently misplaced, but which had been prepared and filed, initialed and charted by a part-time employee who worked only one day a week and would remember nothing. The Medcor computer carried Alma Purdy's fictional record of office visits, diagnostic entries, lab work, and treatment summary. When the chart was found it would show she had known Dr. Royal for over a year, and it would prove adequate unless the woman's records turned up in the files of another doctor.

He'd invented a rather well documented condition of aggravated arthritic pain to explain the spurious history of past visits. The X rays of a prosthesis-wearer's amputated arm, which he'd inserted into her chart, were a particularly nice touch.

That evening, after the clinic was empty but before the nighttime custodial people arrived, he backed Kamen's car up to the office side door and, under cover of his privacy wall in back of the clinic, loaded the body into the trunk. After that it would briefly occupy part of the two-car garage in Royal's empty rental property a few blocks away. From there the late Mr. Kamen would go to dwell in the newly planted "garden" in Royal's basement, perhaps not all at once, but piecemeal.

The contents of the Hebe's briefcase were nothing: ancient, blurry photos, renderings that resembled Dr. Royal not in the least, notes of haphazard conjecture, fumbling guesswork. He could imagine what the regional law agencies had. Little or nothing. The object mailed by Mrs. Talianoff remained a small, loose cannon.

The car itself would also present no problem. Without undue trouble he could drive the vehicle out to the backwater's edge after dark. Leave it at the edge of the incoming river. Plan a nearby house call. Invent some car trouble. His patients wouldn't blink an eye if he requested a lift into town. Nothing major, much less insurmountable.

It was past his bedtime and he was physically exhausted but his keen mind still turned over variables. He knew the woman had alerted this Aaron Kamen, who would have taken his story to the authorities, but so what? This was no spearhead of a search team from the K-group or the Mossad. This was an old crone and an inept amateur. Two moron Jews.

His Royal identity, in concert with cosmetic surgery, his language proficiency, intellect, and background in the community, they amounted to an impenetrable shield. It was best not to plan these things out too painstakingly, he supposed. Weigh the probabilities of course, but let the element of chance factor itself into the mix to some extent. Go with the harmonics.

He decided he'd take a Seconal or two, almost too exhausted to sleep, and within a few minutes was slumbering peacefully.

She'd started trying to reach her father by phone late Saturday, calling him a number of times Sunday afternoon and evening, and then putting it out of her mind Monday, with the pressures of work to contend with. But the fact he'd been out of touch all weekend tugged subliminally, and by late afternoon Monday, Sharon started calling the motel in earnest. No answer. That night she dialed several times again. Nothing.

She tried to read. Listen to music. Paint. She couldn't disengage her mind. How could her father get lost in Bayou City?

At times like this, as she prowled her apartment, feeling the walls closing in on her a bit, she would get quick, uncomfortable flashes of insight into just how much damage had been done to her psyche by the thing at the shelter.

The cop and his ominous warnings about sticking to her story of the shooting . . . the cold formalities with the police interviews that left her feeling dirty and confused . . . the frightening business of having to get legal counsel and then depose . . . stand trial . . . terrifying moments after long months of waiting. When she was finally exonerated there was no sense of real relief, only anticlimax. The guilt was still with her, the feelings that a self-defense acquittal could never expunge. At such moments as these she'd realize how far she still had to come to shake loose from it.

At 9:48 P.M., after the fifth call of the evening, letting it ring twenty times or more, she rang the Bayou City motel office, asking the manager to make sure her father was all right. After some discussion, the woman relented and took a passkey, returning after what seemed like ten minutes to the telephone that Sharon insisted she not hang up.

"Hello?"

"I'm still here."

"Well, Mr. Kamen apparently hasn't been back to his room for a day or so."

"Why do you say that?"

"Because our maid didn't show up today and I had to do all the beds and clean the rooms myself. His bed is still made up from the weekend and I don't think he's been back in the room."

She thanked the woman, and as soon as she had a dial tone tried the Bayou City police. A deputy or assistant of some sort answered and she asked for the person in charge, was told he wasn't available, and was given the opportunity of leaving a message. She explained the nature of the emergency, the fact that her father, who was looking into the disappearance of a Bayou City resident, had not returned to his motel room for at least two days. The man on the other end was maddeningly calm and infuriatingly placating in tone.

Think! What should she do first? She phoned her superior at the Coalition and briefly explained the situation. She would have to leave immediately. Could she please arrange to notify the office? They'd cover her absence and handle everything. She assured her boss she'd call as soon as she knew something, rang off, and dialed the motel again, telling the manager not to worry if the police contacted them. It didn't necessarily mean anything bad. Her dad had been conducting a private investigation and may have simply become too involved to return, and so forth.

Sharon forced herself to breathe deeply, count to ten, and get hold of her emotions. She suddenly felt as if she were coming apart at the seams. It was absurd. Her dad would show up tomorrow with an explanation and tell her she'd been childish to worry. She was behaving idiotically.

She went in and started doing every dirty dish in the place, realizing, as she wiped plates and utensils, she'd been grinding her teeth together. She unclenched her jaw and went into the bedroom and started throwing things into a bag, including the packages and mail she'd picked up from her father's apartment during the noon hour—a whirlwind of movement, churning inside.

By 10:45 P.M. she was on her way to an all-night service station, pulling into the self-service lane, getting out, unlocking the gas cap, so nervous she could hardly disengage the pump, hands shaking.

Sharon chilled at the mental image of her dad saying "I'm on to one of the big boys," the phrase immediately filling her with the helplessness she always experienced when he talked about the war criminals. "I smell a rat."

"Someone around here?" she'd asked.

"Down in the Bootheel," he'd told her, referring to the southernmost tip of the state.

But her worst moment was yet to come. Maybe an hour later, driving in a semi-trance, it occurred to Sharon that the first thing the police in Bayou City would do would be to check *her* out, and they'd discover she'd shot and killed a man.

She played with that one half the way to Bayou City.

33

Bayou City

Sleep came like an old, comfortable pair of pajamas one pulls on and encased him in a blanket of warm and seductive familiarity. There was the period of the body's surcease from labor, regeneration, and as he gave himself easily to it, his thoughts became a mosaic of assimilated memory. If he remembered the beginnings of the dream he would attribute it to a clumsy piece he'd been reading. The image of comfortable pajamas and the acronym for the *Journal of the American Medical Association* converged and pooled into a pa-JAMA shape, as the article on deanimation coagulants and neuro-suspension melted toward the fringe of a dream. It was a natural bridge to transfusion and discorporation techniques and his mind made the jump, then to the DNA breakthroughs of some decades later, placing the history around his own contributions.

Early in the morning he penetrated the inversion layer and a question rattled through the corridors of his sleeping consciousness. Does he see something? Is it shadow or bloodsplatter? He sees it above him.

Dreaming below a wall hanging that appears to depict acquatic Lentibulariaceae, alive with vesicular floats and hungry insect traps, he imagined his own eyeblink and pulse rapidity. The appalling grotesquerie under which he slumbered drooped, festooned, bulged obscenely, swagged in the center as the billowing middle of it loomed drippingly above his face. The chameleon's eye blinked and the bladderwort dripped into his snoring, open mouth. His shoulder burned, ached. Involuntarily, he swallowed.

How could he fail to recognize the unmistakably salty, metallic bloodtaste? Flanking the drippy Utricularia, the wall above his bed was splattered red with arterial fluid, veiny crimson, dark scarlet lifejuice. He knew full well that it was hers . . . her blood, gore, and grue. He knew immediately he'd find her acephalous and dead beside him. His alert mind continued to catalog options, and map escape routes.

Sleep-cudgeled senses registered danger, intruder, violence. It shocked him out of his lethargy and he awakened and saw that it was only a wall hanging above him, that the splatter was naught but shadow, that the clutched object was a pillow not a child's torso with partial head, so for a second he thought it was all a dream. In the next eyeblink, in the next heartbeat, he remembered the details of the hag who recognized him and the Jew she sent to confront him. He knew which part was real now, and permitted himself to slide back down into the cradle of deep sleep.

He hoped he could conjure up the little girlchild, Marta, again. Pick up where he left off in a twisted fantasy, but stop it this time before the death scene. Linger with her, a fragment of delicious domination saved in his collection of monstrous artifacts, a small vignette of sadism he reinvented and played with over and over.

Emil Shtolz's self-protective urges and his pleasure-pain linkages made for restive bedfellows, however, and he could not fasten onto the pleasing parts of the dream. As he dropped back into sleep a corner of his sentient mind wondered who would come for him next. He supposed, incorrectly, it would be a policeman of some kind.

34

Bayou City

"Miss Kamen," the police chief said, taking her hand, "I'm Jimmie Randall." She shook his hand firmly. He sucked in his stomach slightly, a thing she noticed guys did sometimes when they saw her. She was too tired to be even faintly amused.

"I guess you got my message?" she asked.

"Yeah. I checked at the motel several times and left word. It doesn't look as if he's been back for two, three days. His clothes and things are still there."

"I know," she said, starting to lose it.

"Listen," he said, seeing that she was on the verge of tears, "we've got a quiet alert out for your father, but I want you to know that I am concerned." He was picking up the phone even as he spoke calmly to her. He dialed.

She bit her lip, nodding, not knowing what to say. She watched him make his phone call.

"Lemme talk to the boss man. Thanks. Hey, bud, how's things? I have Sharon Kamen in my office. . . . Yeah . . ." A long pause. "I'm gonna call Bob. . . . Yeah. We have to bring 'em all the way in now, I think. . . . Okay" He rang off and placed another call before he spoke to her again. "Bob Petergill, please. Bob, this is Jimmie Randall. . . . Fine. There's another development in the Shtolz business. Nobody's had any contact with Mr. Aaron Kamen for about three days it looks like. We got him in Sikeston—" he glanced over at a stack of notes on his desk. "Uh, let's see . . . four days ago, or thereabouts. I think he may have, yes." She didn't like the sound of that. "All right, sir. I'll be here." He hung up the instrument.

"That's the head of the bureau in Cape," he said. "We've got a real good relationship with the FBI here, Sharon, and we need to get all the big guns on this, I think. Might still be that your father is off somewhere and we'll find he's perfectly okay, you know?" She nodded again. She noticed he was no hick cop. In a few moments he'd done everything that could be done, passed the ball, put himself on a first name basis with her but not the other way around, and unless she'd misread him, he was now gently dismissing her.

She wasn't quite so easily finessed. She asked some more questions, most of them dumb, but at least she hadn't started sobbing. Mostly she found herself volunteering a lot of information about herself, the way one often does in a prolonged conversation with an experienced law officer. She decided the smart move would be to get a few hours' sleep and begin anew. How lost could one get in Bayou City?

Apparently, if Alma Purdy and her father were examples, one could get altogether lost. Sharon came away from the city administration building with a couple of facts she hadn't had going in. She had a missing persons sheet on the Purdy woman and was surprised how relatively young the lady was. Her photo made her appear twenty years older. Second, she had the circular her dad had prepared for the rat hunt.

Back at the motel, all of three blocks from the police headquarters, Sharon shed her clothing and filled the tub, easing her tired body into it and loving the instant gratification of the soapy heat. She was an inveterate shower person but at this moment a hot bath and a long soak were in order. Just a couple, three hours shut-eye and she'd be recharged.

She looked at one of the circulars as she relaxed. Beneath the blowups of the likenesses of the Boy Butcher, Emil Shtolz, Aaron Kamen had added thoughts about the possibilities of reconstructive surgery:

Photograph One: Dr. Emil Shtolz the way he looked when he left Germany in the mid-1940s. Note birthmark.

Photograph Two: Dr. Emil Shtolz's photograph by the time he obtained a driver's license in the postwar 1940s (South America). Identical to photo used by War Crimes Tribunal when Shtolz was tried and convicted in absentia. By the time Shtolz had come to South America he had had cosmetic surgery. **Note removal of "Tear of Satan" facial birthmark.** Presumably his left arm might also show evidence of the removal of official Waffen-SS blood group tattoo. Following standard escape procedures employed, it is a reasonable assumption that upon Shtolz's emigration to North America additional plastic surgery would have been sought. Subject may no longer resemble photographs.

Kamen had also appended the following:

General Note: Intellectual capacity and language fluency will render this individual extremely difficult to identify physically if further cosmetic facial restructuring has been employed. (See dental records.)

Look for someone working either as a clinician, doctor, teacher, medical assistant, veterinarian, dentist, researcher, or in a related field such as pharmacology, biochemistry, etc. He may have an unusual number of pets, or in some way volunteer his services to help animals, children, and/or the elderly. Shtolz might do charity work for an animal organization such as the Humane Society, or work around livestock in some capacity. He might run a day care center or work for such organizations as the Boy Scouts of America. He might be posing as a priest or minister, or volunteer to work with church, school, day nursery, or nursing home groups.

He may wish to display proficiency in one of the scientific disciplines, for example, a laborer whose hobby is some avenue of clinical experimentation or a blue-collar worker who has treated illnesses. He will seek out contacts with young children, developmentally impaired people, senior citizens, animals, and those he considers vulnerable.

There were no further notes about checking out the man's paper trail for a fraudulent resumé or references that wouldn't stand up to close scrutiny, because that was basic to any investigation. It was the first thing one did as a hunter, one followed the trail.

The circulars were thin sheets of paper but they had a weight she couldn't believe. The weight pushed her down, made her ache inside, shudder, and she jerked her head, trembling, as she felt her face sliding down in the bathwater. How long had she been asleep in the tub? God! Unbelievable.

Sharon got out of the now cool water and rubbed vigorously with a huge, rough bath towel. The motel room had felt quite warm when she first entered it but the air dried on her now, making her tremble again, every pore of skin tingling. She was afraid and wasn't completely sure she should be. You could think about things in a way that might perhaps influence them. She jumped into bed and pulled up the scratchy blanket and the spread that smelled of tobacco smoke and was asleep before her beautiful, silky hair hit the pillow. She did not hear the rain that was pounding outside in accompaniment to her deep breathing.

35

New Madrid Levee

Daniel Bunkowski dreams of his third bit inside the House of Pain, which was one of the names the inmates gave to the Marion, Illinois, federal penitentiary.

Dr. Norman, in charge of the program that originally shoehorned Chaingang out of the maximum security side, enjoyed a unique position within the penal system, and his ties to clandestine intelligence, the military, and the law-enforcement community had, in a direct, odd way, filtered down to his principal charge: the only inmate within the federal system with a Level 7 rating.

The unprecedented cartes blanches this anomaly was given transmuted in strange ways. The correctional guards found the special procedures loathsome, but what the guard nicknamed Spanish felt toward Bunkowski could only be termed unnatural. It was a fierce, mad, irregular sickness that ate away at the man.

He never missed an opportunity to be cruel to the occupant of cell 10, in the violent unit of disciplinary segregation—D Seg being prison jargon for solitary. It had begun with words, stories of animal cruelty and child abuse that he hoped would enrage the thing kept in restraints, cuffs, boxes, irons, and a biter. He graduated to photographs: shots of a kitten being tortured and sadistic kiddie porn. The guard had studied Bunkowski's dossier, on advice of various jailhouse "docs," the specialists in the more depraved extremes of sadomasochistic behavior.

The pictures had an effect opposite to the one he desired, however. When the monster saw them he simply turned to stone, and never again showed his antagonist any sign of

135

response. The mistreatment then changed, taking on a physical edge, and Spanish began to beat on Chaingang when he knew he could get away with it. When Dr. Norman was out of town, as he was on this occasion, the opportunity was too good to ignore.

Warden Dickett put his trust in Captain Lawler, a brutal and by-the-numbers dope entrepreneur, who delegated to McCullough, Brock, and Lopez the daily responsibilities of prison business. They, in turn, farmed out the routine work. Thus, Spanish Rodriguez, through his bud Lieutenant Lopez, was able to cut himself a huss.

With quid pro quo in various currencies having greased his entrée, Rodriguez took a baton and wrapped it carefully in thick rolls of newspaper. When it was properly prepared he headed for the house where the beast was caged.

That particular date, the violent unit had just been repainted, and, like the rest of D Seg, it glistened with a fresh second coat of rather prepossessing institutional beige. The behemoth's house was unlike the others, however, as it was not only restricted with respect to personal contact, the cell bore its own unique caveat:

WARNING!

To all personnel/Effective immediately/TFN:
The following rules shall be rigidly adhered to regarding the maintenance of the occupant of Cell 10, **MAX D SEG VIOLENT** Unit: <u>NO PERSONNEL SHALL ENTER THIS CELL FOR ANY REASON AT ANY TIME UNLESS ACCOMPANIED BY ONE OF THE FOLLOWING SUPERVISORS:</u>

1. Dr. Norman
2. Captain Lawler
3. Correctional Officer McCullough
4. Correctional Officer Brock
5. Lieutenant Lopez
6. Myself

BUTCHER

Spanish ignored the warning. His palms were sweating.
"Crack Ten," he shouted to the officer manning the
controls, his voice hoarse.

"Hey, man, we're not supposed to—"

"Lawler knows, goddammit, and the fag is outta town,
so crack the sum-bitch, aw'right?"

The other officer shrugged and unlocked the cell door,
bearing its stenciled unit number and the rules, which
were posted under a large sign reading Violent. The
massive steel door also housed a special feeding and
hygiene port, the operation of which was governed by its
own set of security regulations. None of this mattered to
Rodriguez. He wiped his perspiring hands on the sides of
his pants and entered, pulling the heavy door closed
behind him.

"How you doin' ya fat fuck?" he asked, his voice soft,
almost loving, as he struck the huge, bound figure across
one of its legs. "That feel pretty good?" It turned him on to
put his weight into a baton swing like that. He swung
again with all his might, aiming lower and connecting
against the side of the beast's weak ankle. The muffled oof
of pain was like a lover's orgasmic scream to the little
man. "You behave, blimp, and when I finish with you we'll
let the doctor check you out for these little aches and
pains." He drew back and swung again. Hard.

It was painful for Bunkowski to remember such moments. The vividness of the guard whacking away at him
was irritating. Why, when he could recall nothing else,
did he have to seize on that hurtful event to replay in his
head? The way he tried to dodge the baton strikes,
moving ever so slightly at the last instant; the guard's
body odor, heavy as his own; the plan that germinated
with the first clubbing; all sharp, clear memories.

137

His impaired mental computer also recalled the visit to the prison shrink called Hodge, although the memory of it was out of sequence with the beating. It became part of the same plan, but that was later. Or, was he confused again? Had he escaped that time or had he been set free intentionally? It was too complex to sort out the chronologies. It hurt him to concentrate. The flashback, more of a blurback really, reconstructed a moment of wounded time.

Dr. Hodge, another of the zillion faceless sissies who'd been so fascinated with him over the years, resented Dr. Norman terribly, and all but throbbed with delight at the chance to have a session with the much whispered about occupant of cell 10 in D Seg of maximum security—the hole.

First there was the parade from the hole to Hodge's office, Daniel "Chaingang" Bunkowski, a quarter ton of dead weight, bound and gagged by every means possible. Even the handcuffs had their own boxes, as this inmate was notoriously monkey-pawed. A squad of strong, well-trained correctional officers shared the collective responsibility for controlling the occupant of cell 10 whenever he was moved. They were known as the SCUT squad, Special Convict Transport squad being the official title, but no army latrine honey-dipper or mental institution nut-wrangler ever faced such dangerous scut work. There was no letting down when you were within reach of the predaceous monster who lived in D Seg.

Chaingang, restrained and masked, had a badly swollen ankle and a cracked rib. The nonsequential illogic of the injuries defied analysis. Perhaps there had been other equally severe beatings. *In any event he was transported to Dr. Hodge's office, rather painfully, but showed nothing in the hard black marbles that were his eyes.*

"So, Dan . . ." the doctor began.

Dan? No one, not even sissy Dr. Norman, had ever used such a name on him. It would be like walking up to a rogue elephant with blood on its tusks and saying "Hi there, Jumbo."

Abject hatred flickered in the hard black orbs. "Let's talk about your mother, shall we?"

If a worse beginning could have been devised, it would be difficult to imagine.

"You loved her and hated her, is that fair to say? I mean your case history is quite classic in that respect. Your stepfather abused you something awful, beating you, keeping you under the bed in a punishment trunk, only bringing you out to assault you sexually, forcing his perverted attentions on you as your mother stood by. God, no wonder you hated her. Still, she was your mother. So all the long hours while you were kept inside the darkened closet, what sort of confused and bitter thoughts must you have entertained?" Dr. Hodge was enamored of his own rhetoric and continued at some length. Daniel, of course, was examining the room for opportunities.

"But why the hearts? That's the part I don't quite understand. Eating . . ." he made an ugly face of distaste, ". . . a heart! Why, Dan? Why did you eat the hearts after you killed your victims? What's that all about, can you tell me?"

He remembered that in their own way the sessions with Hodge were harder to take than the amateur beatings he'd been given.

He set his mind to work on various projects, waiting for an opportune moment when the idiot prison psychiatrist was briefly called out of the office. Finally, it came. Instantly he went into his belly stash. Chaingang could barely move his fingers, but he possessed incredible dexterity as well as strength. Deftly, with the greatest precision and focus, his fingertips found temporary freedom, curling down under his apron of belly fat, and producing a horde of tiny objects. A plastic thing that opened into a hinged hook, which was tied to a short length of stout monofilament line, a tiny stoppered vial, a stub of pencil.

After six attempts he was able to catch the grapple hook over the edge of the nearby wastebasket and with the greatest focus slide it over within reach of his fingers. His luck held and it did not tip over. Quickly, hoping time would also be on his side, he pulled the metal container up to where he could sort through it, looking for something he might use as a weapon, a metal nail file or rusty razor blade, anything. There was nothing of interest. Only the shrink's discarded junk mail.

Out of disgust he found a clean envelope and took a stamp from his tiny vial, wetting it with perspiration and applying it over the cancelled one. Dr. Hodge's address was on a peel-off label, which is why Chaingang had selected it. He removed the label and retrieved a junk novelty catalog from the trash. Skimmed the pages quickly until he'd found something, then removed the order form and filled in a number with his pencil stub, using the doctor's MasterCard number from a discarded receipt.

He was about to seal the envelope that would send away for the joke novelty item, when he saw something that made his coal black eyes sparkle with momentary interest: a harmless-appearing toy called Slingshot & Water-balloon Game!

"Wouldn't it be fun if you could launch your water balloons 300, even 400 feet into the air?" the catalog copy asked, breathlessly. "Now you can! The Slingshot & Water-balloon Game was designed by a professional marksman to smack the target dead center every time! Competition-grade launchings can achieve super velocities of up to 250 miles an hour, just pull back the firing cradle, put your muscles behind it, and wing those water balloons skyward. Warning: Do Not Aim At People Or Pets! Made in USA and 100% biodegradable. Comes with instructions, Poly-Vordex grips, rubber tubing, and nylon ammo cradle, plus water-balloon starter kit. Targets not included." It was priced at $23.95. Chaingang thought it was a bargain.

There were two accessories to the game offered: one was a gross of heavy-duty balloons, which he ordered to go with his weapon, and a set of targets, which he didn't need. He already had a target in mind.

All these details were deliciously fresh. Daniel had no

idea that the basic events had taken place nearly three years before and were unrelated to his present condition. They were, nevertheless, pleasantly comforting memories, albeit out of context and asynchronous. He recalled his ambivalence at finding the toy as it meant he would have to forgo the fun of sending for the gag item.

The peel-off label was reapplied to the order form. Thick fingers that could tear a human jaw loose took the stub of pencil, erased the item lot number he'd written, and ordered the slingshot and balloon set in its stead, crudely sealed the envelope, and daintily flipped it into the Out tray of correspondence on the nearby desk.

One other slight change had been made: the order would be paid as a charge to Hodge's credit card, but while it would still be sent to the penitentiary, it was now coming to the personal attention of a trustee whose con name was Mousie. Chaingang had something Mousie wanted. Free enterprise will always rule. There would be some trade-offs. Bunkowski would end up with a weapon that he could transport with him wherever he went. Not rubber, nylon, plastic, nor "Poly-Vordex" would set off a metal detector. And while the hacks looked in Bunkowski's every orifice, there was one place no one, not even Dr. Norman, had thought to look: under his fat roll!

There were even prescribed methodologies for such unthinkable, unspeakable, unnatural acts as the monitoring of cell 10 occupant's bowel movements, the cleaning of and disposal of dejecta, and the post-excremental inspection of his anal aperture. (Talk about your scut work! But in these matters no stone could be left unturd.) A record of the occupant's feces production and wiping patterns was seriously kept and examined. It was known colloquially as the log log. Rectal, nostril, oral checks, and routine examinations of Bunkowski's head, armpit, and pubic hair were made by unlucky correctional personnel. They parted his toes, looked up his nose, and made him spread his rose looking for . . . well, anything. He found their efforts embarrassingly amateurish.

No one considered that anything of practical use could be hidden under a mountain of surplus gut. After all, he was constantly subjected to metal detectors, and, frankly, if anyone had looked the experience would have been traumatizing in the extreme. The beast was careful never to wash there, cultivating a moldy green scum of toxic tummy-jam that gave off a powerful stink when exposed to air. Sewer shit, sour diapers, and gas line breaks were Chanel No. 5 by comparison to the paint-peeling, stinging, blindingly odoriferous nightmare of Chaingang's belly-stash stench. By the time Dr. Hodge returned, the mini-grapple and line were neatly tucked away under the mastadon's rubbery truck-tire-sized fat apron.

"Well now, where were we? Oh, yes, Dan, we were discussing your mother—" The doctor jumped at a loud sound escaping through the biter mask. It sounded like a lanyard being pulled on a chainsaw, the startling noise that Bunkowski made in lieu of a human laugh. He couldn't help himself. The bound, shackled inmate was amused at the thought of catalog number V-C-1238 arriving. He wished he could have sent Dr. Hodge the practical joke item from Illinois Novelties, Inc. It was fun to imagine the good doctor opening a package, finding Chaingang's "gift donor" card, and then the "realistic bloody heart."

36

Clearwater Levee Road

A kind of unusual thing, not a bad thing, but certainly out of the ordinary, surprised Keith Glenn and his father Thursday night, the twenty-third. They were watching a Goldie Hawn movie Keith had seen before but his dad hadn't, and he was mildly annoyed to hear the doorbell, till he discovered it was Doc Royal. Surprised, to be sure, because there was no sound of a vehicle out in the road.

"Hey, Doc! What-chew doin' out here in the rain?"

"Evening, Keith," the older man said, in his friendly tone of voice.

"Doc Royal?" came a loud call from behind the young, bearded man. "Get yourself in here, man. Keith, *get outta the way!*" his father bellowed cheerfully.

"I can't. Let me stand here. This heat feels good." He took off his rain hat and hung it up on one of the pegs by the door, taking a handkerchief out to mop his face. "I love a good old wood stove."

"Come on *in here!*" J. G. Glenn extended his hand and Royal shook it. The man put his arm around Royal as if he weren't wearing a dripping raincoat. "Gladaseeya! We didn't hear your car." He pulled the doctor into the living area.

"I'm down the road a ways." Royal gestured vaguely.

"Come in and watch TV with us," the son said.

"I can't, Keith. My boots are muddy and—"

"Get yourself in here. Keith, get that blamed thing off." J.G. hopped around turning on lights, pushing a chair over. "Sit here. Get outta that coat." The man issued an

143

incessant stream of orders to anyone within earshot, as was his habit.

"Go on and watch your program. I thought I'd drop in just for a second. Don't let me interrupt. Keep your program on."

"We wasn't watching nothing," Glenn the elder said, scurrying around putting water in a pot and setting it over the flame. "Keith, get in here and scare up something for the man to eat."

"I'm not—"

"How about some Girl Scout cookies? Daddy just bawt ten boxes off of Andy Henry's girl and ain't no way in hell we gonna eat 'em all. Here, take a box home." He placed a box of unopened cookies in front of Royal on the nearby table.

"You two been doing all right?" the white-haired man asked, hoping the answer would not be drawn out. He was rather in a hurry to go about his business.

"We been getting along fine, me and the boy," J.G. Glenn said.

"Time helps heal."

"It surely does." The man got moist eyed as he talked about Myrtle Glenn, who'd eventually died from a number of debilitating diseases including disseminated sclerosis, for which Royal had treated her the last eight years of her life. It was easy for the doctor to commiserate. He'd shared the loss.

There hadn't been a day of those years she'd been entirely free from severe pain, and this expert in manufactured anguish, this man who knew and comprehended the complexities of the nervous system and the mysterious codes of the brain, had made her into a pet. Watching, measuring, testing, savoring her days of tremors, killing headaches, pneumonia, paralysis, and finally the death that came to mercifully claim her.

Mistaking his motives and never knowing his secret brutalities, the men thought of him as a saint, who'd given of his time selflessly to help their loved one.

"J.G., I wonder if I could impose on your kindness?"

"Whatcha need, Doc?"

"I know this is a big imposition, but I was wondering, could I ask Keith to give me a lift into town?" He could as easily have asked to borrow five hundred dollars, the man's best suit, anything imaginable, and the answer would have been an immediate, unconditional yes. They'd both told him often enough how they would appreciate it if he'd ask for something—anything—to help lessen the sense of debt they felt toward Doc Royal.

Even as he made his gratuitous thank-yous he was being escorted to the truck, helped into the front seat, a cup of coffee and a box of Girl Scout cookies in his hands. Keith was putting the key in the ignition and J.G. was yelling instructions and orders from the front door.

"Say, by the way," he added as a smiling afterthought, "don't say too much about me being around here at night like this. I get yelled at by everybody when they find out I drive after dark." Both men chuckled knowingly.

"You come here any time, Doc, night or day," J.G. hollered, giving a big stage wink, a clowning co-conspirator, "and we won't say *nothin!*" They waved a fond good-bye and Keith Glenn pulled onto the darkened blacktop. "Don't be so long before you—" he could hear the man still shouting from his doorway as they drove off into the wet night.

～ 37

Bayou City

Ray Meara came across the levee road slower than usual, trying not to think about the water that seemed to draw closer by the hour as he splashed through the punishing potholes. But what would he do? If he lost this crop he'd

owe for last year and this one as well. It took thirty to
forty large just to get fifty to sixty back. How could he
make it? He'd end up going to the man and putting his
farm up. Wouldn't that be a bitch? Gamble with his
ground just to pay debts? What was the point of thinking
about it? He flipped the radio on.

"—woman looking through a trash bin in north St.
Louis found the body of her twelve-year-old daughter
this morning, according to police. The mother of the girl
had found a trail of bl—" He flipped to a station playing
music, and mashed the gas medal.

He supposed he could do something with Sandy. Make
a major move of some kind. The mere suggestion of it
jabbed him in the guts.

He went about ninety all the way to town and pulled
up across from the bank in an awful mood, shaken from
angst and his own driving. He was in an even worse
mood when he came out of the bank, and decided he
might as well go in Pete's Hardware next door and take
care of that, too. He could look at all the tools and
mellow out.

Sharon Kamen woke up irritated with herself. She
hadn't been coping well. She was being paranoid and
realized it, and she'd taken everything that happened as a
personal defeat. She was mad at her fears, mad at the
cops who were probably making jokes about the gun-
slinger with the big boobs by now. Mad at her father.
Mad at herself for being mad at her father, but when she
looked at his things neatly spread out in the room, she
knew she had to get moving, get out of there and do it
now.

She threw some clothes on and set out to find the local
post office, which was all of ten blocks away. The Bayou
City post office smelled like the motel room, a lovely
aroma of tobacco, disinfectant, and carpet cleaner. She
stood in line behind what must have been every other
soul in the town.

The sound of a drum beat made her turn and look back

in the direction of her car. A parade of sorts—a dozen or so people in uniform, Bayou City cop cars, probably every one the town owned, fore and aft. She left the line and went out on the sidewalk, wondering if she should try to move her car.

Young men with shaved heads. Someone carrying a bright red Nazi flag and wearing armbands. One of them was shouting something over a bullhorn. She caught the word Jews and it exploded inside her head as she saw the dreaded symbol on their flag. Her mounting anger, paranoia, fear, anguish, sadness, worry, confusion, and irritation blew up in a furious rage as she ran to pull the awful obscenity down. This nonviolent woman, once again, had been pushed over the edge by circumstance into an act of violence.

Meara was getting into his pickup parked in front of the hardware store when he saw a fabulous-looking woman come running out in the street and grab at the pole supporting a large Nazi flag one of the skinheads was carrying. Nazi flags didn't do anything to Ray one way or the other, but when the woman grabbed at the flagpole the kid holding it put his hand into her face and pushed her down into the street. The people watching from the sidewalk roared with laughter.

He couldn't believe it. These jerks thought they were at a damn circus! They laughed at a woman getting hurt as if it were a clown act. He churned out into the makeshift parade like a madman, a newly purchased shovel at port arms, smashing through skinheads to try to reach the woman, who was still down on the pavement.

As is the case with all violence it happened too quickly to sort out. Later, he'd retain an impression of people coming into the streets blocking off the cops on either side of the Nazis.

"Come on," he said, roughly, "I'll get you outta here," pulling her through the crowd of milling bodies and noise. He saw the face of that grinning kid, the one with Sandy out at the barrow pit, the kid trying to grab at him as he pulled her through the mob scene, and he brought that hardwood handle sharp into the kid's solar plexus, the two of them running through the screams.

"Slide over," he said, throwing her halfway across the front seat. No time for social graces as he pulled out into the alley next to the bank, watching the mirror for cops, who'd almost certainly be hard on their tail. He mumbled something about getting her to a hospital.

"No!" she yelled, with startling force. "No hospital. Please." She had a vision of The Woman Who Shot The Guy, complaining her father was missing, talking of Nazis, now starting a fight at a parade. My God! They'd lock her in an asylum.

"You sure?"

"I'm all right, really." She felt a drafty shiver of worry blow through the truck. He glanced over at her. A real stunner, but kind of folded in on herself, hunched over, legs pressed together, clothing torn and dirty, hair a mess. But she was captivatingly gorgeous, scared body language or not.

"My name's Raymond Meara." He said it in as calming a voice as he could, putting a smile on his scarred face. "Don't worry," he said, because it was the only thing he could think of.

Everything was spectacular. He didn't let himself really look over at her yet. The long neck. The beautiful face. The shapely body. Long, fabulous legs. A high-class woman sitting beside him.

Sharon just wanted to go back to the motel and sleep. She was halfway through framing her demand that he stop the truck when the man's name found its way through her fog.

"Thanks for coming to my rescue," she said. "Did you say your name was Raymond Meara?"

"That's me."

"I'm Sharon Kamen."

"Sharon," he said, obviously not making the connection. "It's real good to meet you. You're not from here, are you?"

"I'm Aaron Kamen's daughter, Mr. Meara."

He didn't say anything for a moment, then said, too brightly, "Oh!" Clearly he didn't know her dad.

"I guess I may have the wrong name. My Dad said he was talking with a man named Meara about this missing woman he was looking for."

"Oh, sure! I'm sorry," Meara said, snapping out of it. "I'm not too good on names. Yeah, sure. Mr. Kamen. Yeah, I just saw your dad a few days ago. How's he doing?"

"I don't know," she said, in a hollow, pained voice. She told him everything, and he listened carefully, sympathetically, not paying attention to where he was going as he automatically headed back toward the farm. She stopped her running narrative, finally, and realized that she was more addled than she'd thought, and also had no idea where they were.

"Where are we, Mr. Meara? I need to go back," she said.

"Uh, we're on the way to my farm. I didn't know where else to go." He shrugged. "Listen, could I make a suggestion?"

"Okay."

"I know you don't want to go to the hospital but I don't think you should— That is, why don't we go on to the farm? We're not that far away, you can take it easy for a bit, we can talk about Mr. Kamen, and when you feel up to it I'll run you back anywhere you say. How's that for a plan?" he asked. He took her shrug and sigh for a yes.

Sharon Kamen did pretty well until Meara escorted her inside the house. She tried to protest when he wrapped her in a heavy quilt and tucked her into a big easy chair, but she was very ill all of a sudden and she felt both nausea and a terrible chill that had her visibly shaking under the warm cover.

"I'm so c-c-c-cold," she said in a quiet voice.

"Um," Meara said, thinking it might be shock as he examined her head gently. "I don't think you busted anything. 'Course, the sidewalk was cracked pretty good." The house was uncomfortably hot, if anything.

"Thanks a lot," she said, laughing through a shudder.

"Just sit here and relax," he said, moving into the kitchen and putting water into the coffee pot, "you'll be okay."

"What was all that about back there?" Sharon asked.

"Huh?"

"Nazi flag 'n' stuff?"

"Skinheads. They got a permit to demonstrate. I don't follow politics much."

"Can I use your bathroom?" she asked in a small voice.

"Sure. Right through there and the first door to the left."

She struggled up out of the quilt and found her way into the bathroom, which was surprisingly clean and homey, with cattails-and-ducks wallpaper.

She came out in the kitchen without the quilt, a bit warmer, but still shaking inside. "I appreciate you helping me like that. It was kind of you."

"Sure," he said. The swirling hair and lovely face had him speechless, as if his ideal woman had materialized out of nowhere.

"As long as I've forced myself on you this way," she said, "I'd be grateful if you'd let me pick your brain a little more, Mr. Meara."

"Please, it's Ray."

"Thanks. I'm Sharon," she said, smiling in a matter-of-fact way. "Ray, I'm at loose ends with Dad being missing. The police don't seem to know anything." She gestured with only her fingers, the pressures evident in every aspect of her demeanor.

He nodded. "I already told the cops what little I know. I had a call yesterday from our police chief. He said Mr. Kamen had been tracking a guy who was a wanted war criminal from the Nazi era. He asked me a bunch of questions and that was about it. Sure a lot of Nazis all of a sudden. Nazi demonstrators, a Nazi flag, a Nazi war criminal."

"Do you think the one my dad's looking for could be involved with the ones in town?"

"I don't know." He shrugged. "Possible, I guess. Kinda' doubt it. They don't trust anybody over twenty-five. Nah, I don't think so." He couldn't think much of anything with her up close. The epitome of a woman: velvety-looking skin that would feel like the finest silk or the most expensive cashmere. He imagined what it would be like to kiss her, to run his hand up those long legs.

"Please tell me exactly what he asked you," she said, conscious of his eyes burning her and fighting to ignore it. She was used to the hot stares of men, but not under these conditions. She tried to ignore his frank gaze, and fought the impulse to stereotype him.

"He thought he'd located this dude who was some kind of a doctor during World War II, that he was around here somewhere. He thought the man was around seventy years old but could look a good deal younger."

As Meara talked, Sharon noticed how he positioned himself at an angle, sitting so that the deep scars across the side of his face and head would be hidden. He was one of those men she'd never want to meet on a darkened street. He gave off something, an aura of potential violence or crudeness. Whatever it was, she found it distasteful.

"He wanted to know about Mrs. Purdy," Meara said, "the old gal who'd written him or called him about spotting the German. I told him what I'd heard around town and so on. Nobody knew where she was." His large shoulders went up. "Everybody figured she'd gone off to visit relatives or something. She didn't come into contact with other people that much."

"But didn't she have anybody here, neighbors or someone, who would worry about her sudden absence?" Sharon asked.

"Not that I know of. Like I told your father, she kept to herself."

"I mean, it seems like the sort of thing that would have made the papers. Maybe the police wouldn't say anything, but I'd think the gossip, the local grapevine, whatever you call it, would be buzzing about missing persons, you know?"

"I'm sure there was some concern, Sharon, but I don't think people really knew, outside the cops and one or two others. I doubt if anybody outside local law enforcement, me, and the folks at the motel where he was staying even knew your father. Only those he had contacted. Jimmie Randall, he knows to keep his mouth shut about stuff, and I 'magine anybody wants to hold a job with him does likewise." Ray Meara was in his forties, deeply tanned, and might have been a decent-looking man except for a day's growth of wiry beard and the thick ropy scar that disfigured the side of his head and disappeared down the neck of his T-shirt. Perhaps he only looked mean. She knew not to judge a person by his physical appearance.

"What type of questions did Dad ask you about Mrs. Purdy, Ray?" She kept her eyes on his stare, working not to be defensive. She needed this man's input and his help, but she could already feel herself starting to dislike him.

"He didn't ask that much. Just what contacts did she have around town . . . I told him it would be like delivery guys, some box-boy at the grocer's." He stopped a yawn in time. "Milkman. The mail carrier. Guy at the post office. The bare minimum. Mostly what he wanted was for me to make a list of names."

"Do what, now?" she asked.

"Names of guys who'd be old enough to fit who he was tracking. He wanted a list of who worked in hospitals in Cape, Sikeston, uh, the nursing homes like Bayou City, East Prairie, Charleston, Bertrand, or New Madrid. Physicians. I remember he said that word, you know, not doctors but physicians, who were over fifty and working either as vets, dentists, chiropractors, eye doctors, anything that had a medical tie-in. He wanted to know who all the coroners or medical examiners were, who worked in the funeral homes, and he asked weird stuff, too." He smiled a dangerous smile.

"What do you mean?"

"Oh, off-the-wall things. Like he asked if I knew anybody bought cats and dogs."

Sharon just stared at him. The statement was totally out of left field. "Bought cats and dogs?"

"Yeah. To experiment on," he explained patiently, in the tone one might use with a slow child. "I told him there are some old boys round up van loads for the labs in St. Louis. There was this guy at the pound used to sell 'em, too. He was interested in all those names, and wanted me to make up a list for him."

"You made the list?"

"Yep. Gave it a shot."

"Could I ask you to make me that same list? I know it's a lot of trouble—"

"It's no big deal. Sure."

"I'd really be grateful," she said with a smile that showed just the tip of her tongue. He thought it was so sexy he nearly came unglued. The mental governor in his head spotted a fantasy starting and nipped it hard in the bud. He swallowed and told her he'd think on it.

"Could you give it to me now? I don't mind waiting a while."

"I can't. I was supposed to go over to the set-back pasture and help this guy with some cattle," he looked up at the kitchen clock, "and I'm already way behind."

"Oh, I'm awfully sorry." She felt like an oaf. "Let me call a taxi. Can I get a cab to come out here?"

"No, don't worry about that. The pasture is only a mile or two away from the highway," he lied smoothly. "I can take you back to your car or wherever you say. Are you at the motel out on the highway?"

"Yeah, but I can't impose—"

"If you feel fit enough to ride, we'll go on in." He got

up awkwardly, hoping he didn't sound as if he were kicking her out.

"I am so sorry for inconveniencing you."

"Hey, you aren't a bit," he said, a little too emphatically, as they went outside. "It's no bother. Tomorrow I gotta come back by the motel there, and I'll leave the list off, okay?"

"Are you *sure?*"

"No bother," he told her, holding the door open.

But she bothered him plenty, this mysterious lady with her exquisite femininity and little tongue trick, her big-city manners, blondish hair, and dynamite, pale green eyes. He knew, of course, that Sharon was Jewish. Aaron Kamen had mentioned it enough. Meara suspected she was a beautifully natural blonde, which, so far as his experience went, was pretty rare for a Jewish woman. It was one of many unusual things about Sharon.

Ray would have been chilled to read her thoughts at that moment. She was far more shaken than she appeared, and at that instant, getting in his pickup truck, she was making a mental note to tell the authorities about Mr. Meara as a possible suspect, and about the list he claimed to have made for her father. Doubtless they knew anyway but she wasn't going to overlook anything.

The day had turned spooky and then very strange. By the time they arrived at where her car was parked her mind was back on the Nazi demonstrators, and she was suddenly glad again for the presence of the rather frightening man beside her. "I hope those Neo-Nazis aren't going to be angry with you because of the way you helped me, Ray. That one—you know—you hit with the shovel?"

Meara looked over at her with a lopsided laugh. "That punk? Forget about it," he said, genuinely amused. She wondered what had happened to *Mrs.* Meara, shuddering slightly as chilled rain splashed against the bug-smeared windshield.

38

Sharon Kamen began the day in a go-get-'em mood, resolved she'd find her dad within the next eight hours. He was somewhere not too far away, St. Louis maybe, working on the Nazi. She sat at the table under the window of room 6, working on the checklist for the day, looking out at the steady rain that showed no signs of abating, making notes, and clock watching. The second it hit 9:00 A.M. she picked up the phone and asked the office to get the operator for her.

She placed a call to work and a voice she didn't recognize answered. After she identified herself, she spoke briefly with her Coalition stand-in, then asked if she might speak with Wendy or Gloria. A moment later she smiled to hear, "When you comin' back? D'jew find your father? Are you aw-right or what?" Ditzy but lovable Wendy had never sounded better to her. She needed a friendly voice in her ear.

"I want a favor," she told Wendy. "A big one."

"You got it. Hey—you okay?"

"Yeah. I'm fine." She smiled. Wendy's familiar speech pattern lifted her spirits. "Listen, I've put a couple of keys in the mail to you at the office. Could I please ask you to go over to my apartment and get the mail?"

"Yeah! Of course. No problem."

"And I know it's a lot to ask, but would you please go over and pick up my dad's too?" Sharon explained the details, what to do with the keys afterward, to put everything in the big envelope she'd sent. There were labels in the envelope too, to apply to any boxes. Money for postage. No, she didn't think Wendy would need to do it more than one time. It was in case something came that might help her father, but Wendy was sweet to offer.

She'd finished up on the phone when she saw the truck pull up in the space next to her car, and when she saw Raymond Meara getting out she hurried to the door and opened it.

"Hi," she said.

"Morning."

"Come in," she said, with no other option since it was raining.

"Yeah," he said, but as he stepped barely into the doorway he also seemed to be in an all-business mood. "If you don't mind me asking, what have you got planned for today?" She told him briefly and he surprised her by saying, "I got a suggestion for ya."

"Oh?"

"I've put together a list that's close to what I gave Mr. Kamen, as best as I can recollect." He unfolded a thick wad of ruled tablet pages. The pages were covered in heavy black pencil marks, neatly printed company names and the names of doctors, then a page of addresses, all of this alphabetized. He'd obviously gone to a lot of work, reconstructing the list, then alphabetizing it and printing out all the addresses.

"I really appreciate this. You didn't have to go to all that work. My gosh—"

"No big deal. Anyway, what I thought was, we'd go around to some of these places together. You know, you could ask if your father had been there and if he had we could establish who he'd seen and who he hadn't seen, what time and so on, and you could give that to the cops. Might find out something they missed. Anyway that was my idea."

"It's a good idea, but Ray, really, I can handle this on my own. I do appreciate your willingness to come with me but I can find the places. This list is what I needed." Her tone was trying to dismiss him.

"Look. You'd best let me help you. I got nothing I have to do. This is a slack time for me. I could take you around and it wouldn't be a bit of trouble. I really want to help find out what happened to your father," he said, and kept going before she could say no again, "and, you know, it's gettin' to be a problem on some of the highways. I'm familiar with the area and you're not, and I know which places to try first before the roads get closed off by the water. Also we can get to places in the truck, might be a problem for that little car of yours, low as it sits. Two heads are better than one." It was a long speech for him and he looked serious.

"That's really kind of you but—" She stopped the sentence in midair, shaking her head no. She didn't want or need the hassle, even though it was logical enough. "I couldn't ask you to do that." Having rescued her, did he now feel responsible? That was the last thing she wanted.

"You didn't ask me to do that," he said. She was shaking her head again, a smile in place, obviously convinced it was a bad idea. "What I think we should do first is hit the ones in Cape." He leaned over her shoulder and pointed to the list. "Here. Here. This guy. And the sooner we get going the sooner we can get it done."

She turned her face up to his but knew she was going to let him help and the refusal was never articulated. He was putting the list back together and sort of angling toward the door, trying to make it as easy for her to agree as he could. "Mm—" she made a small moan of protest but he was hearing none of it.

"If we're lucky we can finish up in Cape Girardeau by late afternoon, but one of these is near Jackson. That's a good piece of driving and the water's already over the interstate in two places so by tonight that highway's going to start to be a problem."

"You sure?"

"Let's go," he said, somewhat abruptly. "Come on."

She got up and got her raincoat and purse. "This is really kind of—" But he was already outside and getting into the truck.

Ten minutes later, sandwiched into the midst of a convoy of giant semis, she was glad Meara had volunteered his help. Water was already over the highway, as he'd predicted, but it didn't seem to have stopped anybody.

She studied Ray's notes:

ANNISTON COMMUNITY CENTER	Dr. Paul J. Childress
BERTRAND HOSPICE	Dr. William Syre
CONSOLIDATED RESEARCH LABS, INC. (Sikeston)	Dr. Mishna Vyodnek
CHARLESTON MEDICAL ASSN.	Dr. Claude E. Romanowski
DELTA GENERAL (Sikeston)	Dr. Raoul Babajarh
FLETCHER, N.J. (New Madrid)	Dr. N. J. Fletcher [Retired from private practice]
FUTRELL ANIMAL CLINIC (Hwy. 61)	Dr. Homer Thuey
FUTRELL, C. Z. (retired) (Kewanee)	Dr. Charles Z. Futrell [Retired veterinarian]
HOSPICE OF NEW MADRID	Dr. Donald Henry
MOODY VETERINARY (Sikeston)	Dr. Preston Moody
ST. JOSEPH'S HOSPITAL (Cape Girardeau)	Dr. Clement Puyear
TROUTT, OTIS (retired) DENTIST (Bayou City)	Dr. Otis Troutt [Retired dentist]
TATUM, BARNABUS G. (retired) (Cape Girardeau)	Dr. Barnabus G. Tatum [Retired D.O.]
ST. LUKE'S MEDICAL CENTER (Cape Girardeau)	Dr. Howard Southmore

This seemed an unlikely way to go about finding her father, from a stranger's arbitrary list, and her pessimism was scarcely diminished by her companion. Sharon glanced surreptitiously at the badly scarred man beside her.

"Ray, how did you know all these doctors, and all the different places and everything? And what made Dad so sure this man would be a doctor, just because he'd been a doctor for the Nazis?"

"Well—"

"It seems like such guesswork, you know?"

"Your dad thought this guy'd be one of those, what-yacallem—ego freaks? Figured he couldn't stand it if he couldn't practice medicine or experiment on things. In small towns like this everybody knows about all the doctors, what their reputations are, where they came from. That's all people do around here is talk medicine, discuss their operations, or who's going out with whose wife. See, here's what I figure. This guy's got to be pretty old. Even if he was like twenty in 1944 you can see he'd be past retirement age. That narrows it some. Like that retired dude Barnaby something?"

"Barnabus Tatum," she read from the list. "Retired D.O."

"What's D.O.?"

"Ophthalmology—no, that's the eye. Osteopathy, that's it."

"Thing is . . ." He picked and chose his words carefully before he spoke. What Meara was thinking he wasn't about to verbalize. He knew she didn't have a snowball's chance in hell of finding anything out, but he wasn't going to be the one to break the news. "This was the direction your father was heading, anyway." He left the rest of it unsaid. If her father had got himself jammed up in a bad scene, at least it proved one thing. He'd looked under the right rock.

39

Cape Girardeau

It took them an hour and seventeen minutes to get from the door of Sharon Kamen's motel on the outskirts of Bayou City to the home where Dr. Tatum lived. He was very old and quite ill. She never found out what else he was suffering from other than acute emphysema and didn't care to have his illness diagnosed. She was inside the home five minutes tops, and when she came back to the truck her face looked ashen. Bloodless.

"Let's go, please," she said, and slammed the passenger-side door.

"You wanna go by the hospital next?"

"Sure, fine."

"That didn't take long."

She didn't say anything, put her head against the seat, facing away from him, and began sobbing bitterly.

He thought he really had a dandy effect on her. Ray fought the impulse to touch or console her, focused his mind on the rainy streets and dangerously stupid Cape motorists, and kept his mouth shut.

Finally she brought herself under control. "You know," she said, blowing her nose and trying to smile, "it's funny. I'm not a crier normally. I don't tend to cry much. You caught me in a slump." This struck her as absurd and she laughed. "It's all so impossible. . . . I don't know. That man in there is a dying invalid. His wife said Dad hadn't been to see them and suddenly it seemed as if there was no hope. I know something's happened—I know it has." She blew her nose again.

"Hey, I understand," he spoke quietly. "But your dad looked to me like the kind of person could handle himself. Don't jump to any conclusions yet. This is only the beginning. The fact he didn't get to the Tatum house doesn't mean anything bad."

"Okay."

Three stops later, midafternoon, the weather having warmed up and the rain having slackened, Meara still sat in the truck, waiting. Ever since this lady got into his pickup that morning he'd been self-conscious about how dirty the interior of the truck was.

He started to get out and stretch and saw her coming out of the building, striding toward where he was parked on her long, gorgeous legs, and she took his breath away with the flawless geometry of limb and the artwork of pore and follicle. But he was beginning to realize there was more than beauty that made her so intensely attractive to him.

"Hey, listen," she said, in a bossy, businesslike tone, as if she'd read his mind, "this is really taking way too much of your time, Ray. Please take me to a taxi and I'll make my own way back, huh? You've been super, but this is fine."

"I'm not going anywhere," he said. "Where to next?"

"Oh, well," she said, letting a lot of breath out as if in disgust. When she inhaled deeply, Meara couldn't help but watch her chest push the sweater out and fill it. Why was he doing this to himself?

Again, Sharon was uncomfortably aware of his attention, and the last thing she needed was someone coming on to her. She was smart enough to know, however, that she was a woman who was capable of unconscious provocation and this was the sort of routine interpersonal moment she dismissed. She knew things by taste, background, and instinct: how to appear warmly feminine, for instance, without crossing the line and becoming unduly provocative. She also knew the reverse, and she could chill a man without half trying. With her concerns about her father, the kind of look Meara had given her virtually negated all his kindesses to the moment. She about tore the raincoat off in her haste to pull it around her, and to hell with what he thought.

He felt, appropriately, as if he'd acted like a boorish pig, and it was clear she was going to end up hating him if he didn't get his act together. He could hear words coming out of his mouth, something about Sikeston and Anniston. Bertrand. Dr. Syre. Just words in a business-like tone. He couldn't get his mind right, and glanced at her again.

Ridiculously, she could feel herself responding to his gaze. Ludicrous. It angered her and she felt soiled sitting in his filthy, moronic truck with its country and western music on the radio. She felt tired, too, and vulnerable, and her breasts were quite sensitive under the blouse and sweater, as if he'd reached across and touched her. She didn't understand or welcome the feeling, rejected it wholly, trying to keep it out of her eyes and keep the heat out of her face.

"I don't care which," she said, reading his thoughts and telling him "no way" with her mind, tone, and body language. She did everything but print No Chance in the accumulated dust on the dash.

"Let me study on it a minute," he said, guilelessly, in what he thought sounded like the voice of a man strangling on his own lowbrow thoughts. "It's—uh—you know, hard . . ." Hard. Jesus. "Hard to know—" He was closer to her than he had been. How had he accomplished that? Ray was behind the wheel and she hadn't moved. Maybe it only seemed closer.

To him she smelled like flowers in a springtime garden. He was getting drunk on her and it was hard . . . hard to breathe. He cracked a window. He knew she read all of this somehow, on the wavelength where a woman's intuition operates, and he imagined her recoiling as if she'd seen a snake slither out of the glove compartment. All of this in a half second, and at least he had the wit to sense he'd conducted himself rudely, and with a woman looking for her missing loved one. He wrenched his thoughts out of the absurdly adolescent male fantasy.

"Charleston's out of the way. Let's head back this way," he pointed, "and we can swing on back through East Prairie and Bayou City."

"All right," she said icily.

"We could go to Sikeston, back down sixty-one to Kewanee, and swing back through New Madrid, then take you back to the motel. You want to do that?"

"Okay, let's try Sikeston," she said, "and we can see how it goes from there." Sharon pushed all thoughts away but those of her father's whereabouts.

How many contacts would it take before she generated a single positive lead? Quite casually, a hideous thought intruded, and she realized a very frightening portal had been unlocked inside her mind. The crushing fear that something was terribly wrong returned and wrapped itself tightly around her.

The pickup truck smelled of leather, oil, Ray's aftershave, and something she couldn't place. She guessed it was her own anxiety.

Sikeston proved to be the reverse of Cape; everywhere they went, Aaron Kamen had already been there. When she left the last location she was exhausted, and they went back to Bayou City directly.

She thanked Meara, he said he was glad to help, and they each left it at that. She went inside and took two showers, one hot and one cool, crawled into bed, found an easy-listening station on the FM, turned the music down to enough of a murmur that it could compete with the cowpokes ramrodding the eighteen-wheel longhorns down Highway 80, and fell fast asleep.

Meara sped away from the motel and within minutes was knocking on Rosemary James's mobile-home door. Her friend Brenda opened it and nodded a bored hello, screaming "Rosie" down the length of the trailer. "You got company!"

"Hi!" she said, coming out of the bathroom, her hair wrapped in a towel. "What a nice surprise. What are—"

He shut her lips with a hard kiss, pulling her with him, laughing, as they moved down the hallway to the bedroom.

"Tell Brenda you'll see her tomorrow."

"Brenda, I'll see you tomorrow," she called out, and Brenda was running her mouth about something, but the door was shut, and they weren't listening, concentrating on touching each other with heat and urgency, as he locked the door and eased her back on the bed.

Maybe forty, forty-five seconds later he said, "Sorry about that."

"*Ray*mond," she said, and changed the sheets. They undressed fully, cuddling in the bed together. Before long her body curves and warmth had heated him up again and she felt him stiffen and enter her.

They made love oddly, at least for them, him tucked into her from the back, and then he was spent and pulling his Levis and boots back on, telling her adios.

Rosemary's neck ached from trying to kiss him over her shoulder and she said to him as he went out the door, "Come again any time," actually one of her funniest remarks, while she rubbed her neck and followed him out.

Meara was surprised to find Brenda still sitting in the living room, working a crossword puzzle.

"I'm just leaving," she said, without looking up.

"Don't go on my account," he murmured, saying to Rosemary, "Later," and kissing her good-bye. She stood in the doorway until the truck was out of sight.

"Don't that beat all?" Brenda sneered.

"That's my love life for ya," Rosemary said, half smiling. It was her day to think of funny things. "A pain in the neck and a pain in the ass."

40

New Madrid County

Meara was up before dawn and on Sharon Kamen's case for real. He watched the rain break before sunrise and the red ball came up casting fiery rays of scarlet, crimson, pink, purple, lilac, and lavender light across the ribboned rain clouds of dark blue and gray.

Sharon was dressed, luckily, had hung up the phone moments before, and was writing a quick note, when someone knocked on her door. She was genuinely taken aback to see Ray standing there.

"Hope I didn't wake you?" he said, a polite questioning tone in his voice.

Yeah, she thought, I always sleep fully clothed. She shook her head no.

"There's flash flood watches forecast and it's probably gonna get a little hairy around here. I talked to this old boy I know, me and him go way back, and I asked him about this guy who lives in New Madrid. He's about seventy. I told your dad about him but I didn't think to put his name on your list. He's a river rat. Got these two boys meaner'n snakes, and a couple girls worse than they are. They poach. Dynamite fish." He then said a word she didn't recognize. "I know they jacklight, bunch dogs—pick up strays, all that good stuff. If he was the guy and your dad braced him about it, well I think we might ought to go to Sheriff Pritchett with it, the guy in New Madrid, too."

"We?" She still didn't get it.

"There's another old guy in New Madrid would be

165

worth talking to, and this would be a chance to drive in. You might have to boat there if you don't go now." He made boating in sound like something incredibly tedious and complicated. "Better we go ahead and get started, if you think you want to."

"Let me think for a second," she said. He had a point. She'd barely been able to hear on the phone. That would probably be the next thing—the phones would go. "Maybe we could just call down there?" But he was moving toward the parking lot.

"Water's already in a lot of the terminals. Come on, Sharon. Might be your only shot for a while if that river pushes on in."

She got her purse and slammed the door. "I need to come back right away, though, Ray. I've got scads of stuff to get done today." Her tone was not particularly gracious and she didn't care.

Neither did he, apparently, as he didn't bother to reply. She got in the truck, which didn't seem quite as dirty as it had the day before, and shut the passenger door. A young, male, adenoidal jock's voice sing-songed through rip 'n' read weather news:

"It's the wettest on record. Thirteen inches for the month. We had our wettest day yesterday, with eight point twenty-seven inches. Flash-flood watches forecast for the Missouri Bootheel and southern Ill—" Meara stabbed at the station selector but it was as if the second station were an unbroken continuation of the first.

"—above flood stage at Frankfort and portions of the parkway are closed this morning. Evacuation is under way along the Cumberland where many communities are flooded as the rivers reach record levels. The flooding—" he hit the button again and got some pleasant music, which she wished he'd left on, hit it again, and a female counterpart of the first two male voices added her two cents' worth.

"—moderate to heavy rainfall forecast. Heavy echoes on the radar, with rain moving south and record heat on the way. Eighty-four in Tampa yesterday. Atlanta had seventy-nine. St. Louis is cold this morning with—" He killed the power to the box of bad news.

"Bayou Ridge, where the farm is," he said, "is in what they call the spillway or the floodway. The Army Corps of Engineers have this deal they're talking about doing, this project—" he couldn't get it out. It stuck in his throat like a big, sharp bone. He swallowed. "If the river reaches a certain point they cut the levee and my ground is at the bottom of the Mississippi."

"That's terrible, Ray! Can they do that?"

"The Army Corps of Engineers?" He laughed and looked over at her as if she were kidding him.

"Am I crazy or are we going opposite from Charleston?" She was totally turned around.

"Yeah."

"I thought you said we should go talk to Sheriff Pritchett in Charleston?"

"Yeah, later. We're going to see the New Madrid County sheriff, Gunny Hughes. New Madrid is in New Madrid County. We're still in Mississippi County. Then we can run on by the old man's place, the retired guy."

"Okay. Hey, Ray? Thanks." It was the first civil thing she'd said to him. Sharon realized she'd been bitchy, prickly, overly sensitive, and really didn't give a big Scarlett damn. The weight of her dad's absence was now a pair of blue ghosts that sat perched on each shoulder.

Women, even beautiful ones such as Sharon, have ugly days. Short days. Fat days. Bitchy days. Drab days. Stupid days. Bad hair days. This morning, all of them had come around and snuck in bed with her while she slept, and she'd woken up wearing all those undesirable personas. She also felt remarkably dense.

"No big deal," he said.

It took about twenty minutes to reach New Madrid, with water standing in the surrounding fields and the road ditches completely filled. It appeared that another light rain would push everything under water. The truck had to slow several times as Meara negotiated fairly deep water over the road.

He finally pulled up in front of the New Madrid County Jail. "You don't need to come in," he said. "I can handle this if you want to wait."

"Not necessary, Ray. We'll go together, okay?" She had come down off her high horse, and Meara had decided to give her all the real help he could and cut out the nonsense. They went in with the mutual feeling the air had cleared between them.

The jail appeared to be a one-man show that morning, with a single male officer behind the front desk acting as clerk, receptionist, secretary, dispatcher, and factotum law-enforcement representative. Gunny Hughes would be back shortly and what did they want to see the sheriff "in reference to?"

Meara gave a general summary to the deputy jack-of-all-trades while the occupants of the jail watched them, or seemed to, from a bank of television monitors behind the dispatcher's switchboard.

They left and called on Dr. Fletcher, but he was asleep and could they come back later? They could. When they returned to the sheriff's headquarters, Hughes was in, along with three other men, all of whom devoured Sharon with their eyes as Ray talked to the lawman in charge. Hughes asked her to have a seat while he took Ray inside his office, and, even on a short, fat, drab, ugly, bad hair day, Sharon Kamen sitting down and demurely crossing her legs had to be the most erotic spectacle ever put on display in the New Madrid County Sheriff's Office.

She blocked her surroundings out and sat there, very still, on hold, as phrases drifted out to her from the closed office.

"—called Bob Petergill in Cape and he's—"

"—that ole boy's a complete butt-hole! So is—"

"—keep her out of this. Could be risky to—"

"Okay, Raymond," the sheriff said, opening the door and shaking hands with Meara. "I appreciate you comin' by." He leveled cop's eyes on Sharon. "And you, Miss

Kamen, we'll stay close to this. You going to be staying in Bayou City, or you going back home to Kansas City?"

"I don't know, sheriff. I guess I'll stay here until I find Dad," she said.

"I understand," he said, and gave her a friendly smile. Then they were in the truck and driving back toward the Fletcher residence. Meara parked in front. They still had a few minutes to kill. Apparently, the sheriff had been open with Ray about the case, and, for whatever reason, had excluded her from his counsel.

Sharon thought that living in this part of the country would be, for a woman, like living in feudal Japan or something, but she kept the thought unspoken.

"What was the story?" she asked Meara. "I just heard fragments."

"The river rat thing—he didn't buy it a bit. They got an eyeball on 'em all the time. He didn't go for my theory at all. On the other hand, I gotta' tell you, Sharon, he's very concerned about your dad having come in and tried to run an investigation on his own.

"He thinks something might have happened. In other words, he thinks it's entirely possible that your dad found the guy."

She felt the words clutch at her heart. She didn't say anything, and Ray continued. "He's also concerned about you asking questions. Going around to the same places your dad went. They're in a funny position. It's not their place to tell you that you can't, since there's no proof any crime has been committed, but what he said was, this woman needs to be careful. In other words, stay out of it and let the law do their job.

"The feds are already deep into it. They been looking for your dad from the start, way I get it. So I said to him, whose case is this, anyway? Jimmie's? Yours? The FBI's? Kick Pritchett's? And he said the answer is yes. The sheriffs, him and Kick, they run the whole show down here. In these little communities they rule; they run the Highway Patrol, the local police department or Public

Safety people, whoever. That's the way it works in Missouri. A crime on private property, a missing-persons case, or a homicide, the sheriff rules. He said if the FBI wants to take over a federal crime they can, but right now, since there is no physical evidence, the element of jurisdiction doesn't enter into it." He added, as softly as he could, "Without proof of a crime, is what he was saying."

He brought her back to the motel the same way they'd come, after a brief meeting with Dr. Fletcher, who'd filled them in on her father's visit. He repeated his admonitions about ministers and salesmen, and, again, pointed out Dr. Royal as the source for a list of the "real old timers" still around. On the way back up the set-back levee she asked Ray who Royal was and would it be worth a visit to talk with him.

"Nah. Old Doc Royal's a fine feller. He was our family doctor for about a hundred years. I got sick when I came back from overseas and Doc Royal helped me. He's good people but I doubt if he could give us anything. He retired a couple years ago, but he got bored fishin' and went back to work. I think he sees patients one or two days a week or something. He's got to be seventy if he's a day."

Sharon added the name to her list.

"It wouldn't hurt to go see him, I guess," Meara said.

They were quiet for a long time, driving along the levee high above the rising river's overflow. They pulled into the motel parking lot and he turned to her. "Well, I know you got a lot to do and so do I, so, I'll see you sometime." *Get real,* he told himself, looking at a woman he knew he could never have. "Be careful, Sharon." *You're history, Ray.*

"I sure do appreciate everything. It was really sweet of you. Thanks a lot," she said, getting out of the truck.

"Hey, no problem. Look, if I don't see you again, good luck, okay?"

"Thanks," she said, slamming the pickup door with an

empty heart. He nodded and pulled back out into traffic. She closed the motel door and was shocked to find she felt devastated at the idea of not seeing him again. It was so off the wall, such an alien emotion, that she sighed and slumped back against the metal door, feeling short, fat, ugly, stupid, and now, alone and more than a little confused.

She was so fearful for her dad she'd begun hallucinating rednecks. She shook it off and got on with her day.

41

New Madrid Levee

How long had the beast been asleep? How long had he been in these weeds? He clawed at filthy skin covered in dried blood and insect welts. He needed food, a hot shower, more food, a bath. Other powerful, gnawing hungers flowed through him with a heat that he could taste.

Daniel Bunkowski tried to assimilate. Concentrate. Motivate. Nothing operated. He peered, blinking like a bear coming out of hibernation, a one-eyed bear who'd definitely seen better days.

To see wildlife, to see nature in the raw, become unconscious in deep weeds. The wildlife will sense that you are no longer a threat and go about the routine business of survival, assuming the weeds in which you slumber are far enough from the beaten path.

He vaguely recalled regaining consciousness and seeing a mink, of all things. He remembered cattle egrets, abundant and ghostly, static across a pasture laden with mist. The word Presley in the distance—hallucinated?

No. Simply a common local trade name. A rusty Delta Corn sign made of tin crowned a barbed wire fence. He saw rabbit sign nearby. All of this through a thick sleeve of serious pain.

Beaver are far below in a still ditch about to overflow its banks, but he intuits their presence and eventually sees the dam, testing his operational eye. He makes the first demands on his system, tries again to remember.

Squirrel nests sit high in old oak overhead. Deer sign, lots of game sign; the nearby water and food supplies draw animals, and abundant roadkill marks the proximity of wheeled traffic.

A couple of very young mockingbirds, one on a rock, the other on a post, cry for food in unison.

Mother comes, pokes something in one of the open maws, gone even as the food is transferred, already busy at first light, scrounging food for the babies. A good mother. Not like some—human ones for instance.

"Dan?" A voice echoes.

"Dan?"

A red wave washes through the fogbank. *"How did it feel?"* One of the imbecile shrinks at Marion. *"How did it feel, Dan, to have your mother allow the Snake Man to sexually molest you in that way?"*

"Dan? . . . Why do you take their hearts, Dan?" Had he really escaped or merely hallucinated it? Presley's Farm Market was real enough.

He watched for signs of the monkey men in the immediate perimeter, and as he faded back into sleep, his battered topsy-turvy computer did its best to survey and report:

Mink.
Egret.
Cattle.
Beaver.
Squirrel.
Deer.
Roadkill.

Mother.

The folks back at Marion Pen . . . Dr. Norman.

Breakfast, in other words, not to mention lunch and dinner.

His mindscreen fought itself, working overtime while the huge beast slept again, his gyro standing a death-watch for Dan.

The beating had been severe, and where he'd shrugged them off in the past, this one he could not. He'd escaped by luck, pure will, and raw animal power. Addled, suffering from a number of serious aspects of trauma ranging from blood loss to concussion, he realized it was miraculous his bumbling, wounded escape had got him out the sally port, much less this far.

His survival instincts were not those of a normal man, to be sure. Surviving was a religion about which Chaingang was most devout, and his drive was that of a fanatic. It was the part of his life-support system that had saved him countless times.

Spanish had tried to hurt him and been partially successful—no small achievement in itself. Daniel could not see clearly. The vision in his left eye, where he'd been struck, had suffered badly. In the rearview mirror of the stolen car he'd surprised himself by pulling his left eyelid down and watching a sudden spill of blood overflow the eye onto the cheek. He was injured, and the potential damage level was high.

He'd seen cattle egrets, rusty farm signs, nests high in century-old oaks through mashed lashes of the right eye, occluded oculomotor response, a haze, a foggy day in London town. Peering intently through the petroleum jelly of pain he misattributed the source.

Had he been driving when the wheel of whirling white light tightened into a shaft of brightness that short-circuited his surge suppressors, overloaded his main-frame, and transported him back inside?

He dreamed he was inside looking out, but instead of towering walls, rolls of razor wire, and sharpshooters, he sees a distant highway billboard from another state, the state of misery: Southeast Missouri Farmers Have A Friend At Security Trust.

The haywire computer sees it in his mind, registers the word security, and scans the words of a forgotten manual:

"Possessing no offensive capability patrols must rely extensively upon security measures, both administrative and tactical."

(1.) En route to area of operations: false landings, feints, and circuitous routes.

This eludes him.

(2.) In objective area: proper organization for movement, cover, concealment, camouflage; light, noise, and odor discipline.

He tried to force a fart and could not.

Odor discipline. He had practiced the martial technique known as the Breath of Death for many years, as it was particularly well suited to a man kept chained, manacled, and in a biter mask. He had learned controlled halitotic/ periodontic-type exhalation, and various expectoration techniques.

Every con in the Max, D Seg, had his own handcuff key. There was a guy who made them for dust, a pro who ran a metal lathe and could turn out a tiny steel key that would pop a Teflon Smith & Wesson set quickly as you could say it. Bunkowski had one fashioned out of hard plastic that he carried in his stinking hidey-hole crease under the blubber that overhung his groin.

Chaingang allowed a blow to knock him to the cement floor where he released the key and palmed it. He'd practiced with the black box on a thousand times, and Spanish was getting so worked up he could have done anything with his paws so long as they were behind his back.

When everything was in place and Rodriguez was catching his breath, Chaingang made his move. His brain held another fragment of gold: something he'd overheard about Captain Lawler and one of the cons, but he switched it to Rodriguez's sixteen-year-old sister, and, with the biter off, blood dripping into his mouth, he croaked out what the boss bull had done one day while he was strip searching her.

Spanish lost his head and began punching wildly at the handcuffed man. Chaingang took what he had to, and allowed the tiny piece of plastic straw to drop into position from where he'd held it during the rain of vicious head blows. It was loaded with a fleshette made of melted sprue and feathered in rodent hair. Chaingang had personally eaten the mouse that he'd used for the fletching.

Summoning up the Breath of Death from the center of his guts, hauling an immense tubful of air into the lungs with such force that it also caused his testicles to ascend, he spat the miniature dart into the left eye of Spanish Rodriguez, coming after him like an enraged rhino, Chaingang Bunkowski—loose! Immobilizing the guard in a reversed skein of cuffs and restraints.

He had no intention of killing the man. No, he wanted to keep this boy alive. He knew the kind of dues that would be paid when they had to tell Dr. Norman his boy had broken out again. Shit rolls downhill, and Rodriguez would be in line for all of it.

Other details of the escape blurred.

There'd been another major piece of luck. The guy on the D Seg gate had been there about ten minutes, a transfer from the infirmary over on minimum security side, and what with one thing and another, Bunkowski made it to the outside once again. Slick as Big Mr. Dick.

Chaingang had stolen a car.

Now, hidden in deep weeds, his brain malfunctioning, his enormous poundage shook with the tremors of fever and shock.

The diminutive Latino guard had hit him many times, using things that would addle, but that would not break the skin.

The stolen car came in and out of view, racing across

his mindscreen. He began to remember—to really remember for the first time.

The beating from the guard was two, three years back in time. It held no relevance. He hadn't escaped, and there was no escape now. With Dr. Norman's technology Chaingang lived in a perpetual prison. Even through the pain he could feel the implant back in the rolls of fat that cushioned his skull and unique brain. They controlled him, Norman and the others, by means of an implanted locator.

His hearing popped in and out as if he were experiencing pressurizing and depressurizing aboard an aircraft or submarine, and, similarly, the car roared into view again. What was it about that car?

Bunkowski concentrated fiercely and saw the other car coming. He'd been in Kansas City, fucking Kansas City! The mindscreen fed him his map, fighting for clarity of recall: I-70 east for two hundred fifty-two miles from K.C. to St. Louis. I-64 east to I-57. Then on to Marion for his rendezvous with Dr. Norman. But in St. Louis, where construction had detoured all the major roads, he'd somehow found his itinerary bollixed by the rerouting, and he was southbound on I-55 suddenly, when he noticed a light bar on the roof of the vehicle two cars behind, and no legal place to turn, without exiting into a knotted jumble of crowded exit lanes, underpasses, overpasses, and who-knows-what impasses. He was doing the speed limit plus two. He went around a car, the cop went around a car. He became ultra-cautious, and by the time the heat turned onto an exit lane he was too far south to go back.

The map was a familiar one. He'd played in killing fields in Missouri's hinterlands once before, in Waterton, and he decided to hang tough on 55 until he could cross the river, then head back over to 57 and up to Marion. He was looking at his map, in fact, when the drunk driver in the Olds 98 swung out into his lane. Not even Chaingang's lightning hand-to-eye coordination was quick enough to swerve completely out of harm's way, and the two cars slamdanced off the interstate, rolling, bouncing, crashing; steel, glass, plastic, fiberglass crumpling, shattering, tearing ass every which way.

Chaingang remembered lights on and off, a mob of hands lifting, hearing himself laugh as he was dropped rudely, coming to in a cramped ambulance, and he recalled parts of the memory coming back, earlier, bass-ackwards and out of kilter.

He remembered being offloaded. Many hands. Curses. Jokes about dead weight, "eat your Wheaties," paramedic banter—something about him being his own driver's-side air bag.

There was food, garbage so disgusting even a gourmand with a penchant for the odd, uncooked pulmonary artery was repelled. He recalled thinking what the cops would do as soon as they I.D.'d him; relived the cool air on his rear rotundities as he waddled through a hallway of protesting voices; recollected his impromptu exfiltration. A purloined ride, cramped of course, minutes or hours of driving while he fought against blacking out, and then, much later, regaining consciousness.

But for the first time in battered memory there was a desire that burned even more than hunger. At least hunger for the ordinary fast-food sustenance. The image of the sissy doctor who was at the root of all his troubles was an itch he couldn't yet reach. As he recuperated he would think on the sissy and come up with something appropriate. He never underestimated enemies, however; Chaingang was a planner.

There were those within the penal system and the tentacles of intelligence, the military, and law-enforcement communities, who seemingly answered to no one. Norman appeared to be such an individual, at least on the level of their quasi-scientist/guinea-pig relationship.

Inside Marion there were whispers of ties to DDI, CIA, other national security outfits. Bunkowski was part of the far stranger truth. In the mid '60s, Norman had been recruited by a component of the mil-intel network then calling itself the Special Advisory Unit/Combined Operations Group. Just who they advised was never totally clear, but for a brief time USMACVSAUCOG, their full nomenclature, was the lash-up responsible for "sensitive wet ops in Southeast Asia." Assassinations and terror campaigns run against Laos and Cambodia "across the fence"—illegal ops. It meant clandestine executions of *South* Viets, allies, at least on paper, whom someone had marked bad. It meant trips north into the Z and beyond, hazardous sanctions requiring "sanitized" (untraceable, unidentifiable, unattributable) bods. The most expendable form of covert grunts undertook actions so bizarre and surreal that the nature of the missions could never be made public. A stateside school for sanctioned killers had been one of the wet dreams that almost eventuated.

Dr. Norman was in charge of finding certain candidates whose histories, talents, and proclivities suited them to the work and who could be sacrificed without undue fuss. He had told underlings, "As distasteful as the program was, it was necessary for our country's prosecution of the war effort."

Enter Daniel Edward Flowers Bunkowski: four hundred and sixty to five hundred pounds, six feet seven inches to six feet nine inches, depending on which dossier you believed. Born in 1950, 1951, or 1952. An abused and tortured child who'd lived and evolved into the strangest, most monstrous killer in American history; a heart eater and serial murderer of despicable vileness, who had an intelligence quotient so high it warped every curve. A man mountain of hatred who was presentient, who'd learned somehow to sense impending danger.

Norman termed him, "That rare form of human being, a physical precognate." He thought Chaingang could sense danger before it occurred.

The awesome devourer of hearts had supposedly told his captors, under drug-and-hypnosis therapy, that he thought he'd probably taken "about four hundred and fifty to five hundred lives," a human life for every pound of his weight.

Chaingang Bunkowski had fit the program's profile to a Tyrannosaurus T. Skilled assassin, stalker supreme, with a built-in survival system and network of defense mechanisms beyond peer, he was a man who hated *everybody*. He killed out of pure pleasure. These factors made him the ultimate hunter-killer unit.

Norman saw in Bunkowski his own link to immortality. His discovery and experiments would stand as a unique cornerstone to the work being done in his field of medicine. And when the technology had permitted it, he'd supervised the first brain implant of its type. Laser surgery had been performed successfully, and a sophisticated piece of microelectronics was inserted. It linked Daniel to the Omni D F MEGAplex Secure Transceiver Auto-lock locator Relay unit and movement detection monitor—OMEGASTAR.

But Chaingang would not be so easily controlled. He knew, now, that he would be all right. The leviathan closed its eyes, content and relaxed again, and slept restfully, gathering its great strength. This time the beast dreamt of a spider.

42

The golden orb was back. It had spent the summer in a web that was visible from the small hinged port that was sometimes left open to provide air for the windowless enclosure. A beam of light regularly found its way to the underside of the duct where the web had been spun, and in the evening this light attracted its share of bugs, so the golden orb could dine on found objects at its leisure. Two days ago the golden orb had vanished. It was either a sign of approaching winter, he reasoned, or the spider had fallen prey to something else. But now it had returned.

Her significant other had never been in evidence. Presumably he had been destroyed after the mating process, or had gone south for the season. Through the long days of summer she had managed to engineer a magnificent pouch nearly as large as her own body, an egg sac, so if she survived the coming months, by spring she would deliver.

A distant cousin, Loxosceles recluses, gave the occasional nasty lesion to inmates, who were routinely treated with cortisone IVs.

Daniel had a vested interest in mastering the identification of such insects, not only their appearance, but the symptoms of and treatment for the lesions they inflicted. This was golden orb intelligence if you lived in the land of killer spiders and queens who ate their men.

There might come a time when the ability to simulate a poisonous spider bite, or to inflict the semblance of such a wound, might give one the edge.

The scenario might go thus: coincidentally with Dr. Norman's absence on one of his frequent trips to D.C. or terra incognita, Dr. Hodge would be told by some lackey in the prison hospital that the occupant of cell 10 was desirous of communication. A heart-to-heart, as it were. (The spider would provide the hospital ticket.)

In Dr. Hodge's office, Daniel would dip into his tummy vault for the slingshot and water balloon game. One of the balloons would hold a sealed condom filled with Solution A. The balloon itself had a small quantity of Solution B. These, A and B, were inert until they were mixed. At that point . . .

The laboriously concocted dream of spider and balloon began to disintegrate, the bits and pieces dissolving into Chaingang's reality.

His only contacts were spiders, cockroaches, ants, mice, flies, Dr. Norman, Dr. Hodge, his feeders and inspectors, the D Seg violent-ward hacks, and Mousie. There would be no trade this time. His hallucinated scenario, cooked up on a broken mental computer, had overlooked the fact that all incoming prison mail was inspected.

His powers were coming back, even as he rested. His flawless inner clock had repaired itself and was ticking again. The normally unflappable thermostat that regulated his temperature was back on the job, and he was ice cold. He snuggled down into the folds of the filthy bush tarp that encased him. The hunger that generally drove him was back with a vengeance, and would goad him awake soon, a raging and mad appetite that had a life of its own.

Chaingang's mighty mindscreen worked once again, and as it surveyed the ambient factors that affected or might chance to affect him, sensors filed sitreps to the computer terminal, as his brain examined shards of broken data through the healing neural system.

At the northernmost edge of the Mississippi alluvial plains, southeast Missouri's lowest point drops down in the shape of the devil's hoof, or, as the inhabitants prefer to analogize it, the heel of a boot. As vast ocean receded, glacial plains evolved into dense swamp, which grew large stands of timber. Much of this was cleared for farming as the Mississippi lowlands area became what is now known as the Bootheel.

The mindscreen imprinted lowlands, searched for trace and transfer cross matches, and printed the findings: "In the sandy fringe of rice paddies that borders the Annamese cordillera as it descends to the South China Sea, the lowlands shelter and feed the provinces of Quang Tri and Thua Thien." It was odd, when one got down to it, one killing field was pretty much the same as another.

His hard black eye blinked open. A spider was crawling across him. He flicked it away.

> Come into my webworld,
> Said the orbster to the fly,
> I'll fuck you apart,
> And take your heart,
> And watch you slowly die.

He thought of the very fly Dr. Norman, smiling hideously as, across a wet green rice field, he saw the ma 'n' pa bait shop.

He got up. Pain savaged him but he simply bit down and ignored it, concentrating on matters of consequence. He found the car, a Pontiac as filthy as he was, rather well hidden all things considered. He stowed the huge bush tarp and started to get in the car, but his sensors nudged him. Leave the vehicle for the moment, they told him. He hoisted a duffel heavier than two ordinary men could carry, and headed in the direction of food.

He could think of only one thing: Surely they must possess a microwave. He had a mental picture of himself stuffing microwavable ham-and-cheese-sandwich packages, one after another, dozen after dozen, into the microwave, cooking them for a few seconds, opening the little door, eating, spitting plastic. Consuming huge bags of chips, pork rinds, packaged crunchy-munchies of dubious vintage, shoving Slim Jim Beef Jerky sticks into his mouth, feeding them into his maw like edible pencils shoved into an automatic pencil sharpener. Gobbling, sucking, swilling down liters of cold brand X cola—he had to stop. He was salivating and blowing like a St. Bernard waiting for the Pavlovian timer to ping. He had to jerk his mind off the food before he choked on his own saliva.

He fed, instead, operational options and potential threats to his brain: the construction project, bright with blue Amoco insulation; the farmyard with its rusty red pump and part of a wagon wheel beside a fake well; For Sale—Wellman Realty on the front lawn of an obviously occupied dwelling; a private drive flanked by the halves of two black rubber truck tires; Garberg For Assessor, Reelect Joe D. Davis County Commissioner—old leftovers from a hickburg political campaign. A kid blew by him with Wilson Pickett blaring from the truck radio. Custom Welding, and the word that had caught his eye on the sign 4 Corners Gas *Eats* Bait Gun Shop.

This was not a town where men stared at one another, but even here they gawked at the apparition that quite suddenly materialized in their midst, a monster-sized thing that waddled in demanding food, paying for it with the dirtiest, funkiest pile of bills any of them had seen.

He resembled—what?—a cross between the Pillsbury doughboy on steroids and some mutation of Behemoth Wrestlemania that had gone terribly awry. Immense. Grotesquely ugly. A tower of hard, dirty, mean fat. Eyes that were like the heart of black marble, no dimension or soul. A killer's eyes in a baby's doughy face. Not a visage to inspire confidence.

Godzilla parted hillbillies and began snatching at racked foodstuffs, popping the plastic top and penetrating the foil seal of some Pringles with a finger the size and density of a steel cigar, then tapping out half an entire tube into a plate-sized mitt and consuming the whole thing in a single crunch, all but redlining on the ingestion of pure sodium.

They simply didn't know what to think. The monstrosity began tearing the wrappers off Mrs. Abner's egg salad and tuna melt sandwiches, not eating them but shoving them into the aperture in its face, sucking them down whole in nasty, wet glurps; opening a Dr Pepper on its teeth and chugging it; ripping open wax cartons of milk and orange and grape drink. They were experienced men, but this was beyond their experience. It eyed the guns, paid for the rampage of feeding, and waddled out the door in a noxious downdraft of sewer stench.

They were still discussing the apparition when, several minutes later, it reappeared, driving a battered, dirt-encrusted Pontiac the color of mud, lurching out into the parking lot and pumping unleaded into the car's gas tank. By the time he clomped back in to pay, they'd grown tired of speculating about him.

This was a place where hardworking men, or hardly working men in some instances, came to buy bait or ammo, swap guns or sea stories, drink a few brews, bitch or brag about crops and women, and they were not overly interested in their fellows. Chaingang would draw stares anywhere, but if there was a place he could halfway blend in, rather fortuitously he'd found it. The Gas Eats Bait shop had added its wares, as the sign outside showed, incrementally. Guns had found their way to this casual marketplace, and when the beast had calmed its hunger, slaked its thirst, and decided to chance tanking up the hot car as well, it was toward weaponry his attention was drawn.

The duffel was as much ordnance and firearms as anything else, but he never missed an opportunity to stock up on accessible tools when they were so easy to acquire off the books. There was a modest rack of shotguns and rifles for sale. He hated rifles and immediately dismissed them. A shotgun, properly reworked, could be a pleasantly effective up-close tool that was as disposable as such weapons could get. He passed over two expensive models for three used shotguns that could serve his needs: a Mossberg, a Remington, and a Winchester.

He asked to look at the Mossberg, and behind him a

loud voice said, "That's a damn fine shotgun, son. That's my gun. I slayed me some damn birds with that sumbitch. If I hadn't got laid off at Ryker's I'd never sold it. Here I am doing $18,590, okay? This year Ryker's works me a hundred and seventeen hours more but they *pay* me $17,300. Are you *following* this shit? Can you believe this damn shit?" The man behind him had turned from the Goliath-size figure, no longer interested in what he believed, and was telling the other guys in the store the old complaint. A television played a soap opera loudly from a back room. Chaingang put the Mossberg down and examined the Remington's action. He didn't trust it at all. "I need $17,300 and a hundred and seventeen more hours like I need another crack in my ass, okay?" He was nearly as tall as Bunkowski, but trim and hard, sunburnt a deep rosewood color, white hair, with dark Elvis burns and Coors on his belt buckle. Everybody but Chaingang wore a cap with advertising on it.

The door crashed open and a young, wiseass-looking guy strode in, wearing metal-shod cowboy boots, slapping a long leather quirt against his leg. He looked like somebody spoiling for a fight.

"Gimme a pint a' blackjack," he snarled.

Two young men on horses were visible through the open front door. The three had ridden up and nobody inside except Bunkowski had heard them. He was examining the Winchester twelve gauge. The punk paid for his Jack Daniel's and stomped out, not bothering to close the door. Chaingang saw him leap onto the nearest horse and use the quirt on it, unnecessarily, as the trio rode off.

"Fucker killed two horses last year, I heard. Mean mutha friggin' sumbitch. Anyway, Ryker's is working me a hundred—"

"How much?" Chaingang asked in a deep basso rumble. The proprietor told him, and was rewarded with more filthy bills.

"I can always drive produce for Lamonica or the Wallace boys, but shit, they want you to go outside or run around them scales and you can't do that shit now and keep your friggin' CDL."

"Give me a box of shells. Double 0."

This took the man aback. Nobody bought double 0. "I don't have an entire box. I got, oh, maybe ten or so." He pawed through an open box of loose shells.

"I'll take what you have."

"You don't pay a damn speeding ticket they'll jerk your CDL now. Hell, I'd work for Lamonica but he's liable to tell you to go run outside the friggin' scales, you know?"

Chaingang pocketed his change, and asked the proprietor in a quieter voice, "That kid on the horse? What's that boy's name?" His tone implying he'd known the fellow and forgotten his name.

"Jerry, you mean? The Rice boy?"

"Jerry Rice, sure. Does he still live in town?"

"Naw," the man eyed him suspiciously. "He's never lived in town that I knowed of. He lives right down at the end of the gravel road where he's always lived." The older man pointed.

"Ah! He ain't who I was thinkin' of, then," Chaingang said conversationally, making small talk until he could see the suspicion drain from the man's eyes. When the mood struck him he could be notoriously deft as a con artist, even muster an array of rather disarming social skills, bolstered by the unique talents of a natural actor, the unerring ear of a mimic, and his eidetic recall of stored observational minutiae. When he determined it was safe to do so, he took his purchases out to the car and drove away, not turning down the gravel road. That would come later, after dark.

The rain opened up again, splashing onto the stolen car. He was pleased in one way, as he'd neglected to clean off the windshield or refill the container of wiper fluid under the hood. However, it would also make the tags easier to read. He'd changed them once, but by now both sets would doubtless be on the hotsheet. He needed a fresh ride as soon as it became feasible. He needed soap.

A real bed. Real food. His stomach rumbled, and seemed to be answered by a thunderclap.

The storms had moved with him, and he remembered the slick bridges, rain-soaked highways, and limited visibility that preceded the run-in with the drunk driver. It had rained since he'd left Kansas City. He normally enjoyed driving in rain, but the wet roads had probably helped bring about the mishap. The weather patterns, moving from the west, had accompanied his journey; it appeared that he'd brought the flooding rivers with him.

43

Bayou City

She woke up running from someone and successfully getting away and was almost free of her pursuer when the jarring, jangling telephone caused her to sit bolt upright, caught in a tangle of covers, completely disoriented and befogged, lurching around to find the unfamiliar instrument and snatching out at it as she tried to unfog her sleep-drugged mind.

"'lo."

"Mizz Kamen?" A voice she didn't recognize.

"This is she speaking," she tried to say through a mouth like cotton.

"Did I disturb you, ma'am?"

"No. No. Not at all."

"Good. I wanted to see if by any chance you'd heard anything about your father's whereabouts since you were in Chief Randall's office?" The voice sounded distant and hollow.

"No. I haven't heard anything. Who did you say this

was?" She was still groggy, she noticed, as her fingers fumbled instinctively to remove an earring she wasn't wearing as she tried to press the phone closer.

"This is Sheriff Pritchett, Mizz Kamen, I'm . . ." Whatever the man said next was lost in an electro-spasm of crackling static.

"Hello? Can you hear me?" she asked.

"I think the line's about to go, ma'am. Can you hear me okay?"

"Fine. Did you hear anything about Da—my father?"

"Surely haven't. We're intensifying our search. I take it you haven't heard anything more?" he asked her for the second time, a hard cop edge to his tone.

"No. I'd certainly call the authorities if I learned anything—"

"We've placed him in New Madrid," the sheriff continued smoothly, his voice growing fainter as he spoke, "but after that we've been—" *crackle* "—cover where he went next. We'll find him. Listen, uh, what exactly did Mr. Kamen say to you the last time you had contact, as far as any plans he had, or what other cities he might be traveling to?"

"Well, let's see. He said he was going to head back Monday at the latest. He was going back to St. Louis first and he said he had some business there, and then he was coming home."

"Where was he going in St. Louis?"

"He didn't tell me," Sharon said.

"Was that usual for your father? Didn't he ordinarily tell you where he was going when he went out of town?"

"He always made it a rule not to discuss the cases—his investigations."

"Would there be anyone he might have talked with down here beside Chief Randall and myself, in law enforcement? For instance, did he mention any contacts in New Madrid or Clearwater counties?"

"No, I can't think of anyone." She'd never heard him speak of his unofficial contacts, what she'd once teasingly called the Old Goy Network.

"Okay. So he was going to St. Louis today, he said, then coming back home immediately. Is it possible he'd come back tonight and not phone in the interim if he'd had a change in where he went?"

"Yes, I suppose so. It isn't likely, but it's certainly possible. He didn't plan to come home that soon anyway, Sheriff. He was going to St. Louis today to take care of some business, then coming on back to Kansas City either Wednesday or Thursday, I think he said." It was hard to recall specific conversations, and she was beginning to doubt her memory.

"But if he drew a blank on his investigation, he could have headed on up to St. Louis, huh?"

"His things are still here. I think something's happened to him." It made Sharon suddenly cold to put voice to it. She was wide awake and frightened.

"All right. Well, stay in touch with me and we'll be talking soon."

She assured the sheriff she would, as the spitting phone line went dead in her hand.

Her wristwatch revealed an astonishing piece of information, as she glanced at it to check the time. It was morning. How long had she slept? Twelve, thirteen hours? She rubbed sleep out of her eyes and walked over to the heavy curtains, peering around into the parking lot and street beyond. Rain was sluicing down in torrents, and she'd been in such a fog she hadn't realized it, though it was audible inside the motel room. The fact she wasn't totally functioning at the top of her abilities descended on her like cold rain. She watched a vehicle splash by and thought, *Daddy's out in that mess, somewhere.*

Sharon went in and peed, came back, sat on the edge of the bed, and tried to marshal her strength and street smarts. There was work to be done. She had to snap out of it.

She forced herself into action, picking up the phone and asking for Raymond's number. It rang and rang. While she listened to the buzzing, crackling line, she made a scribbled note, something she'd forgotten to tell the sheriff a minute ago. Called Jimmie Randall, two other county sheriffs, and, finally, the FBI office in Cape Girardeau. Dressed. Wrote a letter. Back to the phone. Tried Meara again. Phoned Kansas City, a couple of numbers in St. Louis, and Meara's line a third time. The ringing was loud and hollow, and nobody answered.

"Office," the woman at the motel desk said for the umpteenth time.

"I was wondering, do you know where Mr. Ray Meara's farm is located?"

"Yes."

"Could you give me directions on how to get there? I know some of the roads are getting bad."

"Highway 80's closed, I just heard this morning."

"I see."

"I can tell you how to go around the back way. It's a little longer but you shouldn't have to drive through much water."

"Yeah." Wonderful. "Please, I'd appreciate it."

"Well, first go through town to 102 and take a right at the levee," she began. Fine, Sharon thought, but what's a levee? Her mind simply would not kick in. She would kill for a cup of strong, black coffee. "Then you take the second gravel road after 740 and when you come to the next fork—"

The more convinced Sharon became that something had happened to her father, the more she tried to push the bad thoughts out of her mind. She could almost step back and watch herself begin to deal with it the same way she had with the shooting at the shelter. By simply shutting down.

She sat by the phone, wondering if she should try Ray again, listening to the hum of traffic moving through the rain. She kept thinking about the scarred, solid face of her rescuer as he took her arm and lifted her off the hard pavement, pulling her to safety.

Sharon rejected the notion, but she imagined she could conjure up this strange man's smell, the powerful and distinctive aroma of a pair of leather cowboy chaps, she decided. A dumb western fantasy she was having. *Romance on the Range.* Even though she rejected the notion of Meara out of hand, laughed at the idea of anything between them, and thought he could never mean anything to her, he was in her nose like a fragrance she craved but couldn't afford. Go figure.

She forced herself into action, slamming the door and dashing for the car. The rain was solidifying, a soaking downpour, and as she started the vehicle and pulled away, the windshield wipers were already fighting to keep the glass clear enough for her to see.

By the time she was through Bayou City, heading east, she hoped, the blades had been turned to maximum speed and they responded angrily, with a slapping noise that sounded inanely like *hyper-wiper, hyper-wiper, hyper-wiper.* She realized two things: she was psyching herself out, and she was driving way the hell too fast.

Sharon slowed the car, making a conscious effort to relax her mind. After a few more miles there was nothing. The farmhouses stopped and there was only the white line and blacktop, and the silvery gray of the rain-drenched fields. No farmers or tractors. No traffic. Just the road and the sound of the wipers, the song of the tires, and steady, hard rain against a sky the color of a destroyer. Visibility extremely limited.

About the time she started to consider pulling over, the rain stopped, and she quickly cut the annoying wipers. Not a car or truck was on the road beside her. Zero population. Just soybean and wheat fields. Milo. Corn. Rice. Immense expanses of flatland tilled for grain crops or cotton, the staples of the Bible Belt.

If a tire rolled over a nail out here, if a radiator hose came loose, if a fan belt did whatever fan belts do, she'd be alone. A pretty woman trapped in a car. Isolated. Victim written all over her. Nobody would hear her screams out in these desolate boonies. Screams? Hell, you wouldn't hear dynamite out here.

And then, standing by itself at the side of the road, a

two-story sign! Surreal and mind-bending out in the silvery nothingness:

KEHOE'S PLACE

in immense white letters on a black background. As she drew closer she realized it wasn't at the side of the road but out in a field a quarter of a mile or more away.

My God! What sort of an ego needed their name visible like that? It was an advertisement for someone's screaming need: Hey, look at me, folks. I'm successful! Admire me!

It got worse the closer one came and she could make out dots that the poor visibility had obscured, dots between the letters. P L A C E was an acronym and further on down the road one could see the massive archway over a private drive, doubtless inspired by *Giant,* Tara, and a lot of bad episodic TV. Kehoe's P.L.A.C.E.—Petroleum, Land, And Cattle Enterprises.

Wow, she thought, almost skidding as she braked, startled by a pickup truck that roared out of nowhere as if it were going to charge out onto the highway, but braked just in time. She had a glimpse of three laughing faces in the truck cab.

The weekly Bayou City newspaper lay on the seat beside her: "VIRGO (Aug. 23–Sept. 22)," her horoscope read. "Invigorating travel helps unravel mystery."

44

New Madrid Levee

Less than twenty-five minutes by car, but an experiential universe away from Sharon Kamen and her travail, the beast was back.

He too, however, was on a trail. Anyone else wounded and recovering from a car wreck would have foregone the hunt, but Chaingang's needs were beyond the ordinary. They'd taken him down a gravel road and set him back in dark weeds. Two hours of still, fiercely resolute surveillance had finally been rewarded. He'd seen movement inside the small, tar-papered house.

Still itching, tired, filthy, hunting might have been low on his immediate priorities but for one thing: Vengeance was inseparable from the healing process. Of all the cruelties and inequities of life, the two things that would send Bunkowski instantly bugfuck were child molestation or animal cruelty. The shrinks had lots of names for his identification with animals, but, explanations and psychobabble aside, remembered pleasure was everything for the beast, whether it was raw sex or raw meat. Nothing was as delicious as raw revenge.

When the punk had whipped his horse cruelly in front of a hungry Chaingang, he'd added Jerry Rice's name to the stained Boorum & Pease accounts receivable ledger that the human exterminator had carried since his days in Southeast Asia. The bulk of the entries fit the homemade title Utility Escapes, but in the back pages were names, accounts, clippings, addresses, reminders of judges, CEOs, dog bunchers, baby rapers, freaks, punks, molestors, and torturers, the worst of the monkeys, the ones who needed to be found and erased with extreme prejudice. Richard Shmelman, CEO of the soap monolith Myers and Gumble; Judge Robert Watkins, who punished the good mother and sent daughter back to the arms of her torturer; Edmund Furst, president of ACME, the notorious American Cosmetics Manufacturers Executive; the woman who sold her kids into slavery; the man who condoned his kids' "harmless" slaughter of a petting zoo, and the judge who backed him; the humane folks who do product testing on animals; the Taiwanese merchants; the Bangkok kiddie pimps. A random page or two of yellowed newspaper clippings contained more offhand animal cruelty than a Mexican rodeo, more stories of child abuse than a major city's DFS file cabinet. Mr. Bunkowski's shit list. Names he could recite like a rosary.

Inside the tar-papered shack a bright explosion of light suddenly spilled out of an open door into the yard. Loud voices carried. Two men left on a bike, in a roar of unmuffled, gravel-spitting acceleration, and when all was still again he moved from the shadows. The horses were saddled and tethered where they still stood, presumably, from that afternoon. Starving. Unwatered. Shaking.

He waited for a long time, conscious of the sound the twelve gauge would make and how the noise would carry. Then, when he knew the time was right, he blasted the piece of shit through a window, paying back the drunken asshole who closed his eye, the Snake Man, the girls who'd laughed at him that time as they sailed by in their daddy's convertible, the people who made hospital gowns, Spanish Rodriguez, Mommy, Dr. Norman, the designers of cars who made them for fucking dwarves, the seven goddam dwarves themselves and the cunt who dropped them, Norwegian whalers, Japanese sailors, Illinois jailers, the whole shit parade, the double-zero buck punching a nice wet hole in the middle of all that trash.

Quick resupply. A fast gathering of money, food,

weapons, this and that. He cut the horses loose and waddled back toward the ride.

As he pulled off the gravel the fucking car was limping—a flat. He sighed, heaved his tonnage out of the vehicle, opened the trunk. Nothing. The asshole hadn't even been carrying a spare. He left the thing where it sat, his duffel and weapons case in his hand, and started down the road toward the nearest heartbeat.

The kill had been satisfying in one respect but Bunkowski was less than devoted to firearms. They were never his weapon of choice in ambush situations, where he preferred a killing chain, his hands, a club, or his fighting Bowie. Grenades and shaped charges were next on the list, and, finally, guns. Shotguns were accessible, cheap, and disposable, but they were noisy. The one exception, a suppressed street-sweeper with poisoned shell loads, had grown difficult to obtain for field-exigency situations. Even distant neighbors would have heard this ruckus. He shrugged it off.

The ma 'n' pa bait-food-crackerbarrel-gunsmith-dog pound-shit hole never closed, apparently. He propped the used shotgun up against the wall by the screen door, opened the door, and clomped in, his ankle now one more point of hurt. He was beginning to drop back into one of his dangerously ill-tempered moods.

"Hey, big boy!" the proprietor called to him. Chaingang's face crinkled in its deadliest configuration, a malevolently beaming ear-to-ear grin. The President of the United States mouthed platitudes and promises in the background darkness. "Come on in. I been watchin' that fuckin' liar on TV," the older man said, viciously. "Them sons of fuckin' bitch'n crooks in War-shing-ton—" he began a tirade about politics in Missouri pidgin English, as Chaingang fumed. While the store owner ranted he noticed mud on the giant's booties.

"I know what you been up to," he said, knowingly. "You the one, all right. You behind the Winchester *shoot!*"

How could he have known? Obviously someone had found the body already. Perhaps it had been on the news, a television bulletin, or the noise of the blasts had . . . he was too exhausted and irritated to aggravate himself with the illogic of it. A yard-long steel snake that slept in a specially reinforced canvas pocket dangled from the beast's hand. Taped steel links the size of cigarette packs chainsnapped the idiot into oblivion.

Daniel stepped over the body and without preamble searched the premises, taking some money, another shotgun, and the keys to the man's pickup. He placed the Winchester, wiped, not that it mattered, back on the rack of firearms for sale, and, almost as an afterthought, added the weapons he'd taken from the punk's shack.

The truck was a real piece of crap, but the tires were fairly round, at least before Chaingang threw his elephantine load into the front seat with a crash and groan of old springs. He got the seat back, arranged his duffel and weapons case, and drove to the pumps. After filling the rusty pickup with gas, he wedged his bulk back in behind the wheel, started up the sewing machine engine again, and gunned it into life, driving down the road in newly acquired wheels which he knew he'd have to dump immediately.

About a mile and a half down the blacktop there was a muddy access road that led up over a nearby levee, where it disappeared. It was near the river, probably a place frequented by local hunters and fishermen. The small sign by the road told the whole story: Winchester Chute.

Nobody's perfect.

The loud vocal bark that was his approximation of a human laugh snapped forth involuntarily.

Bayou Ridge

By late morning Meara was working on a piece of fence out behind the house. The sky was a wet-looking gray at the horizon, and the sun had come out for a time, but the pollution of industry from Clearwater to the south scumbled the blue with semiopaque, dirty smoke. The clouds and smog gave everything an ominous overcast layer of foreboding.

He saw a speck down on the Mark Road and was trying to place the car as it drove past the big willows and came winding down the gravel in his direction.

Ray realized it was Sharon Kamen's car and in spite of himself he could feel his heart pounding like a little kid's on a springtime Saturday night. What a fool! But by the time she pulled up on the chat driveway he had a big smile plastered across his tough, scarred face.

"Hi!" she called out, getting out of the car.

"Hi," he said. God, she looked good.

"I tried to phone but you were outside, I guess."

"Yeah?" He couldn't imagine what had happened to bring her out there. "Did you locate your father?"

"No."

"Oh. I thought maybe . . ." he trailed off.

"No, I just wanted to, you know, talk. I thought I'd call, but when I tried to phone three or four times this morning . . ."

"How'd you get through the water on Highway 80?"

"The woman in the motel office told me how to come around the back way." She gestured.

Hair. Chest. Face. Meara struggled with his involuntary reactions to her slightest movements. He tried to keep what he was feeling out of his eyes. "Good," he managed to articulate. Jesus. Eyes. Mouth. He was so drawn to her.

"You have a nice farm," she said, feeling like an imbecile. "Oh, did you see the paper?"

"Uh-uh, I haven't."

"I brought one," she said, and he followed her back around the side of the car as she reached in. He looked at the back of her legs.

She had on high-heeled shoes—in the country! The women here wore flat shoes, or what the guys called hag-pussy shoes, big old thick, clunky jobs favored by wrinkled country grannies, therapeutic boondockers to go over their ugly, wide-ankled support hosiery.

A few inches of the backs of her legs were visible, smoothly muscled, slick, tanned flesh under pantyhose or sheer stockings that curved up from trim, perfect ankles to flawless calves. He held the door as she turned and handed him the paper.

Ray assumed it would be something about the Neo-Nazis and the scuffle but it was the write-up on her dad:

DISAPPEARANCE IN BOOTHEEL
LINKED TO SEARCH

The search for a fugitive German war criminal, Nazi scientist Emil Shtolz, may be connected to the disappearance of celebrated Missouri Nazi hunter Aaron Kamen, of Kansas City, and a Bayou City resident, according to law-enforcement sources.

"Well," he said, after he'd skimmed the rest of the story and found nothing on the skinheads, "it finally made the papers." He handed the newspaper back to her.

"Look, Ray, I know I have no right to ask, but I was wondering," the green eyes reached into him, burning him, "if you'd consider being my chauffeur some more. I want to keep asking about Dad." Not batting her eyes or even using them. Not blinking her "Gee, officer, could you let me off with a warning?" eyes.

"Sure, if you really think that's what you want to do."

"I don't see anything else I can do. I want to give it my best shot."

"Well," he said, exhaling a lot of air and then puffing his cheeks out, "I'll help any way I can." He made a move with his hand the way she'd seen him do several times since they'd met. It was a characteristic movement that seemed to say to Sharon, *I know what these scars make me look like.* She found it a touchingly vulnerable thing for him to do. "Speaking of your best shot, come here a minute. I want to show you something." He turned away and started walking.

She caught up with him. Her heels sank into the mud. "What are you going to show me?"

"It's over here," he said, motioning across the field toward a huge, old barn that stood beside a weather-beaten tractor shed. They walked in silence for a few seconds, Sharon doing her best to stay on a crude board walkway that spanned the muddy ground.

"Vanishing Americana," she said to him, her words surprisingly loud in the stillness of the Bootheel boonies.

"Hm?"

"Old barns. Part of the past. They always seem to make a powerful statement about yesteryear to me. Do you feel that way, too?"

"Barns just mean a lot of work to me. I think of stock when I see one. Livestock's one endless headache."

"You mean barns are only for farm animals down here? We had hay barns where I was raised."

"Nah. They have grain barns here, but I mean in the old days everybody had some stock. I used to run about fifty head of cattle myself, here and on my other pasture land. So I look at the barn and that's what I see—all that work."

"It's immense."

"Watch your step here," he said, as they went through

where stairs had once been, stepping through a framed doorway, walking on a floor of old straw. "It's all hand-hewn cypress. Man could build himself a hell of a little cabin out of this. You'd have your fireplace out of the foundation. All that rock was hauled down here from the Black River. So there's all your stones. You got enough cypress the termites haven't ate, you'd have your walls. And you could burn those others in your fireplace after you built it." He pointed up at the roof high above them. "Those are Shaker shingles. They'd be your kindling."

"You should do it. Build yourself an old log cabin— My God, *Ray?*" He was holding a pistol in his hand.

"It's okay. You're not afraid of firearms are you?"

"Yes," she said, "I certainly am. Where did that come from?"

"Under my arm."

"You carry a *gun?*"

To answer her he pulled open his jacket and she saw the leather shoulder holster, but her eyes were riveted on the deadly looking object in his hand. "Why do you carry a gun?" She was frozen in terror.

"Habit, I guess. It's a good idea, being afraid of firearms, but they're like saws or hammers or vehicles. Tools to do a job with. You don't play with them, you treat them with respect and take care of them and then, when you need them, you have the tool to help you." He'd misinterpreted her fear.

"Please put it away. I hate guns." Sharon's voice sounded as small and helpless as that of a scared child.

"I don't want you to be scared of it, Sharon. A little fear isn't bad. It's okay. A healthy respect. But don't be scared to use it if you have to. Have you ever fired a handgun?"

"Yes, as it happens, I have. I won't again. Not ever."

"Why's that?"

"I just won't." She wanted to tell him about Stacey and her boyfriend Duane, why she'd never touch a gun again.

But she couldn't talk about it. Instead, she said, quietly, "I hate violence and violent things. I don't believe in guns."

"You probably fired a forty-five or something that made a lot of noise, and had a heavy kick, and it made your wrist sore or whatever." He continued to misread her reaction. "But sometimes a firearm can save your life, or someone else's. In the old days they called 'em equalizers. If you're going up against some old Nazi who may be an experienced killer, you better be holding some protection."

"I have protection, Ray. God is my protection."

"That's fine. But a little iron is good, too, for insurance." There was a small white paper square stuck in some rotting hay bales that stood against the far wall of the barn. "Imagine that a feller who meant to do you harm was standing over there." He pointed. "This is my friend, Irma," it sounded as if he said, as he held the pistol, finger off the trigger. "This is my baby. She's an ERMA EX-CAM, RX-22. Fires long rifle rounds. CCI Stingers." He turned and did not appear to aim, his hand and arm and body sort of pointed toward the hay bales and the weapon barked twice. It was deafeningly loud and Sharon turned and ran, tripping over the sill of the doorway, *falling, getting up, falling again, screaming, crying, letting it all come crashing down around her, all the fake toughness, the pain of missing her dad and knowing he might be in grave danger, of being all alone and trying to stay strong and failing, the pain of a thousand Duanes and Staceys and river rats and cops and robbers and he was holding her and she was letting him, not caring, not caring about anything, sobbing, shaking, wishing she were back in their nice snug home, Mom in the kitchen, Dad not knowing from Nazis, everybody nice and safe.*

She finally got quieted down to a soft snuffling, and he held her in his arms as gently as he could, rocking her a bit, or perhaps she imagined it, and then she felt one of his hands touch her, dipping beneath her hair, cupping the nape of her neck, and she read his desire in the heat of his palm, and it fed her somehow and she looked up at him and her full lips were so perfect, the wide inverted V a model's pout, an actress's temptation from a zillion seduction scenes, but when you're near it and you can touch it the pull is more magnetic than any gravity.

Sex with anybody, Raymond Meara or whomever, was so far from Sharon's conscious desires she'd have bet anything such a turn of events was out of the question. Her father might have perished, there was a monster of an old Nazi out there somewhere . . . but sometimes the act of lovemaking can be a release or a physical pressure valve. There are times when it becomes an astonishing, life-affirming reaction.

The first kiss took him under and her with it, and against all odds and reason they were inside the barn, touching, tasting, holding, kissing, enflaming, exploring, swallowing each other in the searing heat of tongue and caress and passion that spurted out, melting whatever it touched, brooking no arguments, taking no prisoners.

It was the oldest equation on earth and totally unsupported by math, common sense, logic, or science, but it still worked. The old heat-plus-mass formula, its impossible arithmetic continuing to defy law by cognition. Two into one equals one.

46

Marion, Illinois

"Yes, sir," Dr. Norman said, in what was for him a nearly obsequious tone, "that was my intention when I phoned you." The old man to whom he was speaking was one of the most powerful leaders in the world, yet few knew his name. The force behind the throne of several former and present monarchs, CEOs, and U.S. presidents, he had personally mandated the organization known as SAUCOG, in an executive session of the National Security Council, which he had then headed.

"So, *nu?*"

"When we were getting Special Covert Action printouts over the Newton Secure/Comsec System I saw the operation in southeast Missouri. So I phoned the gentleman at Justice and confirmed the status of that particular situation," Dr. Norman explained. The scrambled landline was silent for a moment.

"They want this old Nazi sanctioned?" the old man asked, using the passé jargon for an execution.

"That's correct. It seems he's built a new identity and become such a pillar of the community that Justice is afraid they might not be able to get him through channels. They might not make a sufficiently tight case against him. The gentleman also said if such a person was tried and the thing backfired, like the Ivan the Terrible case did, it could have a chilling effect on future sightings. They want him brought down in a public way. Messy . . . I'm quoting," Norman said.

"What?"

"Messy was the word he used," Dr. Norman said again. "I don't care how messy your man makes it."

"So how was this left?"

"I told him I had a man there. Once I found out all the details of the Nazi's past history, I knew I could motivate him easily . . . and to get his operatives out of the way. That we'd handle it."

"You sure this is prudent considering your man's, uh, instability?"

"Well, sir, I think it's perfect for us. If it works, and he accomplishes the mission, it proves our case. We redeem ourselves in the sense that we have proof such an individual can be manipulated to perform jobs of this type. It ratifies and validates everything we've done: the brain implant of the locator, the technology, the efficacy of my drug Alpha Group II, the concept itself. If it doesn't, then our man at large has outlived his usefulness and we'll take steps to dispose of both the matters."

There was another pause while the scrambled linkage sizzled across time zones.

"All right," the old man said.

Norman thanked him, promised progress bulletins, and disconnected.

He was mildly annoyed by one aspect of the new plan. He'd have liked to allow his pet subject more rest and relaxation time after the automobile accident he'd had, but Dr. Norman was familiar enough with Daniel's Herculean recuperative powers to know he'd bounce back sufficiently for this simple task. It would be a form of R & R for him.

The doctor had known what he had to do the second he'd first learned of a Justice op within a few miles of Daniel's current turf. He had to make the most of what might become an unfortunate coincidence. In Dr. Norman's opinion, Daniel's protection superseded all other considerations. He couldn't take a chance on his treasured human experiment running around in someone else's kill zone. Bad enough if it had just been Justice, but *this* group? No way would he permit it to happen.

Too bad about Shtolz, in a way. He'd been familiar with the man's dossier for years and, frankly, admired his accomplishments. He'd done some brilliant work on brain-host discorporation. Pity the two of them would never be able to discuss such things.

Everything was dovetailing beautifully. Norman's job was suddenly so much easier. He could instantly imagine Daniel's reaction to photos of the doctor's early experiments. Norman had, in his own collection, quite a stack of grisly mutilation shots. The clinical torture murders of babies and animals would send his big friend up the nearest wall. There was one in particular where they'd had their brains removed while they were still alive and the three host subjects were wide eyed, as if living, but with the tops of the little skulls sawn open and empty, that would evoke an interesting rage. Nor would his man at large be at all amused by the image of the puppy with the top of its head cut off.

On paper, it appeared to be a by-the-numbers mission. Potentially, at least. Send a team in, create a diversion, and inject Daniel by dart gun, or whatever means. While the Alpha Group II was taking hold, show him the old Nazi's experiments on children and animals, and simply point him in the right direction. At that juncture one only had to get out of the line of fire, which is why Norman had phoned the old man.

It was one thing to pull Justice off a covert op, but quite another to interdict a serious running mission by the Israelis, who were sure to have assets in place. If we knew, one could be certain they knew, and it would take a personal call from the old man to stop the otherwise unstoppable Mossad.

~ 47

Bayou Ridge

They were in Meara's farmhouse when Ray's phone rang.
It was Jimmie Randall. Could Meara stop in to the office
this afternoon? Afternoon in Bayou City could mean
anything from 12:01 P.M. to anytime it wasn't too dark to
farm without headlights. Sharon had things to do and
they said their good-byes, with Meara following her back
to town.

A lot of rain was coming. You could tell from the air
and from the sky. It stunk of fish and worms and
stagnant ponds; a funky, festering rankness that fumed
up out of the turgid road ditches to meet the humid,
malodorous promise of the descending rain clouds.

Only a few hours later, but hours of a day that had been
so long and eventful that it already seemed like the next
day, Ray was pulling up in front of the motel. Sharon
heard his now familiar truck motor outside the door and
was peering out around the curtains when he knocked.

"Come in," she said.

He dripped in out of the wetness. "Hi."

"Um, hello," she said, as he kissed her.

"Thought I'd stop by on the way home. Guess who I
talked to today?"

"FBI."

"You got it. They'd just finished with you. There they
were in the Bayou City police chief's office. Asked me a
lotta' questions about *you*, girl."

"That's nice. You told them I was an okay person?" He
moved over close and leaned down for another kiss.

"I told them you were very okay," he said, breathing in the fragrance of the woman who was all he thought about now.

It was a long, soulful kiss, but it wasn't quite the same as earlier in the barn, and then in the house. Some of the heat had cooled.

Sharon reached up and touched his face and smiled, and moved over to the window, seemingly preoccupied, pushing the curtains aside and looking at the sky. In between the buildings across the road you could glimpse the horizon. The flatlands were all cottony looking with a misty look to the blue tree line, and where Sol was beginning to set there were slashes of blood and flesh-tone pink across the bruised black and blue cloud banks.

"Thinking about your dad?"

"Mm." She nodded.

He put his hands on her shoulders very gently, coming up behind her, and she tightened a little. "S'matter?"

"Nothing."

"Sure?"

"Just tired."

"I wish I could say something—you know—optimistic. Promising. Give you an encouraging word."

"Thanks." She smiled. You could hear the television laugh track on the speaker in the next room.

"I just thought I'd stick my head in the door on the way home. Tell you I was thinking about you."

"You're a nice guy. Very sweet." She smiled again but her mind was blank. She knew she should invite him in or something, but it was the "or something" she wasn't in the mood for. "Don't mind me, Ray. Women are too strange."

"Tell me about it. I never could figure them out."

"Now hold on a second, we're strange but not impenetrable."

" 'Zat so?"

"All we want is perdurable love from a caring person. That's not so hard to figure out."

"It is if you don't know what the per-thing is," he said.

"Perdurable," she smiled prettily, "my dear, means permanent. Lasting. Very durable. A love that won't pale over time, one that won't wear out through all the female mood swings."

"Fine, Sharon. Very durable. Why not say that in the first place?"

"Because we think in words," she said, too pooped to realize he'd been teasing her.

"That's a heavy concept."

"Come on. Perdurable. Good word. Expand your mental horizons. How many words can you name that begin with the p-e-r prefix? Perform. Performance. Pertinent. Perky. Perfect. Come on."

"Person . . . purple." They laughed. "I'm going home," he said and started out.

"Keep going," she said, softly. "Percolate. Permanent. Pertain."

"I got one," he said, putting his big hands on her shoulders. She looked exquisitely beautiful framed there in the doorway. Tired or not, she was so spectacular. "Perdurable," he said, in a hoarse whisper.

"No way," she said. "You can't use my word." She looked about seventeen at that second, and he leaned over and kissed her right below the ear on the throat and held her like that, then kissed her again, gently as he could, on the nape of the neck and whispered, "Perfume."

At one of the stop signs on his way home, a car full of boys, so Bayou City bored they could only booze 'n' cruise, jumped the stop and nearly rammed him. He watched them roar away, remembering what it was like to wait for thunder so you could spring into your ride and chase the night lightning. His first truck had Riders On The Storm painted on it.

Face it, killer, he told himself, you've finally found something worthwhile. He realized he was grinning idiotically.

According to TV, the investigations into the "4 Corners Murder" of Brother Beauton, who ran the 4 Corners Gas Station, and the murder of Jerry Rice, had so far "yielded no leads." The day didn't look too promising either. Meara, an early riser, had taken to leaving all his news sources blasting through the small farmhouse, and as he walked from bathroom to kitchen to living room, the scanner, big radio, and television fed news and weather snippets.

"—Bayou City schools are also closed—"

"—flash flooding, swelling rivers and overflowing drainage ditches, have become serious hazards for motorists. Many homes and businesses are finding themselves in deep trouble—"

"In deep shit," Meara said back to the radio.

"Road banks are overflowing along the highways into Sikeston, Dexter, East Prairie, Bayou City, and many of the surrounding communities. . . ." A female reporter was doing a locally televised stand-up. "Captain Dave Vineyard of the Public Safety Department says it looks bad."

A uniformed man spoke. "It's the worst I remember it in fifteen years on the job. This is the only time I can recall when old Highway 61 was completely under water. If this keeps up, we'll start evacuating Sikeston in the morning."

Meara cursed and stomped out of the house.

The river stages looked bad. They were talking about

how it was going to crest in twenty-four hours, but that was the standard meteorological line of bullshit. They'd predict a crest, then revise it upward, then predict another crest. They didn't know jack-o-logical shit about the river.

Water was already above the flood stage at Cairo and pushing in fast. A few more inches and the back way would be closed, and it would be a mess. Nobody could go in or out past Big Oak, even in a flatbed, yet it'd be too shallow to put a boat in.

The water was no longer just a silver gray ribbon along the far horizon. You could look way down in the fields to the south of the Meara ground and see that big silvery-blue-gray mass of water pushing in. That far away it looked as still as a sheet of glass, but up close it was powerful and always moving, the river currents making it slither like a million serpents, filling the low spots, coursing through the trees and over the ditch banks, all of it aiming at Raymond.

The stoutest bailing wire he had on the place was about the consistency of a steel rod. But he had a big loop of that new, triple-thick barbed wire, and he got down under the house and started working. He'd be damned if he'd let that river have the house.

It took him all day to sink four railroad ties wired to the foundation. Four of those big, creosoted crossties, each wound in three strands of triple-thick, the wire going up under the foundation and twisting around back under the ties, which he sank as far down as he could get.

It was rough work, with no room to use the posthole digger or get full movement of the shovel. He had to angle it and it took its toll in scratched hands and barked knuckles. Then there was the barbed wire. It was like razor wire, it slashed anything it touched, and when Meara crawled out from under the house he'd ruined the knees of his Levis, his shirt, and both new leather work gloves. On top of that, when he was pulling his tools and what was left of the wire out from underneath, he raised up too soon and drove a rusty nail about an eighth of an inch into his skull.

For about five minutes he didn't know whether to cry, cuss, shit, or go blind, he was in so much pain. He ended up sitting on the old wooden porch feeling his sore head and wondering if he should go in and get a tetanus shot, because the way the day was going, the way his luck was running, he'd have lockjaw by morning.

When he went inside, the telephone was ringing and he actually had a few seconds of fleeting hope. It seemed he had entered one of those sweepstakes and—no, there was no catch—he was being phoned long distance from somewhere in Arizona to be informed that he, Ray Meara, had just won a seventeen-foot fiberglass Chimera Jon boat, with seventy-five horse motor, and a new Superglide Trailer. No, he was told, he didn't have to buy a thing.

"As soon as you check in here at Rancho Hacienda we'll be validating your eligibility prize number and you're guaranteed that as soon as you take the tour—" To his credit he neither cursed nor broke the phone into tiny pieces.

It rang immediately, even as he was hanging up, and he picked up the receiver thinking the line had not been disconnected.

"I am not interested," he said.

"Raymond Meara?" The woman's voice was muddied, the connection so bad he could scarcely hear her.

"What?"

"Raymond, this is Marsha at the bank?"

"Oh! I can't hear you too well, Marsha."

"You cashed a check recently for two hundred dollars. It was written by Doug Seifer? That check just came back. It's marked insufficient funds and we need you to take care of the discrepancy please."

"Insufficient? You mean it bounced?" The nail still hurt. Perhaps his brain was leaking out of the hole, slowly evaporating.

"That's right. We need you to make up the two hundred dollars, Ray, plus there is an additional ten-dollar charge for putting the check through. Did you want us to take that out of your account or do you want to come in and pay it?"

"Marsha, may I call you back immediately on this?" he asked. She said yes, and they hung up. He tried to reach Doug and got nothing. He dialed the operator and a phone company employee assured him the lines were still working. He tried the number again and got nothing. Calmly, one hand on his brain hole, he dialed O and this time got an A T & T operator.

"Could you try a number for me please? I'm having difficulty getting it to ring. Water in the terminals, I guess."

"Sorry you're having difficulty, sir. Glad to help." The man told him this in a sincere, pleasant tone. Good ol' efficient A T & T. They'd get this call through, even if the floodwaters were coming. The busy signal rang loud and clear, a fast busy, unlike the ones Meara was used to.

"Uh, listen, could you make sure that number's working? I couldn't get it to ring and, you know, now it's busy."

"You want me to verify if it's busy?"

"Yeah. Please."

"You realize you'll be charged extra for verification of a B-Y sir?"

"*I'll* be charged?"

"Yes, sir. There is an extra charge." The man told him how much.

"You gotta be shittin' me, Jack. I gotta pay extra to find out if a phone is in working order?"

"Yes, sir." Meara told him never mind and hung up. Again he didn't break the phone.

The telephone rang. He hoped it would be Doug straightening the mess out. It was Rosemary, mad as a wet hen.

"Just who in the flaming hell do you think you *are* you

two-timing—" Mercifully the phone lines were going out and he barely heard fragments of her cursing. The phrase "gutless, lying bastard" was an endearment that broke through the crackle. Her voice was suddenly loud and clear. "What kind of weasel are you, Ray?"

"What got under your saddle?" he asked, his voice flat and devoid of emotion.

"I'm getting goddamn sick of hearin' about this bitch from Kansas City you're running around all over town with, and you and I are gonna get one goddamn thing *straight* and I mean—" She was really shrieking at him. It was like a series of poisoned darts entering his left ear, and he was afraid they'd poke through and meet the nail hole, and what little remained of his gray matter would leak out once and for all, so he pulled the phone straight out of the wall.

Rosemary James, A T & T, Sprint, Western Electric, Whatever Sweepstakes, General Electric, Ma Bell, siding salesmen, the nice lady at the bank, the weather girl, teleconferencing boiler rooms, and at least half the assholes working for the phone companies, the Army Corps of Engineers, Rancho Uranus, the Department of Agriculture, the VA, Doug Siefer—he threw the whole taco about a hundred yards out into the field.

Verify *that*.

Shoney's was fairly crowded. A busload of folks on the way to either the Opry or Branson were lined up at the food bar loading plates, and the tables and booths were abuzz with eating sounds.

The waitress named Sherri looked up and saw a nightmarish vision, the stink of him warning her first, but not preparing her for the sight. A vastly fat, humongously big man waddled toward her in stained T-shirt and filthy battle fatigues, oblivious to the folks around him. One poor fellow, who didn't see the human parade float behind him, was almost knocked headlong into the food bar.

It stopped in front of Sherri and sound rumbled from its innards.

"You got pancakes or waffles?"

"Yes, sir," she said, fighting to smile in the poisonous proximity of his stench. "We have pancakes."

"Got blueberry?"

"No, just plain. They're scratch-made, though. Real good," she said.

"How many in an order?"

"Two in the short stack. That's $2.39. Or we have the tall stack, that's three," she said brightly, figuring him for a tall stack.

"Three?" he sneered. "Three pancakes?" He couldn't believe it.

"Yes, sir."

"I'll take a tall stack. No, bring me two tall stacks on the same plate." He'd been ready to order thirty, as an appetizer, but he, too, smelled something. Heat. Probably a plainclothes dick or undercover heat. His vibes were never wrong.

The waitress brought the two tall stacks in due time and he put all the butter pats on the six pancakes, pouring approximately half the jar of syrup onto them one by one as he built a layer. It would do as an appetizer. He stood, wadding up the dripping food, turning to survey the watchers. He'd felt out his audience the way an intuitive actor will. A smile split his face as the shark's mouth opened and accepted the stack of pancakes, butter, and syrup. There was no chewing. He merely swallowed, inhaling the food. Every eye was glued to him, but one man in particular was looking at him funny. The gaze was steadier. Perhaps this was the cop.

Chaingang, his left hand dripping from the pancake snack, smiled at the man and approached his table. People fought back revulsion as his aroma wafted across their plates. He maneuvered himself so that he was to the right of the seated man, leaned over, beaming and friendly, and asked, "Aren't you Ted Goldberg from frannus's?"

"Huh? No," the man said, turning, backing up slightly as the befouled leviathan breathed toxic waste into his face. The thing's massive left paw was patting his shoulder in a warm gesture.

"Oh! I'm sorry," the beast rumbled. "You look like Ted, from the American Legion cremmer. You got a twin," he boomed, waving good-bye. Friendly chap. Big smile. You sure couldn't judge a book by its cover.

Chaingang waddled to the cash register, leaving behind his blinding odor, the image of a two-legged beastman, and an immense sticky handprint of maple syrup on the back of the man's new polyester jacket.

50

New Levee Barrow and Route W

Ferris and Donnie Meuller and Donnie's oldest boy Scott were in Donnie's big silver V-boat. They'd played out the catfish around Stocker's Store and were letting the current take them back, fishing their way back in the fast-moving floodwaters, letting the current scrieve the boat, propelling them downstream.

A man could get into the big, heavyweight outlaw cat real good if he knew where to fish. Hit 'em about half an hour before dawn, go back around five and catch another fine mess before suppertime. They were hitting livers the way the rich gobble caviar—they couldn't get enough of it.

The water gushing through Lyman Hole Lateral sluiced into the St. Petersburg Ditch and overflowed the banks, moving out over 221 and the tree-clogged drain canals where the big boys liked to hang out and feed. From the bottom of the canal, which was Lateral Three on the maps, the St. Pete Ditch carried about eight and a half feet of moving river water, and as the drainage ditches continued to overflow into this fast-moving stream it became a rushing nine-foot-tall wall of water that buried everything in its path.

At the outskirts of Bayou City the nine-foot moving wall, with the power of the Mississippi, Ohio, and Tennessee rivers behind it, smashed across the fifty-four-inch drainage culvert, flooding the banks of the ditches adjacent to the already full Bayou City sewer lagoon, moving out across 218 and the highway bypass that was now the bottom of a swiftly moving lake.

An ever-building, merging, growing wave of water overflowed the Cedar Isle Slough, Old Route 17, Catch-basin Ditch, and the set-back levee itself, joining the backwaters of the Cumberland, Platte, Missouri, and God-only-knows how many overflowing tributaries. This entire mass with a life all its own now swirled, flowed, and intermixed, becoming an unstoppable force of nature, spreading, moving, inching inland over what was no longer dry land, the water seeking its own level, moving higher and higher, putting everything it touched beneath it.

"Oh, *shit!*" Ferris screamed.

"Lookout!" Donnie screamed at Scott, and the three of them tried to strike out at the black thing suddenly looming in the pathway of the V-boat. The first to hit it was Ferris, who caught a good shot on the blade of the oar, catching it against the unyielding steel. The oar splintered as it smacked back into Scott's paddle, knocking it into the water, then smashing him down into the boat as the broken oar whacked him in the nose. Donnie got a halfway good stance but the oar slid over the slick metal as their prow collided with what was later discovered to be the left front fender of a Mercury Marquis. The boat took a hit, shooting Donnie Meuller out into the water, where he plunged over his head, beginning to panic as he could not move in the coat that now felt as if it weighed two hundred pounds, caught in a current too strong to swim against, and only a lucky probe with the broken oar saved him from drowning.

51

Bayou City

Two hours later Scott was having his nose taped, the men had changed clothes, and Sharon Kamen was in the back seat of one of Jimmie Randall's cop cars, on the way to the station.

"Has Chief Randall learned something, do you know —about my father?"

"They just told me to bring you to the office," the uniformed driver, a female cop, said in a flat, noncommittal tone.

The building was a bustling beehive of activity, and she was immediately taken into the chief of police's presence. "Good morning, Sharon," he said. "Let's go in here." He escorted her to a room she hadn't been in before, a bare conference or interview-type room with a heavy steel table and chairs. He asked her to have a seat, and she could hear a conversation on the other side of the open doorway. It was a noisy office, with constantly ringing telephones and a steady murmur of voices and assorted sounds adding to the hubbub.

In a few seconds Randall reentered the room, followed by five other men and the woman officer who'd brought her to the administration building.

"Sharon, this is Special Agent Petergill."

"We've met, Jimmie," the FBI man said.

"Hi."

"How you doin'?" Petergill said, his smile cordial but official looking. Sharon had an awful wave of premonition.

"Fine," she said.

"We've found your father's car," Petergill said. She listened to the explanation of how the vehicle was found. What the circumstances were. Where. Why she couldn't go out there.

"There's not much to see now, anyway, Sharon. Water's almost completely over the car. We put a man in to get the plates and double-check the VIN, but it got too rough to do much more." He left some of the obvious unsaid. "We can't take chances with men diving now in that water. It's coming in too fast. But I doubt if much—uh—evidence could be found." She nodded. "This is not going to be easy, Sharon, but we need to talk seriously about the possibilities. I'm sorry to put you through it, but—"

"I understand. I appreciate everything you're doing to find Dad," she said quietly. There was an awful feeling of pressure in her upper chest, and it seemed suffocatingly warm in the room.

"It doesn't look real good for finding Mr. Kamen. I don't say we can put a lot of stock in the fact we found the car where it was. But the thing is, you see, it is unlikely your father would have been in that area driving before the water pushed in. I think it's possible that somebody wanted to create the impression your father drove into the backwater. Aside from the various ways we know that didn't happen, that road was still being traveled by vehicles three days ago. Obviously, if Mr. Kamen had been around here on an investigation that recently, there would have been some contact."

"But what if Dad had an accident or hit his head or something and got amnesia and he's out there wandering around?"

"Sharon," the FBI man said, speaking so softly she had to strain to hear each word, "true amnesia's so rare it's hardly worth considering. I think because of the nature of what your father was trying to do, we have to at least face the possibility that something has happened. I know it's tough, but I'm afraid that's what it's beginning to look like. I would have been more optimistic *not* finding his car. But," he shook his head again, "it doesn't look good."

"No, I understand. I can see that."

"Now I think it's incumbent on you to start taking precautions accordingly. I know you've worked very hard to find some trace of your father, and you've handled this in a professional—" Somebody had come in and whispered to the woman officer and she in turn said something to the FBI man.

Sharon caught "—Raymond Meara."

"We'll be a few minutes," he said, and the uniformed men left. He turned back to Sharon. "Your friend Mr. Meara's out there. As I was saying, you both have been trying to help, but at this point the best thing is to let us handle it. We don't want to—" he chose his phrase, "create unnecessary problems."

"Are you in charge of the investigation?" she asked.

"Ah!" His face took on a pained expression. "In communities like this we don't generally get into jurisdictional hairsplitting. It's better to work together until we see what shakes loose. There's actually been no crime here, so the investigation is a missing-persons case officially, until such a time as it becomes a federal matter for the Bureau. But we naturally will give any help to Chief Randall, or the state and county people, that we can." He smiled at her. She had the impression he was a decent, just man. All these guys were decent men. So was her dad—he was decent. "Don't give up on your father yet, though. This doesn't have to mean anything. But you need to understand the potential seriousness and, obviously, from here on you need to let us handle the question-asking. Okay?"

"Sure." She thought about what she'd done so far. Her futile interviews and fruitless travels down the muddy side roads and flooding arterial highways of rural Clearwater, Mississippi, Scott, and New Madrid counties.

Even if the police said they weren't pursuing an investigation, what more could she do? Follow the old New Madrid physician's advice and start making a list of the ministers over fifty? Is that what her dad had done?

The airless, stifling conference room was sapping her spirit. She started to leave, and as she stood, her father's memory was like a needle driven into her soul, painful and debilitating and as paralyzing as a small stroke. The tears came out once again, an involuntary spillage from her inner wellspring, overflowing, in imitation of the rivers. Tears streamed down her face and she blew her nose with a fury. Somehow she found her way out to where Raymond Meara waited.

"I—" She started to make a joke, to tell him she should have known *he'd* be around someplace, but she couldn't get it out, and instead went up to him, letting herself crumple against his strong body.

"Come on," he said, taking her out to the truck. She got in and saw the interior of the pickup was spotlessly clean and she blew her nose again.

"Oh, boy," she said. Meara started up and they drove back to the motel.

"I heard about it on the scanner. My phone is completely out." Out in the field. "The back way's closed. I took the truck out last night and slept in the cab for maybe an hour or so. There's still not enough water to put a boat in, but maybe by this afternoon there will be."

"Where's your boat?"

"It's over at a guy's house on this side of the water. He'll take it down to the water's edge for me and pull the trailer on back so nobody steals it."

"Oh," she said. They pulled up in front of her motel room. "Come on in," she invited, wiping her eyes. But when they went in she left him sitting in a chair by the window and went into the bathroom, weeping uncontrollably. God, she hated this weakness in herself. Sharon felt shame and disgust as much as pain.

She freshened up and came back in the room to find

Ray sound asleep in the chair. She pulled the spread off the bed and covered him with it, kicked her shoes off and got into bed clothed, pulling the woolen blanket around her and hoping that sleep would come and hold her.

~ **52**

His scarred countenance was the first thing she saw when her eyes opened.

"'lo," she said in a sleepy voice.

"Have a good nap?"

"I must have. You should have slept in the bed."

"I didn't do much more'n close my eyes and I was sound asleep. Sorry about that."

"I was glad you were with me." Her voice was soft and muffled.

"You look like a little girl in your sleep."

"Do I?"

"Mm hm."

She sat on the edge of the bed and brushed her hair. He wanted to tell her not to touch it, to say that her hair was so beautiful and sexy the way it was. He wanted to say a lot of things but he sat there, wisely keeping his mouth shut.

"What did they say to you about Dad today?"

"Nothing. They think it looks bad because of the car turning up like that. I'm sure they went through all that with you."

"The FBI man thinks it was planted there," she said.

"Yeah, well . . . if that's true, it was a stupid goddamn thing for somebody to do."

"What do you mean?"

"Who would have ever known that something happened if they'd just hid the car? Put it in the river or whatever. Now it looks like, as the cop said, foul play. Somebody trying to cover their tracks. Real dumb."

"You think Dad's—" It stuck and the pressure welled up again, but she inhaled deeply and rubbed sleep from the corner of her eye. "You think he found the Nazi?"

"He might have gotten close, yeah. The guy's been lucky up to now. I mean, nobody knew anything. They didn't know Alma Purdy, they hadn't seen your father—"

"What did you just say?" Her eyes widened.

"I said they hadn't seen him or—"

"No. Before that."

"I said they didn't know anything. They didn't know Mrs. Purdy, they hadn't seen your father."

Sharon picked up the phone and started to ask the office to connect her to the police station and then decided against it and asked for the time, thanking the woman at the desk. "When the car was left where it was, Dad's Mercury, there was no way to get through to New Madrid, right?"

"Not on that road, no." She was going through some maps. She couldn't find what she wanted and got keys out of her voluminous purse, opened the door, and unlocked the car. Meara waited in the chair, his legs stretched straight out in front of him. "Okay," she said, sitting down beside him and opening the maps. "Show me where the car was."

"I can show you about where it was. Um—it'd have to have been right along in here. There's W and the levee road."

"And all this was water?"

"When the car was left there? Yeah."

"And the roads to Cape are closed now, right?"

"Yeah."

"How about here? Or Sikeston? The interstate? Could anybody come around that way with the car?"

"It's possible. I mean, you want to be sneaky, you

could hook the car to a chain, drag it in with a flatbed, drop it, and maybe drive the truck out afterward."

"Okay," she said, "but what about these FBI guys and the state patrol? How did they get in?"

"Boat, I suppose. State rods might have come in through Charleston. Regional HQ is at Satellite E, not all that far. They could have spent the night here or come in by boat."

"Point is, if somebody did something to Dad they've got to be around *here*. Bayou City."

"Mm. They might have come through before the water was that deep, come in two days ago and left it there. See, let's say two people were working together, one drives a truck and the other rides shotgun. They come in the back, move your dad's car from wherever it's been stashed. Leave it at the water's edge, go back out, cross the shallow water over the highway to Charleston. If you knew the roads, wanted to gamble, you could have made it."

"This guy's seventy years old or something. How would he know someone with a big truck?" She was grasping for anything.

"Whoa, Sharon. You're making a case for something that's got a big hole in it. The Nazi, first, who says he's alone? If he's managed to deep-six an old gal and . . . evade an experienced manhunter without leaving tracks, odds are he's got somebody helping him. Maybe these Nazi skinhead punks, maybe one of them, I dunno. It's too . . . whatyacallit?"

"Hm?"

"Too perdurous? What's the stupid word. Per*dur*able, that's it." He smiled. "Too problematical. Is that a word?"

She laughed in spite of herself. "Last time I looked." She smiled back at him.

"I guess you don't want to fool around, eh?" He wanted to kiss those green eyes of hers shut and work his way down.

"Maybe later." She smiled affectionately at him. What a character. What was not to like?

"Okay. Take a raincheck. Hey, let's go get something to eat."

"I'm not hungry."

"I am. Keep me company. Cup of coffee won't hurt."

"Okay." What else could she do? Start building an ark?

The restaurant was called the Crystal Cafe, a homey place filled with guys wearing caps. The two waitresses called everybody by their first names and ran around with trays full of blue-plate specials and home cooking.

Sharon looked at Meara. What am I doing? Is this the mutual gravitational pull of two binary stars, or just a shoulder in the crowd? An umbrella in the storm?

Tyson-Spinks. Clay-Liston. Doakes-Weaver. Buckley-Vidal. Would Kamen-Meara rank among the all-time classic quickies?

It was cozy and pleasant in the Crystal Cafe. Warm. She felt safe with Ray, and sat there, the object of stares that more or less bounced off her awareness, until a shadow loomed over them. He was bigger than Meara, and, if possible, even rougher looking.

What happened next was odd. He sat down, not saying excuse me, never so much as glancing at her, scooting a chair up to Ray's side and beginning a long, fairly animated conversation they conducted in whispers she couldn't hear. Mostly it was the guy doing the talking, whispering in Meara's ear while Sharon tried to look at her coffee and the walls, doing her damnedest not to drum her fingernails.

"I'm sorry, man," she heard him say.

"Don't sweat it," Meara told him. The man left as abruptly as he'd intruded, never so much as nodding to her.

Meara paid for his chopped steak, mashed potatoes, and steamed green beans just like Mom used to make, and they got up to leave. As soon as they were outside she asked him, "Who was the mystery man?"

"You mean Doug? Oh, he's just a friend. Doug Seifer. He just wanted to let me know about something."

"Oh."

When they pulled into the small motel parking lot the woman in the office stepped outside and waved at Sharon to come over. She walked into the office and the innkeeper told her, "Young's Pharmacy called while you were out. They want you to come by. Said it was important."

"Young's Pharmacy?"

"Uh-huh. They said they got a package addressed to you in care of the motel. Young's gets our packages."

"Okay. Thanks."

"I think they said it's from your father."

 **53**

Meara could sense the excitement in Sharon as they headed for Young's. It filled the truck like heat.

"Ray," she said in a funny voice, and he looked over. She was looking at him with those green eyes deep like ice on a frozen pond. "Is that where Dr. Fletcher told us about?" They had just passed the sign in front of the Royal Clinic.

"Yeah."

"Can we drop back by there after we get the package?"

"I reckon so. Don't see why not, but what's the point?"

"What's to lose?"

"That's true, I suppose. They said they didn't want you going anywhere alone, though. So I'm comin' in with you."

"Thanks." She smiled at him, feeling glad he was with her. Young's was pharmacy, drugstore, novelty and gift shop, card shop, high school hangout, and all-purpose dime store. USPS packages were delivered in the normal way in Bayou City, but some of the express carriers used the pharmacy as a pick-up and delivery point. There was a package waiting for her. The return address was marked with her father's address, but in Wendy's girlish, loopy hand. So much for the package from her dad.

"Bad news," she said to Ray, getting back in the truck. "Just some stuff forwarded by a co-worker back home."

He stopped in front of the clinic and they went in.

"Hi-dee," the woman called to Ray.

"Hello. I was wonderin' if Doc would have time to see me and this friend of mine."

"Why, shore. I'll ask him."

"Ask if we could just have half a minute." He explained briefly why they were there, and they were told to take a seat. They sat next to several other waiting patients.

"Ray, water got you yet?" one of the men said over a copy of a sportsman's magazine, and they were still in conversation when Sharon looked up to see a kindly man in bifocals.

"Raymond, my boy."

"Hey! Doc." He stood. "I want you to meet a friend of mine, Sharon Kamen. Sharon this is Doc Royal. Sharon's dad is the one who dis—"

But the older man was moving, heading toward the door, where a vehicle was just pulling in front of the building, the passenger door open under the clinic's protective portico. "Please call me," the doctor said to them, his hands spread in the stick-up victim's pose. "I can't stop to talk now. Marie and Walter Binksley were just in a fire," he said, going out the door. Everyone in the waiting room moaned their sympathy. "Water got into the floor furnace and shorted—" The door slammed on his words and he was gone.

"We'll get him another time, Sharon. Damn! Walter's a fine old gentleman. Those damn floor furnaces." He shook his head and thanked the woman at the desk.

"That's him," Sharon said.

"That's him," Ray said, misunderstanding. "Good ol' Doc."

"That's Emil *Shtolz,*" she hissed, shaking, shuddering, knowing as she uttered the words aloud she'd just seen evil up close. She'd seen the man her dad had been chasing. She knew at that instant her father was gone. "Take me to the police, Ray."

"Huh?"

"Please. Let's go." She was dead serious. He looked at her to make sure she wasn't putting him on.

"Hey, Sharon. You kidding me?" He was smiling.

"Please." The word leaked out so angrily, between her pretty clenched teeth, that he just sighed and started the truck.

"I know you're really under a lot of stress, babe, so—" He could feel her fear and frustrated anger so he let it drop, but he knew what a big mistake she was making. He went into the city administration building with her but let her do her thing with Jimmie alone.

He felt sorry for her. Within a few seconds he could see a familiar look on Randall's face and pretty soon the chief's loud laughter could be heard through the glass. Not long after, she slammed out of there and he was following her, saying in a placating tone, "—and I'll have more'n thirty candles on my next birthday cake, Sharon, and he delivered me. Doc's been here all his life." Chuckling. "I promise you he's all right."

"He hasn't been here all his life. He has a foreign accent, he's a Nazi in hiding, and he probably killed Alma Purdy and my *father,* goddammit!" The door cracked like a gunshot when she hit it.

"She's under a lot of stress, Jimmie," Meara said to the smiling cop.

"Yeah, I know that, Ray. Just try to keep her in the motel, though, will ya? She's in no state of mind to be out talking to folks."

"Okay."

"Catch ya later," Randall said, pleasantly.

"Right." Meara went out the door. Sharon was standing beside the truck, so mad she didn't know what to do. She saw Ray and got in and slammed the door. They rode back to the motel in silence.

"Do you think I'm a *moron?*" she shouted the moment they pulled into the parking lot, slamming the truck door again and running toward the motel room.

"No, I don't," he said, staying with her so she couldn't slam the door on him. She whirled.

"I don't mean only you. I mean *all* of you. I know that's the Nazi bastard Shtolz and I know he's done something to Dad. I know you think he walks on water and so on, but I promise you I know what I'm talking about." She turned and started throwing things around, scattering papers as she looked for something. He wished he could give her pills to calm her down. "That voice—I know that accent. He's a German. That's a German accent. Very polished, very continental and all. But—no wonder nobody's caught him. You think he's the bloody *Pope* around here!"

"Hey, don't get pissed at me. I didn't do anything."

"Look at this," she said, having found one of the circulars.

"Yeah?"

"Shit, don't you see. That could easily be Shtolz. God almightly I don't believe this."

Ray picked up the piece of paper and looked at it. "That could easily be Shtolz? That *is* Shtolz, Sharon. What are you saying?"

"I mean *Royal,* goddammit hell shit, *Royal Royal* DOCTOR ROYAL AHHH *Royal* AWWWW—" into a wail of sobbing, gasping, pure, unadulterated rage. He tried to hold her and she jerked away, stomping into the bathroom and slamming the door so hard that a man in the adjacent room, a visiting salesman out of Allen, Texas, thought for a second that a car had crashed through the wall.

Meara stood there looking stupid, shaking his head, thinking what a way he had with women, then went out the door to take care of business.

By the time he returned to the motel the woman who opened the door was a calmer Sharon Kamen. She'd pulled herself together.

"Come on in, Ray," she said, a bit sheepishly. "I just got—weirded out."

"I understand," he said, going in and sitting down on the edge of one of the chairs.

"Upset over Dad. Sorry I took it out on you."

"No big deal."

"Over and done with," she said, sitting down in the other sling chair. There was a small, laminated-plastic-top table, two cultures, and half a generation—maybe eight hundred miles—between them, and Meara felt chilled, and wanted desperately to aid her in some way. To be of value.

"I wish I could help you, babe."

"I know you do," she said, and reached for his hand, lightly touching hers against the back of his. "You're a honeybun. You've been a big help. A big help." She seemed crestfallen.

"Listen, how'd you like to go for a boat ride? Just to get your mind off things for a while?"

"Thanks." She shook her head. "I just think I want to be by myself, Ray. You mind?"

"No, of course not." He got up and she was at the door with him. "I'm going on in, so, if you want or need me for anything, let me give you a number."

She said fine, got a pen, and wrote down the number at his friend's house.

"That's Pee Wee Kimbro. His place is at Mark Forks, where the water begins. If you need me just tell Pee Wee or Betty, all right? They'll come get me."

"Thanks," she said, and turned her face up for a kiss, but when he kissed her she didn't put anything into it. He didn't care and kissed her again, trying to inject all the promise there was into the kiss. He told her he'd see her tomorrow and left.

The second she heard his pickup growl out of the motel parking lot she was back in the bathroom with the book. Sharon knew now that whatever got done she would have to do alone. Nobody would believe her. She *had* to force Emil Shtolz into action. When her rage subsided again and a ray of logic penetrated the anger, she realized how unwise it was to confront him by herself, but as her father had been drawn to the clinic alone, so she now felt committed to pursuing him. What were her options? Neither the local cops nor Ray would give her the benefit of the doubt.

She thought about the words Young's Pharmacy on what had presumably been a package containing prescription medicines, shipped to her father from St. Louis. A pile of junk mail and a package bearing a St. Louis USPS rubber stamp: Opened and Remailed By Bulk Shipping Center, the drugstore name visible underneath. It had originally been sent from Bayou City.

She held the book, a diary or journal in German. Two hundred pages. Small: four by six inches. Three quarters of an inch thick. Faded, soiled green leather. Brass metal corners and a brass lock, which was unlocked.

An ornate eagle with spread wings, seated atop a circular emblem with a swastika on it, was stamped in gold. Below the Nazi symbol, deeply stamped in Germanic black letters: *NATIONALSOZIALISTISCHE DEUTSCHE ARBEITERPARTEI,* and in large, flowing letters in embossed gold—

LEBENSBORN

She leafed through a few pages of writing, recognizing the word *Geheim*. She could make out isolated phrases here and there but she cursed her inability to read the journal as her father could have. It apparently was the diary of the missing woman, something she'd managed to ship to Sharon's father before they both disappeared.

This had ended up in the hands of the bulk shippers, whoever they were, in St. Louis. Perhaps it had come open in transit. This explained the delay in its being forwarded.

She tried to think. The title meant something like life force or love force: born of love, born of life, fountain of the newborn? Living birth? She tried to force a plausible translation, her frustration mounting. Whom could she show this to?

There was a number she had once written down in her directory at home. A mysterious phone number that her father had been so serious about—someone who was to be called only by him, and only in emergency situations. He'd made vague allusions at the time, implying the guy was maybe Mossad, and it had frightened Sharon. She wished she had the number now.

She felt zombie-like. It was as if she were in some limbo world where life hung suspended. She could move, talk, see, react, do things, but her actions affected nothing. The real world spun on as she playacted out her inconsequential moves . . . a chess game with an invisible, intangible player. If she only had the balls to do what her dad would have done under similar circumstances. She wished she hadn't been so quick to condemn his old-fashioned ways. Sometimes the old ways were the only ways. The German phrase he'd once taught her, *verdrängte schuld,* repressed guilt, came back to taunt her.

The anger and frustration welled up inside and she snatched at the slim Bayou City–East Prairie–Charleston phone directory and began flipping through pages to the Rs. There the bastard was—twice:

ROYAL, Solomon D.O., Royal Clinic, and the number. Below that, Residence 709 West Vine and the phone number. She dialed furiously, then remembered she had to call the operator first, and dialed nine.

"Desk?"

"Please dial a number for me, a local call." She gave

the home phone. She'd tell that son of a bitch she knew who he was. She was on his trail. Make the bastard sweat.

The line was ringing. She knew it was a recording even before she heard the voice say, "I am away from the telephone right now. If this is a medical emergency, please call the following numbers—" Probably something he put on the phone in the evenings so he wouldn't be bothered. She'd bother his Nazi ass, all right.

She knew she could find West Vine easily. And just as certainly she knew Royal had done something to her dad. He'd pay in spades.

First things first. She got the lady back on the telephone and said, "I have something I want given to Mr. Meara. I was wondering, could I ask you to hold a package for him?"

"Sure," she said.

Sharon thanked her and asked for the number Ray had given her. She'd decided how she'd proceed, just in those fleeting seconds of coming to terms with her own repressed guilt.

"Yea-lo," a woman's voice sang out on the other end of the line.

"Hello. Is this the Pee Wee Kimbro residence?"

"Yes?" the woman answered suspiciously.

"Is Pee Wee there?"

"Yes," she said, almost grudgingly.

"May I speak with him please?"

"Who's this?"

"My name's Sharon Kamen." Nothing. "I'm a friend of Raymond Meara."

"Oh! Ray's friend. Why didn't you say so, Sharon. I'm sorry, we don't like some of these sales pitches that you get now from strangers."

"Sure. Me either. I wanted to tell Pee Wee something."

"Sharon, Pee Wee done left already. He said he was havin' trouble with the trailer so he's gone on down to the water to wait for Ray."

"You think Ray might come by there first?"

"He might."

"If he does, would you tell him something, and this is real important, Mrs. Kimbro. There's a package I want him to do something about. It's at the motel office." She sensed the message would be so confused by the time he got it there'd be no point in trying to explain further. She'd put a note in about getting it translated and so forth. "Please tell Ray the package is waiting for him at the motel office, will you?"

The woman repeated the message back and Sharon thanked her.

54

Although Chaingang had body parts that could be described as merely larger than normal, his torso, arms, and legs were so big that sometimes, when he was at his heaviest weight, he at first resembled a Macy's float that had broken loose from its tethers. A killer blimp with legs the size of giant tree trunks could hardly stuff its parts into off-the-rack clothing. The beast had a twenty-six-inch neck, for example, and his upper biceps, if flexed, would simply rip the seams from any sleeve of a standard work shirt, however extra stout.

At the time he was first heading east across Missouri, he'd changed to his driving clothes, a white T-shirt size XXXXXL, size fifty-eight fatigue pants, and 15EEEEE work boots.

The duffel and weapons case were filled with ordnance, ammo, a torn-down piece, claymore mines, det gear, Tupperware-housed emergency edibles, and the staples of daily living, his bush tarp, poncho, fighting Bowie, a small tool shop, a mobile triage, all his survival equipment that permitted him to rove as a one-man gang, the whole nine yards from toilet paper to Tabasco sauce. There were some spare socks, shorts, odds and ends, but he tended to operate with few changes of clothing.

The stuff he was wearing had reached its limit. His clothes were about to fall off him and, even after a cold sponge bath perched on the muddy edge of a swollen creek bed, he was so rank he was even grossing out his own olfactory senses. He had to get clean and get pretty.

It was time to find one of the special outlets that catered to the superhumongous. He pulled off to the side of the road and found a pair of small directories chained to an old-time pay telephone. His flawless gyro was once again operational and he deduced that a big man's clothier was within driving distance.

He got back in the vehicle, which was irritating him more and more by the mile, and continued on, a posted sign warning him as he approached a bridge, Over 36 Tons 15MPH. It was hard to read.

He felt himself growing more pissed by the second. He slobbered on his fingers and savagely wiped them across the encrusted lid of his bad eye. After some hard wiping the eye reluctantly opened. His vision was hazy but at least he could see better. Oh, yes, someone would pay for all this shit. He gritted his shark fangs and kept driving. Over the next slight hill, as if to further goad him, he drove into water. A solid sheet of water covered the highway completely.

Anyone else would have turned around. He didn't pause for a heartbeat, simply gripped the old pickup's steering wheel in a tight ten o'clock, eased up slightly on the gas pedal, and aimed her into the blue. Somehow his compass kept him on the unfamiliar road and in a couple of minutes he drove out of it. A mile later he came to another stream but it was faster-moving and obviously deeper. What the fuck, he thought, and roared into it full tilt, the truck smoking as if it were on fire.

Water shot from the prow of the pickup in two high

and rather disconcerting wings. No way was he going to make it. Should he go back? No, he decided. Quickly as he could, wedged under a steering wheel by his massive gut and Detroit's midget draftsmen, he managed to wiggle out of his combat booties and socks, which he placed on the passenger seat. His timing was unerring: within a few seconds the high water drowned out the engine. It was a good fifty yards to the other side. He wrapped the shotgun and weapons case in the huge bush tarp, jammed that and his boots into the top of the massive duffel, retrieved some duct tape from the bag as an afterthought, and taped the edge of the bush tarp as tight around the outside top of the whole container as he could, smashing the driver's side door open.

It was all he could do to muscle the door back enough to get out in the moving water and he got two shocks, first when the cold water hit groin level with an icy slap, and second when he grabbed the towering load and stepped out into the water. The force of the current nearly took him off his feet.

Tall, stout trees of various types, ages, and sizes grew nearby in the road ditches, but nothing short of the threat of drowning could have induced him to try to unwrap the taped bush tarp and balance a stolen Remington and the weapons case while he rummaged for his big blade. He decided to improvise. He worked the previously owned shotgun out, racked shells into the water, and used the empty weapon as a makeshift cane, the duffel and weapons case slung over his shoulder. With a fireplug-thick arm curled around his gear, one hand helping to steady his bulk, he began to negotiate the swift-moving water with dainty little steps, his bare feet on the pavement, an ox yoked to an elongated duffel bag.

He made it out of the water and sat on his stuff, exhausted from the effort, rubbing the muscles in his powerful legs. A lesser man would have had to swim toward the nearest down-current bank, but Chaingang's legs were used to routinely lifting and moving a quarter-ton load and they stood up under the challenge.

When he'd rested for a bit he dried his feet, put on socks and boots, pitched the Remington, and began humping down the road in his rather comical waddling, limping gait. An eternity later he was at the Bayou City shopping mall.

Porky's Big Fashions occupied a boxcar-like space between a video store and an empty storefront, and when he squinted his good eye, the sign looked like Porky Pig Fatshits to him. Even the signage was poking at him, conspiring to enrage the clownish bear. They would pay dearly, all of them. He spat, belched expansively, a mighty halitotic regurgitation that fouled the air around him, adjusted both his load and his package, and waddled toward Porky's, cutting wet farts.

What must the store owner and his clerk have thought when this . . . *thing* blew into their sanctum sanctorum? The manager-owner, young Ryan Sneeden, was back in his office and Mrs. Schecter was at the cash register working on receipts. Wynton Marsalis's "The Very Thought of You" and central heat whooshed at roughly equal decibel levels. Suddenly there was a loud slam as a huge, incredibly dirty person blundered through the doors.

"May I help you?" Mrs. Schecter asked in the frosty tone she reserved for people who came in looking to use the bathroom and so on. No response. The thing was lumbering through the store, seemingly oblivious to her, *touching* the garments as he moved by the clothing racks, leaving his scent everywhere. He was like a steer or bull or something, an animal that had wandered in off the street. A rank stench, not of sewers, but an equally sulfurous and deadly toxicity of unthinkable body odor assaulted her patrician nose. "Are you looking for something?"

He pulled apparel off racks. Anything that looked big enough. He was trying things on before she could stop him. This monstrosity of a blubber gut in a filthy T-shirt with . . . was that *blood* on it?

Ryan Sneeden sensed, perhaps smelled, something

foul and came out blinking, a curly headed little boy of a young man in his mid twenties, a big fake stewardess smile in place. "Hi. How you doing today?" Neither he nor Mrs. Schecter had ever seen a creature such as this in the store, nor had they been ignored in so rude a manner. Sneeden found it quite distasteful and went back in his office, shutting and locking the door.

The intruder had a pair of bib overalls that looked like about a size fifty-eight. A pair of XXXXXL jeans that appeared to be about six feet across the ass. T-shirts. A belt made from the entire length of a large dead cow. He plopped them up on the counter, frightening Mrs. Schecter half to death. She didn't know whether to ask would there be anything else, would it be cash or charge, or please go away and permit me to inhale. The beastly stink was quite unbearable up close.

Chaingang's black marbles cross-haired the woman behind the counter for the first time, an old douchebag about fifty-something with dark hair bifurcated by a silver-white streak. It made her look like a cartoon skunk to him; Porky Pig's skunk woman. She was wearing an expensive red dress, weighed a fast ninety-five pounds, and was really a rather decent-looking old bitch, he decided. The glint of gold and diamonds against her out-of-season tan winked at his good eye. He was usually uninterested in such things, but he needed to resupply and his mindscreen was planning for certain contingencies that might require a hefty bit of barter material.

He went back and selected a suit, an act that in itself was something to see, as he pulled on a four-hundred-dollar banker's gray job and admired himself in one of the three-way mirrors: suitcoat over damp fatigues and slaughterhouse T-shirt. He looked like the drummer in a punk-rock house band at an institution for the criminally insane. He found a couple of shirts with broad stripes, a tie with bright stars, perhaps five feet long, and some underpants to see him through the perilous night. Deposited all of this on the counter with his other purchases and let Skunkie sack it up for him in a nice, tasteful container.

"How do you wish to pay? Cash or charge?" she intoned, trying not to breathe any more than necessary.

He eyed the street and the rest of the store in the shoplifting security mirrors, as he pulled out a disreputable hunk of moist cash.

"Do you have somewhere I could make wee-wee?" he asked, his bass voice rumbling like a Hammond organ in the enclosure. His breath was as potently malodorous as the rest of him, and she blinked in disgust.

"I beg your pardon?"

"Wee-wee. You know," he said, having a bit of fun with her, "drain the old liz." He cupped his package.

She didn't find off-color behavior amusing in the least, and let him know with her stare, which had withered many a man. Oh, the clientele they sometimes had to put up with. Fortunately most of the chubbies who came in were, well, gentlemen at least.

"We don't have public facilities," she said, a stern frown drawing down the corners of her mouth.

"Do *you* ever wee-wee or has that old hole of yours dried up completely?" he whispered, something snaking out of his right hand and shutting off all the sights and sounds and smells in her little world.

Skunkie dropped back against some XXXL turtlenecks like a steer getting kissed with the bolt gun. Even before she quit twitching, he was waddling back to the office where the young chap had run to hide earlier.

His odd brain was working a mile a minute as he moved quickly around the leather wing chairs and dressing mirrors. A fist the size of a twenty-two-pound cannonball knocked once on the door and Ryan Sneeden jumped up.

"Yes?"

"Fellatio you look at this cranmus of mine for a sexer? The lady up front didn't fress to change, so I was hoping that you could." He heard the fellow fumble with the lock and saw the door open. Chaingang's face was contorted into his parody of a human smile.

"Just doing my books," Sneeden said, with bravado. "Whatcha' need there, big guy?" He exuded polish and self-confidence. Just the kind of little asshole Bunkowski liked to hurt.

"Ah, well," he rumbled, "for openers I need to see if you can catch up with Skunkie?"

"Pardon?"

"You'll have to hurry. She's on the way to *hell*," Chaingang said, as he hammered a bottomfist into the youngster's face, hitting him right between the eyes. The blow went *Thock!* just like a Porky Pig cartoon sound effect. If his Bowie hadn't been under wraps, parked in the taped-up duffel, he could have partaken of the delicious opportunities, but for now he concentrated on resupply. The young man had no keys, so he would not be able to lock the store. Shame. He went through the desk rapidly, found the cashbox and took it. Took the young fellow's billfold, money clip, ring. Felt his neck, groin, spine, and ankles for surprise treasures, found none, and unzipped. He actually did have to wee-wee and did so on the lad, who'd fallen with his head at an angle that suggested he might not be rallying, unless there was an afterlife.

Chaingang checked the back door: locked, no keys in it. Went to the front and kicked Skunkie under the counter. She fit there as neatly as if she'd been designed to tuck into that available space.

With a loud grunt he squatted down and took off her bracelet and two absolutely killer diamonds. Some old man had paid for his thrills. He idly toed her skirt back and appreciated the good, if slightly skinny, legs, and checked out her old saddlebag ass. At the very end, he noted with amusement, Skunkie had made wee-wee.

He rang up a sale on the register, cleaned it out, and was stuffing bills and things here and there when a young bloke of perhaps twenty came in and saw a giant behind the counter. He still had on the gray coat over his T-shirt, which looked hip enough to the kid.

"Hi."

"Sor-ry," Chaingang simpered, in his most effeminate caricature. "We're *clothed* until tomorrow. In-ven-to-ree!" He pouted, with big, fat pursed lips.

"Um, okay," the kid said, leaving. God, he thought, there were tons of fags everywhere.

Bunkowski hoisted his purchases, saddled up, and walked back out into the parking lot of the mall, in quest of appropriate transportation. Behind him, Marsalis's "A Sleeping Bee" serenaded the dead.

55

They were parked in a black Dodge van with privacy glass and Virginia tags, in front of an overgrown lot on the nearest side street intersecting the main thoroughfare where the shopping mall was located. They'd driven all night, the wheelman good, but of a more garrulous nature than some. She'd excused herself and crashed in the back. She was a lady who had to grab her Zs while she could.

Watchers always wonder if *they* have watchers, and not without good cause. Watching watchers is part of the game in what is often disdainfully regarded as the intelligence community. That's what they did, people like the man and woman in the muddy black van. The spook version of internal affairs, crossed with what the former Soviet citizenry had once termed Smersh, was their adoptive parent company.

If they in turn had been observed, their watchers would have seen a rather dirty Dodge van with out-of-state plates pull up and an attractive, slim, thirty-something woman in slacks get out and stretch. Vacationers, probably, in the area visiting relatives. She walked to the corner of the video store and looked around, as if waiting for a friend, changed her mind apparently, and returned to the vehicle. A watcher would have observed nothing more.

The van stayed put, and inside, the glow of the OMEGASTAR mobile locator/tracker stayed locked onto their target, who at the moment was less than two hundred feet away. It was a judgment call. Doing somebody in a crowded shopping center wasn't out of the question but there was a lot to factor in.

They were still there when the target came out in his limping waddle, loaded with clothing purchases it looked like, and walked out into the busy parking lot.

Here is what they saw: They saw him chat with some old friends, stand around chewing the fat, looking as if he'd misplaced his ride, then suddenly wave as he spotted the car. They saw him walk up to the vehicle, laugh about his momentary mental lapse with the driver, toss an enormous duffel bag in the back seat, get in the car, and pull out. From a few hundred feet away it appeared the person who'd been in the driver's seat had moved over and the target had driven away. For some reason the other person's head was no longer visible above the seat.

Nobody could do fakes like Bunkowski. He had all the actor's skills, from mimicry to observational brilliance, but his physical presence and organic sense of how to move in order to manipulate, confuse, boggle, and convince, was second to none. It was as if a great stage actor with the gifts of a young Brando, Olivier, or, more accurately, Jackie Gleason, had decided to become a serial killer. Think of the ways they could mislead, bewitch, and persuade with their communication capabilities turned on full. Chaingang could make a person feel as if he alone in all the world could help him in his fumbling, clownish moment of need. As with Gleason, the physical package only added to the power of the act, especially when he assumed an underdog's helpless persona. The rubbery face, the baby-fat guileless smile, the disarming moves—he was an actor's actor.

Had the watchers been nearer they might have heard bits and pieces of conversation floating their way on the scented, wet Bayou City pollution. "—visited my son. He's stationed at Fort Sill." *Why, what a coincidence,* he might have replied. *I just got back from Oklahoma too!* as his mindscreen began to spin a scenario that would be impossible to move away from. They could have heard how easily he inserted himself into a life, created a plausible chain of events that bumped against the other person's experience, listened to him scrandle a frace of doublespiel that could, if you were unlucky, leave you very surprised and dead.

Even as he dealt with the dopey-looking middle-aged man sitting at the wheel of the Plymouth, obviously waiting for his better half to emerge from a store, he felt the dual pulls typical of his brief moments of human interfacing. He hated the monkey people but every time he heard them speak or peered into their nothing lives he found the fragments totally fascinating. After all, that part of him that had remained human identified with the species of which he had once been born.

"Hah doo. I was wonderin' canna fanna ansellation?" Forget the sense of it, it wasn't communication intended for the vic he was about to hurt, it was for onlookers, the watchers whose proximity to his awareness was a sharp burr. To an observer, the tone and openness and body language completely masked his intent. The watchers would not observe his head inside the car, the Breath of Death in some poor man's face, and, as he recoiled, the snap of the neck as giant paws took the victim below the line of sight. "You slide on over there, podna," the beast might ad-lib, smiling, as he wedged his girth behind the wheel.

There was never a sense of threat, nothing observable. How the hell were the watchers supposed to know what was going on? It was only when they saw one head instead of two that they realized what they'd witnessed. Damn! The big fucker was so slick. They'd have to tranq the rogue elephant elsewhere. The money was exceptionally good, but it was stressful work.

They settled back and let the Plymouth vanish from sight, then the wheelman turned on the ignition and they followed the signal from the target's locator, pulling the Dodge van back onto the blacktop road, and hoping they wouldn't have to drive through much more water.

 **56**

She first thought of getting a cop to go with her while she forced some sort of showdown with Dr. Royal, but the madder she became the more such a confrontation seemed pointless. He was sneaky smart. In that kind of refereed face-to-face encounter he would be cooly articulate, as mock understanding effused from his Nazi mouth, the filthy, murdering son of a bitch! She would be the wild, violent one. The thought of yet another stereotyped judgment call by the redneck constabulary was sufficient to rekindle the heat of her rage.

She put the Lebensborn book back in the paper it had been wrapped in, took a black marking pen from her purse, noted the time, and quickly printed a note:

I'm going to make "Dr. Royal" (Shtolz) tell what he did

with Dad. If anything happens, make sure the police arrest him for murder! Love, S.

In her thirty years on the planet, Sharon had been involved in two acts of violence, but as she printed her initial, it was as if Aaron Kamen's daughter no longer existed. This was someone else, a dark being pulled from Sharon's guts by anguish and anger. This stranger now went back out to the car, opened the trunk, and grabbed the first weapon she saw—a tire iron, tossed it into the front seat, got in, started the car, and sped off into the rain.

She marked the numbers seven-zero-nine on her mental slate, and concentrated on finding the street address and nothing else. No planning. Just do it. She drove through the arc of a sodium lamp, rain splashing hard on the windshield, and the poor visibility parted the curtain of her rage enough to allow her to flip the wipers on.

There it was, 709 West Vine. Her arms prickled as she realized this bastard had been sleeping a few blocks away from her. She stopped, made sure of the house number again, then backed about fifty yards down the street and pulled against the curb, killing the lights and the motor.

Fate always has her way. Another time and the mad-woman who'd taken possession of Sharon Kamen's body might have waited a few hours, given up, cooled, gone home, calmed down, and things might have ended differently. But fate had settled around Sharon, sealing her destiny.

For two hours she waited. First she'd roll the window down on the passenger side when the windshield fogged up, then it would get wet and cold and she'd run the engine. Then she'd turn it off and the windows would fog up again, and she'd roll the window down. It kept on this way as the rain stopped, started, pounded, slackened off, stopped, started. . . . It was a long, angry, perhaps even insane, two hours.

Eventually, Dr. Solomon Royal chanced to emerge from his home, and it was a grimly determined woman who sat in chilly silence, the tire iron comfortingly close at hand.

He opened an umbrella and spryly moved down the steps from his front porch, unlocked the door of his car, closed the umbrella, placing it on the floorboard of the back seat, got in, and started the motor. When he drove away she was right behind him, letting her fury press down on the accelerator. He turned, with her on top of him, and when he braked at the stop sign in front of Bayou City Episcopalian, she came up behind and gave him a hard smack in the bumper.

"How's that feel, you Nazi son of a bitching *shit?*" she shouted, inflamed by the rush of adrenaline and power, her beautiful chest heaving. It was consuming her that the man in the car in front of her had murdered her father, and she was about to slam into him again when he pulled out from the four-way stop in a fishtailing squeal of wet rubber, and she floored the gas pedal, coming up on his rear again.

He knew, of course, what the situation was the second he saw the woman's face in the car behind him. It was a stroke of luck that she was stalking him. What lovely timing. Small towns have no secrets, and he'd known about her from the moment she first verbalized her suspicions to the police. Just what one would expect from a family of fucking kikes—like father like daughter.

It was resolving itself so perfectly. The only concern he had now was to make absolutely certain it wasn't some kind of a setup that these bothersome imbeciles had concocted. The odd detective or boyfriend lurking about to witness his reactions.

He wished he could get her to the house, where the options would have been so numerous. First the drugs, chloral hydrate at one end and the most toxic poisons at the other. A coffee cup and drinking glasses that he kept prepared and refreshed in his special kitchen cabinet. There were other nice insurance policies against subjugation by an adversary, such as a relatively benign hypo full of pain-killer or the loose newel post on the stairwell, filled with a lead center, that could swiftly crush a skull.

Then there were the proofs that had overflowed his office and now filled his home with decades of irrefutable history. Dusty photos, awards, framed newspaper stories, magazine covers, full-page pictorials of a young Sol Royal treating GIs. Checkable, impeccable proof that he was who he claimed to be.

He could be infuriatingly calm and logical while she accused him of this and that. Sit in front of the big picture window with a nice cup of tea or coffee, elegant and unruffled in his drawing room. The spider could spin his fine web, talking gently and sympathetically as he poured her cup, his voice a cultured, lilting, hypnotic instrument. She would listen to the rhythmic and measured responses, and perhaps drop her guard at last, acknowledging her awful mistake as she reached for her cup.

He'd continue to placate and convince, his voice soft and well modulated, his demeanor reasonable, his idiomatic grasp facile, with only the slightest accent and hint of gutturalness in his speech.

Bright headlight glare in the rearview was dangerously close and it snapped him out of his brief fantasy. He knew what he had to do and shrugged off the thought of a witness as he headed for the floodwater.

She was right there with him, her lights horrible in the gathering darkness, blinding him. The rain was compounding the hazard. He had no choice.

The instant he got to Andrews Road he slowed automatically and she smacked into him. *Hard.* His head snapped as if it were on the end of a whip. *Twisted Jesus* he would make this Jew cunt pay. Just keep calm.

He hit the water too fast, almost flooding his engine, the Jewess twat inches off his bumper, both of them roaring over the road, smoke steaming from the hoods of the cars as he gunned it up the incline of 1140, watching the line of road, concentrating to stay on pavement, the mirror now tilted straight up to deflect the bright lights.

She tried to crash into him again as he came to the shallow part of the water but he was ready this time, and able to absorb the impact better, and he floored it as he hit dry pavement, shooting forward. He tapped the brake. Nothing. The brakes were wet. He trod on the pedal with all his strength and the car almost rolled, swerving wildly back and forth as the steaming vehicle screamed to a stop on the high part of the road.

He lurched from the car just as she plowed into it, hitting his automobile a vicious carom shot. His "knuckles" were under the dashboard, as was a loaded Luger. He started back around the car to get a weapon but as he saw her backing the other car up for another run at him, he moved away as fast as he was able, keeping the solidity of the engine block and chassis between them.

She backed up too far and one of the tires slid off the soft shoulder. She stupidly floored the gas pedal, in her panic, sinking a radial into several inches of Missouri gumbo. It was all he could do not to laugh with glee. He started back toward the weapons.

But who would have thought she could run so fast? The buxom young Jew bitch was screaming at him, almost on him, "You fucking Nazi killer! What did you do with my *father?*" and he never saw the tire iron. On the word father, a sharp shock of pain exploded down through his shoulder and he fell to the wet pavement.

"Don't! Please! I'm not—" he pleaded.

"You bastard son of a—" She was raising the iron back again when he grabbed a slim ankle, yanking savagely. The woman's arms broke her fall but the tire iron went clattering away.

She tried to kick him between the legs as he struggled to his feet and a pointed, high-heeled shoe caught him solidly on the inside of the left leg, just missing his groin. He screamed and smashed a fist towards her face, which she somehow deflected, scratching his arm as she tried to get at his eyes, and then they had hold of each other, screaming and panting as they rolled across the blacktop and into a muddy ditch.

The woman was fighting for her life but so was he. She'd lost a shoe, and managed to kick the other one off, but in doing so lost her balance and he got away and started up the ditch. She grabbed for his legs, trying to pull him back down, but he was able to kick her in the face and scrambled for the car as she ran up the ditch bank behind him.

Emil Shtolz was covered in mud. There was blood dripping from his left arm. His right shoulder felt as if it might be broken. He was limping. His glasses were broken. He was gasping as if he were about to have a coronary. But he made it to the car before she did and grabbed for the grip of the Luger just as she pulled him backward.

They were back on the pavement. Muddy and bloody and fighting like animals or little children, screaming and kicking and scratching, untrained combatants suddenly learning what it was like to battle tooth and nail. He kicked at her as he racked a shell into the gun, more frightened than he'd ever been in his life, knowing that if he dropped the gun she would kill him.

He fired as she leaped at him and, even as close as they were, he managed to miss. She grabbed for the gun and he shot her in the hand and wrist. She fell back, and he shot her again, but he got her with the next one. Hit her dead center.

He knew several things in that instant: he'd won, he knew that. He knew she was dead. He didn't need to check for vital signs, he'd seen innumerable Jews die, and one more had joined their ranks. He had to resist the temptation to blow her apart inch by inch, because he was going to have to do something with this meddlesome sheenie and her car as well. He knew he had chains in the trunk.

All of this flashed through his head like lightning as he

wobbled around and somehow regained his feet. His right hand could scarcely hold the damned Luger, so he took it in his blood-encrusted but uninjured left hand and carefully moved around to where he could administer a coup de grace to her head. As he was starting to bring the front sight up even with her temple under its wet mop of hair, a truck appeared in the distance.

Why should he take the chance of moving her and the car as well? Suddenly it was all too much trouble. No one would be able to prove any connection between himself and the dead girl, no matter how much they cared to speculate. His reputation would protect him—these were his people, after all. He hurried to his car, got in, started the motor, cut the wheel as sharply as his condition permitted, and floored the gas pedal, roaring back in the direction he'd come.

Shtolz' eyes were riveted on the approaching truck. Would the driver notice her? Would he stop to help, or assume that since no one was behind the wheel of the vehicle that the person had gone for a tow truck? Was it someone who would recognize his car? He sighed deeply when the truck turned as it reached the nearest corner, and devoted his attention to making it back through the deep water and, above all else, not driving off the road.

Once he was on the other side he tested the brakes. This time they held after a few taps. He stopped, backed to the water's edge, and got out, aching but with a strong sense of relief. His problems were almost over. When he was sure no one was observing him he took the Luger by the barrel and, with his good arm, flung the weapon out into the moving stream of water. He got back in the car and headed toward his house. He would give himself a chemical bath, patch himself up, and by the time the authorities came around with questions he'd have an airtight alibi scenario for them.

Sharon Kamen no longer thought of Dr. Royal or avenging her father. She felt herself turning cold, sculpturelike, coming unhinged at the pit of her stomach, abdomen, and chest, coming apart like one of Jean Ipousteguy's reclining bronze nudes. She knew she was fading fast, her arms raised, legs in an unladylike sprawl, too weak to stop the wounds that bled onto the hard surface. She could only think of the woman in *La Femme au Bain,* recumbent, weird, cold, unhinged . . . and very still now in the rain.

57

Wedged under the wheel of a four-year-old family Plymouth, Chaingang observed a spill of treasures in the seat beside him. His duffel and weapons case, a pile of packages bearing the high-concept imprint, "Porky's Big Fashions—elegance for the extra large, tall, and portly." He made a few quick pit stops: behind a bustling gas station (Goin' Fishin'? We Got Your Bait Here), where he loaded a hundred and forty pounds of innocent bystander into a dumpster, and at a tire-repair place (We Aim to Please so *Retire* Here!), where he made more than full use of the rest room.

He took a careless sponge bath of sorts using a piece of tarp for a towel and the lukewarm faucet water, then changed into strange long-legged boxer-jockeys that fit in the crotch like a massive diaper for an incontinent sumo wrestler, the largest bib overalls ever made, and a fresh T-shirt. When he left the men's room it looked as if someone had attempted to give his seal a bath in the wash basin.

These needs met, his thoughts turned to his growling

gut. He was ravenous for decent munchies. He drove past Esther's Cafe (Home of Famous Bayou Catfish), only because he counted fourteen trucks in the postage-stamp lot and he wasn't sure he had that much ammo. Finally he wheeled into the drive-up lane of a Fastfood.

"Welcome to Fastfood. May we take your order?" the intercom rasped.

"Gimme six Swiss with mushroom, six triple curly-crisps, six mondo munchburgers, six hacienda grandes, six beef 'n' bean burritos, and six large conquistadores."

"What would you like to drink?" the box asked, but he was already driving toward the food window, salivating like a bear coming out of hibernation and smelling salmon.

"That'll be sixty-six dollars and sixty cents, sir," a girl announced through a small crack in the security window, getting a look at the leviathan whose arm, a massive, rock-hard, hairy-pelted thing with a skillet-size paw on the end, was extending payment even as she spoke. She had to force herself to touch the money. An arm roughly the size of a railroad tie rested on the sill, huge fingers drumming impatiently while she filled the security port with numerous sacks of food and his change. "Thank you, and come back," she said, insincerely, as he stacked the food sacks across the floorboard of the Plymouth, where the corpse of its previous owner had recently rested.

She shuddered as the big thing drove away, a hand shoving mushroom-'n'-Swiss-triple-curly-somethings in-to its gaping maw. Snaggleteeth meant to wrest meat from bone and bite the caps off beer bottles tore into six sacks of fast food in a salivating, frenzied greaseorama of feasting. Next best thing to a live one.

The watchers meant him no serious, permanent harm. They were not there to destroy him, and that was perhaps one reason why his sensors didn't nudge him. Also, he was feeding, and food was what he lived for.

They'd watched the pulse indicate two stops, but when a couple of minutes went by without any movement they did what they always did, they moved in close enough to eyeball the target through binocs.

"He's *eating!*" the woman said, the word loaded with unusual portent.

"There you go," the wheelman said, unnecessarily. She already had the door open and was on her way toward a nearby copse. The target was on the other side. Parked.

An observer watching the watchers would have seen, again, an ordinary looking, fairly attractive woman get out of a van and walk into some trees. She was carrying a case that might have held a musical instrument or a fishing pole, and was dressed in a way that would cause no raised eyebrows. She was moving at a trot, but who walks slowly in the rain?

She ripped a perfectly good pair of slacks but made her way into position and wasted no time getting the piece out and sling-wrapped against a tree trunk. At that range he was in the bank. The lady happened to be a world-class handgun, skeet, and rifle shot—SAUCOG's secret sniper.

Chaingang was chewing one minute, spitting food the next, fighting to get the driver's-side door open and then charging out on tree-trunk legs, the killer chain in his hand, looking for whoever shot him. Trouble was, she was far away, already running back toward the Dodge van, the expendable, silent air gun still lashed to its indigenous firing stanchion.

"Call it in!" she shouted from the edge of the trees, and the wheelman was instantly on the radio, speaking the code phrase that let the meat wagon know their package was ready. She got in the van and they took off, as she gave specific directions.

He'd pulled up behind a discount store and ma 'n' pa grocer's to have his munchies. He'd almost made it to the stand of trees when the ultra-potent Alpha Group II hammered him to the ground like a felled water buff.

The surveillance team pitied the guys who had to load him.

～ 58

"Dan?"

Nothing.

"Dan?"

An immense, unforgiving hand picks up an imaginary ice pick and stabs it down into the center of a block of ice exactly the shape of a human brain.

"Danny?"

"Danny are you there?"

"Oh, Danny Boy, the ice, the ice is cracking," someone sings in a thin, sissified soprano.

"Is anyone home?"

Cracks in the ice cobweb out and complete two perfect hemispheres that now split, revealing an object the shape of an egg, translucent and made of ice, at the center.

"Daniel?"

The egg is at the center of Daniel Edward Flowers Bunkowski's brain.

"CAN can can cancancan . . ."
"YOU you youyouyou . . ."
"HEAR hear hear ? ? . . ."

"ME me me me me MIMI MIMI MIMI memememe mememememememememememememememememe . . . mememe

memem…memememememem…MEMEMEMEMEMEME
MEMEMEMEMEMEMEME?"

The question echoes unmercifully and the egg of
translucent ice cracks open.
CRUNCH!
A tiny monster with a face familiar to occupant slithers
out, a newborn mutant, who squawks in a high voice
filled with profound intuitive unsimplemindedness and
profoundly intuitive simple Simonizedness, lists dangerously. Argh, matey, she's grocery-listing dangerfieldly to
starboard. Fart up the shortarms and jerk off the yard-
arms you pedagogic poltroonish pusillanimous pussies of
quotidian quiddity.
Pedagogic: of or about teaching. Second G is hard J
sound.
Poltroonish: characterized by cowardice.
Pusillanimous: lacking courage and resolution. Con-
temptibly timid.
Quotidian: commonplace, ordinary; daily occurrence.
You forgot Pussies, the computer tells him, chiding
him, stabbing down into the hole in his unconscious-
ness.
A perfectly formed poem slithers out of this same
black hole:

Gothic daymare	pallid daylight	quotidian quiddity
snake oil payoff	diffused sun	cracked ice
huckster transport	filtered images	poltroonish hucksters
monster Johnsons	misty shroud	master my johnson
frozen seaspittle	shadow phantoms	pusillanimous pussies
drenched doubleknits	silent stalk	submerged gravesites
heartsick castle	final reality	newborn icebrains
wet fog	distant ocean	pedagogic hardjays
dangerous cliché	screaming gulls	pussied bluejays
of secrets	gathering darkness	craven ravens
submerged reefs	obscene promises	sunken junkers
name translates	killer love	bloated humans
coughing bark	silken silver	contemptible cadavers

excessive consonants	razor bites	jungle catgrowls
600 steps	curving kisses	666 doubleburgers
sheer precipice	arcing flash	arctic brainjob
stone cliffs	sharpened steel	frozen blowjob
ancient rumors	snake oil daymare	freezing handjob
rumored horrors	heartsick cliché	freaking knobjob
icy exhaustion	shadow secrets	fucking oddjob
bracken green	wet gorse	flogging slobjob
Heather gorse	killer fog	dark perspectives
jackhammer heartbeat	icy horrors	nasty oneiromancy
last rays	huckster payoff	Nancy o-NI-ro-mancy

The disjointed phrases slither back down into the egg and it seals itself as it is swallowed whole by the black hole, swallowed hole by the black whole, hollowed hole in a holy bowl.

"Daniel? Can you hear me? It's your friend, Dr. Norman." The tape will repeat many times.

He's visited these sunken cadavers many times before, a part of memory lodged at a particular juncture of the hippo's hippocampus that the drug probes first, a watery world of dead faces wired into his demolition derby for the deceased. He tries to slam the door on it and lacks the strength.

"Occupant is algolagnic," the doctor told someone once. It was overheard by the beast, who set about to learn the meaning. It proved to be that he took pleasure in inflicting pain. The fat lady on TV said, "Them serial killers get boners hurting and mutilating people." Well, that was a bit general and imprecise. He could not recall a time when he'd got a boner simply because he was inflicting pain or cutting something off. . . . Well, come to think of it, yes, there was one . . . one time when it made him come to think of it.

A cold wind blows over the black hole that conceals his mass grave of underwater corpses.

"—a particular target that you will wish to dispose of, Daniel. He was a scientist who worked in a research program during World War Two. A dossier is available and we have prepared color slides of some of this man's experiments involving the torture of animals, babies, and young children. I know you will—" Norman's words floating in and out. "Dr. Norman is your friend, Daniel. He deeply regrets that you—" Oneiromancy: divination by means of dreams. "—allows you to have great personal freedom, and—" The voice coloring, the blackest part of the hole puddling now, taking on a new configuration and values, a field of red, the black outline of a cordiform, a black heart, on blood red.

"—dogs and monkeys, which were found like this. These children had also been mutilated while they were still breathing. The apparatus was hooked up to the brain before—" Chaingang would never forget the puppy with the top of its skull off. The infant cadavers, the looks on their helpless faces. The smiling man showing off his experimentation. The lion coughed and twitched, pushing at restraints that were not there.

"Here are more photos from his experimentation program. A mass grave . . . one hundred and fifty cats, over eight hundred puppies, three hundred monkeys, an unknown number of . . ." A wave of nausea, partly from the powerful drug, partly from the subject matter, "Look at this little boy, Daniel. Who does he look like?" It could have been a close-up of Daniel, age eight, fresh from punishment by the Snake Man, his mouth agape in pain and terror, perfectly normal in appearance until one's eyes reached the sawn-open skullcap. *Occupant is algolagnic.*

"This man is revered by the community of Bayou City, Missouri, where you are currently located. Feel free to destroy him in any manner that gives you pleasure, Daniel. When you're done with him I hope you'll leave that state, and I'd like to suggest you take some time to rest and get your strength back after your accident. I was awfully sorry to learn you were injured. Remember always, Dr. Norman has your best interests at heart. He

would never do anything to hurt his friend Daniel."
Norman had begun doing some experimentation of his
own. Slowly, he was dropping third-person references
when he spoke to Chaingang, although he still referred
to himself in the third person about half the time.
Bunkowski noted the changes in personal pronoun us-
age, the familiar you and your, in addition to the use of
his first name. One day soon his friend Daniel would
dine on that forked tongue.

"Be very careful in dealing with this old man. He is
resourceful and has many friends. Young men of a white
supremacy organization called the New American-
German Enterprise for Reunification and Solidarity, or
NEW AGERS, sometimes help protect him.

"Remember, too, for your own good the drug we've
employed is extremely powerful, so it will cause a brief
period of disorientation as it wears off. You'll appear to
return to a fully operational state, but you'll be slightly
groggy and may not have total physical control. The
grogginess may come and go. In addition to lack of
coordination you may notice certain behavioral lapses
. . . low-key behavior that you'll find irritating when you
initially interact with others. This will wear off quickly,
so don't be alarmed. Soon you'll be able to behave as you
normally do. Take care, my friend," the voice said,
lovingly. Inside the broken ice egg the mutant screamed
in rage.

When he awoke after another prolonged respite he was in a strange place but felt none of the warning signs that alerted him to impending threats to his safety. The humans had left him. He remembered the awful color slides all too vividly, and he saw what they'd left behind, a recorder with a cassette in it. He touched nothing.

He walked outside, feeling around for his chain, which he'd left in the pocket of his fatigues. Where were his fatigue pants and why was he wearing gray suit trousers? There was his newly appropriated Plymouth. He opened the trunk and found the tarp-wrapped duffel. The weapons case was intact. He checked his SMG, made a cursory inventory of ordnance and ammo, patted his pocket and felt the bulge of chain, and realized he'd hallucinated the gray trou, took another step backward and fell right on his vast fat ass.

The sensation of falling was heightened by a rush of Alpha Group II through his life-support system. Neurons picked up strange signals as the molecular pump that regulates dopamine gave him a flood of something that produced a floating feeling. The spark plugs of his engine misfired as he tried to zoom in on his surroundings.

He was sitting on cracked tarmac. An overgrown parking lot. No. Runway. The sign on the safe house where he'd had his little drugged briefing read Feld's Charter on a peeling board. Overgrown runways. Blue around him on three sides. The edge of the little shithole, no doubt.

Chaingang made it to his feet again, slammed the trunk, got in and started the car, drove until he found a pay phone. Looked up Shtolz, regained his senses, looked up Royal, tried both numbers. Man was gone. Looked up the Neo-Nazi security outfit and tried there, logic over discretion.

"New Agers," a guttural voice sneered.

"Is Dr. Royal present?"

"Huh?"

He repeated the question, and some punk told him he had the wrong number, slamming the telephone receiver down.

He made a note of all three addresses and got back in the car, passed out cold, but regained consciousness almost instantly. He sat, poleaxed by the punch of the drug, and finally shook it off sufficiently to drive. The combination of the recent car mishap and now this. He was barely functioning.

He decided he'd kill for a cold one. Where was he, what was he doing? Something about a puppy, little children, open brainpans.

Numerical analysis.

Symbolic math.

Parsing of equations.

Random solution purging.

Charting abstract algebraic transformation nodes—no problem. His was a mind that could command virtually any situation, and assimilate and retain any understandable fact, but figuring out where he was had proved to be beyond his grasp.

He drove until he ran into water, turned, drove some more. Put gas in the tank. Showed the nice service station man his three addresses and inquired which was nearest. The pleasant chap pointed him toward the skinheads' hangout.

There were four toughs lounging around the storefront office. Under ordinary circumstances Chaingang could have kicked their collective butts to Mars, asked his questions, and planted the last survivor. As it was he meekly knocked, entered, and smiled pleasantly, his attitude toward the youths rather loving and open.

"—so this fucking bear grabs the rabbit and goes, do you get shit on your fur when you wipe? And the rabbit goes no, so the bear picks him up and wipes his ass with the fucker!" The young men with shaved skulls laughed uproariously.

"Yeah?" one of the punks asked. The one who'd just told his joke sat on a scarred table piled with papers. Behind him a black, red, and white flag sported a Germanic-looking eagle and the name NEW AGERS. Boxes of white-supremacist nonsense were piled everywhere in lieu of chairs.

"May I speak with Dr. Royal, please?"

"Hey, tubby, you the guy called a while ago?" one of the others sneered.

"Yes."

"You got wax in your ears? What the fuck's wrong with you, asshole?" He was a big one, right in Daniel's face. The skinhead didn't like the fat fuck's looks. He was old but had a haircut kind of like theirs, sort of making fun of them, coming in and asking shit about the doc when he'd done been told. "You a tough boy?"

"Yes," Daniel said, pleasantly. The kid slapped him. Hard. Right across the face. Chaingang put a hand up to ward off further blows and that was all it took. The four of them were on him with fists and boots. One of them had recently been hurt during a ruckus after their parade, and they weren't swallowing any more redneck horseshit.

They pounded the crap out of Daniel, the second real kick-ass beating he'd had in his adult life, and when they got tired they dumped him out in the alley, which was the hard part. Beating him up was a snap, but carrying the fat son of a bitch was nigh impossible for the four of them. Bunkowski as dead weight was a pallbearer's nightmare.

Unlike the memories of the worst go-round at the merciless hands of Spanish Rodriguez, or the aftermath of the bad accident, the recollection of this ass-kicking actually had a feelgood side effect. He came to in a pulpy, turnip-headed state of joyous bliss at first, as some body chemistry unlocked by his physical defense mechanisms blended with the Alpha Group II. The end product was sort of a heroin high. Eventually, still on the nod, he found the car, managed to get in, and started the damned thing.

He wheeled out into the light traffic, his mind a whirlpool of confusion. He tried concentrating on reading signs and watching the vehicles: Gas For Less; a silver Acura; bread; cigarettes; Just Add Bacardi; a maroon Gran Prix; Burlington Northern—Hydracushion—Santa Fe; a log truck; a red Celica; Raymond Meara; a Nissan Stanza—RAYMOND MEARA cut through the junk from out of nowhere. He kicked the thing into a hard illegal U and roared back. It was Meara. From a hundred years ago in the Nam. Alive and getting into a beat-up pickup, that bastard Meara!

Only four SAUCOG survivors made it back to the world counting Chaingang: Michael Hora, a dead fucking sniper named Bobby Price, and this boy. He was sure it was Meara. If it was—there was the answer to his ordnance resupply needs. Old Ray would have some goodies stashed round and about here and there.

The last time he'd seen Meara alive and well had been back at base camp where a worthless fuck named McClanahan had briefed them down in his private trailer. The man had offered them up to the little people as a sacrifice, and his mind's eye pictured the two flags and pennant furled around the tall bamboo flagpole above the berm hole that led to his air-conditioned bomb shelter, the U.S. flag, South Vietnam's buttwipe, and the pirate skull flag of their phony recon outfit. The fucked-up monkey men playing soldier.

It took an eternity for Meara to get wherever he was headed, but Chaingang had tremendous patience and he used the time to nurture himself on the poisons that coursed through him, taking the bruises and humiliation of this latest beating and using it to forge new strength.

Tailing Meara to the water's edge was child's play. Nobody could stay on a vehicle or a subject the way Bunkowski could. He lagged way back, now and then allowing the red dots or yellow headlights to wink out briefly, but the sudden stop almost made him overrun his man. He was barely able to wheel into a gravel side road in time. Meara was getting into a boat.

Chaingang was out of the ride and moving—a wad-dling run—surprisingly fast, faster in fact than anyone alive had ever seen him move. He could run very fast for very short distances, and his tree-trunk legs of steel propelled him down the mud road. Meara had his back to the road and was yanking on an outboard motor lanyard when he heard the deep rumble in his ear.

"Don't move anything if you want to live," Chaingang said, puffing. The smell alone might have cut through and warned him, but Meara stunk a little himself. The voice, once heard, was not one a person ever forgot.

"Right," Meara said, chilly.

It was a professional frisk job, and when Chaingang Bunkowski patted you down it was almost a sex act. He got the ERMA .22, the pocket knife, even Meara's keychain.

"Listen up. You know who I am?"

"Yeah. Bunkow—"

"Good. Nobody gets hurt here. I need resupply: gre-nades, claymores, satchel charges, haversacks. What have you got and don't fuck with me, I'm paying." Money scattered over Meara's shoulder, symbolically.

Meara did not give up his ordnance because of any particular threat, but because of who was behind him. When fucking Chaingang materialized suddenly, thun-dering up behind you in huge splayed bare feet, big as a sewer culvert, demanding claymores and grenades, you did not screw around, you gave up the claymores and grenades even if you had to go home and make the freaking things. Meara didn't need the pain. He knew the monster personally. He'd seen some of his work. Up close.

"In my barn. Buried under the floor of the barn. I'll dig them up."

"Good. Let's go." The voice carried on the water's edge. A quarter ton stepped daintily down into the small boat and it damn near capsized before he could center his weight. Meara got a glimpse of something in Chaingang's right paw, but he did not let himself look directly at the man or his weapon. Pistol. Bowie the size of a large machete. Chain. What was the difference? If he decided to hurt you with something that was it.

The motor caught and they were moving into darkened trees. Meara would have at least considered taking a shot when they moved through the darkest overhang of willows and big oak, had it been anyone else, from Jesus SanDiego to Jesus himself. But there was never even a glimmer. You didn't think such things in Mr. Bunkowski's presence. The Dai Uy had drilled him good on the essentials long before they'd met. "Never fuck with him; never speak to him by name; never eyeball him; but above all, *never* fuck with him."

Ray'd been a spear carrier, a half-assed merc, but he knew how good this fucking brainiac was. The problem was, even after he'd given up the goods, there was no way Meara would walk away from this. His brain worked at triple time and a half during the silent boat ride.

They reached the other side, Meara cut the motor, tilted up the propeller, and they coasted into a flooded road ditch until the keel scraped muddy bottom. Chaingang hopped out, agile as a mountain goat but for his bad ankle, grabbed the coiled rope in the bow and pulled the boat, gear, Meara, and the outboard up onto land as if the whole shebang weighed fifty pounds instead of five hundred and fifty. Meara got out and they headed up the road toward his barn, the barefooted beast waddling along behind him.

Chaingang could technically get resupplied simply by communicating his needs to Dr. Norman, his hated nemesis. He was never without weapons. There was a haversack of military high explosive in his duffel, and some shaped charges and det gear. The weapons case in his back-breakingly heavy mobile house included such goodies as a submachine gun; a customized mail-order hybrid, which he carried broken down, barrel and shroud, firing assembly, crudely stamped receiver, over-large trigger housing, and grips shaped to accommodate one of his massive mitts; as well as a small supply of partially-loaded magazines of 9mm military ball ammo. Why aggravate himself to steal a used Winchester, then Remington, shotgun? And why this business with Meara?

Because Chaingang was a planner. He believed in the soldierly axiom that if one planned hard, one fought easy. He had hard plans for Dr. Norman and whomever else might be in the line of fire, and when he was finished in this floating turd of a hickburg, he wanted his munitions and weaponry cocked and locked. He was always going to pick up disposable shooters, such as the bait shop shotguns, and when he saw Meara, a notorious ordnance freak, he smelled instant resupply. These punks, who'd had the temerity to assault him when he was befuddled by the drug, and the elderly Nazi needed killing. He would stock up with field expedient necessities.

Meara was convinced he had one chance: boogie. They reached the barn, went inside its dark confines, and he made his move, McClanahan's unforgettable warning echoing in his head.

"Some stuff on this side, some stuff under those corner boards," he told the man, and bent to start unearthing the first silenced AK-47. The second he saw the huge shadow move toward the other side of the barn he took off running for his life. The shot never came, which was almost as scary as if he'd felt lead whacking into him, but Chaingang was smart. He knew it would take x amount of time to unearth the munitions and if he fired, one: he might not hit Meara, who was a fast runner; two: the shot might compromise the time he had to resupply. He analyzed Raymond Meara as a low-priority threat and decided, since the fool could hardly go to the cops about illegal guns he'd hidden, to let him go. Also, the drug's aftereffects still exerted some gentling influence on the killer. He wasn't really paying for the stuff, so perhaps this was quid pro quo.

As he was digging and pulling up goodies, he heard Meara splashing around out in the water nearby. The sound was oddly touching to him for reasons he'd not have been able to verbalize, even if he'd cared to, but as he loaded up for grizzly he dug around in his pockets and found a little trinket, which he tossed into the empty cache hole. He was paying for the goods after all. Next time old Raymond was down in the barn he'd discover a token from his good buddy Daniel—the smaller of the rocks belonging to Porky Pig's late and lamented Skunkie. Maybe $25,000, give or take, but meaningless to Chaingang.

Would he have whacked Ray had the asshole not been smart enough to run? Is bird shit white?

Fifty minutes later the big man was back at the water's edge. Somebody else who lived on or near Bayou Ridge had a big metal V-boat with a monster muscle motor on the back. Not rinky-dink like Meara's tippy piece of shit. Chaingang stepped carelessly into the larger boat, nearly sinking it, and deposited his heavy load of goodies, then his own heavy load, choked the motor, yanked the starter with a vengeance, and the thing wisely started on the first pull.

Down in the woods, where a freezing Raymond Meara was hiding, the sound of his neighbor's Evinrude was the loveliest thing he'd heard in years. It meant, *a,* that enormous bastard was leaving, and *b,* he wasn't taking Ray's boat.

Then again, he thought, he'd stay down in the woods a while longer, just in case that had been the sound of Chaingang laughing.

~~ 60

Bayou Ridge

Meara was fucking freezing. Chaingang be damned, he had to get out of the water. Silently as he could, he worked his way around to where he could see the boat. It would be just like that fat shit to start an outboard and send another boat out into the backwater with a wired throttle and . . . Paranoia was getting the better of him. If Bunkowski had wanted his ass in the grass he'd be planted. Meara looked into the boat and didn't see any new holes but—who knew? He pulled it up a bit further and staked it.

On the way back he saw his .22 in the mud. That settled it. Unless the big boy had tampered with his piece he wouldn't leave a weapon around somebody he was going to plant. Meara wiped it off, racked the thing back, and a .22 slid into the pipe. He removed the mag, ejected the live round, cleared it, peered up the spout at moonlight. Put the magazine back in and reloaded the weapon. He noticed he was shaking a little.

The house looked and felt empty. Spooky but empty. He made himself go down to the barn while he was gutted up for it. Nobody home. In the open weapons cache he spotted something shiny and picked up his paycheck. It appeared to be real enough but, again, who knew?

He went back to the house, built a roaring fire, changed into dry clothes, and sat huddled up in bed with a pile of blankets on, the .22 still in his right fist. Shit. You could probably put a round into the big boy's brain and he'd still rip your pump out. He put the piece away and went to bed, but the shakes kept him from sleeping. He couldn't get warm.

He got up and brought his blankets in and sat huddled close to the blazing wood stove. Burning up and freezing simultaneously, dead tired and too stoked to sleep. *Chaingang* in his fucking life from out of the black. How had he found him? Why had he come to look for him? What did it mean? Suddenly he remembered a couple of news stories about recent Bayou City killings and shuddered as he perspired profusely under the blankets. There'd be no reason for him to bother Meara again. He'd taken what he wanted.

Ray thought about being with Sharon again. He wanted to show her how much she meant to him. He wondered if she'd like the ring. On the other hand . . . Jesus! Think where it might have come from. Who wanted to know? Perhaps he could sell it or trade it to a jeweler and . . .

He woke up drenched in sweat, still in front of the stove, inside a wet cocoon of blankets, sick inside as if he were coming down with a bad virus, gripped by a terrible headache and the notion that it was later than he thought. He cursed aloud when he looked at the clock.

Eleven o'clock. Eleven in the fucking *morning?* He hadn't slept past nine in years. He had a distorted memory of having dropped off to sleep around five-thirty. His neck and head felt as if Fritz von Chaingang had held him in an iron claw all night long. He felt like hammered shit. He got up, sat back down, and tried to think.

Meara got up again, with some effort, and looked out the window. Judas! It was raining. He flung clothes on, pulled hip boots on, and topped the ensemble with a poncho, hurrying outside and slogging down the road to the boat. It was a short walk, as the water had pushed further in, and he was relieved he'd pulled the boat up thirty feet into the drain ditch. It was already sitting anchored out in the backwater, and by that evening he'd have to come in through the woods and tie up in the field behind the house. Thank God his folks had built on a high knoll.

It was the richest kind of bottom land one found in the Bootheel, but it could be costly to farm there. Backwater alone could push in during wetter years, leaving in its postdiluvian wake a stinking mudhole covered in water-logged trees. Even if they didn't blow the levee, this much water already meant Meara would spend a butt-kicking month hauling logs, picking up chunks, and doing the hard manual labor that would be necessary to farm in the flood's nasty aftermath.

Ray was not one to complain or give in to illnesses. He thought most people ran to the doctor for the least little thing, and he believed a man could will himself to stay well. When he felt bad he'd toss back a straight shot, chase it with a big glass of cold orange juice, gobble a few aspirin, and drive on. This was something else. He was sick as a dog, so much so that it was overpowering his efforts to reclaim the boat, and he shook it off as best he could.

The boat was completely full of rainwater. He tried to start bailing with the milk jug but gave up. Too much water and he was in too deep to tip it, so he untied the boat and turned to pull it back out of the water but lost his footing and stepped off into the ditch, plunging down into icy water, the mud seizing his hip boot and damn near drowning him before he could get himself unen-cumbered. He was beyond swearing. A quiet, slow anger was starting to build inside.

He got the boots off, tried to clean out what mud he could, gave up, and jammed them back on, sitting in the middle of the road, drenched, shivering in the rain, finally emptying the water from the boat and getting in. He got it pushed off at last and started the motor, easing the boat out the drain canal past the large oak trees and into the rainy chop.

Nobody would believe what it was like here. You could have a piece of farm ground one day and a lake the next. The wind had picked up some, and the boat was going pretty good, bouncing over the whitecaps. He was going against the current, the prow standing out of the water with his weight and the weight of the big Johnson offsetting the boat's balance. Suddenly there was a noise and the engine stopped dead. Had that fat shit monkey-wrenched him?

What now? He had the sinking sensation of being out of gas but when he looked he discovered he'd sheared off a freaking motherjamming cotter pin. He had nothing. He patted pockets, scrambled around in the recesses of the boat. He'd dumped the small nails he carried for that purpose when he'd emptied the water.

Any small piece of wire or whatever would fix it temporarily. Surely he could come up with a mere fishhook or paper clip? No. Nothing. It was starting to rain harder and he was freezing again and the current was taking him back to the big oaks. And he hadn't had any coffee, much less orange juice. And it was already noon. The day was half over and he was sitting in a boat filling with water out in the middle of what used to be his beans.

It took him fifty-seven minutes to paddle across. He was exhausted from paddling against the current and shaking from the cold. By the time he had pushed through the clog of willows on the other side he didn't have any strength left in his arms, shoulders, or back. He'd only thought he had a headache and neck ache when he woke up. *This* was a headache. It wouldn't have surprised him to see Chaingang waiting to snuff him.

He finally made it to the bank, reached his paddle out, and felt the wood strike good old solid roadway underneath, so he stepped out of the boat. Later, much later, he'd recount the incident and speculate that what he'd done was hit the bridge rail with the paddle. When Ray stepped out he also stepped off the Southeast Mark Road Bridge, dropping down thirty-seven feet in ice-cold water.

He was instantly traumatized. He'd never completely recall how he escaped the death grip of the wet poncho, only the vague sense of swimming into willows where he was found, clinging for his life, in shock, when Wendall Chastain came along and saved his life, hauling him into his boat and taking him back to shore.

"I'll be fine, Wendall," he kept arguing with the man. "Just let Pee Wee Kimbro know and he'll fix my motor and bring it across to me."

"Bullshit, Ray. Now get in there and get dry clothes on before you catch your death. I'm going to run back across, but I'll be right back for you in about ten minutes. Now git!" the man commanded.

Meara didn't even thank him. He turned and trudged up the road, fighting a wave of nausea. What he wanted to do was fix a few stiff drinks and sit in front of his stove for about six days. He managed to get inside, change clothes, crack the seal on a half pint, and take a couple of shots with bottled water, although his well was sunk so deep he could have probably drunk the tap water safely. He was already sicker than any tainted wellspring could make him. He forced himself to pull a leather jacket on and went back out in the rain.

Chastain had just tied up and was starting up the road to get him when Meara came out of the house. Big pieces of the day would come back to him later as deep, dark holes, and this was one. He had zero memory of crossing back with Chastain or making his way to Kimbro's. He remembered ringing their doorbell.

One of their dogs, a strange-colored semi-hound, came barking out from behind the house and bit Meara on the back of the right leg before he could kick it away. He didn't even care.

"Hi, Ray," Betty said, opening the door, and he sneezed in her face by way of answering. "You look like you're getting a cold. Come on in."

"Howdy," Pee Wee's mother-in-law said. "Pee Wee ain't here."

"He had to go in to the blacksmith's, Ray."

"Can I have my keys, please?"

"Uh—I think Pee Wee's got 'em."

"Oh." He sneezed again.

"You're gonna give us your germs," Pee Wee's mother-in-law told him sternly.

"I'll wait outside," he said.

"I don't know when he'll be back. You know Pee Wee."

"That's all right."

"Say, Ray, your—uh—lady called and said to give you a message." She went over to the phone. "Come on in," she said as an afterthought, ignoring the look from her mother.

He opened the door. "Sharon? Sharon Kamen called?"

"I got a note here someplace," she said, rummaging through loose scraps of paper by the telephone.

"Could I use your phone while I'm here, Betty?"

"Sure. Go ahead." He picked it up and dialed the motel.

"Thanks," he said, as the line rang. He heard Betty Kimbro's mother mumble something about how his germs would be in the mouthpiece of the phone and they should take Lysol to it.

Meara asked for Sharon's room number and listened to the phone ring over and over. Betty came over beside him and laid a crudely printed note down beside the phone. He could make out the word package.

"She left a package for you at the motel," Betty told him when he eventually hung up. It brought another big shiver.

Ray thanked her and went to Pee Wee's barn and got some wire, jimmied his truck door open, and hot-wired the ignition.

"Reckon he found his keys," Betty Kimbro said to her mother, as they turned the volume back up on the soap opera they were watching. Meara's truck could be heard starting up and roaring off in the direction of town.

"Better hope he didn't give us any of his germs," her mother said, absentmindedly.

61

Bayou City

It was a pleasant night in Bayou City. No traffic. One cop car. Plenty of shadows. Chaingang's kind of scene.

A dainty quarter ton of avenger carrying a case full of happy surprises tippytoed out of the deepest pocket of darkness and penetrated a shabby storefront bearing the NEW AGERS emblem and the legend New American-German Enterprise for Reunification and Solidarity. The door had a cheap lock. What was there to steal inside, after all? A cruddy flag and some cast-off furniture? Who'd have thought someone would want to break in? Break out, maybe, but in?

Chaingang glided in soundlessly, a graceful clown bear easing in through the darkness, bearing enough *plastique* to blow a bridge.

He found an address sheet with the members' names as soon as he gained entry, and was about to leave his surprise when a loud noise startled him and the home-made submachine gun's ugly snout automatically pointed in the direction of the sound. A human snore.

A closed wooden door. He'd assumed it was the club shitter, but as he carefully turned the knob and eased the door open a crack he saw three young men, two asleep on cots, one on the floor, the tiny crash pad awash in graffiti, Nazi symbols, and trash. The three biggest pieces of trash were sleeping so soundly, amid a couple of cartons of empties, that even as the door squeaked loudly they continued to slumber. One of them was really sawing logs, but he suddenly woke up, wide eyed, a size 15EEEEE bata boot having cut off his air supply.

The snorer began to thrash around until he saw the eye of a 9mm firearm a couple of inches away from his own right eye. His hands released their grip on the ankle of the massive boot, but his protesting whimpers woke the others.

"Hello, lads," Daniel said, smiling his most dangerous grin. "Remember me?" Two of them had been part of the group that gave him his beating and only the weapon kept them from trying to rush him. All they could see was a ventilated barrel shroud, bore, and the front of a trigger housing, a long Parkerized-type magazine sticking from its underside. It looked like a Mattel or Hasbro toy, dwarfed as it was by the enormous paws that held it.

They watched him slowly, carelessly, switch the weapon to his left hand, reaching for something with his right.

The huge beast felt a jolt of Alpha Group II course through him and said, in a goofy caricature of his own rumbling basso profundo, "This is N.B.C., the National Buttkicking Corporation," at which point he tenderly whomped all three punks with his immense chain, trying to bonk them on the head as if their melons were the NBC chimes, bing, bang, bong, playing with them. He only thumped the first one on the head, but caught the other two with glancing blows that still left them partially paralyzed. His second attempt was more accurate. One of them, he recognized, was the joker, who'd been particularly annoying. He saved him to enjoy.

Chaingang wrapped the taped tractor-strength chain rather loosely around the joker's throat, with the skinhead facing away from him. The last vestiges of the drug, as Norman had predicted, were causing Daniel to behave weirdly, but since it put him at no risk, he didn't worry about it. He was concentrating on something, and during the interim asked the joke teller how to get to certain addresses on the club roster, quizzing the young man about who lived with whom, what their role was in the organization, and their ties to the old Nazi doctor. The joker, who had just watched this elephantine destroyer kill two of his buds without breaking a sweat, was frightened for the first time in his dim-witted life, and volunteered more information than he was asked, in the hope of saving himself.

The one wrapped in chains heard a strange noise behind him. It was the big fat one grunting. Then there was a stench unlike anything the skinhead had ever known, worse than any backed-up septic tank or sewer smell. He was about to retch when he heard the beast speak.

"A bear and a rabbit are taking a dump in the woods. The bear says to the rabbit, 'Say, listen, when you take a dump does shit ever stick to your fur?' The rabbit goes, no! 'Good,' the bear says, and he picks the rabbit up and wipes with him." The joker almost cried when he felt himself being pulled backward.

When Chaingang finished his business with the big one, he pulled up his britches, said good-bye to the bitches, and went into the other room. What a dump.

He left another calling card, so to speak, this one comprised of military high ex, a detonator, and a trip wire. The closed door to the crash pad, the beat-up table, and one of the stacks of skinhead illiterature, each maintained pressure on the spoons of a trio of short-fused 'nades. The shaped charges were superfluous. The place was already beginning to stink to the point of lethal toxicity. Bunkowski was one of the only serial killers for whom the police jargon "dump site" had more than one meaning.

Chaingang closed the outer door on his work, waddled to his ride, and got in. Enough for one day . . . he was pooped.

62

By nine the next morning, Bunkowski was at the door of a home in the Bayou City low-income housing projects, a maze of identical buildings within Parabellum bullet distance from the heart of what he thought of as Turdtown. One of the youths who'd assaulted him was a kid named John Stephens, and it was housecall time.

The door was unlocked and standing partially open, and a loud TV blared on the other side, giving him a good excuse not to knock. He had a silenced .22 under his humongous T-shirt, and he hoped he wouldn't have to use it. The killing chain and a large pocket knife were more to his taste at that moment, and taste was what this visit was all about.

He turned the knob and quickly stepped inside, a disarming smile in place.

"What the hell you think you're—" an older man started to ask, but the smiling behemoth shushed him with his finger.

"It's a surprise for John . . . from the guys," he grinned conspiratorially. "Is he asleep?"

"Yeah," the woman said in a loud voice, "but who the hell—" He gave her a quick thud on the skull with his bottomfist, which felled her back down to the sofa, a pile of quivering Jell-O. The man tried to get up, but his reflexes were a tad slow and he, too, took a hard thump to the head.

No follow-through with the chain. He wanted to save them.

He found the young punk John sleeping it off in his

trash-and-clothing-strewn bedroom, which was decorated in Third Reich repros, and rock star pussy posters.

"Wake up, sweetheart," he said to the kid. No response. "Fine." The boy was sleeping on a mattress bare of sheets or blankets. Chaingang wished for Superglue, but had none on him, and, somewhat irritated, he chainsnapped the sleeping punk and returned to ma 'n' pa.

There was a good bit of slicing and dicing and miscellaneous mayhem for the next half hour. Dr. Bunkowski tried a couple of organ transplants but the donors rejected the work. Open-heart surgery is tiring, and by a quarter to ten the beast had disposed of the wannabe Adolph and was kicked back on the living room sofa, feet up, watching a talk show about the obese. He was fascinated.

The man in the suit and tie beamed insincerely at the camera. He had very white teeth and a manicured mustache.

"Porkchop weighs over nine hundred pounds—" he paused for dramatic effect while the audience let out an audible gasp, "and Porkchop is what he *likes* to be called, right?"

"Yeah. That's my name. Porkchop." The viewers at home and those watching the studio monitors saw a hugely obese figure sprawled out face down on a stack of mattresses. Only his head and bare arms could be seen. His body was covered in two blankets which had been sewn together. The man's head appeared to be disproportionately small in comparison to the enormous mound under the blankets.

"Believe it or not, folks," the host of the show continued, "Porkchop is married to a beautiful woman. Dasheeka, are you there?"

"Here I am," a woman said. She was an attractive woman, and as the shot widened out the audience could see her seated on the mattresses next to the huge man.

"Porkchop, you and Dasheeka have given us permission to inquire publicly about a very personal matter. We want to ask you about your intimate relationship together." He lowered his voice to a soft, pseudo-concerned-sounding caricature of sensitivity. "How can you two have sex?" The audience held its breath in unison.

"It's easy," the man on the mattresses said. "You just gotta work it out, you know? Me and Dasheeka are a perfect fit. She's hung like a donut and I'm hung like a donut hole." The audience whooped and hollered as laughter filled millions of living rooms.

"We'll be right back," the talk-show host said, pretending to be shocked at the man's remark.

"Do you have an opinion about today's program?" an announcer's voice asked, as a nine hundred number was scrolled across the television screens. "Call us at 1-900-SPEAK UP. Each call costs fifty cents, and you must be eighteen or older. Let's hear your opinion."

Daniel flipped the audio off with a remote control. He got up heavily from the sofa where he'd been watching television, wedged between the man and woman of the house. "You two behave yourselves." He clomped across the carpet, his 15EEEEE feet making nasty squishing sounds as he walked to the telephone and dialed.

He listened for the instructions and gave the telephone number. When he heard the tone he made his recorded message.

"Hello. My name is Bill Stephens," he said, giving the name of the man who was watching silently from the sofa, "and my wife and I just saw the show with Porkchop and Dasheeka. It just *killed* us. It was so funny," the deep basso profundo rumbled, without a hint of mirth, "we died laughing." He hung up, and walked back through the pools of coagulating blood.

When his bare feet were nice and wet he walked over to the dining-room table, and with some effort hoisted his butt up onto it. Carefully positioning himself he then made one footprint after another on the wall, lying on his back as he walked up the wallpaper as high as he could.

Mr. and Mrs. William Stephens, of Turdtown, Missouri, eyes taped open and heads duct-taped to the sofa itself, observed their human centerpiece—unseeing—as he left bloody tracks, then sat up with a grunt and began wiping his feet with the wet towels he'd arranged nearby. With that accomplished, he hopped off the table and walked across scattered pieces of clean cardboard to the bathroom.

Tomorrow, the next day, someone would find the three corpses. Whoever or whatever had ripped their hearts out had then apparently walked across the room, up the wall, and dematerialized.

The talk show had put him in a playful mood.

 **63**

By the next day it was business as usual at the doctor's office. The waters were pushing in closer and it seemed there had been a rash of terrible explosions. So far, eleven persons were dead. By coincidence, most of them were members of a local white-supremacy outfit.

Dr. Royal could have canceled his appointments easily. He was semi-retired, and no one would have thought a thing of it. The idea tempted him mightily but it was no time to get lazy. The last thing he wanted was to commit any act that might fit a profile the authorities would surely have by now designed to match up with the actions of their elusive Nazi, as they'd have clumsily put the facts together.

He was full of pain-killer, but still much the worse for his encounter with the Jew bitch. It was all he could do to keep his avuncular smile in place while JoNelle Lanahan ran her ugly mouth about her problems, reassured her about the diet he'd prescribed for her enlarged thyroid, and got the heart attack survivor out of his office. He'd seen one more old patient, Bess Cosgrove, whose crippling arthritis was worsening. He prescribed a special pillow, changed her medicine, and gave her the obligatory pain shot, which would wear off almost immediately. Somehow he made it through the midday. He told his nurse, "I'll probably be back around one, but don't schedule many. I want to quit early today."

"Sure. Two-thirty all right?"

"Fine," he said, glancing at his watch. It wasn't even eleven yet. He'd nap for an hour. Eat a bowl of soup. He went out his private office exit, closing the door, checking to make sure it had locked, and turned to see a familiar face waiting there in the parking lot of the clinic.

If Ray Meara hadn't been tired and ill to begin with, he'd have taken a clearer look at the bedside clock and seen that it was not shortly before eleven but more like two minutes before nine, and that his clock had stopped at eleven the night before. Had he started the day armed with this small piece of knowledge he might not have hurried, and he probably wouldn't have ended up stepping off the submerged guardrail of the Mark Road Bridge.

But Meara did hurry, and he did step from a boat directly into a deep ditch filled with ice-cold river water, and he was still in shock, not to mention injured (though unbeknownst to him at the time), when he found the frightening note and book left for him at the motel office. Within minutes he knew that Sharon had never returned from her foolhardy confrontation, that the cops were not about to lock Dr. Royal up for murder, and that Royal and Shtolz were one.

Meara, still on his feet but barely operating, simply refused to grasp the fact that such a note as he held in his hand, together with the missing-persons list that now included Sharon, were insufficient evidence to cause the constabulary to immediately arrest the town's leading citizen as a mass murderer.

He fought back the urge to scream in Jimmie Randall's face. He knew the reaction that would cause. The cops were "concerned," and Doc would be brought in for "intensive questioning," but it was "too early" to be sure Sharon Kamen had disappeared, and the words began to form a bullshit cloud, hanging oppressively in the air that Meara was finding more difficult to breathe by the minute. He finally dialed a local lawyer named Stephen Ellis, whom he'd heard was gutsy and aggressive.

In a breathless avalanche of words he sketched it out for Ellis. "I wanna do something. I got to stop this guy. What about a citizen's arrest? Isn't there such a thing?"

"Sure. You can arrest somebody. You arrest Doc Royal, let's say. He gets a lawyer and countersues you for false arrest. Now the jury awards him your farm. That's the way that could work."

"But he might be getting set to disappear himself. What if he gets away with this shit? I gotta do something. I know he's done something to Sharon and—" He was beside himself. "I gotta *stop* him!"

"Okay. I'll be down there as soon as I can. Stay at the motel and wait for me. We'll go to the courthouse and—" on and on. Papers. Warrants. A U.S. marshal would blah blah. The sheriff would do such. He would make bail. You would do this, he would do that. Meara thanked the man and hung up, went outside, and tried to breathe as the bullshit cloud filled the room behind him.

Double pneumonia, both lungs, overpoweringly potent even in its incipiency, ravaged Meara's system, which was already unbalanced by the trauma of the boating accident. Later, he'd learn that as he stepped off the bridge rail, left foot first, the weight of the boat had brought some three to four hundred pounds of steel rushing up to clip him on the spine, then again at the base of the skull, as the tippy boat fought to right itself. The plunge into frigid water had shocked him so totally that he never identified or remembered the two fast blows as he went over the side.

The massive shock of realization that the town's leading citizen, a kindly man he'd known for years, had a monstrous alter ego—this, and Sharon's situation—combined with his physical deterioration to pull him further down.

Once again, a quirk of timing played a part. Had Meara begun his day in a normal fashion, and showed up at Jimmie Randall's office only a short while later, things might have proceeded in a far different way. Twenty-one minutes after Meara left the city administration building to return to Sharon's motel, praying she'd suddenly appear or call, a truck driver found Sharon and called the police, the Bayou City ambulance service, and the Clearwater County sheriff's office. But Ray's timing was bad.

It was a brain-addled, desperate, and violently angry Raymond Meara, both physically and mentally impaired, who stumbled from his pickup in front of the Royal Clinic at 10:43 A.M. He figured it was after noon, and his plan was to wait for the man to return from lunch and arrest him for the murders.

His brain signals were malfunctioning and all he could think of was revenge. Royal must not be permitted to escape. He reached in and unholstered the pistol in the glove compartment, holding it down under the dash as he racked a round into the chamber and thumbed the safety off. Cocked and locked.

He turned, shock, grief, pain, trauma, double pneumonia taking him under, as the man he was after appeared at the side of the building, saying something to him and laughing, and very slowly, as if in a drugged state, every move on slo-mo, he laboriously pulled the weapon from his belt and said to his old friend, saintly Doc Royal, "You're under arrest you son of a bitch," pointing his firearm at him as he'd been trained to do, the words sounding inside his head as if they'd been pulled through axle grease and molasses.

"*YOU'RE UNDER ARREST YOU SONNNNNN*NNNNNNNNnnnnnnnnnnnnnnnnnnnnnnn nnnnnn and on and on, a long, unending nnnnnnnNNN NNNNNNNNNNNNNNNNNN〰〰〰〰〰〰〰〰〰 of pain that became a **WALL OF SCREAMING NOISE THAT WAS BOTH QUIET PISTOL SHOT AND WOMAN'S TERROR-STRICKEN SCREAM.**

How the finger touched the trigger and why he felt as if he were passing out and what made him squeeze that trigger before he fainted he could never be certain.

Ray retained hazy images of a man and woman there in the parking lot, the woman screaming again and again as if someone had dropped a mouse down her dress, and somebody else looking at him from the passenger side of a parked car.

He looked down at old Doc, either dead or very close to dying, with a CCI Stinger having just gone in through the face, exploding the brain on its way out, or so it appeared, Raymond shivering, not fainting after all, finding the strength to go back and put the gun on the floorboard beside a small, leather-bound book that he'd knocked off the seat.

He sat in the truck waiting to hear the siren, wondering who would show up first, Jimmie Randall or Eddie Roddenberg or some other asshole, coughing, looking at the weapon and the book, the word Lebensborn mocking him with its golden eagle and swastika.

64

Clearwater County Jail

Meara was a man deep in confusion. Hurt held him pinned. On the physical level he ached from a beating, but he'd had a few beatings before. At least one rib was broken, but he'd broken his share of ribs. The confusion —that was new: a muddy, inconscient thing that pushed at the limits of his sanity, washing across him in dirty waves of disorientation.

The man next to him whispered in a strange, hoarse voice, "—and you know, man, it ain't bad, but you're putting in all these hours and that's when you get hurt 'n' shit, when you don't *concentrate.*" Concentrate, the man whispered, and Meara, whose wrists, ankles, and waist were joined by jailhouse iron, tried to concentrate. The hurt stabbed his chest when he inhaled, held his chest like a vise, throbbed across the side of his head. His tongue found another point of soreness.

"So this big sumbitch comes back where we wuz playin' poker 'n' he goes, kin I put my stuff over here? And this one ole boy, he says shit no, you cain't dump on nat, it's *my* bunk, shitbird. And hell, man, you know how it iz inna Navy, it's root hog or *grunt!*" The man laughed in his strange, whispery rasp.

The sign to Meara's left read Out Of Bounds.

"So, shit, I stand up 'n' say to this big dufus, we got rules here, boy. This dufus goes whatdyamean, man? And I say, hey, dufus, it's root hog or die, motherfucker!"

Behind them an authoritative flat voice barked, "No talking, assholes." Meara filed it away for future reference.

284

To the left was out of bounds, and in this place there were no talking assholes permitted. As if to underscore this wisdom, heavy steel slammed behind them. Meara took a deep breath and winced from the sharp pain. A sign in front of him proclaimed Danger. Below that: Stand Clear While Gate Is In Motion.

This was more information than he could digest. The lights were dim. He fell, but there was no sensation when he smacked the hard surface, wrapped in perplexing ignominy and jailhouse iron. By the time he regained consciousness he was a news story. The front page of a sixteen-page newspaper:

BAYOU CITY MAN CHARGED IN SHOOTING
by Isabel Santora of the *Bootheel-Republic* staff

A Bayou City man has been charged in the attempted murder of retired physician Solomon Royal, 70, of the Royal Clinic of Bayou City.

The man is Raymond Meara, whose address is listed as Star Route, and who is said to live on a farm approximately twelve miles south of Bayou City, in the community of Bayou Ridge. Meara has been charged with attempted homicide.

He is accused of shooting Royal in front of his clinic at West Vine and Petrie streets at about 10:45 A.M. yesterday.

Sheriff Pritchett said, "From what we can tell, Mr. Meara was carrying a pistol with him and had parked near the clinic. Eyewitnesses say he walked up to Doc Royal and shot at him, point blank. Fortunately he's a lousy shot and the bullet barely grazed Doc on the side of the face. He lost a lot of blood but they got him patched up real good. Meara didn't attempt to resist arrest."

No motive has been established for the shooting, but Meara was believed to have been distressed over the Clearwater Trench Spillway project, which involves an area surrounding his farm.

The accused man was reportedly given a severe

beating by inmates in the Clearwater County Jail when it was learned that he had shot Dr. Royal. A nurse, Earline Chambers, said that Meara was probably suffering from pneumonia at the time the beating occurred, and was probably ill when the shooting was committed.

Later that evening, when Ray woke up to receive medication, he had weird, remarkably clear memories of a conversation between Sharon and himself. He couldn't be sure if it was real or imagined.

"Don't be so violent in your reactions, Ray," he could have sworn she'd said, trying to teach him. "You're not a stupid man so why react so narrowly to things? It only limits your perspectives and trashes your values in the process." He knew he could never have made up such an elegantly turned phrase. "Life is worthless without decent values. Forget the macho rhetoric a second. Think! We live in a world of constant fighting: Muslim against Jew, Catholic against Protestant, Christian versus Christian, and so on. If we don't learn to live together we're going to kill off the human race, you know?"

"I don't agree," he'd said, in a bullheaded mood. "Sometimes hard-core payback is the only answer. Look at your Israelis, you call them nonviolent? And I say good for them."

"Forget the vengeful stuff, Ray. The only steps that have advanced mankind in the last century were those taken by nonviolent leaders such as Gandhi and the civil rights leaders. No exceptions. The ancient moral values are the only ones that make sense: nonviolence, strong personal ethics, truth, and keeping to one's principles."

He'd sure learned that lesson well. Still, sick and hurting as he was, he realized how much he'd learned from Sharon in a short time. She'd already managed to sensitize him to deeply felt, subtle things he'd never bothered to consider before.

Meara closed his eyes and tried to visualize her there in the small cell with him: five feet, six inches of lovely woman. Dark-hued, velvety smooth skin, pale gem-green eyes, and the most provocative mouth of any woman he'd ever known.

The back page of the local newspaper stared up at him when he opened his eyes. He forced himself to pick up the paper and scan the horoscopes. There it was:

"SCORPIO (Oct. 24–Nov. 22) This is an ideal time to redecorate your surroundings. Emphasis is on authority figures. But resist the temptation to run away."

～ 65

Sharon is walking across his front lawn. Not in high heels but sandals. Bare, tanned legs, long and sleekly muscled and inviting, walking with the insinuating hip-swinging stride that is the patented walk of sexy young women the world over. Still sophisticated looking but in a thin, flowered summer dress, and sandals. Pretty as a picture.

Her arms are bare and she has rather slender arms, and this, too, is very sexy. He remembers other girls, some of whom had large breasts and relatively small arms. Inside his head he sees the medal of a proficient marksman and the line "expert in small arms."

Sharon's hair is long, loose, a spill of sensuousness, a cascade of silky femininity that flows onto her shoulder. He might ask her to let her hair grow and to wear it hanging to her waist, like his grandmother had, and he would help her give it a hundred strokes every night.

He feels his hands on her shoulders as he comes up behind her. Sees her turn and smile into his face, her eyes wide and the color of perfect emeralds. Eyes of desire.

Did he ever know a girl like her, a mere child of the

farm community, perhaps, struggling to pull her child's grass sack through the rows of cotton? Did such a beauty learn beside him, as the smaller boys and girls were taught the rigors of front and back chopping and blocking the plants? Not here.

He had never known a Sharon. Never fumbled with one in the back seat of a car. Never walked one home from school. He had no memories of anyone remotely like her, a mystical, perfect, idealized dream girl who had blown in—and out—of his life.

There was scarcely enough of Sharon inside his head to construct a decent mental picture. The best he could do was a kind of half dream, part reality and part imagination, woven from the crude threads of a jailhouse fantasy.

 **66**

The Swift Trench

A faint chill mist has descended over the party of men, tiny droplets of moisture touching skin, hair, fabric, plastics, beading on the oiled metal surfaces, feeding foliage, dropping into the floodwater beneath the boats. Skinheads, most of them.

Two boats. The one in front a sleek fiber-glass V, and the man in the prow signals. A chopping motion with the hand. The one seated behind him turns and blinks his flashlight once, a long, bright flash at the larger boat behind them. Five men. Equipment.

Both engines stop in a dying purr. Jesus SanDiego, in the prow of the V, absorbs the noises into the pores of his skin. Offended by their pathetic performance. What a joke, these loud, incompetent assholes are. He shrugs it off. No problem. He hears fifty sounds in the unquiet silence.

They are floating in the mouth of the Swift Trench, a black and oily pipeline full of goosenecks and elbow joints that curves up from New Madrid past the Clearwater Trench, forking out toward Barne's Ridge and St. James's Bayou. They're maybe a couple of miles from their destination if they were going in on a straight shot. They're not. They are snaking in from the southwest, out of the cover of a long, thick treeline that runs from the set-back levee clean to the trench itself.

The boats have come upstream from Clearwater, staying west of the levees, running as silently as they could. No lights. One long blink for stop. Noise for go. The V is packed and muffled down. The thirty-footer has a relatively quiet 120-horse on her.

Sandy sniffs the wet night air, wormy and rank, listening to a truck or car rattling across the Kielheimer Bridge, moving up over the levee. He turns, nods, and the kid behind him throttles forward, and the low, throaty 120 rumbles like the glass-packs in his uncle's antique Fairlane, as it coughs into the black wake of churning water they leave behind.

It goes back to way before Farmington, this thing that made Sandy bad. The drugs that burnt him out were what the doctors blamed everything on, but truth be told they only heightened what was already there, twisted and dark, inside a man whose only secret wish had been a hard, unswervingly pernicious death dream. When a man can kill and get away with it—hell, be praised for it—well, then, chief, why not do it? It feels so good and you know what they say . . . nobody stops. The people he works for treasure him for what he is.

The man in the prow of the V feels the chill spit hit him lightly in the face like a wet kiss, and his mind wanders back into a fantasy about guns.

Sandy loves guns. Somewhere under all this water old

shooter Ray has got him a case or two of Alpha Kilos: sweet, neat, wiped, and piped. Custom suppressors. Assault rifles that have been combat proven in every conceivable terrain. Bitchin' fine cap-crackers that SanDiego can almost taste, hot and sweet like physical desire. Free for the taking. Ray sure can't use them.

Old Ray will have them beautifully turned, fitted to a fine hello, packed like the Hope diamond, and hidden someplace real dumb. Mad Man Meara, a thousand times crazier than SanDiego, so fucking stupid in an age when even the most inexperienced gunrunner knows you use Ma Bell's landlines, only Ray still makes home deliveries! Begs to be taken off. Aches to be ripped.

Jesus is powerfully built, black silk bandanna over skinhead top and whitewalls, rat down the back, black and silver-flecked muscle shirt, red rag armband with his animal count, bat-belt, chute pants, 14E felony flyers, loyalties tattooed on his biceps, emotions on his knuckles. Thickly muscled arms cradling a Ray Meara special, as he prays for a night game.

They reach the willows and he fast-forwards his fantasy to the moment where he asks Ray where the guns are hidden. Meara starts to wise off and he sees himself jamming steel in the asshole's mouth, like a big, hard dick. Meara tastes 3-in-1 oil and his own blood. Sandy busts out a few of his teeth with the gun barrel. Lets him eye the death tube.

Perfect night. Almost no moon, and this is the last night they will work in here. The honcho found what he wanted, but they will go in this final time.

The guys with him are wussies. He smiles, wishing he could unleash a burst and watch three or four guys dive like fucking blue marlin. It breaks him up thinking about them diving overboard into eight or nine feet of muddy water. Four cartoon belly-floppers. Wussy assholes.

He chops and the kid stops, blinks, the pontoon boat throttles down and the two boats ease through the trees. On the other side of the willows the water is like four football fields of black glass stretched two by two, end to end. Perfectly still. No wind. The mist is diminishing. Somebody else drives over the Kielheimer. The muffled engines will carry a mile or two out here. He waits for the vehicle to pass.

Water sounds. Fucking frogs. "Do it," he says, and the kid scoots them out across the glass, through Meara's northwest ground and into the woods. The 120 rumbles, penetrates the edge of woods, he motions for both boats to kill their engines. Behind him the big pontoon boat rides treacherously low in the black water.

67

Bayou City

Daniel Edward Flowers Bunkowski had chosen the night to go calling, but the object of his interest, the inappropriately named Jesus, was, sadly, not at home.

Undismayed, the beast penetrated his lair carefully, the cheap lock quickly defeated by a Taylor lock-pick-gun and a few experimental tries. Chaingang's locksmithing and invasion skills were remarkable, in spite of his first mentors' having been failed exponents of the crafts of picking, peeling, breaking, entering, and thievery.

It was as filthy looking a crib as one could imagine. Much as he'd have enjoyed a hands-on experience, it was too nasty a hovel even for Chaingang to wait around in, and he had once lived in a sewer.

Down in the depths of his ruck he found a small rattail file. He removed a little package wrapped in huge T-shirts, shorts, and thick, 15EEEEE socks. Raymond's

Nitrolite. He took the package from its nest, got a roll of duct tape, which he kept in a wrapping of aluminum foil, and slowly, meticulously, began the preparation of a homecoming surprise.

By the time he'd finished with the most demanding work, his appetite had returned. Without thinking he idly opened the noisy refrigerator to see if there might be some unopened or otherwise consumable food. Dead cockroach corpses lay stiff in funky pools of turquoise mildew, illuminated by the refrigerator light. Chaingang wasn't quite that hungry, so he unzipped and urinated into the appliance.

That accomplished, he sighed, farted, flicked the awful dew from his pink lily (what he liked to refer to as his rostenkowski), and tucked it away in Porky's and Skunkie's voluminous boxer-jockeys. He yawned, belched, farted again, scratched his enormous ass, adjusted his package, and gently set about screwing the light bulbs back into their ceiling sockets. He replaced Mr. SanDiego's cheap light fixture and the threaded retainer that held it in place, spat, tried to fart again but drew a blank, hoisted his ruck and left the disgusting crib.

He waddled back to the car, heaved his tonnage in, and drove a block and a half away, where he killed the engine, sprawled back across the front seat, and waited. He wanted to be near enough to watch the fireworks when Jesus returned, blundered into his cave, and hit the living room light switch.

He'd taken the three bulbs out of their sockets and made a tiny aperture in each, just so, using the small file. A glass cutter would have worked better, but he was able to make do with the rattail. Utilizing a fragment of stiff paper for a funnel, he ever-so-delicately filled each of the penetrated bulbs with Nitrolite, which was an explosive substance roughly ten times more powerful than $C_7H_5N_3O_6$, and maybe a hundred times that of black gunpowder.

The handling of Nitrolite is not for amateurs. The stuff has a well-deserved reputation for instability, and he did not know how long it had gestated in four-mil wraps under Meara's rundown barn. But if necessity is the mother of all invention then field expediency is its wayward daughter. He managed to get the Nitrolite in the bulbs without *a,* blowing himself up real good, or, *b,* breaching the ultra-fragile filament wires, which were the found-object detonators for these particular boomers.

Unfortunately Daniel had fallen fast asleep and did not get to watch Mr. SanDiego come home for the last time. He was not able to get his jollies in those seconds of anticipation before Jesus entered his domicile and went to his ultimate reward. His chain-saw snores were interrupted by a concussive force roughly that of—well, imagine being at ground zero in an arc-light B52 strike. Even a block and a half away it hammered the soles of his feet, his bladder, his lungs, his teeth. He tasted it like a mouth full of garlic. It deafened him.

He'd used way too much Nitrolite, *way* too much. It blew up Jesus, the house Jesus's crib was in, Jesus! It blew up the tree in the front yard and about eighteen hundred dollars' worth of glass, and imbedded a joist in the wall of the beauty salon across the street ("We cut great head"), causing the lady who lived next door to frighten the hell out of her partially deaf husband sleeping beside her when she screamed at him, "Wake up, Vern, they just blew the levee! We've got to gather up the cats!"

Oh, well, Chaingang thought, swallowing to get his hearing back, starting the car, shit happens.

He had the radio on low. He dug at his ears, twisting his huge bull neck back and forth, trying to get his hearing to kick back in. The words, "Royal Clinic in Bayou City," got his attention, faraway-sounding and scarcely audible, and he cranked the volume up enough to catch the end of the news item.

"—Dr. Royal is in satisfactory condition and resting

comfortably at—" he paid great attention to the hospital name.

One more loose piece of business and he'd leave this low-rent shithole. He jerked his head savagely and the second and third vertebrae cracked like whiplash.

68

The nurse on station 3 at Delta General answered her phone. "Oh, yes, Dr. Howard." It was the chief of staff of the hospital.

"Has the specialist from Barnes showed up yet?"

"No, sir," she said, having no idea what he was talking about.

"His name is Dr. Fine. He has lost his identification but if, er, when he shows up, it's all right. I can vouch for him. It's all right for him to see Dr. Royal."

"Okay," the nurse said.

"I don't think I've ever seen Dr. Fine. Could you tell me what he looks like?"

"You won't have any trouble recognizing him. He's very large. Big man. I want him to take a look at Dr. Royal."

"All right, sir, we'll watch for him," she said.

The doctor thanked her and handed the receiver back to the enormous beast that held a giant blade over his left nipple.

"Excellent job, Dr. Howard. You may take the rest of the night off," Bunkowski rumbled, circling around in back of the thin, balding man and smashing a bottomfist to the gleaming pate. As the chief of staff of Delta General fell forward, Chaingang grabbed the man with his left hand and sawed through the carotids with the right, then cleaned the massive fighting Bowie on the doctor as a crimson pool spread.

With the big blade tucked away out of sight, he waddled unerringly toward the elevators, having been briefed on the layout of the hospital, and on Dr. Royal's room location, by the head man himself.

Chaingang was in a positively radiant mood. He was leaving Turdburg, Misery, and the world looked simply delightful. If there was anything he loved, it was professional men: doctors, lawyers, chief executives, and such —but doctors foremost. He loved them. He loved to kill them. They represented monkeydom at its zenith. He loved to waste them randomly, to make their deaths as ignominious as possible. Once, in a similarly buoyant mood, he'd killed a dentist with his own floss.

Daniel's primary goal in life was to hurt the monkey people until they died, but since his own operation his focus of rage always returned to one man, Dr. Norman, who'd supervised the Walter Reed implant team. The bull's-eye on which he concentrated was the sissy in charge of the bonebreakers at Marion. He would force Norman to remove the fucking implant and then he'd . . . He had to jerk his mind off the feast, he was salivating badly, drooling like a Neopolitan mastiff watching poodles at the dog show.

Seeing Chaingang up close could be a devastating experience if one weren't prepared, and the nurse on station 3 had been expecting big, not super-gigantic. She almost soiled her panties when something freaky large and rather sour-smelling suddenly towered over the desk, telling her it was Dr. Fine.

"What?" she almost shouted in panic. "Oh, yes! Dr. Fine. We're expecting y—" She was starting to get up but the huge monstrosity was telling her he knew where Royal's room was, thanking her in this booming basso profundo, waddling off down the hall as if he owned the place, the largest white coat she'd ever seen flapping open in his wake.

Had she inspected that coat closely she'd have been alarmed to discover a regular doctor's coat, size XL, split under the arms and up the center of the back, and spliced with white sheet that had been neatly glued in place. It wasn't Brooks Brothers but it got the job done.

The patient in 394 was half awake, when a mastodon-sized person in a white coat, with the nametag Fine, intruded upon his thoughts.

"You must be Dr. Royal," the stranger bellowed, an idiotic smile across his ugly countenance. "I'm Fine, and how are we this lovely evening?" He moved near the prone man, taking what appeared to be strips of cloth from his pockets.

The man started to tie strips of cloth to the sideguards of the hospital bed, as if he were preparing restraints. All of Shtolz's defense mechanisms were instantly attuned. He knew whatever this was about it was bad and he made an effort to leap from the bed, but although he was strong and in excellent condition for a man of his age, the heavyweight towering above him could not be measured by any ordinary rules of biomechanics or biokinesiology. Inhuman paws the size of bedpans forced him back in their steely grip, and he felt his wrists being imprisoned by the strips of stout cloth as he struggled.

"There, there, now, Dr. Royal, please don't excite yourself. You're going to need all your strength." As the second wrist was being secured Shtolz decided he'd try a bloodcurdling scream, but it was as if the gigantus had read his mind. "Take two of these and call me in the morning," Chaingang said, stuffing a couple of the strips into the man's mouth.

The scream for help came out a muffled "Nnh!"

"What's that? Oh, don't be alarmed at the precautions. I don't want you flailing around during the operation. Surely you must have had to tie the dogs and cats and little babies down before you worked on them, right? Well, old boy, same deal. Just relax, and look at the bright side," he said, affectionately, reaching under his T-shirt and pulling out the largest knife Emil Shtolz had ever seen. The bright side of the blade glinted frighteningly.

The surroundings, the sounds of a busy hospital, the pervasive smell of Betadyne, all the ambient elements that had been so reassuring to Shtolz a moment before, were now threatening to him.

"How do you feel about discorporation, Dr. Shtolz?" The word hung in the air between them, rank and offensive as the beast's smell. "Personally, I don't see a future in it. Oh—hey! You're not Jewish, are you? Good. I only operate on Aryans."

With that, a quarter ton of punishment on the hoof raised a massive, muscled arm and chopped the top of Shtolz's head off.

 **69**

Clearwater County Jail

Raymond Meara is alone, in the jungle. Inverse perspectives shimmer and restructure, fractionating in the intense heat that crashes into him, plugging his nostrils so that he cannot breathe. He struggles to his feet and plunges through the thick foliage, breaking through to a clearing that he recognizes as the landing zone in the shadow of Monster Mountain.

A phantom rises from the Perspex and pierced steel like a heat mirage off baking macadam. It whispers to him.

"Bounty Hunter One, this is God Six Actual, do you read me, over?"

"Um. Yeah. Right. Uh, loud and clear, God. Is it really you, God? Where are you? I can't see you. Over?"

"I'm right here in the trailer, Bounty Hunter One. Come in. Door's unlocked."

It is the mobile home, sunk into the base of the mountain, roofed, reinforced, packed in a cozy, sandbagged berm. Meara opens the door.

"Come in, my boy."

"Thanks," Ray says, entering the dark mobile home. A figure sits in the shadows waiting.

"You're just in time for breakfast," it says, as Meara fumbles for a light switch. The smiling, decomposed remains of Dai Uy McClanahan holds out a scorched, dented skillet, proffering food. Meara gets a glimpse of black and silver, some blackened mess in the pan. "Come and get it while it's hot, boy," the thing says to him. He realizes now that the voice is not McClanahan's, but belongs to the wall-size monster who comes out of the shadows behind the corpse. Chaingang!

"Brains and eggs!" Meara's own scream is his alarm clock.

"Hey, Ray," the turnkey sang out cheerfully through the bars. "You sleep good in our hotel?" He was unlocking the cell.

"Like a fuckin' top," Meara said, a sack of screaming nerve ends and lousy luck.

"Well, that's good," he was holding the cell door open, "but looks like you're outta here."

"Huh?" Meara was on his feet.

"Come on, let's go. You're going home, man."

What the fuck? Meara was still sleep goofy, but he moved out. "Say what?" he asked, softly, but swallowed the question so as not to jinx the spell.

He had to go through the formalities of checking out of Heartbreak Hotel, but within minutes he was blinking in the bright sunlight, listening to his young lawyer run it down for him.

"—the book alleges that Doc Royal had been a Nazi,

or so they're saying. We'll have to have our own translation made of it but that will come later. You'll still have
to stand trial for the shooting but I doubt if there's going
to be much of a climate for prosecuting or punishing
you." Ray heard the word justifiable for maybe the fifth
time. "Royal was killed last night. Decapitated in his
hospital room." Meara tried to assimilate the information. "So I guess they figure—" Perhaps he read the
absence of understanding in Meara's eyes. Stephen Ellis
took Meara to his truck.

The young attorney told Meara what he'd heard about
Royal's murder.

"There was a witness who saw the killer. He also killed
and mutilated the chief of staff of Delta General. Big, fat
guy, she said, supposedly a giant. They think it's the
serial killer who may have been responsible for some of
these random murders around here."

Meara shivered.

"Sorry. I shouldn't be talking so much. I can imagine
how you must feel, between the pneumonia and what
you went through back there," Ellis said.

Ray was in bad shape, true enough, with losing Sharon
by far the worst of it, but that wasn't why he shivered. It
was what he knew that he could never talk about, his
all-too-intimate knowledge of Dr. Bunkowski, the pio-
neer in organ surgery without anesthetics.

～ 70

Bayou Ridge

The water was not in the house yet. Maybe six to seven inches away from overflowing the top step. He'd come right up the back drain ditch through the middle of his beans and tied the boat to his doorknob, an odd feeling. This morning he looked out, trying to see how much it had pushed in, but he couldn't tell. The sun off the water was blindingly bright.

He looked around, trying to decide if any of his belongings were worth saving. Perfectly decent appliances and furniture would be ruined. He'd think about it. Study on it. Probably have to move the stuff out in the next twenty-four hours if he was going to do it at all. More rain in sight.

If the river pushed on in, at the very least it would fill the house with mud and crap when it finally went down. He'd cleaned mud out of a place once before. You couldn't hardly live in a place after the water got it bad. Be a damn shame. It was a well-made old house. Oh, well, he shrugged. Whatever was meant to be.

The ground would be there when the water went away. He'd still have the farm. That was something.

He was sitting in the living room with a drink, all the windows open, looking out at what was his private lake now, when he saw the tiny speck come through the willows by the Southeast Mark Road Bridge. He watched the speck become a boat with three men wearing hunting clothes, cammo jackets, and caps. He saw a couple of guns, it looked like.

Ray was in the door as they putted up the ditch in a big, ritzy fiberglass job. It was the Jarrico brothers and Doug Seifer.

"Hey."

"Hey," Meara said.

"You about to drown?" Seifer asked.

"Pretty close. You boys huntin'?"

"Yeah," one of the brothers said. "This morning."

"I'll be back in a minute," Doug said, scrambling up on the prow of Meara's boat and from there to the steps. They went inside.

"Welcome home."

"Thanks."

"I got this dude owes me," Seifer said, cryptically, taking something out of his pocket and handing it to Meara. "Check it out." It was a photocopy of a legal-looking document, like a property abstract. Meara read the heading. I 48-99 Clearwater County Survey/Cl. Trench "N" R-25-26-E.

Ray immediately recognized what it was. Thirty-six squares and rectangles split by a black and white dotted highway line that was the set-back levee road, with a blue element to the south and east, in a familiar configuration. Each one of the rectilinear stairstep plots was some farmer's ground.

"You're there," Doug pointed, unnecessarily. "You're Number One."

"Yeah?"

"Guy was working for Milas."

"Milas Kehoe?"

"Yeah. That's from an abstract. He had a geological survey run on your property a long time ago. Over at the flat and down in your woods. Came in the back way and took samples. When you was in jail, he brought a crew in on a pontoon boat. Came right up into your back woods and sunk a test drill. I reckon you're sittin' on some oil."

"Oil," Meara repeated.

"They had Sandy ridin' shotgun, too, way I hear it."

"SanDiego?"

"Yeah," Seifer said. Meara watched his big jaw muscles tighten around a smile. "I knew you'd enjoy that. Anyway, Kehoe figured you'd do some time for Royal. He was fixin' to buy this. He hired the skinheads and Sandy to come in on the thing against you. Hear tell, he's rightly ripped." They both laughed.

"Way she goes," Meara said.

"You could probably sue that shoat and who knows what? Win a box full of money or somethin'."

"I think I've had my share of tryin' to get even, Doug, ya know?"

"I hear you there. Anyway, thought you'd want to know. Better sink a well down in them woods, man."

"Thanks."

"Oh, here." He handed Meara ten folded twenty-dollar bills. "These won't bounce. Sorry it took so long."

"Hey, no big deal."

"If you want to do anything about our friend," Seifer drooped his eyelids and raised his shoulders, "I'm willing to throw in with you."

"Nah." He shook his head. "Revenge just doesn't cut it. I finally learned that the hard way, Doug."

"Okay." Seifer started for the door.

"But thanks, pard. You've been a good friend," Meara said. Seifer got back in the boat and they pushed off toward the drainage ditch, the motor loud over the expanse of water.

He didn't have Sharon but she'd managed to give him some values anyway. He'd learned that vengeance is empty. He'd finally learned something.

She'd taught him a lot. Gave him a lot to ponder, in the short time they'd had together. He'd have a long while to sort it all out, to think about what she meant to him, and he knew a part of her was going to stay with him.

Ray stood in the open doorway watching the boat disappear into the distance. The drizzle opened up again, and behind the dark clouds the afternoon sun played tricks with the sky, splattering vivid reds across the deep blue. Raymond looked up into it, his face streaked with rain.

Life was nothin' but tricky.

～ 71

Memphis, Tennessee

Bunkowski woke up thinking about the little babies and the animals with their skulls open and the brain cavities empty. He knew that some of those photos were burnt into the deepest wrinkles of his own brain forever. Dr. Norman was to blame for all of this. He was every bit the devil that Emil Shtolz had been, and his government was just as corrupt. We didn't kill Jews, but we killed others. What was the big difference? Man was basically evil. Serial killers and mass murderers—he happened to qualify as both—were, in his opinion, like AIDS or cancer, just doing God's work. Getting rid of the assholes. Cleaning up the Big Experiment That Failed.

He flipped on the television set in the low-rent motel room outside of Memphis and lurched into the shower. The weather map showed the showers that had recently brutalized southeast Missouri clearing out and heading east, right into Memphis. Chaingang was unaware, even as water pelted him in the shower, that his own personal rain clouds were following him. When he emerged, cleaner than he'd been in a long while, he watched a fat female comedian make fun of animal rights activists while he dressed. He was dressing for success: expensive grey suit with striped shirt and microdot tie. Cologne. A close shave.

Daniel turned the sound off and tried mouthing the words along with her, seeing if he could lip-read her jokes. She had a mouth like a knife slash in a face nearly as doughy as his.

He was ugly to begin with and the bad eye had not helped his appearance. It gave him an even more grue-some visage, a sort of Satanic bloodshot look. But, amazingly, he could do all sorts of facial tricks with that rubbery physiognomy. If he held his head at a calculated angle, smiled that beaming doughboy grin just so, the old gunshot wound that puckered his cheek looked more like a big dimple, and the scar visible in his eyebrow became just one more wrinkle, a character line as it were.

His smile was, quite literally, disarming when he wanted it to be, and his talents included the ability to easily manipulate and sway people with his face, voice, and body English, to an astonishing degree.

"Good evening, ladies and gerbils. I'm Allan Hamp-ster," he ad-libbed into the motel-room mirror, his face scrunched up in the parody of a human smile. "I tell ya these animal rights nuts *kill* me." The basso profundo rumbled out in the identical rhythms he'd just seen on television. His mimicry skills were totally profes-sional.

Satisfied with the reflected image, he packed his duffel, left the room with lights on, water running, and a fresh puddle of urine soaking through the mattress, loaded the car, and headed for the other side of Memphis.

Midway to the Executive Suites Hotel out in southeast Memphis, he stopped at a pay telephone and confirmed his reservation under the name Lionel Hampster.

By midmorning he was parking his wheels outside the huge hotel complex and registering. The Executive Suites was a blur of activity, one of the busiest hotels he'd been in, a perfect hiding spot. How does one hide when one weighs a quarter ton, stands nearly seven feet tall, and has a puss like an exploded pizza? One doesn't.

If a person wishes to hide an object, as the old saying

goes, the best way to do so is to hide it in plain sight. The easier it is to see, the harder it will be to find. Who looks for a stash in the centerpiece on the dining-room table?

A black girl fresh from hostelry school looked up from behind the registration desk to see a grinning clown bear of a man.

"Hi!" he beamed. "Man, I loves that brown sugar— mm! The darker the cherry the sweeter the meat." He was so stupid she couldn't help but smile. "No offense, but if I was thirty years younger and a ton lighter, I'd jump right on your bones. I'd jump on them now but they'd never *find* you later." Everybody behind the counter laughed. "Ladies and gerbils, I'm Lionel Hampster, and I demand service." He snapped his fingers in a young man's face. "Oh, there you are. What took you so long? Gimme my room key thing and point me toward the bar."

"Would you like a bellman, sir?"

"No thanks, I'm trying to quit." They laughed again. "Have someone take my bags up, please. But right now I need you to find me four or five strong men and put me on a baggage cart and *wheel* me to the drinks." Laughter. Lionel was already a hit at the Executive Suites.

"Here's your key card, sir. Now don't lose it!" the girl joked with him.

"No," he said, as a tongue the length of a tongue in a pair of shoes and the color of fresh lox lizarded out. He placed the room opener on this horrible appendage, retracted it into his mouth, made a show of swallowing, gulped, and opened his mouth to show it empty. "It's nice and safe now where I won't lose it." Nobody made a sound. They'd never seen anything like this in their lives. Suddenly, he reached over and goosed the bellman, who let out an involuntary scream. "Ooh!" He held up the key card in his right mitt. "Good thing I brought a duplicate along." The people behind and gathered around the desk applauded as one, and the huge man waddled off, swaying from side to side like Chaplin, the sound of laughter music to his cauliflower ears.

No, they would not soon forget Lionel Hampster the entertainer, there at the hotel's reservation desk. But Lionel Hampster a wanted fugitive? Nah. He was hidden in plain sight, a ton of fun on the run.

He spent a great first night in his suite, ordering one hundred and twenty-four dollars' worth of room service from Guido Lucci's Italian restaurant down in the inner courtyard of fountains and fake rock. Tournedos buona fortuna, stacked filets of beef béarnaise with march-and de vin, baby duck salad made with Italian spinach, and fettuccine Alfredo ("named after the weak Cor-leone brother," he told the room service waiter), and visions of baked pasta danced in his massive head as he slumbered behind a Do Not Disturb sign for thir-teen hours.

Lionel Hampster would stay there for a week, eating, feasting, drinking, sleeping, riding up and down in the elevators, resting and recuperating, and then he would go make Dr. Norman remove his fucking implant, after which he'd suck out the sissy's bone marrow for dessert.

He donned his finery and went out to do a bit of re-con and resupply, and felt the first pings and twinges of something. Watchers, perhaps? Probably not. He shrugged it off, in too good a mood to permit thoughts of a dark nature to intrude. He concentrated on finding beer, snacks, and the planning of his menu for the next gargantuan meal.

Was there a more delicious beer than ice-cold St. Pauli Girl? If there was, well then, God help him, his duty was to seek it out, buy it, and bring a large quantity back to the room. His thoughts were of hops and barley and delicious foodstuffs, so he did not allow his vibes to warn him of the unmarked vans and their escort cars from the Shelby County Justice Center, downtown at Third and Poplar, that pulled into the busy parking area of the hotel as soon as the target cleared the place. Nor did he dwell